Hotel
LAGUNA

ALSO BY NICOLA HARRISON

Montauk

The Show Girl

Hotel
LAGUNA

NICOLA HARRISON

ST. MARTIN'S PRESS
NEW YORK

First published in the United States by St. Martin's Press,
an imprint of St. Martin's Publishing Group

HOTEL LAGUNA. Copyright © 2023 by Nicola Harrison. All rights reserved.
Printed in the United States of America. For information, address
St. Martin's Publishing Group, 120 Broadway, New York, NY 10271.

www.stmartins.com

Library of Congress Cataloging-in-Publication Data

Names: Harrison, Nicola, 1979– author.
Title: Hotel Laguna / Nicola Harrison.
Description: First edition. | New York : St. Martin's Press, 2023.
Identifiers: LCCN 2022058241 | ISBN 9781250277381 (hardcover) |
    ISBN 9781250277398 (ebook)
Subjects: LCGFT: Novels.
Classification: LCC PS3608.A7835785 H68 2023 | DDC 813/.6—
    dc23/eng/20221206
LC record available at https://lccn.loc.gov/2022058241

Our books may be purchased in bulk for promotional, educational,
or business use. Please contact your local bookseller or the Macmillan Corporate
and Premium Sales Department at 1-800-221-7945, extension 5442,
or by email at MacmillanSpecialMarkets@macmillan.com.

First Edition: 2023

10 9 8 7 6 5 4 3 2 1

*For my parents,
who brought art into my life and
introduced me to beautiful Laguna Beach.*

Hotel
LAGUNA

CHAPTER 1

Laguna Beach, California—February 1946

I STEPPED OFF THE COACH, DIRECTLY IN FRONT OF THE BOARDWALK, and was immediately struck by the colors. Everything sun-drenched and vivid—from the towering palm trees shooting up into the cloudless blue sky to the polished shine of the automobiles lined up along the curb. On my left was a large, white hotel with Mission-style details and scalloped parapets, and just beyond, the ocean glistened green and blue, fronted by striped beach umbrellas dotting the sand.

"Wowsers," I said to myself, as I took it all in.

The coach pulled away and I looked back, feeling the weight of my suitcase in hand. Everything I owned was packed into that small rectangular case, and the remainder of my wages from the airplane factory were tucked into the waistline of my trousers. I carried my case down the boardwalk, past a ballroom and a café, to a wooden bench, where I sat and considered my next move. It was almost two o'clock in the afternoon, and before the day was over I needed to find a place to sleep and a job to pay my way.

A young boy walked down the boardwalk calling out, "Chocolate sodas, malted milkshakes, hot beef sandwiches. Come and get one at Walter McQuinn's Ice Cream Parlor."

My stomach growled at the thought of food.

"Shoestring licorice, root beer barrels. Get your sweet-tooth fix at Walter McQuinn's Ice Cream Parlor."

I waved him over. "Excuse me, does this place Walter McQuinn's sell newspapers?"

"Yes, ma'am. Newspapers, magazines, Mary Janes, Sugar Daddies, Coca-Cola floats."

"And where is Walter McQuinn's Ice Cream Parlor exactly?" I asked.

"Walter McQuinn's Ice Cream Parlor," he called out for all to hear, "located on the corner of Forest Avenue and South Coast Boulevard, just across from the beach!" He turned, pointed, and continued on, "Banana splits, Brown Cows, tutti-frutti sundaes."

"Thank you," I said, picking up my belongings and heading over in that direction.

Perched on a stool at the granite soda fountain, I went straight to the classified section of the *South Coast News*. I scanned and scanned. *Carpenter wanted, inside and outside work, must have materials and tools . . . Installers needed for cesspools and septic tanks. Experience a plus . . . Housing needed for veterans, list your vacancies with American Legion . . . Housekeeper needed, two days a week.*

I sighed and circled the last one. I was capable of so much more after the work I'd done over the past few years at Douglas Aircraft. I knew my way around a toolbox just as well as the fellas, but now that the war was over and the men were back from overseas, the women who'd been doing these jobs had been thanked and sent on their way. There was no more demand for us to work a man's job, and they'd let us know how they felt loud and clear.

"Go on home, go back to being a mother and a good housewife," our plant manager had said, and some women were thrilled to do just that.

Not me. I had no home to go back to.

CHAPTER 2

Wichita, Kansas—September 1942

THE SATURDAY NIGHT BEFORE A FRESH GROUP OF LOCAL BOYS SHIPPED
out, several of us met at the Wichita bowling alley for an unofficial fare-
well party to all those who'd enlisted. Davie Hankel was there flirting
with Julie Hartright, barely paying me any attention, and Bobby Watson was there too, like a loyal puppy hanging around my ankles. Bobby
had been kind to me after my mother passed away: he brought over his
mother's green bean casserole and on several occasions knocked on my
door to see if I needed help, or some company. I'd known him since nurs-
ery school, and after high school he worked in his father's service shop
in town. His kindness was a comfort and a welcome relief, since most of
my girlfriends had married or gone off to college.

I had one week left before I was to hand over the house keys to the
landlord, and I'd spent the last of my mother's savings to keep the roof
over my head. Bobby promised to help me move my belongings into
the room for let above the diner where I waitressed seven days a week,
though now I'd have to do that alone, since he was set to leave for training on Monday morning.

I'd been to the movie theater with Davie Hankel a couple of Saturday
nights in a row, and I'd thought it meant something, but the following
weekend I'd waited on him and Julie Hartright at the diner. They ordered malted milkshakes and french fries and my whole being was filled
with jealousy. Looking back on it now, I can't believe I was even able to

think about boys and going on dates so soon after my mother died, but I think I'd been looking for a distraction, for another emotion to take over from the grief and sadness—burning love, passion, raging jealousy—anything to take my mind off the idea that I was alone in the world now, completely and utterly alone.

That night at the bowling alley I told Bobby I wanted a smoke, and I never smoked, but he found one for me and we went out to the parking lot. I leaned against his car waiting for him to light it, but instead he went in for a kiss.

"Bobby!" I said, pulling away, shocked at how he'd misread the situation.

"I'm sorry," he said, looking away. "I thought . . . it's just that . . . well, I'm leaving tomorrow, and what if I don't come back, what if I don't have the chance to see you again, what if I don't . . ."

"Stop that talk," I said, realizing that he might be a little tipsy, that maybe he drank his beer too fast, that maybe he was afraid. "You're going to be fine, everything's going to be just fine." I put my hand on his arm and squeezed.

He tried again, leaning in, putting his lips on mine, and this time I let him, but his touch was all gentle and sweet as if he were scared he might be doing it wrong. I wasn't in the mood for romantic nonsense, I was too worked up after seeing Davie Hankel and Julie Hartright together, so I took his hand and slipped it up my shirt. His eyes widened as if he were a little boy who'd been given free rein in a candy shop, not a young man about to be shipped out to fight a war.

Now he kissed me back with more certainty as he inched his hand up my stomach and toward my peach satin bra. The idea of kissing Bobby Watson had never crossed my mind in all the years I'd known him, and when I sensed his excitement, I felt a strange thrill run through me.

"I want to give you something," I said, reaching for the door handle of his car and nudging him inside. "A memory to take with you."

As I said it, I didn't even know how far I was willing to go—just kissing, or maybe a little more—but once we were in the driver's seat, Bobby reached his hands around to the back of my bra and managed to unclasp the whole thing. His hands felt soft and warm, and soon he climbed into the back seat, pulling me with him.

"There's more space back here," he said.

He unbuckled his belt, unzipped his trousers, and then began fumbling with my undergarments. I was shocked—at him, at myself, at how this whole thing was unfolding—and I thought about stopping him, telling him that he'd got this all wrong. I'd never done anything like this before, and yet part of me wanted to feel something, even if it was pain.

"Hazel," he whispered. "Are you sure?"

I only knew how this was supposed to go from books and picked-up conversation with the girls in town. I knew it was going to hurt, and it did, a shooting pain as he pressed himself into me, but I was also high from the power of it all, how I'd controlled him with just a touch, a quick feel of my skin, a hint of what might come next. Soon the pain subsided enough for me to feel a warmth, a rush; he pushed his face into my chest and breathed deeply into my skin. I laid my head back, my eyes squeezed shut. I imagined it was Davie Hankel that I had this power over, that it was Davie I was making breathe heavily, that it was Davie enjoying this moment until he couldn't take it anymore.

"Sweet Jesus," he yelled out, quickly pulling himself off me and covering himself with a handkerchief. He threw his head back against the seat, his eyes closed, his face transformed. "My God," he said, breathing deeply. "I love you."

I knew then I'd gone too far. He was a good boy from a good churchgoing family—he would have been content with a few kisses and a letter now and then to keep him company while he was away at war, but instead I'd given him a whole lot more.

I quickly climbed back into the passenger seat and stared through the window. Everything I'd felt just moments earlier transformed into a slowly rising panic. What had I done? What did this mean? All these boys being shipped off to war, all these couples quickly planning weddings or professing their love to each other, I'd got caught up in it all. I was already nineteen, I didn't have a sweetheart, and now that all the young men I knew were leaving for God knew how long, I probably never would. I had wanted to know what all the fuss was about, I quickly justified to myself. Though, deep down, I also knew I'd wanted to make Davie Hankel notice—it was him I burned for, not Bobby Watson. Well, now I knew what the fuss was about, and it wasn't all it was chalked up to be.

I adjusted the rearview mirror and studied myself to see if I looked different, more womanly. I didn't. I just looked stunned, like a child, an irresponsible child.

"Hazel," Bobby said finally. "You are the most spectacular woman on God's green earth." He took my hand in his and kissed it, a gentlemanly gesture that didn't fit the activities that had just taken place in the back seat of his car. "I don't think you realize that I've been thinking of this moment my whole life, for as long as I've known you. Well." He smiled bashfully. "I didn't think it would happen like that. But it was perfect, it was so swell, and we'll have our whole lives for more romantic moments."

I looked at him, scared of all the promises I'd made by that one careless action.

"I'm going to get back here as soon as I can, and I'm going to marry you, Hazel Francis. I'm going to make you my wife."

I tried to swallow, to think of something to say, but my throat was dry. I got out of the car, smoked that cigarette, and walked back into the bowling alley. Then, as soon as I could, I slipped away.

The next day Bobby knocked on the door of my mother's empty house and presented me with a thin gold ring that belonged to his mother. "I want you to wear this," he said. "And think of me every time you see it. I promise I'll take you to the chapel just as soon as I get back home."

There was no turning back. How could I tell this boy who was being sent off to war that I didn't love him? How could I tell him that I'd made a mistake, that I didn't want to be tied to him and this small town for the rest of my life, that I had plans, big plans, I just didn't know what they were yet. That afternoon I dutifully went to Bobby Watson's family home and blinked away the tears as his mother, father, sister, and neighbors all congratulated us on our engagement, hugged me, and welcomed me into the family.

"Your mama would've been proud," his mother said in a whisper as she served a dollop of mashed potatoes onto my plate at dinner. "And I'm sure your father would have been too."

I'd never known my father. He left this earth when I was just a baby. But I was quite sure my mother would not be proud of me in this moment. We had been dirt broke, my mother and I, but she'd always taught me to be kind, to be honest, and to be true, and I was being none of those things.

I didn't move into the room for let above the diner; instead, his family insisted I move into Bobby Watson's childhood bedroom. I didn't know how to say no to them. I felt as if I were some sort of consolation prize for Bobby being sent to war and that I should do my part. They were not a wealthy family, but his mother made sure I was well-fed and comfortable. She treated me as if I were already her daughter-in-law. I continued to work at the diner, taking as many shifts as they'd give me just to stay out of the house, away from the oppressiveness of it all. But when I was there all she wanted to talk about was my future with Bobby, and I couldn't blame her. She'd pick out baby names, boy and girl names, that she thought Bobby would approve of, and she talked a blue streak about the wedding, which she envisioned as elaborate at first. As the weeks and months went by, though, it became a small, no-frills ceremony that she'd arrange when Bobby was allowed to come home on leave. The whole thing made me sick with nerves.

Posters around town and full-page announcements in the papers were persuasive: KEEP 'EM SMILING WITH LETTERS FROM FOLKS AT HOME they said. WRITE TODAY AND OFTEN. It was our job as women at home to keep up the morale of the soldiers overseas. We had an obligation to raise their spirits, so I returned Bobby's letters with as much enthusiasm as I could muster, all the while feeling horribly cruel for stringing him along, for allowing him to believe that we could be happy, that he would be content to wed someone who didn't actually love him, someone who had shared classrooms and playgrounds with him his whole life but who barely knew him at all. I could never tell him the truth in a letter, but it felt wretched to keep up the lies. God only knew how long this war would go on—it could be months, years even. How could I let him think that he had a loving bride-to-be to come home to? Surely that would be worse. And even if I went along with it, even if I married poor Bobby Watson out of obligation, obligation to a hero, that wouldn't be fair to him either. There were plenty of girls around here who'd fall in love with him, and he deserved that. There were plenty of girls who were dizzy with the lack of male attention since the men were drafted. They'd be hungry for someone like Bobby Watson to whisk them off to the chapel. But not me. I would be nothing but a disappointment.

I'd seen ads for women to work at Beech Aircraft in Wichita. Plastered on the outside of the diner there was a picture of a woman holding

letters to her chest, with a caption that read LONGING WON'T BRING
HIM BACK SOONER. GET A WAR JOB! Recruitment pamphlets came in
the mail making promises to housewives that the work in airplane factories was similar to work performed daily about the home. "Operating a
metal stamping machine is not unlike cutting cookies," "painting aircraft
parts is just like painting the porch," and "using a rivet gun is similar to
using an iron," they'd read. I considered leaving the waitressing job behind for the promise of better pay, but it wasn't going to change the lies
I was writing to Bobby Watson, or the act I was putting on in his family
home. And then in the paper one day I saw a small advertisement by the
Office of War Information for Douglas Aircraft in California. WOMAN
POWER WAS NEVER SO IMPORTANT it read, showing an image of an at-
tractive woman working inside a bubble-style Plexiglas bomber nose. She
looked decisive, essential, and strangely glamorous. At the bottom it said,
EARN MONEY FOR BONDS, FOR FUTURE STUDY, OR FOR A PEACETIME
VACATION. WRITE OR CALL TODAY FOR A JOB INFORMATION BOOK-
LET AND A FREE TICKET TO CALIFORNIA.

It was the first moment in a very long time that I started to see a way out.

CHAPTER 3

Laguna Beach, California – February 1946

"YOU HAVE TO BUY SOMETHING IF YOU WANT TO SIT HERE," THE man behind the counter at Walter McQuinn's said, adjusting the white apron over his white shirt and trousers, all immaculately clean.

"Oh yes, of course," I said. "I'll take a malted milkshake." Then I paused, thinking of the meager change in my purse. "Actually, just a hot coffee, thank you."

At the end of the counter sat two women, one slurping a malted, the other digging into a banana split. My stomach growled at the sight of them.

"He was a miserable geezer," the woman closer to me said. "Rude, wearing dirty old duds, and he had the audacity to say I didn't look the part, he said my roundness was the problem. Roundness!" She shoveled a spoonful of ice cream into her mouth, and I couldn't help but notice how her round bottom spilled over the edges of the counter stool. "Why do I need to be slender to be some old fuddy-duddy's assistant?"

Her friend nodded. "Terribly rude."

"I should burn this," the banana split lady said, crumpling up a piece of paper she had in her hand, then discarding it on the counter. "What a waste of my morning."

I sipped my coffee and turned the pages of the newspaper slowly. When the two ladies got up to leave, I walked to the end of the counter where they'd been sitting, casually picked up the crumpled paper, and slipped it into my pocketbook. I'd never worked as an assistant before, but after watching my pennies since the paychecks stopped coming in, one thing I had going for me was a slender figure.

"Can I get you something to eat?" the man behind the counter asked.

"Just finishing my coffee," I said. He raised his eyebrows as if I'd already been taking up counter space for too long. I slipped the wad of paper out of my bag and spread it open on my lap.

"Professional artist seeks assistant in Laguna Beach. Must reside in the area. Good pay for right candidate."

I looked at the phone booth in the back of the parlor, then counted the change in my purse. An assistant. I thought about that for a moment. I'd failed my shorthand class in school and as a result hadn't been offered a spot in the stenography class, but I could take notes the old-fashioned way, and I'd done all kinds of jobs at the factory that I never would have thought I was capable of. Working as someone's assistant—how hard could that be?

I walked to the phone booth in the back of the parlor and asked the operator to put me through to the number in the listing.

"Yes," a man's voice answered.

"I'm calling about the ad in the paper for an assistant."

"All right," he said.

"I wondered if perhaps there was still an opening."

"There is. Do you have experience?"

I thought fast. I had three years of experience working at the airplane factory: I knew how to fire a rivet gun, position a bucking bar, spot-weld tail fins, and I'd even used the hydraulic press a few times. He didn't ask for specific experience, so I answered him honestly.

"I do," I said.

"Come for an interview on Thursday, two o'clock P.M."

It was Monday.

"Is it possible to come today?" I asked.

"Today?" He groaned and let out a loud sigh.

I hesitated; I only had today. I had no plan, and I couldn't cool my heels here for three more days on the slight chance he might hire me. I had nowhere to stay, and I was determined not to delve into my emergency fund—a modest stash of cash I'd been saving from my wages each week. Not yet anyway.

"Today would be best; in fact, it's the only day that would work."
There was silence on the line, and I wondered if he'd hung up.

"Fine," he said gruffly. He gave me the address, and I thought I heard
a click.

"Hello?" I said. "Are you still there? What time would you like me?"
But he was already gone.

The clock on the wall said 3:15, and in a couple of hours it would be
getting dark. I had no time to spare. This was my only job prospect, and I
had to make it work. The counter guy gave me directions and even drew a
simple map on the back of a paper napkin—turn left out of the soda joint,
walk up Coast Boulevard, and turn right on Cleo Street. But when I arrived at the address, I was sure I was in the wrong place. The front yard was
so overgrown, I had to swat my way through weeds and stray branches as
I opened the gate and walked up the pathway. I checked the address I'd
written down, now crumpled in my palm: 120 Cleo Street—that's what
it said on the mailbox. Turquoise paint curled off the front door of what
looked like a small house from the front but seemed to extend back a long
way. A rusty door knocker with a lion's face looked as if it hadn't been used
in years, and it took some effort to get it to move. I knocked. Nothing. Not
a sound, not a creak. I waited. Looked around, rechecked the address, then
knocked again. This time I heard something from the back of the house,
the yard perhaps. An opening and closing of a door, a shuffle coming closer.

Bolts were being unlocked, one, two, three. The door handle turned
and then a jolt, followed by a loud bang as if someone kicked the door,
another tug, and the door creaked open. A scruffy man appeared and
looked at me with dismay. He had a broad, mottled face surrounded by
shots of gray hair.

"What?" he asked, clearly irritated. "What?"

He was unshaven, in paint-covered overalls that looked as if they
hadn't been washed in years, and his hands were filthy, speckled with
paint, his nails black with dirt. He might look like an artist, but he was
not at all what I was expecting. I was so stunned by the whole encounter, I could barely bring myself to speak.

"What is it, woman?" he said, louder now.

"I, um, I telephoned you, about . . ." I held up the newspaper clipping
since words seemed to fail me.

He squinted and leaned toward me. I got a strong whiff of whiskey and stepped back, tripping on the uneven stone pathway.

"I said next week." He swatted me away and began to turn and head back into the house.

"Well actually, we agreed on today," I said, regaining my footing and my composure. I really needed a job and wasn't about to give up this easily.

"Today's no good," he said. "I'm in the middle of something. Come back another day, and for Christ's sake come around the back next time, nobody bangs on this door!" He tried to shut the door but, in a moment of panic, I put my foot out to stop him.

"I can't come back another day," I said. "Please, I've traveled quite a way and . . ."

"You have to live here," he snapped, as if he'd caught me out and wouldn't have to bother with this whole interview after all. "It says it right there." He took the newspaper clipping from my hand and flicked the page.

"I will live here, if the opportunity is right." I felt desperate, and an embarrassing tingling sensation hit my nose and my eyes as if I was about to cry. I would live anywhere. I'd come all this way, alone. This might not be right for me, but it was the only thing I had right now. I took a deep breath and managed to pull myself together. "I can't wait until next week to interview for the position, unfortunately. But I do think I will make an excellent assistant. I'm a fast learner, I'm quick with my hands." I racked my brain for anything else I'd been complimented on at the factory that might apply to becoming an assistant. "I'm willing to do whatever it takes to get the job done and—" I thought about what I'd overheard at the ice cream parlor, decided against it, but then, as a last-ditch effort, I blurted out, "And I take my appearance seriously." This caught his attention. "I try to stay slender." I cringed when I heard myself say it out loud, feeling I'd betrayed the girl at the counter. But I went on anyway, wondering if he'd be requiring me to work on his yard or do housework, given the state of the place. "If I am to work with you, that might be of concern." With this he laughed, but he didn't slam the door shut as he'd threatened just moments earlier. He sighed, put one hand up on the doorframe, and leaned on it as if he were giving this some thought.

"All right," he said finally, easing up a little. "You've got determination in your veins." He slipped a small silver flask out of the pocket of his overalls and took a swig. "Come back tomorrow, though, will you? I've had too much of the good stuff to discuss all this today."

My eyes must have widened, and I was about to tell him again, impatiently this time, that it was not possible, but thankfully he stopped me before I had the chance.

"Relax, relax," he said. "Stay at the Hotel Laguna. It's in town next to the boardwalk. You can't miss it—big sign on top. Come back tomorrow at eleven. No, make it twelve."

I didn't know who this man thought his candidates would be—some rich ladies who could stay in hotels and lounge around as they pleased? This was a job interview, not a seaside holiday. I couldn't afford to stay in a hotel. "It sounds lovely," I said quietly. "I saw the hotel when I arrived in town earlier today, but I don't think I can . . ."

"Put it on my tab—the room, food, whatever. Enjoy yourself, for Christ's sake." He laughed a deep throaty laugh that turned into a cough.

"But I don't even know your name."

"Hanson," he said. "Hanson Radcliff."

"Nice to meet you, Mr. Radcliff, I'm Hazel . . ." But before I could even finish, the door was slammed shut.

CHAPTER 4

Wichita, Kansas—December 1942

I PACKED MY BAGS QUIETLY AFTER EVERYONE HAD GONE TO BED and caught a train to Los Angeles at 6 A.M. I left a note on the kitchen table for Bobby's mother. It was cowardly not to tell her in person that I was leaving, but I knew she'd try to talk me out of it, or at least ask me to stay until after Christmas. At that point I was only looking at my very next move, or two steps ahead at best, and the idea of Christmas with Bobby's family felt stifling. In the letter, I told her I felt compelled to help in the war effort, that more hands on deck could help bring the boys home faster, though I think I knew, deep down, that I had no intention to return. I explained that the pay was better in California, which it was, and I promised to send money back to the family, which I justified would repay her for feeding and housing me for the previous three months. On the train ride to California I wrote a similar note to Bobby and told him I'd write more once I arrived.

Several other girls boarded the train along the way. Nina Lee and a handful of girls from Alabama were already on board, sitting in the colored section of the train car. It seemed wrong that they had to ride with their luggage under their feet and in their way while we could stack ours on the luggage rack. Patricia and Mary Ellen hopped on in Texas, and Carol, who went by Rusty on account of her flaming red hair, boarded in New Mexico. There was a nervous excitement on the train, everyone leaving their vastly different lives behind to set off for a new adventure.

Soon we were all sharing our stories, and by the time we rode through Arizona, we were all sitting together in the back section with the girls from Alabama, our faces pressed to the window in amazement, marveling at palm trees shooting out of the flat terrain unapologetically, standing tall and bold, their wild fronds waving at us from the tops of their spindly trunks.

We disembarked at Union Station, Los Angeles, and were met by Marion, a middle-aged Douglas Aircraft employee who was assigned to help the new girls get situated. As she shuffled us through the station, I was struck by the high, white stone ceilings and dramatic arched windows outlined in bright terra-cotta brick.

"Oh boy," Rusty said alongside me. "We're in glory land now."

A bus took us straight to the dormitories, where we were instructed to double up.

"We've got so many girls signing up that we don't have enough cots," Marion said. "So, for now, you'll be hot-bedding it." Someone in our group sighed at the sound of it, but I had no idea what that meant. "That's right, you'll be sharing a bed for the time being. One of you girls will work the night shift and one of you will work the day shift; the other will keep the bed warm."

I didn't care one bit, I was just thrilled to be there.

"Training starts tomorrow morning at eight sharp. I'll be here to pick you up at seven thirty, so tonight just sleep wherever you can until your shifts are assigned. There are some chairs in the hallway and extra blankets under the beds." We nodded, picked up our bags, and began to couple up. "Alabama girls," Marion called out, "you're this way," and she walked them off to a separate dormitory next door.

The next morning, we took the Red Car line to El Segundo. It was full of women all going to the same place, their hair divided in two and rolled on each side of their heads or neatly pinned up and away from their faces.

"There are so many ladies here already, do you think they'll have a job for all of us?" I asked Mary Ellen, sitting next to me.

A perfectly coiffed, rouge-lipped woman, with a navy scarf tied around her head, turned in the seat in front of us. "Oh honey, there is so much work to do here, gals are getting recruited by the busload. They'll give you triple shifts if you'll take them."

"I'll take 'em," I said, excited by the taste of possibility.

Once inside the factory gates, Marion led us toward a cluster of three huge buildings, all covered with some kind of green-and-brown netting.

"We have lunch here," Marion said, pointing to the benches set up under a part of the mesh that formed a giant canopy. "We eat in shifts. There are thousands of girls working, and we rotate fast so there's never a minute, night or day, that aircraft are not getting made."

"Is this supposed to make us feel like we're actually in battle?" one of the girls asked, laughing as she looked at the camouflage netting covering the buildings and the outdoor area.

"Hardly," Marion said, glaring at the young woman who'd asked the question. "It's to keep us camouflaged, so the enemy can't see what this building is if they fly overhead. We'd be a target, you know, just like they targeted Pearl Harbor."

Someone in the group gasped and I shot her a look. I for one didn't want anyone at the factory to think I was scared and not up for the job.

"We're building bombers, ladies," Marion said sternly. "SBD Dauntless dive-bombers, A-20 Havoc attack planes. If the enemy knew what we were doing and where, they'd happily blow us to pieces."

Back in Wichita, the war had felt far away. The ration stamps were real, the victory gardens we planted were real, the mothers who sat at home worried sick, that was all too real, but the idea of enemy planes and potential targets here in the United States, in California, where I was about to start living and working, that was new thinking to me.

She walked us into a massive hangar that must have been ten stories high. Partially built aircraft were lined up at perfect forty-five-degree angles, with men and women working on various parts of the planes. Some were inside the body of the aircraft with a drill, others under it with a rolling toolbox at their sides; someone was on a ladder working on the wing. I'd never seen such a thing: men and women working side by side, doing the same work—or at least that's how it seemed. Everyone looked important, each with their own task.

In another room, this one full of tables, women were bent over, sorting through boxes of debris in front of them.

"They're sorting the wheat from the chaff," Marion said. "Hundreds of nuts, bolts, and rivets skitter across the floor each day. They get swept up, and we have to sort through the metal shavings and trash to put the lost fasteners back into service. Saves us hundreds of dollars, and we have the perfect-sized fingers to do the sorting."

"Do we get to decide what job we're assigned to?" one of the gals asked her. I was wondering the same thing, hoping I'd be assigned to work inside a plane.

"Mr. Lockhart, your supervisor, will decide that when he sees how you do on your rivet test," Marion said.

The girls in the group started whispering to one another. I wasn't overly concerned. Growing up, just my mother and me, I had to learn to help around the house at an early age. When the kitchen sink was leaking, I was under there with a wrench tightening up the faucet nut. When the chair to the two-person dinner table broke, I screwed the legs back in place. When our car wouldn't start—and that was every other day since it was such a beater—I was the one standing on a step stool, my head under the hood. My mother would cook and clean and sew, but I enjoyed fixing things when they were broken.

Though I didn't remember him at all, my mother told me I inherited my handyman instincts from my father. He worked as a train engineer. Each shift on the locomotive was at least twenty-four hours, and he'd be in charge of transporting 20,000 tons of freight from one part of the country to another—often flammable liquids, crude oil, chlorine, or ammonia. "Special Dangerous" was what they called that kind of freight. My mother told me that he was gone so often and at home so infrequently that they never really had the chance to live like man and wife in the traditional sense, that he was far more comfortable on the trains, moving, fixing, on the go. Even when he was home, she said, he spent most of his time outside or in the garage. So when a hand brake malfunctioned and sent sparks off the wheels, causing a fire on board that lit up those flammables, we didn't fully feel the loss of him right away. My mother said she was used to having just the two of us at home. But as I got older and saw other kids with their fathers, I became consumed by a slow-burning grief, a yearning for what might have been.

I was too young to have learned any engineering or mechanical skills from him, but I always thought of my father when I worked on the car. I wondered if he'd have been proud of me. If he were to walk back into our lives right then, would he be shocked to see me comfortably working under the hood? Would he nod his head in approval? I'd often search other men's faces as I walked down the street, particularly the strong-looking ones—not the ones in suits and ties, the ones in work clothes with grease under their nails—and I'd imagine that their face was his face, and I'd wonder if that was how it might have felt when he smiled back at me.

"Here's where we change and keep our lunch pails," Marion said when we reached the end of the sorting room, and she took us to the lockers. She opened a door to a room full of cots. "If you work a double shift, you'll get a thirty-minute break to take a nap. It's exhausting work, you have to concentrate at all times, so you'll need a chance to rest your eyes if you double up. But let's not forget you're saving lives by working here. The faster and more efficiently you work, the faster we can bring our men back home where they belong." Marion touched a small pendant around her neck. "So don't let each other down," she said. "Now, time to learn what you'll actually be doing here." She gave each of us a set of earplugs and a pair of goggles and led us out to the factory floor.

"We need buckers, and we need riveters," she said. "Riveters stand on one side and slide the metal pins through to fasten the metal sheets together; buckers, they stand on the other side of the line, opposite, and they buck the rivet when it's inserted. You're going to pair up with someone who already works the line, they'll show you what to do, and then you'll take a test."

Everyone was in formation, and an eruption of noise rose into the huge open space—drilling, hammering, metal against metal. I quickly put my earplugs in and watched in awe as hundreds of synchronized women worked at their stations in the assembly line.

"I'm Lou Anne," a tall, slim woman yelled as she approached me.

"Hazel," I shouted back.

She nodded to the round goggles in my hand. "Put those on," she said as she pulled hers off her forehead and positioned them over her eyes. "If you want to keep your eyeballs intact."

She led me to an open spot in the assembly line. It was bright inside, lit by overhead fluorescent lighting, but to protect us from becoming a target, the building was completely devoid of windows. She adjusted my goggles, helping me position them correctly, turning my head from one side to the other. "Your hair is fine pulled back like that, but tomorrow make sure it's wrapped—it's safer that way. You don't want to get that pretty hair of yours ripped off." She looked down at my thick-soled boots, which I'd bought as soon as the information package arrived in Kansas along with my application. "Don't wear anything but those around here, can't tell you how many rivets have gone right through a gal's foot." She was really yelling loud, but I could just barely hear her over the noise of the place, so I watched her lips to make out what she was saying.

"I'll be over there, on the other side of you, using one of these rivet guns." She pointed to a long row of guns on pulleys above our heads. "You're going to line up the bucking bar to the hole, hold it until I drive the rivet in, and it will fasten these two parts together." She held up two squares of aluminum with about a hundred punched holes. "Now, I'm not going to be able to hear you at all when I'm on the other side, so check if it's in good—if it is, give me two taps with the bucker; if it needs more, tap once and I'll punch it again. Now, if you hold the bucking bar crooked, I'm gonna have to drill the rivet out and drive a new one in, and if the hole gets too big, it's gonna have to be patched. So don't let that happen because it will slow us down."

"Got it," I said, looking up at the large rivet guns hanging overhead. I may have worked with a hammer and even a drill in the past, but I'd never handled large machinery like this before, and I hoped I'd get it right.

"Practice a couple on here," she said, holding up a bit of scrap metal, "and then we'll do your test. Once you're halfway through, we'll switch places, and you can be the riveter."

Lou Anne walked all the way to the end of the line and back up the other side until she was opposite me, and we began, slowly at first until I got the hang of it, but soon we were tearing along, my arm vibrating each time she punched the gun. It was repetitive work, but there was a seriousness to it, an intense concentration that I liked.

When I was done, Marion came by, looked at my work, and gave me what seemed to be a nod of approval, which flooded me with relief.

"This way," she said, taking me and my metal square to Mr. Lockhart's office.

"Name?" he asked the second I walked in.

"Hazel Francis," I said, standing at attention in his small, immaculately organized office. He was a short man, but he had a commanding presence and a no-nonsense attitude.

He looked at the metal rectangle I handed him and studied it. "Nice work," he said. "I hear you worked fast with no mistakes. That's what we need around here."

I stood a little taller with his words of encouragement.

"I'll put you on as a riveter and we'll see how that goes," he said. "But you take it seriously, you hear me, no gabbing with the girls or you'll be ejected off the line faster than you knew what hit you. One missed rivet and you could be responsible for the metal peeling mid-flight. Do you want to be responsible for a bomber going down with someone's husband or brother in it?"

"No, sir."

"Good." He handed me some paperwork to fill out. "You have someone in the forces?" He glanced down at my left hand, his eyes settling on the thin gold band. "You got a boy deployed." It was a statement more than a question.

"Yes," I said awkwardly. "He's, um, my friend, well, fiancé." That word felt all wrong coming out of my mouth, and I was ashamed that I could barely bring myself to say it. "He's stationed in France, I believe."

Mr. Lockhart nodded. "Well, then you know. No talking about what you do here. Loose lips sink ships." He pointed to a poster on his office wall of a ship engulfed in black smoke going down into a blue ocean. "No talking when you're on the line. No jewelry, we don't want anything that could get caught in the machinery." I was relieved at having an excuse to take the gold ring off my finger. "And coveralls or trousers only, pinned at the ankle, no excess fabric, no pockets or buttons, and no skirts or dresses." He sighed. "But put some lipstick on your face so we can tell you apart from the fellas. All these trousers walking about the place these days, and we can barely tell who's who."

Something about him, and the factory itself, intimidated me—he was a hard-liner, the hangars were enormous—but I hoped he didn't pick up on my trepidation. I wanted him to know that I planned to take this job very seriously, as if my life depended on it. He handed me a pen and nodded to the chair where I could sit to fill out my information.

"Pay is sixty-five cents an hour to start." I looked up, wide-eyed. I'd been working back home as a waitress part-time for only thirty cents an hour and the occasional skimpy tip. "That can improve depending on how you do. And we encourage our workers to purchase war bonds through our payroll deduction plan if you can, to help with the war effort," he said, his tone serious. I nodded. "But this is no charity. You'll be working seven days a week, ten-hour days, no time off except Christmas. Thanksgiving is a workday. This is man's work you're gonna be doing to help keep these fellas alive."

"Yes, sir. It's an honor to be here," I said, looking back at my paperwork. Sixty-five cents to start!

CHAPTER 5

Laguna Beach, California — February 1946

HOTEL LAGUNA WAS A MISSION-STYLE BUILDING RIGHT ON THE beach with a bell tower and a large sign announcing itself at 17 South Coast Boulevard. On the walls of the lobby there were signed photographs of Humphrey Bogart and Lauren Bacall, Errol Flynn, and John Barrymore, all dining or lounging at the hotel. The whole place was like something out of the pictures. Based on my meeting with Mr. Radcliff and the fact that he'd clearly been hitting the sauce all day, I had my doubts that our interview the next day would actually lead to a paying job, but at least I had a place to sleep that night and, if it didn't work out, it gave me an extra day to search for some other work.

I was determined to do exactly as he'd suggested and enjoy myself. I walked in, gave the man at the front desk Mr. Radcliff's name, and, with no fuss at all, was shown to a small but immaculate guest room, filled with the warm afternoon sun from a window looking directly out to the ocean. Two large paintings decorated the walls—one a beach scene, the other a view from some hills with the tiniest triangle of ocean visible in the distance. I opened the drawers of the dresser, pushed open a door that led to a private bathroom, then allowed myself to fall back on the bed, smoothing my hands over the soft cotton sheets and the plush bedspread. This was spectacular.

After unpacking my outfit for the following day and hanging it in the closet, I walked downstairs to see the rest of the hotel. It was an L-shaped building with an open courtyard in the center, a fountain surrounded by gardens, and a set of table and chairs. There was a restaurant and a lounge, and at the back of the hotel a walkway took me directly to Main Beach. I took off my shoes and let my feet sink into the cool, soft sand.

The landscape here was rugged and complex. This beach was tucked into a cove, with houses dotted on the cliffs above, alongside palm and eucalyptus trees. Little shops and restaurants lined the boardwalk, a quaint town was just beyond, and rising above it all were steep hills that hugged this part of the coastline, as if protecting it. I could see why so many artists were drawn to this part of the Southern California coast.

As I approached the water's edge, white sea-foam rushed up and washed over my toes, the icy water startling me. After seeing the sun glisten on its surface, I had expected it to be warmer. A gentle breeze blew off the ocean, and I wrapped my arms around myself, noticing how quickly the temperature dropped once the sun began to go down.

By six o'clock I was starving. I walked back along the boardwalk to South Coast Boulevard and was met by a shaggy-haired man in a red shirt and gray trousers standing on the corner.

"Halloo," he called out, waving madly, his ruddy face with its thick beard looking right at me. "Delighted to see you!"

I turned around to see if he was talking to someone else, but he pointed his cane in my direction. "You!" he said, smiling like a crazy person. "Are you alive?"

"I believe so," I said, continuing to walk, but he blocked my way.

"You're new here," he said.

"Um, yes, I just arrived yesterday."

"Welcome to Laguna Beach," he said. "You're going to love it here." A car driving by honked its horn, and he waved at the driver. "Halloo, how *are* you?" he boomed.

I put my head down and kept walking.

"Some people have millions of dollars and no friends," he called out after me. "I have nothing, but I have thousands of friends who walk and drive by to greet me. I am the lucky one, me!"

When I reached the hotel, I looked back and saw he had moved on to bother someone else, waving frantically and pointing his cane. This town sure had some interesting characters. After a brief visit to the powder room, where I applied some rouge and tried to smooth down my hair, I walked as confidently as I could into the dark oak-lined restaurant.

"Table for one, please," I asked meekly. I'd never stayed in a hotel before, let alone eaten in a restaurant by myself. If they balked at the idea, I'd immediately apologize and back out of there, and I'd eat at the diner instead. In fact, I thought maybe I should do that anyway, save myself the humiliation of being turned away, but when I added, almost in a whisper, that I was a guest of Hanson Radcliff, the maître d' clasped his hands together, picked up a menu that looked as if it belonged in the library, and ushered me to a booth with red leather seats.

I'd planned to select something small—my eyes went to the soup du jour, or perhaps the sliced eggs with Russian dressing—but when I saw the full menu, my hunger got the best of me. The only thing I'd put in my stomach all day was the cup of coffee at the ice cream parlor.

"I'll take the beef tenderloin sauté stroganoff over baked rice and a cup of tea please," I said to the waiter. "And a baked potato with butter and chives." I looked down quickly, embarrassed at my order, fit for a man.

"Very good," the waiter said, writing it down.

"Oh, and it's on Mr. Radcliff's tab," I said, making certain there wasn't going to be a misunderstanding.

"Of course," he said and walked back to the kitchen.

When the food arrived, I devoured it. I ate half and set my fork down for a moment. I didn't want anyone to see me tear through a beef stroganoff like that, it wasn't ladylike. But my goodness, I hadn't eaten a meal like that in years. After polishing off the rest in daintier bites, I headed to my room through the lobby but was lured by the sound of jazz pouring down a long hallway. I followed it, peeking into the hotel bar—a sign read LA CONCHA COCKTAIL LOUNGE. It had a front-row view of the sea dancing under the night sky. I stood there for a moment, in the middle of the crowded bar, watching the midnight-blue waves crashing right in front of me. When I looked up, the bartender was waving me over.

"Gets you every time, doesn't it?" he said. "A chair just opened up, want to take it?" He pointed to a seat at the end of the bar. I felt uneasy about sitting by myself in such an establishment, but the music, the view, and the relaxed feel of the place made me want to stay. Glancing around,

I noticed an older woman sitting alone at the other end of the bar, so I allowed myself to do the same.

"Thank you," I said.

"Jimmy," he said, sticking out his hand.

"Hazel."

"Beautiful, isn't it?" He stood with his hands in his pockets.

"It certainly is."

"So, what brings you to Hotel Laguna?"

"I'm here for a job interview."

"Swell. What can I get for you?"

"Just a water, please."

He raised an eyebrow. "Sorry, but you can't take a ringside seat at this hour if you only drink water," he said with a laugh.

"Oh," I said, embarrassed. "I don't want to add to the tab. I mean, the artist I'm interviewing with is putting me up here. I just ate at the restaurant, but I don't think it will look good to put an alcoholic beverage on the tab."

"Who's the artist?" he asked, wiping down the dark wood bar in front of me and setting down a napkin.

"It's Mr. Radcliff," I said, taking the newspaper clipping out of my pocket and flipping it over to where I'd scribbled down his name. "Mr. Hanson Radcliff."

"Ahh." He laughed and nodded. "I think you're fine. He's a regular—he will not care at all, believe me."

"But it doesn't seem right."

"Tell you what, this one's on me," he said in a whisper. "How about a French 75?"

Jimmy was tall and broad shouldered, and I could see the muscles working under his white button-down shirt as he moved around the bar quickly, pouring from bottles, putting them back again, getting down one glass then deciding on another. Finally, he made a big fuss of delivering the bubbly, opaque drink with a lemon garnish.

"A champagne cocktail named after the French seventy-five-millimeter field gun and its powerful kick," he said with a smile.

I couldn't help but laugh. "A cocktail with a tale. Thank you, that was quite a display."

"I live to entertain." He smiled, revealing a dimple on his left cheek, then he was called away to a patron at the other end of the bar. I sipped my drink as I looked out at the crashing waves and was surprised by the sweet and sour notes.

This artist, Hanson Radcliff, seemed like a real crumb. Our meeting the next day would probably amount to nothing, and this time tomorrow I'd be figuring out my next move, likely boarding a train to someplace new, but boy, this town sure would be a nice place to call home for a while.

"Sorry about that," Jimmy said. "I had to make some drinks."

"Quite all right. I can see you're busy." He wiped down the bar again and replaced my untouched napkin with a fresh one.

"I invited you to sit here, so it would be ungentlemanly of me to leave you alone." He took down a wineglass from above the bar and wiped it with a towel, then started on another. "So, what's the job?"

"Honestly, I'm not really sure," I said. "An assistant of some sort."

He raised an eyebrow.

"What is it?" I asked.

"He's a real nice guy, comes in here frequently, very talented artist and well respected in that regard. I get along with him great, we've had some deep conversations . . . In fact, he's been more than kind to me."

"But?"

"Some people around here are . . ." He seemed to be looking for the right word. "A little afraid of him."

"Afraid?"

He shrugged. "He can be abrupt, that's all, but you just have to get to know him. Being behind the bar as much as I am, I hear a lot of talk."

Suddenly I was second-guessing myself for responding to the ad, but it wasn't as if I had any other options.

"Well, I'll take my chances," I said. "I've been working at an airplane plant up in Los Angeles, and now that the men are back and we don't need to produce so many planes, I'm out of a job. I need to make some money and figure out what I'm going to do next."

"I know the feeling," he said. "But once you get settled, I think you'll really like it here."

"You know, you're the second person to say that to me today. When

I was walking to the hotel, some crazy man outside stopped me in the street and wanted to talk my ear off."

"Oh," Jimmy said with a smile. "That's just Eiler Larsen, he's the town's greeter."

"The town has a greeter?"

"Unofficial, I suppose, but he's out there every single day welcoming people to Laguna and generally just spreading goodwill."

"He seemed a little off the cob to me," I said.

"Maybe a little, but he's harmless. Anyway, you'll see what I mean about this town: after a while, everyone starts to feel like family."

"Sounds nice," I said, taking another sip of my drink.

"What did they have you doing at the factory?"

"All kinds of things: riveting, welding, I even worked on attack bombers." Just describing it made me miss it. "I loved every minute of it. Working a real job like that, a job that meant something, and paid well. I wish it could have gone on forever." I looked up at him and quickly regretted saying that. He looked a few years older than me, and he was certainly able-bodied, must have served somewhere.

"Sorry, I didn't mean it like that," I said. "Of course I'm glad it's over, I just wish it didn't mean those kinds of jobs were closed to women like me."

"Don't worry." He smiled. "I understand what you're saying."

"How did the war treat you?" I asked.

"I was right here at the beginning, training for the marines. I'm from New York."

"New York?" I perked up.

"Well, Queens, and I was stationed not far from here, at the El Toro marine base, where they showed us the ropes before they shipped us out. Some of the officers were actually housed here in the hotel. I took one look at this place, and I said I'm coming back. A view like this, balmy seventy to eighty degrees pretty much year-round, I'll take it. It's relaxed, everyone's happy and nice to be around." He smiled. He really did look happy. "Once the war ended, I disembarked in San Francisco, and I got on the train and headed straight down here to this hotel. Told them I'd do anything they wanted: clean the floors, make the beds, peel potatoes. I didn't care. They had me start out wiping down tables, windows, even bathrooms, and now I work the bar four nights a week. I'm still learning the cocktails, so if it doesn't taste right, keep it to yourself."

I smiled and took another sip. "It's perfect," I said, even though it was a touch too tart.

That night I slept like a baby. The bed was spacious, the sheets were soft, and the room was quiet and heavenly. But best of all, I wasn't keeping the bed warm for anyone coming in off the night shift.

CHAPTER 6

I ARRIVED AT 120 CLEO STREET AT EXACTLY TWELVE NOON. THIS time I knew to walk around the side of the house, and I found the door ajar. I saw Mr. Radcliff inside a large room, all windows, whistling.

"Hello," I said quietly, not wanting to startle him. "Mr. Radcliff," I said, louder this time, knocking on the open door. Finally, he turned around and saw me, a bucket in his hands.

"Good God, what are you doing standing there?" he said. "Come in, have a seat." He motioned to an old armchair covered with books and magazines.

He had combed his hair back from his face and was dressed in trousers, a shirt with the sleeves rolled up, and a vest. He still had a wildness to him, but he looked more respectable, as if he might at least have showered.

"You're here about the ad I placed. What was your name again?" he said, walking toward me and putting his hand out.

"Hazel Francis," I said, shaking his hand. It was rough with speckles of paint that looked as if they'd never come off no matter how much he scrubbed.

"You want something to drink?"

"No, no thank you," I said, perhaps a little too fast.

"I'm having a 7 Up," he said.

"Oh, all right, that would be nice, thank you."

He walked out of the room, which was more like an adjoining sunroom added to the back of the house. This must have been his studio: there were canvases everywhere, mounted on the walls, stacked on the floor, leaning on each other—landscapes and seascapes mostly. I stopped in front of one—a mountain range painted bright red and orange as if the hills were on fire. In the foreground were blackened silhouettes of spindly tree branches. Next to it, a bright turquoise ocean pulled back at low tide, revealing green and purple tide pools. Most of the paintings I'd seen before were dark, somber, and serious. These were unnatural, in unrealistic colors, and yet they were exciting, somehow believable, as if the sun had been especially bright that day, making things glow and reflect.

I suddenly felt his eyes on me as I studied his work, and he walked back into the room.

"So," he said, handing me a small green bottle with a straw. "You want to be an assistant?"

"Yes," I said.

"And you have experience?"

"I worked at Douglas Aircraft for three years building airplane parts and, most recently, after production stopped, working odd jobs at the plant, secretarial, that kind of thing."

He nodded, picked up a few paintbrushes lying on the ledge of an easel, and took them over to a sink in the corner of the room.

"You don't have any experience in the art world then?"

I shook my head then quickly added, "I'm a fast learner."

He put his hand to his chin and pulled at the gray stubble.

"You've got a look about you," he said.

I didn't know what to say to that, but his gaze didn't leave me, and I began to feel uncomfortable.

"It's very beautiful, your art," I said. "Very colorful."

"It's because I pay attention. I paint things the way I see them, not the way you think they should be seen," he said. "Don't you want to sit down?"

"I'm fine," I said. It felt strange to sit if he was wandering around his studio cleaning up, and, besides, everything was a mess and there was nowhere to sit. "I'm used to being on my feet all day at the factory."

"Well, that's good," he said. "If this works out, you'd be on your feet for hours at a time."

"That wouldn't be a problem," I said.

"Good. And I keep sporadic hours—you might say I'm a little erratic—so I'd need you available whenever I need you. That's why it's a unique situation, not everyone can do it. Do you have someone who'd be waiting for you at home? A husband, children?"

"No."

"A boyfriend?"

I shook my head.

"Good." He looked at me and then cocked his head a little, as if he was just noticing something for the first time.

"How often do you urinate?"

"Excuse me?" I clenched my purse to my chest.

"It's a personal question, I know," he went on. "But I can't have distractions all day. I need someone who is in control of their body, not running to the lavatory every five minutes."

I shook my head, baffled. "I, I would say about the same as anyone else really. Actually, when I worked on the line at the factory, we had to work incredibly fast with the rivet gun, and the bucker opposite couldn't work if I wasn't at my station, so bathroom breaks were few and far between," I said, proud of myself for coming up with such a fitting response, but he had walked to the other side of the room.

"You'd need to be close by," he went on. "It won't work for you to be in Los Angeles anymore."

"I understand," I said.

"Good. And you'll need to be resourceful."

"Of course," I said. "May I ask what the salary would be?"

"Before we talk money, let's see if you're up to the task. I need to make sure I know what I'll be working with."

"Oh," I said, surprised. "Oh, yes, of course."

"But if it works out, I could pay sixty dollars a week," he said.

My eyes almost popped out of my head—that was a lot more than what I was making at the airplane plant, where I had to work seventy hours a week, and it was far higher pay than I would have made in any other job available to me. "Wow," I said, not meaning to actually say that out loud. "That would be fine."

"Okay, then," he said, pulling out a large drawing pad from under a table pushed against the wall and arranging it on his easel. "Should we

get started? You can change in the washroom, it's through that door." He
pointed toward the house where he'd gone earlier to retrieve the 7 Ups.

"Oh," I said, turning to look in the direction he was pointing, then
back to him. "What exactly would you like me to do?"

"A sitting," he said.

"A sitting?"

"Posing, modeling, whatever you want to call it." He nodded, taking
out a piece of charcoal and holding the tip up to his eyes, putting it back,
and taking out another.

"I'm sorry, Mr. Radcliff, there seems to be some misunderstanding.
I'm no model."

"That's all right, as long as you can sit still and stay in position for an
hour or two, maybe three, it should be fine. I can direct you to get into position, but if you fidget, move your arm, the angle of your face, it changes
everything: the skin tone, the shadows, the perspective."

"But you said you were looking for an assistant."

"Yes, you'll be assisting me with various things, whatever the day
calls for. Some days that means you'll be assisting me by posing so I can
work on my portraiture."

"But I thought you did landscapes."

"Good God, woman, so many questions!" He was glaring at me. "What
difference does it make to you?" he said gruffly. I could see why people
might be afraid of him. "No real artist gets too comfortable painting just
one thing; it becomes dull. True artists see things deeply, we reimagine
them, and enhance our understanding of them. I've accomplished that in
some of my seascapes and landscapes. You saw it yourself; I watched you
studying my paintings just now. I've captured the rage of the ocean and
her intent. Now I will improve my understanding of the female form."

Despite his tone, it all sounded quite beautiful, what he said. I wasn't
sure I completely followed, but there was something thrilling about it
nonetheless. I supposed I could sit for him if that was all he wanted—he
didn't seem disturbed by my lack of experience in that regard—and I
imagined it would be easy work to simply sit there. Maybe I could read
a book or something to pass the time.

"You can change in the washroom," he said, pointing with the charcoal in his hand. He was getting impatient, but I could tell he was trying

to remain calm. Surely, he could recognize that he had caught me completely off guard with this request.

"All right," I said, quickly turning and walking toward the house, then hesitating. "And, I'm sorry, what did you want me to change into?"

He peered around the easel and glared at me. "Nothing," he said. "That's the whole point."

My arms flew around my midsection, and I froze. I can't imagine what my face must have revealed. I felt ridiculous for not having picked up on it earlier and horrified that I'd been so caught up by this whole situation without having any notion what it would entail. He wanted me to take my clothes off! To pose completely nude in front of him, so he could draw my naked body. This was repulsive; he was an old man with a drinking problem, a degenerate for all I knew. He stared at me a moment longer and raised his shoulders, waiting for me to do or say something, but nothing came out; there was just a look of horror etched on my face.

"Jesus Christ." He took the charcoal he had in his hand and threw it against the wall. "A waste of my goddamned time!" He got up, barged past me, flung the door open, and marched into the house. I paused for a moment in shock, then left the way I'd come in.

Half an hour later I stood on the boardwalk looking out to the ocean, hands in fists, furious. A family walked past me with a baby carriage and the woman laughed, probably at something her husband had said, but it felt as if they were laughing at me. My skin crawled with humiliation. And to think that the whole time we talked he'd been eyeing me, picturing me as a nude model, as if I would disrobe for a total stranger like that. Horrified and embarrassed at my naivete, I tried to shake the conversation from my mind. *What did you want me to change into? Nothing, that's the whole point.* I felt so ignorant, I wanted to throw something. I marched to the water's edge and looked for a rock, a pebble, something, but there was nothing, just sand. I found a piece of seaweed, long and snakelike. I picked it up and threw it into the water, but it wasn't satisfying. I wanted something with weight.

I'd paid so much attention to my hair that morning, I'd tried to impress him with my tasks at the factory, when all he wanted was to look at my naked body. I shuddered at the thought and quickly began walking toward the hotel. There was no point staying here a minute longer.

I would pack my things and leave this ridiculous town with its ridiculous people and their absurd requests.

Another wave of mortification swept over me as I walked through the lobby of the hotel, so beautiful and grand, and recalled how I'd enjoyed my evening—a decadent dinner, a cocktail watching the ocean, a conversation with a stranger behind the bar. All paid for by a man who expected me to take my clothes off for his enjoyment.

"Hazel, is that you?" a familiar voice called out behind me as I was about to climb the stairs to vacate my room. It was Jimmy, the bartender from the previous evening. "Why the long face? Did the interview not go well?"

I shook my head. "No, it did not go well."

Jimmy sighed. "I'm sorry about that. He can be difficult," he said. "Why don't you let me make you a strong drink to cheer you up? The bar doesn't open for another hour or so, and I'm working on a new concoction."

"It's barely three in the afternoon."

He shrugged. "A tea then?"

I managed a tepid smile and followed him to the empty cocktail lounge. I had nowhere else to be.

"What happened?" Jimmy said once he was behind the bar.

I shook my head. "I can't."

"That bad, huh?"

"He said he wanted an assistant, but that's not what he wanted, that's not what he wanted at all." Talking about it made me feel even more humiliated. Good Lord, I had told him I was slender. Slender!

"Well, what did he want?" Jimmy was leaning on the bar, listening intently.

"It's indecent," I said. "He wanted me to . . ." I stared into the tea he'd set in front of me, unable to meet his eyes. "He wanted me to model for him."

"Model, huh? Like pose for him, to draw you or somethin'? Well, that doesn't sound so bad. Forgive me for being so bold, but you're a pretty girl, he must've seen that right away."

I knew it was a compliment, but I just couldn't take anyone else saying something about my appearance. I didn't want anyone to notice me at all. I wanted to shrink, to hide.

"He's an artist," Jimmy went on. "He has an eye for beauty."

"Oh, Jimmy, stop, please stop, I can't take it. I feel so wretched about the whole thing and how I handled it. I was so ignorant. I had no idea that's what he wanted."

Jimmy put his hands up. "I'm sorry, I didn't mean to step out of line. I'm just telling you this is an artists' town, it's filled with people who look for beauty in everyday life, and they find it. It's like magic. They can look at something that you and me might walk past every day, and they see something, they capture it, and then it's permanent, you know, captured forever. I can never quite believe it when I see the paintings in some of these galleries. Not all of them are all that good, in my personal opinion, or maybe I'm just not smart enough to understand them, but Hanson Radcliff, he's a genius, there's no doubting that."

"But you don't understand, he expected me to, to . . ." I couldn't say it, but somehow I thought I'd feel better if I told him, as if I'd be relieving myself of the shame. "He wanted me to take my clothes off," I said finally. But as I replayed the conversation I'd had with Hanson, I didn't feel better; instead, a hopeless feeling took over. "I'm sorry," I said, embarrassed at the tears that were forming at the corners of my eyes. Jimmy placed a napkin in front of me. "I'm sorry, I just really, really wanted this job, I needed this job, the pay was . . . it was very generous." I caught my breath, feeling another gush of emotion come over me. "I have no idea what I'm going to do now. I don't know where to go, I'm almost out of money, and I just really can't go back home. I have no home to go back to!" At this I really did start to cry. "Oh God," I said, trying to get ahold of myself. "I'm sorry."

"Hey, hey, hey," Jimmy said, reaching over the bar and placing his hands on mine. "I don't know about any of that, and I certainly don't know anything about modeling or posing or sitting or whatever you call it, but I do know that it's different here. It's just art, it's part of the process; you'd be part of his art. And surely you wouldn't be doing that all day long."

"No, he said he'd have me helping with things he needed assistance with, so I don't know what that means, but I suppose it couldn't be any worse than taking my clothes off."

Jimmy took a stack of white cloth napkins out from behind the bar and started folding them. "Listen, you've got to do what's right for you, but it sure would be a shame for you to leave town so fast before you've even had a chance to get to know this place. The people here are generally kind and interesting. The weather is perfect; honestly, there's no place I'd rather be. And"—he smiled—"it'd sure be nice if you stuck around."

I managed a small smile back, then I took a napkin and folded it the same way he did. Then another, then another—focusing on something else for a moment helped calm me.

"Hey, Jimmy," I said. "You know, I think I'd like to take you up on that offer of a strong drink, after all."

CHAPTER 7

Los Angeles, California—March 1943

THREE MONTHS INTO MY JOB ON THE ASSEMBLY LINE, MR. LOCKHART tapped me on the shoulder, pointed to me, then flicked his thumb toward his office. Worried, I wanted to ask what it was regarding, but I couldn't hear a thing he was saying on the factory floor. I'd been working hard, concentrating for hours at a time, trying to do everything right. The work might be mindless, after the first few thousand rivets, and my feet and back were throbbing by the end of my shifts, but there was something remarkably satisfying about being one small cog in the wheel of something so much bigger. It gave me a sense of purpose to know that I was contributing to such an important piece of machinery—an SBD Dauntless dive-bomber. It sounded so sinister and violent, yet capable of soaring through the air with precision and force, taking out enemies before they could kill our men.

"I need to take you off the line," Mr. Lockhart said as we entered his office, and he closed the door.

My heart sank. The money was good, and I liked being around all these women. I didn't want to go back to serving coffee and french fries.

"The girl you were filling in for, she's back from leave."

I nodded.

"You're fast; your hand skills are quick, precise. You did above average in the speed test. I'd like to try you in assembly for the cowling."

"Okay." I nodded, trying to keep up.

"The engine cowling." He stood up and we walked from his office, and he led me to a different hangar. "Here, I'll show you what I'm talking about."

Unlike in the previous buildings, where rows of women worked diligently in assembly lines longer than a football field, the hangar we entered had a long row of half-built planes, each at the same midstage of assembly, one after another, reaching from the entrance where we stood all the way to the other end of the hangar.

"We call them 'precompletes,'" he said. "Sections of the plane—we can't put the whole thing together too fast because we won't have room for them, so we build it in pieces." He approached the body of the nearest plane—the wings and tail still unattached—and climbed up a six-stair ladder into the aircraft. "Come on." He looked back at me on the ground. "Keep up."

The top was still open, so we were able to stand, but Mr. Lockhart climbed up to the nose and crouched down.

"See that?" he said, pointing to a large circular rim with an opening in the center that looked as if it might be where the propellers would be attached later. "That's the cowling." There was a series of metal fixtures and bolts and clamps and tubing. "Have you ever used a wrench?"

"Yes."

"Good. And you'll be working on electrical wires," he said, easing his way back out of the aircraft. "It's not a small job; most men who work on these have been doing it for twenty years. It requires patience, diligence, and high dexterity. But I think you can handle it."

We climbed down, and he introduced me to a girl perched on a ladder at the front of the plane. She had a bright floral headscarf tied around her hair. "This here's Phyllis, she's going to train you. She's one of our best, so listen and learn. And don't screw it up."

I didn't screw it up. I focused on my training, I asked questions, and then I did the work, squeezing into the nose of the plane for hours at a time, often cramped and sore, but relishing the fact that I'd been upgraded to something more.

And then, two months later, I was pulled off the job again.

"I'm sending you and some of our top girls to the Long Beach plant for two weeks of training on the A-20 attack bomber," Mr. Lockhart said. "The Havoc. We just got a big order from the military and we need them fast."

"Yes, sir."

"They're heavily armored—eight .50-caliber machine guns in the nose, three machine guns in each wing and two more mounted in both upper and lower turrets."

"Wowsers."

"They are complicated beasts: 165,000 parts need to be assembled, and they're not cheap to make either. Anyway, we need more hands on them if we're to get them made and flown out to the troops. Think you can do it?"

"Yes, sir." I wanted to shout from the rooftops. I had never been more excited to feel part of something so important.

"If you get through training, we'll bump you to seventy-two cents an hour."

I wanted to hug him, but instead I said, "Thank you so much for the opportunity," as calmly as I could manage.

Some of the girls had started going dancing at the USO after our shifts, determined to boost the morale of the troops stationed in Los Angeles, and I'd joined them on several occasions, but after my training was complete, I stopped any late-night shenanigans immediately. My work felt too precarious: one slipup could cost someone their life. I couldn't be tired, I couldn't be distracted, and I sensed that the whole team that worked on these A-20s felt the same way. It baffled me to think that this metal piece of machinery, with a massive engine and eighteen high-powered guns, could fly into the sky. How could it even leave the ground with all that weight?

Many nights, after working for hours, I'd dream I was in the aircraft when it took off. I'd look out the window and see the ground peeling away and I'd feel a thrill that, against all odds, I was the one soaring high. And then I'd wake and feel weighed down with guilt for enjoying the ride. In Bobby's most recent letter, he said he was with his detachment on an island for a week of special training, but he wasn't allowed to say where or what he was doing. I wondered if he was flying in planes like the ones we worked on, or if he might sit in the very aircraft we'd just completed, and it would bring me back to the grim reality of what we were doing: building planes to send young men into the enemy skies with just a hope and a prayer that they'd come back down to earth safe and unharmed.

CHAPTER 8

Laguna Beach, California — February 1946

BACK IN RADCLIFF'S STUDIO, I STOOD FOR A MOMENT, NOT SURE what to do. The sound of movement came from farther inside the house, but I couldn't quite bring myself to let him know I'd returned. A seagull cawed loudly outside, and it jolted me into action—I pushed my shoulders back where they belonged instead of the slumped heap they'd fallen into and made my way to the washroom.

Once inside, door locked, I unbuttoned my blouse, slipping it off, folding it, and placing it on the counter. Unfastening the waist of my skirt, I let it drop to my feet, folding it and placing it with my blouse. I looked at myself in the mirror. Despite not having a comb on hand, I'd managed to keep my center part and the heart-shaped frame it created around my face. The pin curls from the previous day were no longer pronounced, but my dark, shoulder-length hair still had a gentle wave to it. As I stood there in my cream bra and step-ins, I gave myself a little nod—flat stomach, slight curves. He'd be lucky to have me as a subject, I tried to convince myself, though I cringed at the thought of actually doing what would come next. Turning away from the mirror, I dropped the briefs to the floor, unfastened my bra, and dropped that too. A robe hung on the back of the door, so I slipped it on, then, without looking back at the mirror, I walked back into the studio.

"What the hell are you still doing here?" Mr. Radcliff said, standing back at his easel, turning too fast, spilling a splash of brown liquor from the glass in his hand.

"I needed to think about it. But I'm ready to get started now," I said.

He paused and squinted at me, maybe to consider whether the offer was still on the table.

"Do you want to do this?" he asked. "I don't want to sketch someone who doesn't want to be sketched. And I don't want to hear you complaining about it either."

I thought for a moment. If I did this, my reputation could be ruined. If he painted me and then sold those paintings, my naked body would be on display for all to see; I wouldn't be able to take it back. My prospects of marriage would be marred; my chance of having a family would dwindle. But if I didn't take this job, I'd burn through my meager savings in no time or I'd end up cleaning toilets for a living, and that future didn't look too bright either. It didn't feel as if I had a choice.

"I'll need some instruction on poses in the beginning, but I'll get the hang of it," I said.

He sighed and slid a metal chair to the center of the room, then he walked back to his easel and adjusted his stool. "Just sit, find a position that's relatively comfortable, but something you think might be interesting. Take thirty seconds or so to find a pose, and when you get there, stay, don't move."

I walked to the chair, placed my hand on the back of it, and inhaled deeply. I could hear the quiver in my breath, and I made an effort to control it on the way out. I tried picturing anyone but him looking at me, anyone but an old man, in his sixties, maybe even his seventies, about to gaze upon my naked body. I tried to think of someone else—anyone who wasn't him—someone I could focus on. Bobby Watson's face came to mind. No, please; I blinked him away, too terribly sad. Davie Hankel—no, thinking of him made me feel like a child, immature, jealous, hateful. I turned my back to Mr. Radcliff, and I pictured Jimmy, the bartender from the hotel, waving me over to him—the dimple in his left cheek, the big smile, the white teeth. I slipped the robe off my shoulders and let it rest at my elbows. My front was still fairly covered, but my back was bare, almost down to my tailbone. I stayed there for a moment, feeling the air—a cool breeze coming in from the open window, as if someone were running their fingers on my skin, making it prickle.

I took another breath and was about to let the robe drop further, but first I'd settle on a pose. I focused on Jimmy's enthusiasm as he placed the French 75 in front of me, the sour taste I hid when I took my first sip. His eagerness to show that he knew what he was doing behind that bar. I kept my hand on the back of the chair and walked around it, then sat, legs tight together, facing him. My breasts felt cold under the thin cotton robe. I wished my hair were longer, long enough to cover my nipples when the robe was gone. I was sure I looked anxious, uncomfortable, everything clenched. I stared straight ahead, determined not to look at him, but my eyes betrayed me, darting to his face to seek his approval. Mercifully, he was searching a small cardboard box for a piece of charcoal.

I slid my knees around to the left side of the chair so the right side of my body was facing him. I pictured myself sitting at the bar, casual, relaxed. I leaned my arm on the back of the chair and put my fingers in my hair, crossed my right leg over my left. I had my right hand on my thigh, but I let it drop to my side. Stop, I told myself. Stop right there. All right, I would drop the robe. I waited a moment. Should I announce it, should I let him know I was ready, that this felt like it might be a pose, angular, artistic? I shouldn't. To speak would ruin everything, I could sense that much.

"That's it," he said. "Stay right there."

I slowed my breathing and listened: a bird in the tree outside, cicadas, then nothing. Stay right there meant don't move, didn't it? The robe was still hanging on my elbows, still somewhat closed at the front. I would leave it there until he told me to remove it.

Finally, the scratch of charcoal on paper, long, swishing tones, slow at first, long and slow, the outline taking shape. Gradually it grew faster, a quick scrubbing sound, as if shading perhaps. The sound made me feel more comfortable. I stared at a spot on the wall, a nubby bit of uneven paint. I had no idea how long it'd been—five minutes, maybe ten. I tightened my stomach muscles—it felt satisfying somehow—but after twenty or thirty minutes my back was aching. I wished I'd been more upright.

"Change," he called out.

I turned to him, hesitated, then stood up to head back to the bathroom.

"Where are you going?" he asked.

"You wanted me to get changed." It was uncomfortable to be speaking with him half-naked, so I crossed my arms over my chest.

"Change positions," he said. "When I say change, you move into a new pose, completely different from before." He took a swig of his drink, ripped the paper off his easel, and threw it on the floor. I couldn't help wanting to see where it landed, trying to see what he'd seen, what he had drawn, but I knew I shouldn't waste time doing that. I had to think of a new pose.

I sat back down, and, squeezing my legs together at the knees, I shuffled my feet around to the other side of the chair, being careful not to reveal any more of myself than I had to, resuming almost the exact same position on the opposite side.

"Not that," he said. "Turn toward me." He put his hand vertically in front of his face and angled it, directing me. I did as he said, facing him head-on. Knees together, I leaned forward, one arm across my knees, the other hand holding my chin. I stared right at him. If I was really going to do this, I was going to have to own up to it. He was staring at me, studying me as if I weren't a person but an object, a thing. I wanted to look away, I wanted to ask if this was all right, but I told myself not to. I focused on his hair, straight and gray, almost white, hair that didn't want to be ruled by pomade. Eventually the scratching and scraping began, different this time, pencil on paper, higher pitched than charcoal. Quick movements, urgent, a man who had something to prove. I stayed; I didn't move. I don't know how long it took, but it was longer than the first. I could have stayed much longer in this pose, but eventually he ripped the page from the easel and threw it again to the floor, facedown.

"We're done," he said. He looked exhausted, as if the effort had taken it out of him. "Get dressed."

As I put my clothes back on, I was sure I'd ruined my chances. I hadn't posed nude. Even though I'd made the decision that I would do it, I'd kept the robe partially on at all times, covering the most private parts of my body. He hadn't explicitly asked me to drop it, so I hadn't. But I was sure I'd failed the test.

He'd refilled his drink and was sitting on the stool at his easel when I returned.

"When can you start?" he asked quietly.

"Tomorrow," I said.

"All right, come back tomorrow at eleven."

I didn't know if I'd be able to do this again, but the sooner I started working, the sooner I'd start getting paid, and then I could spend some time looking for a more reputable job.

It was past five o'clock when I walked out of his house and toward the town. I had no idea where I was going or what to do next. I had landed the job, and that was the most important hurdle, but I still needed to find somewhere to sleep that night. My suitcase was being held in the lobby of the hotel, so I walked in that direction, and when I got there, I peeked into the bar.

There were only a few patrons, and Jimmy had that start-of-the-shift crispness to him. He was behind the bar, hands in pockets, waiting attentively for someone to need him.

"Hazel," he said when he saw me, a big smile broadening across his clean-shaven face.

"Hey there, Jimmy."

He motioned for me to sit down.

"Oh, no, thanks. I'm about to check out."

His face dropped a little.

"But, um, I took your advice," I said, looking down, unable to meet his eyes. "And, I got the job."

"That's swell. So you'll be sticking around."

I nodded. "I hope so."

"Are you staying here at the hotel?"

"Oh, no," I said, lowering my voice, "I need to find some place that won't break the bank, you know. Once I start working it'll be fine, but things are just a little tight right now."

He nodded. "I'll ask around."

"Thanks," I said, but my face must have betrayed me.

"What's your plan for tonight? Are you going back to Los Angeles?"

"No, I don't really have a place to go back to. I suppose I could try to stay another night here at the hotel, but I don't want to use up the last of my clams." I tapped my pocketbook then shook my head, embarrassed. "I should have thought things through."

He nodded, a concerned crease forming on his perfect brow. "I have an idea. Meet me back here when my shift ends at ten," he said. "I'll help you figure something out."

I wanted to ask more, but he was called to the other end of the bar and started chatting with an elderly couple. I collected my suitcase from the lobby and walked, rather aimlessly, around town. I stopped in front of a bulletin board outside the post office and looked for any mentions of a room to let, but there were only "Housing Wanted" requests, mostly for "fully employed married couples." I headed for the boardwalk, passed by a strip of restaurants and businesses facing the beach—Café Las Ondas, Dante's, the Bath House, and a bowling alley where music flowed out the front door.

With a few hours remaining and nothing to do, I sat on a boardwalk bench and put my suitcase under my legs. The sun was setting, and soon it would be dark. I pulled my cardigan around me and hoped that Jimmy knew of a place for me to stay that night. I hated feeling so unmoored, with no place to call home, but at least I had a job now. I'd work hard, I'd make good money. I vowed to never let myself feel so unsettled again.

CHAPTER 9

Los Angeles, California—October 1943

ONCE THE PRECOMPLETES WERE PUT TOGETHER AND THE PLANE was finished, the final step, before it was rolled out of the huge electric doors onto the tarmac to be fueled and flown to a military installation, was its inspection. Our team lined up to watch and be on hand for any questions that arose. It was the first time I'd seen a completed plane close-up, and I felt as if this were its graduation, a ceremony for this one magnificent beast before it got to go out and do its job.

When the inspector walked out, I was shocked to see that it was a woman. She wore a blue jumpsuit with red piping and a red-and-white patch on her arm that read DOUGLAS AIRCRAFT INSPECTOR: MRS. AU-DREY TARDY. She took her time scrutinizing every part of the plane inside and out, making notes on a clipboard. I could have stood there all day watching her. It seemed to me as if it were the highest level of honor to be a female inspector, tasked with being the final set of eyes on this complicated aircraft. Her knowledge, her expertise, and her level of confidence in herself to know so much—its parts, how they should be assembled, and if it was fit to then be flown—was astounding to me. I knew it required a college degree, probably in engineering, but this woman had achieved it, and she inspected that metal wonder meticulously. I would have done anything to walk in her shoes for a day or two.

The rest of that week I couldn't stop thinking about what it must be like to feel so accomplished, and when I sat down to write my weekly letter to Bobby, I found myself telling him about her, how proud and valued she must feel as a woman to be the final eyes approving this aircraft. Before I even made a conscious decision to do it, I was telling him how I wanted to make a life for myself in which I too felt proud and valued. I didn't know what I wanted to do with my life exactly, but I wanted it to mean something. I told him I wouldn't be returning to Wichita. I told him that I had always liked and respected him, how I thought he was so brave to fight for our country, but I told him that I wasn't in love with him the way I knew I should be if we were to be married. I tried to convince him that he deserved someone who would love him and devote herself to him, that there were so many young women who would be lucky to be his gal, and that it felt cruel to keep pretending that we would get married as soon as he returned, when I knew deep down inside that we wouldn't.

I had not set out to write such a letter; it almost seemed to have written itself. But afterward, I felt relieved, as if a huge weight had been lifted off my shoulders, and at least for a little while, I persuaded myself that he would feel the same way, that he'd be relieved to know he was free to find himself a girl who would appreciate all the good things about him, someone who would love him completely. I went to the post office and mailed the letter.

A month went by, and then another, and I received no response. I suppose I knew he might not respond, but the silence started eating away at me. I worried that I'd done the wrong thing. It had felt honest when I wrote it, and I didn't want to keep stringing him along, allowing him to hold out hope for something to look forward to all these months, only to shatter the façade once he got back home. But I agonized about it now, recognizing that I had been impulsive, most likely to relieve myself of guilt over what my own actions had set in motion back in Kansas. I was haunted by the thought that it might be easier for him to handle any disappointment once he was back home with his family. I prayed that he might still write and let me know he agreed or that he understood. More and more, I needed a sign from him. And then, a few weeks later, sitting in my dormitory room, I received a letter. I turned it over. There was no return address, but I felt my stomach drop. I opened it and saw the neat, slanted handwriting of a woman.

Hazel,

I thought you should know that my dear Bobby was killed in action while stationed in France. Because of you he died heartbroken. He was away from his family, sleeping in God knows what condition, seeing unfathomable things most likely, and yet you saw fit to send him a letter and break his heart and for what? For what I ask you? My boy went off to fight for his country, he was a hero and a patriot, but you, you took away his hope when he needed it most. You are a coward and a disgrace to our country.

It went on, but I couldn't read any more. I closed my eyes and saw his innocent face, his look of surprise when we got in his car, his excited announcement that he'd marry me. I doubled over, felt as if someone had kicked me in the stomach, knocking the wind out of me. I'd wanted to give us both freedom, but instead I'd given him this. His mother was right: it was my fault, I had been a coward, and I deserved every single one of her insults.

I could never go back home.

CHAPTER 10

Laguna Beach, California—February 1946

"HERE, LET ME TAKE THAT," JIMMY SAID, WHEN I WALKED BACK into the bar toward the end of his shift. He looked around a little nervously as he took the suitcase out of my hand and set it behind the bar. There were only two patrons left, and as soon as Jimmy announced last call, they signed their tabs and were gone.

"You can leave your things here," he said, "we'll come back and get them later." I glanced back at my case behind the bar. "Don't worry, it'll be safe, I'm locking up."

He walked me out of the hotel through the back door and onto the beach, where there were several green-and-white-striped beach loungers. "After you," he said, as if we were about to sit at a fine dining establishment. He opened a paper bag and unwrapped a large sandwich and handed me half. "The chef lets the staff make dinner with the leftovers most nights. I'm working on sandwiches, not your usual bread and butter though. I try to get creative."

I didn't want to take his dinner but upon seeing it, I realized I was starving. "Are you sure?"

"Absolutely." He was right, it was an unusual but delicious combination of chicken and mashed potatoes. I nodded my approval. He must have been starving too, because he ate without any attempt to make conversation, which I was grateful for, and when he was done with his half, he pulled out a second paper-wrapped bundle, offering me half of that sandwich too. I declined because I was only partway through the first.

"So," he said when he was done. "I live here." He pointed back toward the hotel. "Upstairs—the top floor is reserved for staff. It's a treat because I get to wake up to this every morning"—he looked out to the water—"but there are six of us to a room, so I haven't made the big leagues just yet."

I laughed.

"I'm not sure if they've changed the bunks since the officers stayed here, but it works. We're on call early mornings, late nights, weddings, parties for movie stars, you name it, and in return I have a roof over my head in one of the most beautiful locations in the world, I'd say."

"Sounds like you've got yourself a solid arrangement," I said. The moon was high over the darkened ocean, and if I didn't figure something out soon, I'd be keeping it company.

"I know you're in a bit of a bind," he said. "So, I was thinking you could sleep here too."

"What!" I said. Obviously I'd given him the wrong impression by confiding in him about the work with Mr. Radcliff.

"No, not where I sleep!" Jimmy said, his face turning pink. "I'm sorry, I didn't explain myself." He whispered this time and pointed behind him. "I mean, in the bar."

"The bar?" I said, a little too loudly.

"Shhh." He looked back at the hotel, but no one was around. "I know it sounds crazy, but it's part of my job each night to bring these beach chairs and loungers into the bar, so they don't get damp or swept away by the waves. Every night I come out here, eat my sandwich, bring in the chairs, lock up, and come back down around six each morning and bring them out onto the beach again. I'm the first one in and the last one out. You'd have to make a quick exit when I come down in the morning, to be sure you don't get caught, but at least you'd have a roof over your head until you find something more permanent."

I must have looked scared, or disappointed, or regretful—all the things I was feeling at once.

"Look, I'm not saying this is a long-term arrangement, but for tonight and until you find something that suits you in your price range, you could hunker down here. These chairs are pretty comfy if you put the footstool out in front like this." He leaned back, his hands behind his head, pretending to get comfortable. If I hadn't been so concerned for my immediate well-being, I might have paid more attention to how handsome he looked when he lay back like that, how his tanned, muscular arms looked sculpted with his sleeves rolled up. "I can bring you some clean blankets, you'll be golden."

"I don't know," I said.

"I know it's not ideal for a young lady like yourself, and not something you'd want to do for too long, but until you get yourself settled . . ."

I stared straight ahead and shook my head. I was starting to feel like a real fool to think I could just make this work, but it had all happened so fast. I'd really held out hope that they'd keep me on at the factory, and when it ended, I had no backup plan. I didn't want to spend the last of my savings on lodging—then I'd feel really destitute.

"Well, that's all I got, I'm afraid." He stood up, brushing the crumbs off himself, then started to fold up some of the nearby chairs. "I'd give you my bed, but I'd get fired, and you wouldn't want to be alone with the fellas I room with."

When Jimmy had said he had a plan earlier, I assumed he knew of a room to let or a friend who'd be willing to let me stay. But it was almost 11 P.M. and this was my only option.

"I'll do it," I said. "I'll be extremely careful, and I'll leave first thing in the morning."

"Swell, you'll have the whole room to yourself once I leave. There are bathrooms, water—maybe don't go swigging the booze, then I'll surely get fired, but other than that it'll be your own private room until the morning."

"Thank you so much," I said. "It's really kind of you, and you barely even know me."

"Well," he said. "If I'm lucky, maybe I'll get to change that."

He held my gaze for a moment, and I felt a flutter in my stomach when he said it. As crazy as these sleeping arrangements seemed, I suddenly felt quite excited by the adventure of it all.

I didn't sleep on the green-and-white-striped beach chair that Jimmy had set up for me; instead, I lay down in a corner booth with burgundy velvet cushions, wrapped up in two white cotton towels. It was more private and hidden than the beach chair. I lay there, smelling a hint of the disinfectant used to clean the tables, and listening to the ocean on the other side of the windows, sure I'd never be able to fall asleep.

When Jimmy unlocked the door at 6 A.M., I jumped up, forgetting where I was for a moment.

"It's just me," he whispered.

Instinctively I patted down my hair and put my hand to my face, embarrassed for him to see me just moments after waking, but he went about his business.

"It'll take me about fifteen minutes to set everything up, so take your time," he said. I nodded and headed to the bathroom to brush my teeth and get dressed for the day.

"How did you sleep?" he asked as I walked out the back door to where he was lining up the chairs.

"Surprisingly well," I said.

"Excellent. I woke up a few times wondering how you were holding up down here, so I'm glad to hear you managed to get some sleep. What are you doing with your day?"

"I have to be at Mr. Radcliff's studio at eleven."

"You've got some time on your hands."

"I can amuse myself," I said. "Want me to help you set up?"

"No, I don't want anyone to see you, so it's best if you scram."

I nodded.

"But I'll meet you back here tonight at ten?" he said.

"Thank you, Jimmy, it's so nice what you're doing for me."

"I'm glad I can help."

I smiled and started walking away. "Oh," I called back. "Is it all right if I borrow this?" I asked, realizing I still had a towel in my arms.

"No problem," he said, and I set off down the beach.

It was a foggy morning, and Jimmy was right, I had hours until I needed to be at Mr. Radcliff's studio, so I walked south for a long time, watching the mist hover over the water's surface. I couldn't see very far in front of me, but from what I could tell no one was around. My only company was a group of small white-and-gray-feathered birds with black bills that stayed close together and ran in short, quick steps to avoid the waves. I laid the towel out on the sand and watched them, fascinated that they managed to outrun the encroaching tide every time, stopping briefly on the wettest sand to shoot their beaks straight down for insects or crabs, then running off again on their short, straight legs.

I walked down to the water's edge, pulled up my pant legs, and waded in until it didn't feel as cold anymore. Finally, I decided to take a chance. I had never swum in the ocean before, only at the local swimming pool as a child. Even when I was at Long Beach, the rigorous training hadn't allowed time for any kind of beach outing. I looked around again, and, seeing no one, I slipped off my trousers and blouse, shimmied out of my undergarments, threw them on my towel, and ran straight into the ocean. Taking my time to acclimate to the temperature wasn't an option without a bathing suit, so I dove in, charging through the waves until I was fully immersed. Once I was past the whitewater I swam straight out to sea, the waves picking me up and carrying me, then sliding me down their smooth sides.

Swimming in that vast ocean without a costume was thrilling—nothing between me and nature, no slip of fabric, no restrictions. I felt wild. I dove under a wave and let myself glide underwater, and when I came to the surface I was laughing. I couldn't believe I was doing this—what had gotten into me?

The farther out I swam, the calmer it became. Beyond the waves, I was able to lie on my back and take it all in—the shoreline, the rocky coves, the few houses high on the cliffs, all shrouded by the white morning fog. It was like a secret, a hidden gem. I swam parallel with the shore, not wanting to drift too far from my towel and my clothes. Things might not be perfect, I still didn't have a permanent place to live, but in that moment, I felt free.

I could have stayed in longer, but I was aware of the time, and the later it got, the more likely it was that others would be out on the beach, so reluctantly I swam to shore, dried off, dressed, and used my compact mirror to arrange myself into something presentable.

At Boyd's Café on Laguna Avenue, I ordered coffee, toast, and bacon, and in the restroom I put on a face, gave myself some rouge, and pinned my hair in the hopes that its dampness would help it take on some form of a wave when it dried. Then I set off for Mr. Radcliff's studio, feeling alive and ready to take on the day.

When he met me at the door, Mr. Radcliff also seemed freshly groomed and raring to go; he even had his easel set up and his paints out, a hot coffee steaming in his hand.

"Let's get one thing straight before we go any further," he said the minute I walked into the studio. "I see you as an object like anything else. Your youthfulness, your figure, your pretty face, they do nothing for me except provide a subject to paint."

"Good," I said, insulted, despite the fact that just yesterday I'd cringed at the thought of an old man like him eyeing my figure. He must have noticed. "I hadn't thought otherwise."

"I just want it to be clear."

I nodded.

"Today it's legs," he continued, his tone lightened a little now that he'd had his say. "Legs and feet."

My legs and feet were tired from walking so far already that day, so I was glad to be still for a while. I put on the robe.

"How would you like me to arrange them?" I asked.

He had me lie on a blanket, raise the robe up to my upper thigh, and cross one leg over the other, then he asked me to cross at the ankle instead. "I don't care what you do with the rest of you—read, look out the window, sleep for all I care—just don't move the legs. The light is good now, I want to capture skin tone."

Once he got to work, he didn't speak. Moving my eyes only, I glanced around his studio, and soon, after I heard him quickly sketch the outline, he put the pencils away and started to paint. The smell of linseed oil was strong and quite pleasant. After a while I became aware of an itch on my back, and the more I thought about it, the more I felt the need to scratch it. I closed my eyes and told myself to relax, but it was intolerable. I took long, slow breaths and finally the desire to move subsided. After what may have been hours, I heard his stool screech across the floor, and I jolted upright.

"Now you can move," he said, laughing. "I don't know about you, but I need a break."

Later that afternoon, while he went into the house and took a short nap, I capped all the squeezed metal paint tubes, reading the names of each color as I went: burnt umber, cerulean blue, sap green, yellow ochre, alizarin crimson. They sounded so exotic, and I marveled at how he could turn those blobs of color on his palette into art.

That night I met Jimmy outside by the beach chairs. We ate sandwiches again, and I told him about my swim and how I'd survived my second attempt at sitting for Mr. Radcliff. I realized as we spoke about our days that I'd been looking forward to seeing him again all day. After we said good night and he locked the door, I went to the bathroom, soaped up as best one can with a small sink in a tiny bar restroom, and once again curled up in the corner booth at the bar. In the silence that fell around me, I could hear the doubts in my mind swirling around and around. I tried to tell myself that everything would work out, that I had done the right thing by taking the job with Hanson Radcliff, and that I wouldn't be hiding out in a bar forever, and then I tried with all my might to fall asleep.

CHAPTER 11

Los Angeles, California—August 1945

WHEN IT WAS ALL OVER, I CRIED.

President Truman announced that the hostilities were over at a little after 7 P.M. on August 14, and all of Los Angeles, it seemed, erupted into a victory roar. Everyone poured out onto the streets and celebrated. Music played on radios, and people danced on the sidewalks.

The next morning on the Red Car line, the women sang and cheered on their way into the factory. Everyone was so happy: all those husbands, sons, fathers—they'd all be coming home.

We were told not to clock in, not to find our posts, but instead to meet in the east hangar, where we were thanked for our service and told that soon we could head out the way we came in. The war effort was over, and our jobs would be handed back to the men upon their return.

Some of the girls from the factory went to the USO that night, but I couldn't bring myself to go. When I turned the handle of the door to my dormitory room, I felt the tears rise up. It was a wave, a rolling wave coming out of nowhere, rushing up from the pit of my stomach, through my chest, pushing on my eyes. I had to let it out, this sudden, desperate sadness, but I couldn't let anyone hear me. What kind of monster cries on such an occasion? How selfish of me to be filled with despair when so many others could finally breathe again, knowing their loved ones were coming home. But that thought only made the tears fight harder.

I'd really believed that the work I was doing would somehow change the course of my life, that things could never go back to the way they'd been. But now it seemed like a sham. We were no longer needed. I was no longer needed. Women could go back to their household duties, but what did I have to go back to? I didn't want to stop working. I didn't want to step away from this feeling of achievement. Now that I had a taste of it, I wanted more.

And then there was Bobby. Boys would be returning home as men. Bobby's family would have to endure the pain of losing him all over again, and it felt as if I were to blame. I should never have sent that awful letter.

I managed to stay on for a few more months—some of us were able to help wind down production until all the men were back. But by the end of January, we were officially told to vacate our roles at the factory.

I knocked on Mr. Lockhart's door after my final shift.

"It's about my position, sir," I said.

"Final checks can be picked up tomorrow," he said, sitting down at his desk and looking at some papers, then back up at me, as if wondering why I was still there.

"I was curious if there might be any other positions available at the plant."

He wrinkled his forehead. "Did you not hear? The war is over." He placed his hands firmly on the desk in front of him. "Miss Francis. There are no positions to be had. The jobs have been returned to the men who left them."

"I know, I'm aware of that, I was just wondering if perhaps there was something else I could do."

"Something else?" He half laughed. "Go home to your husband, tend to your children."

Everyone assumed that at my age I would be married with children and have a house to take care of. I looked down. Thankfully he'd forgotten that I'd been engaged, and I wasn't about to remind him.

"Listen, we are grateful for your service. You ladies stepped up and did things we never thought you could do. You showed skills that, quite honestly, I didn't think a woman could possess. But it's over now, go on home."

I felt a spark of hope that he remembered the work I'd done—or was he saying the women in general had surprised him? Either way, it was some sort of acknowledgment of our tenacity.

"Thank you, sir," I said. "I worked very hard while I was here, and I thoroughly enjoyed the opportunity to aid in the war effort. It was an absolute honor. But I don't have a home to go back to. I want to work. I remember one of the advertisements said that our work here would stand us in good stead after victory, and I wanted to discuss with you what that could mean for someone like me who wants to continue. I would do anything." I sounded desperate, but I couldn't help myself.

Lockhart shook his head and sighed.

"Look, there's nothing for you here. The military contract is over; we don't need to produce what we did before. Do you know how much we held in contracts with the military?"

"No, sir," I said.

"One hundred twenty-nine million dollars. All canceled. Thank the heavens we don't need to keep on fighting, but our work here is done." He paused and stared right at me. "Your work here is done."

"But surely there's someone who needs phones answered or . . ."

"Not here."

"Filing, typing?"

"Miss Francis . . ."

"I'm really a fast learner."

"What I'm trying to tell you," he said, raising his voice a little, "if you'll just listen for a minute, is that there's an airplane plant in San Diego, about sixty miles south of here—Consolidated. They've been working with the navy to build transport for personnel. They've taken their Liberator bomber wings and engines and they've combined them with an expanded fuselage. It's called the Liberator Liner, and they figure they can transport civilians just as well as they can transport sailors, so they're looking to interest the airlines, make cross-country travel available to more people, maybe even intercontinental travel."

"That's a fantastic idea," I said.

"They're onto something. I can put you in touch with a friend who's in charge down there; maybe he'll have something for you, but it's a maybe."

"Oh, I would be so grateful, thank you."

"I can't promise anything. I'll put in a call. Leave your address or an exchange if you've got a telephone at home, and I'll let you know if there's anything for a woman down that way."

I took a deep breath. "Would it be at all possible for you to put in your call now, sir?" It was a bold request, after I was asking so much already, so much beyond what was appropriate, but if I didn't at least try I could lose my chance completely. He stared at me, shocked perhaps that I had the audacity to waltz into his office and make these kinds of demands. I looked right back at him, willing myself not to back down. Finally, he broke my gaze and looked out the window for a second, then walked over to the telephone and picked up the receiver.

"Put me through to Consolidated Vultee Aircraft Corporation in San Diego," he said. "Robert Twyman please." He looked back at me and squinted, as if contemplating whether he'd actually complete the call. "Robert, old man, how are things down there? Good. Good. Listen, I've got a young woman here who worked at the plant and is looking to continue on. I know, I told her that. I know, I know. She's persistent. Unmarried, yes." He looked over at me. "Yes, she's slim. A hard worker too, one of our best over the past few years, even worked on the Pratt-Whitney engine, and the A-20. I know, impressed me too, to be honest." My heart was racing.

"Anyway," he went on. "We've got nothing for her here. I know you've got plans to work with the airlines, so you might have more opportunities. Yes, yes, I wouldn't send her your way if I didn't think she'd be an asset. All right then, good. I'll let her know."

He hung up the receiver and turned back toward me.

"Monday," he said finally. He wrote down the information on a piece of paper and handed it to me. "Go down and see him Monday."

"Oh, my goodness, this is the most wonderful news. Thank you so much, Mr. Lockhart. You won't regret recommending me, it really is the kindest thing anyone's ever done for me."

He nodded and ushered me out the door. "Yes, yes, very good," he said. "Off you go, then. And Miss Francis, best of luck, but find yourself a nice man and settle down, it's the best thing for a woman like you."

I caught the first train out on Monday morning, and I could barely contain my excitement. I had everything I owned packed in my small suitcase in the baggage cabin and my pocketbook next to me. I splurged on a cream soda for breakfast and sat at the wood-paneled quarter circle to drink it, watching a gentleman head into the onboard barbershop for a haircut. Everything felt so civilized and full of possibility. Early that morning before the sun was up, I'd agonized over what to wear—trousers and a smart blouse to show I was factory-ready, or a more feminine day dress in case I'd be starting off with secretarial work. In the end, I decided on a middle-ground, bottle-green utility dress with very slightly puffed shoulders and my low-heeled oxfords that I'd barely worn for the past few years in lieu of my heavy work boots. I did part and roll my hair smoothly as I had for work, but instead of pinning it up in the back I let it hang loosely, trying to achieve a perfectly balanced look of femininity and good work ethic.

After all my planning, I felt that I'd made the right choice as I approached Mr. Twyman's office just before 10 A.M. It was a temporary-looking structure, away from the aircraft hangars, that looked as if it had been assembled in a hurry. I set my suitcase down by my side and knocked.

"Good morning, Mr. Twyman," I said, smiling broadly as soon as he opened the door. "Hazel Francis from Douglas Aircraft."

"Ah, you'd better come in."

Better come in—what kind of welcoming was that?

"I contacted Lockhart, but he said he had no way to reach you."

"Oh yes, I'm sorry about that. I just left my housing arrangement, but not to worry, I'm here now," I said, but he didn't look pleased to see me. "Is now a good time?"

"Well, the job's gone, I'm afraid."

"What do you mean, gone?"

"It's been filled." He shrugged.

"How could it be filled? Mr. Lockhart said that you had a position for me, I heard him tell you that I'm a very good worker, very fast hands . . ." How could he dash my hopes like this? All I needed was a chance.

"I'm sorry, there's nothing I can do."

"I don't understand."

He threw his hands up, exasperated to be forced to have this conversation with me, but I had come all this way, spent my hard-earned money on a train ticket—one way! I deserved a response.

"Look, it was going to be a cleaning position, mostly, polishing the glass noses, getting the metal shavings out of the nooks and crannies of the planes we're testing for commercial airlines, nothing glamorous. I thought it would be a good job for a woman, petite and all, able to get into small spaces, but turns out we had a small-framed man who could handle the job just fine."

"But you promised that job for me," I said.

"Look, lady." With this his tone changed; while he might have been annoyed with my presence before, now he seemed downright insulted. "These men have been to hell and back, and they deserve to have a job waiting for them when they put their feet on the soil in their own country. No skirt is going to walk onto my grounds and tell me what she is or isn't entitled to. Do you understand?"

"Yes, sir," I whispered, realizing that in my alarm I'd spoken out of turn. "I'm sorry." I stood there, trying to think if there was anything else I could possibly say to make a case for myself, but after the tone he'd taken I knew there was no point.

"I'll be on my way, then," I said, picking up my suitcase. I moved slowly, hoping, praying he might change his mind, or suddenly remember some other job that I'd be suited for.

"Look, I'm sorry, but women's work is done," he said as I walked out the door.

"Yes," I said. "That's what I've been told."

I made my way back to the station and bought a ticket to Los Angeles that boarded at noon. I didn't even bother putting my suitcase in the baggage car; I dropped it at my seat and rested my feet on it. I was deflated and defeated. I was taking a train to nowhere. No one would be waiting for me at the other end. Just hours earlier I'd been reveling in everything about the journey south, the motion of the train, catching a glimpse of the ocean out the window, the future that lay ahead. I'd been patting myself on the back for working so hard, telling myself how it had paid off, it had really paid off.

So much for that.

I stared out the window—what could I do? I supposed I could get to Union Station and check the schedule for the next train to Kansas, but that idea, simply crossing my mind, gave me a horrible jolt. I couldn't do it. The shame and guilt about Bobby came flooding back. I'd told him I wanted to make something of myself, build a life for myself in California, but look at me now. No promise, no hope, just a stupid, overzealous girl who'd got too big for her boots. All for nothing.

The conductor spoke up. "Next stop, El Toro Station, connecting coach to Laguna Beach. Next stop, El Toro Station."

Laguna Beach. I'd heard people speak of Laguna Beach at the factory. And soldiers at the USO had talked about visiting the beach town on their day's leave. One young man from Boise thought it was the most beautiful place he'd ever seen. I stood up abruptly and grabbed my suitcase.

"Getting off," I called out loudly to the relatively empty car. "Getting off."

CHAPTER 12

Laguna Beach, California—February 1946

TWO WEEKS INTO THE JOB, I WAS EXPECTING TO RECEIVE MY PAY-
check any day, then I'd get out of the bar and find a room to rent. My
back was sore from sleeping curled up in the booth, and I was in desperate need of more appropriate living arrangements.

I arrived a little before my start time of 11 A.M., but Mr. Radcliff
wasn't in the studio.

"Hello?" I knocked, then peeked through the doorway. "Mr. Radcliff?"

"It's Hanson," he called out. "And I'm in the kitchen."

I'd only ever been in the studio, and I was curious about his adjoining house. I followed the Spanish-tiled hallway past the living room
and dining room, where the table was stacked with canvases. The place
looked as if it could use a good cleaning, but as I made my way toward
the kitchen, where the smell of coffee brewing and bread being toasted
wafted my way, I saw the view—the whole back of the house was a wall
of windows looking out over the cliffs onto the ocean below. I hadn't realized from the street that the house was literally perched on the cliff.

"It's Hanson, for Christ's sake. 'Mr. Radcliff' makes me sound like
an old man," he said gruffly, pouring himself a coffee. "Breakfast?" But
before I could answer, he was getting down a second cup and flipping
open the side of the metal toaster.

"Thank you," I said.

He cracked two eggs into a pot of boiling water and watched them.

"The view," I said, "it's really something." I couldn't take my eyes off it, but he seemed indifferent, or maybe modest. "How long have you lived here?"

"Thirty years or so. I bought it soon after I was married."

"Oh," I said. I hadn't pictured him as the marrying type.

"She's passed now, but left me long before that anyway—I drove her 'round the bend," he said with a laugh. He waited another minute then scooped the eggs out of the water and dropped them onto the buttered toast. He sprinkled some salt and cracked some pepper, then walked out the patio door and came back with a handful of herbs that he quickly chopped and sprinkled on top. He slid the plate in front of me. "Enjoy."

I'd allowed myself to swim for twice as long that morning, with no time to eat at the café, so I was grateful for the food. I was starving but tried not to let it show by digging in right away.

"Go on then," he said, nodding to the eggs, and when I took my first bite, he seemed satisfied. "All right," he said. "I'll be off then."

"Off?"

"I'm heading to the desert with Berg. I told you."

Actually, he'd told me to report to him at 11 A.M. sharp, that he was going to work on "arms," and I'd purposely worn a chemise under my blouse in the hopes that he could sufficiently see my arms in it. But now he and Berg, whoever that was, were heading to the desert. I nodded, trying to appear easygoing, which didn't come naturally. I was counting on a full week of pay, and I almost said as much.

"So," he said as he put on a straw fedora and slung a knapsack over his shoulder. "I'll see you in a few days?"

"A few?" I asked. "Is there something I can do to help while you're gone?"

He looked around his messy house. "No, not that I can think of." He shrugged. "I should be back by Friday, Saturday at the latest."

I'd planned to talk to him at some point that day about my living arrangements, to ask if perhaps he knew of someone who might be renting a room, but he seemed in a rush to leave, and I didn't have an answer ready if he asked me where I'd been staying. I stood up, slipping my pocketbook onto my shoulder.

"Don't rush. Finish your breakfast," he said, walking toward the door. "Just lock up on your way out."

The car engine roared to life outside and I was left in his house—his vast, unruly, disorganized house. I took my time finishing my eggs and toast and looked around in awe. I was curious what lay beyond the kitchen, where the snaking Spanish-tiled hallway would lead. I took my plate to the sink and washed the breakfast dishes as well as a few others that had accumulated in the sink. I wiped the counters and could have kept going. I had an urge to sweep the crumbs from the floor, and then I could mop. I could have this house completely turned around by the time he was back home, and he might feel obligated to pay me for the days he was gone, but I resisted. I'd been hired as an assistant and a model, not a house cleaner, I reminded myself.

When it was time to leave, I knew to pull the door closed so it would lock behind me as he'd asked, but I couldn't quite bring myself to do it, not yet. The thought of wandering aimlessly until Jimmy's shift was done at ten o'clock that night felt awfully depressing. I opened the door to the back patio and decided to wait a little longer, use up some more time before I made my way toward the hotel. I sat down in an iron chair in the shade, but the sun moved quickly, focusing its energy on me. It was hot, and I thought about the possibility of bathing. How luxurious it would feel to bathe in a tub, wash the salt off my skin, the sand from my scalp, and soak for a little while. It would be beneficial to Mr. Radcliff too, I told myself as I went into the house—opening each door in search of a bathroom—to work with a model who bathes regularly rather than washing in the hotel washbasin.

His bedroom was bare. A bed, a small table with an empty glass. Sheets twisted and tossed. More windows looking out to the ocean, and a stack of books taking up one corner of the room. The next room was sparsely furnished too, a single bed tucked against the wall. I closed that door and peeked into the next—I had found it: a large bathtub.

I soaked for over an hour. It felt glorious.

By late afternoon I was feeling much more relaxed. Curious, I continued on down the hallway, wondering how big this house really was and how many paintings an artist would have to sell to afford such a place. The hallway led to a narrow staircase with a closed door at the top. The stairs creaked, and I got the impression they hadn't been used in a while. I turned the door handle, but it was jammed. I pushed my shoulder onto it. I tried again with a little more force, and when it swung open, I gasped.

A woman's figure, rounded, misshapen, sketched with a hurried hand and pinned to the wall. Next to it, another, a woman lying down, her body disproportioned, the outline of her nose exaggerated. It felt vulgar, yet I couldn't peel my eyes away. I felt ashamed for looking, as if I were spying on someone's private, personal moment. On a desk in the middle of the small room there was paper upon paper, what looked like hundreds of drawings, most unfinished, sketched or half-sketched, some simply outlined, some torn in half. There were notebooks on notebooks. I opened one, every page used; another looked as if something had spilled on its pages, swollen, then dried. There were paintings on large canvases and small, loose canvases rolled up, napkins with the outline of a woman sitting at a bar, a woman leaning into a man, a woman's lips, her eyes, her shoulder. Scraps of paper with sketches strewn about everywhere, even an egg carton completely covered. All women. There was a frustration about the room, an impulsiveness. The mess, the disorganization made me tense. I backed out of the room quickly, jammed the door shut again, and, hurriedly, made my way back down the stairs. I grabbed my pocketbook and bolted out the door.

The next morning, I found myself back at Hanson's house after my early morning swim. I'd locked the side door when I left the night before, but I'd woken in the middle of the night in the hotel bar recalling that I'd left the patio door unlocked. I swam, dried, and dressed, and started walking along the beach until I reached Thalia Street, where I climbed the stairway that led from the beach, turned left on Coast Boulevard, and turned onto Cleo Street.

I was strangely fascinated by those images, the secretive nature of that room, something forbidden about the paintings. I returned to it, and this time I looked at the artwork differently. There was a beauty to some of them—the curve of a woman's back, the seduction in something as simple as a shoulder blade—while others were still shocking to my eye. After seeing all of them, I couldn't help but wonder what he sketched when he saw me.

Back downstairs at his studio door, I stood and looked around. It was more of a mess than the house, far worse. There were bottles everywhere, ashtrays full of cigarette butts. He must have had friends join him the night before he left. I wanted to find the sketches he'd done of me that first day, but I'd never find them in this chaos and disorder. They could be anywhere. I peeked at the easel. I looked on the workbench, but it was covered with brushes and booze. I was about to head into the house when I saw ripped-off sheets of paper peeking out from under a desk. I carefully pulled them out and turned them over.

It was me, but the figure he'd drawn was stiff, tense. I could see it in the pose, I could see it translated into the sketch. I'd been nervous, felt tight and uneasy, and he'd drawn what he saw. There was a sharpness to the lines—my shoulder a jagged edge, my neck ridged. The angles, the harshness, the discomfort. I wanted to rip them to shreds. Was this really what he saw in me? No wonder he always looked so defeated when he was finished painting, no wonder he'd seemed so drained. I was a bundle of nerves, an awkward, uncomfortable sight. I shoved the sketches back where I'd found them and backed away. I clenched my jaw. I had thought maybe I was getting it right, posing partially exposed, but I'd been a fool to think that. Plucking up the courage to take off my clothes wasn't enough to make me a good subject. Why did he hire me when I looked like this? If I didn't get this right, my days here were numbered.

I pulled a large garbage can into the center of the room and threw in all the bottles, emptied the ashtrays; I suddenly felt compelled to do something, to clear up the clutter. I couldn't leave the studio like that. I wiped down the table, scrubbed at a spilled, sticky drink on the floor. I found a bucket and mopped the entire studio, then I arranged his paintbrushes in cans. I put charcoals, spread all over one table, back into their box. When I was done I was perspiring, but the studio looked spotless, and I was able to breathe again.

That afternoon I took another bath and wrapped my hair in a towel. When I was finished, I took all the clothes I was wearing and washed them in the soapy water, then I retrieved the robe I used in Mr. Radcliff's painting sessions and put it on while I hung the clothes out to dry. Back in the bathroom I sat down on the edge of the toilet seat and looked at myself in the mirror. I slipped off the robe and moved my shoulders, pushing one forward, then trying the other. I lifted my chin then dropped it, held my hands to my face and lowered them to my side one at a time. Everything felt so silly. I went to the kitchen and looked for something to help me relax, take the edge off. A bottle of bourbon on the counter would have to do, so I poured myself two fingers, and a splash more for good measure, taking a sip as I walked back to the bathroom, then a gulp to speed things along.

I spent the next hour or so practicing poses and sipping bourbon. I took the mirror off the hook on the wall and let it rest on the sink so I could see more of myself. I was starting to get the hang of it, I thought, understanding and feeling how things looked, and recognizing that what felt comfortable or at ease sometimes came across as slumped or lazy, whereas what felt awkward or forced could, at times, look composed, interesting even. I needed to do more of this experimentation if I wanted to succeed.

It must have been nine at night when I was really getting into the swing of things, and after a few more nips of bourbon I had started to wonder if I should just sleep there that night, when all of a sudden, I heard noises coming from the front of the house. I gasped, quickly wrapped myself back up in the robe, hooked the mirror back onto the wall, and raced out of the bathroom to retrieve my clothes, still hanging outside to dry.

"Whoa," an unfamiliar voice called out just as I was passing the kitchen. "What do we have here?"

I looked up and saw a man who certainly wasn't Hanson Radcliff. I screamed, pulling the robe tightly around me, and grabbed a knife off the kitchen counter.

"Stay back," I shouted. "Stay away from me."

The man put his hands up, but he didn't back away. He was in his forties, maybe late thirties, and had sandy blond hair that swept across his face. A pale blue kerchief was tied around his neck. He didn't look like the kind of person who'd rob a house, but then what did I know? He took a step toward the kitchen.

"Get out of here or I'll call the police," I yelled, but the man just laughed. "This is no laughing matter," I said. "This is not your house; you do not belong here."

He composed his face into something of a bashful grin. "I'm sorry, I didn't mean to laugh. Nor did I mean to scare you. But I'm pretty sure this is not your house either, and unless you and Hanson have some kind of arrangement that I don't know about, I think you also may not belong here. I'm Edgar by the way, Edgar Berg." He stuck out his hand to shake mine but almost immediately Hanson walked in behind him, his arms full of painting gear, his hat lopsided on his head.

"What the heck are you doing here?" he asked, placing his bags down and taking off his hat.

Frozen, I stared at him, unable to come up with a single thing to say. He looked down to my robe and back up to me again questioningly.

"I seem to have . . . it's just that I didn't know . . ." I put my hand to my hair, which had dried a frizzy mess after I'd washed it and let it air-dry while I messed around in front of the mirror, then I instinctively looked out the window to my clothes hanging on the back of the outdoor furniture.

"Ah," Mr. Radcliff said, following my gaze, a slight chuckle erupting from his throat. "You stayed here while I was gone, and I wasn't supposed to be back until tomorrow."

"I'm so sorry, Mr. Radcliff, I'm so, so sorry."

"It's Hanson," he said, sounding more irritated by that than by the fact that I'd been making myself comfortable in his house while he was away. "I would have stayed away longer, but this man is intolerable."

Edgar laughed.

"I'm so sorry, I didn't actually sleep here, I slept"—I paused—"somewhere else, but it's not really a good arrangement, and I don't have anything more permanent set up yet, so I admit I did spend some time here during the day, both yesterday and today, and I did bathe here," I said, ashamed, looking down, unable to bring myself to look him in the eyes. "I'm terribly sorry. I did clean up your studio, but I understand if this is grounds for termination . . ."

"For goodness' sake, woman, why didn't you just say you didn't have a place to live?"

"I, well, I was going to try to . . ." I stammered on and glanced over to Edgar, who was watching this whole interaction and seemed to be quite enjoying it.

Hanson sighed and turned back toward the car outside. I was so embarrassed I might have run right out the front door if it weren't for the fact that I was wearing nothing but a robe.

"Give me a hand bringing in some of the canvases, would you?" Hanson said, then stopped and looked at me. "But you'd better put some clothes on first."

I grabbed my still-damp clothes, rushed to the washroom, and wrestled my way into them, then helped Hanson bring the wet paintings into the studio. I apologized profusely again, which Hanson brushed away.

"Bourbon?" he asked back in the kitchen, holding up a glass toward me as he poured one for himself and one for his friend. I glanced at the bottle and feared he'd notice it was emptier than when he'd left.

"No, thank you." I shook my head quickly, desperate to leave. "I must go."

"To where?" Hanson asked.

"To the place where I've been staying," I said, trying to be vague.

He shrugged, and I bolted toward the door, my head down.

"Tomorrow . . ." he said. I looked back, waiting for him to tell me not to bother coming back. "Meet me at 374 North Coast Boulevard. It's just past the hotel, past Victor Hugo's on the right-hand side."

Walking briskly down the boulevard, I hoped I'd make it to the hotel before ten o'clock. I was shaking with humiliation and had a chill from my damp clothes in the cool evening air. Sharing this awful, awful story with anyone was a terrible idea, but I knew that as soon as I sat down in that beach chair, and Jimmy handed me my half of the sandwich, that was exactly what I would do.

CHAPTER 13

THE ADDRESS HANSON HAD GIVEN ME WAS FOR A SMALL GALLERY in a pale blue two-story building, a five-minute walk from the beach. In the window, modest paintings were displayed on a wooden backdrop, clustered together and labeled by the artists. I cupped my hands to the window to peek inside. In the back, a woman stood painting at an easel.

"There she is." Hanson's voice startled me. "The intruder," he said with a laugh. "Are you scoping out your next victim?"

"No!" I said. "I am so sorry for . . ."

"Enough of your jibber jabber," he said. "Enough!" He walked past me, around the side of the gallery, then he turned back. "Are you coming or not?"

I followed him. I'd assumed we were going into the gallery, since that was the address he'd given me, but instead he walked to an almost identical building behind it, and up the rickety wooden stairs that led to a door above. He tried it, but it was locked, so he dug a key out of his pocket and fumbled around until he was finally able to open the door. Inside, he pulled open the blinds.

"It's been empty for some time," he said. "I used it as a studio when my wife was around—to get some peace and quiet. If you can help out in the gallery once or twice a week, when you're not working with me, then you can stay here. Consider it part of your salary."

"Really? That's extremely kind of you!" I had expected him to fire me, but here he was, offering me a place to live. The place was a shambles, but it would be so much better than sleeping in the back of a bar. It looked as if there might even be a separate bedroom.

"It needs some work; you can throw out whatever you don't need. I haven't set foot in here for years, so there's nothing I'll miss." He made his way toward the door. "Stop in downstairs sometime and tell Lillian I sent you. She'll give you some hours."

"This is all more than I could—" I said, hurrying after him as he descended the stairs. "Really, it's very generous, especially after . . ."

"Also, when you see Lillian in the gallery, tell her to take you to the pageant with her. Just go to the meetings, and tell them you're there in my place."

"The pageant?" I said. "A beauty pageant?"

"No," he said with a laugh. "Though that might bring in more crowds! The Pageant of the Masters—it's an art show; the whole town comes together to re-create famous pieces of art with live people in them. Sounds crazy, I know, but they put on a good show, and it brings a lot of people to town." Hanson started coughing and couldn't seem to stop. "It's good," he said, finally standing up straight again. "Very good, very entertaining, I just don't know why I have to get roped into it year after year. But you go, do whatever they need you to do, and try to get me out of as much as you can."

"Okay," I said, not having any idea what he was talking about. Where was this pageant? What time did I need to be there? But he seemed eager to leave.

"Oh, and when you do go, give this to Johnny, the director." He took a small, thin envelope out of his pocket and held it out, then he held out a second one. "And this one's for you." He started to walk away, then turned one more time. He threw the keys toward me. "Catch."

Back inside the apartment, I held my first paycheck to my chest. Things were really looking up.

I got right to work and spent the next several hours stacking up broken crates and boxes, piling up rolls of dusty and mildewed canvas outside the front door, and making several trips to the garbage bin. I cleared the countertops and tables of paper cups and old newspapers. Once I'd removed most of the junk and the layer of dust and grime from the surfaces, I could actually start to see what lay underneath—white walls, wooden beams overhead, large windows in the living room and bedroom filling the space with light.

There was a small kitchen with a table and two chairs, a living room that managed to squeeze in a cozy two-seater and a bookshelf, and a bathroom just barely big enough to fit a bathtub—I marveled at how they must have got the tub up the rickety stairs and in through the tiny front door, but I was happy it was there. I cranked the windows open to air out the space and smiled when I realized I could actually hear the waves breaking on the beach.

After just a few hours of work, it looked remarkably better. There were some boxes in the bedroom. Hanson had said to get rid of everything, but these were full, and some of it looked important. I dug through but didn't feel right throwing out his personal belongings. I saw a flash of silver at the bottom of one of the boxes and pulled out an engraved lighter that looked as if it might be expensive. I placed it on the kitchen counter and made a note to give it to Hanson—I didn't want to be responsible for his valuables—and the rest of the boxes I shoved into the bedroom closet.

ON MONDAY I STOPPED IN AT THE GALLERY ON MY WAY INTO TOWN. Hanson wasn't expecting me until early afternoon.

"Welcome to the Co-Op," a woman said as I walked through the door. "Feel free to browse, unless you're here for something in particular?"

She wore denim overalls, and her hair was pulled into a bun on the top of her head, held in place with a paintbrush.

"I'm staying at the apartment in the back," I said. "I just started working for Mr. Radcliff, he gave me the key." I held it up to prove that I wasn't some interloper.

"Oh," she said, her demeanor changed.

"He said to ask for Lillian. Might that be you?"

"That's me," she said, wiping her hands on a rag hanging off the easel, then down the front of her overalls.

"I'm Hazel," I said. "Apparently I'll be working a shift in the gallery?"

"We desperately need someone on Sundays. We're a cooperative gallery, so all the artists who exhibit here have to take turns working a shift. Hanson owns the building, it's his gallery, but he doesn't work here, obviously."

"Sundays would be fine," I said. I didn't know much about art, and I certainly didn't know how to sell it, but it couldn't be that hard.

"I teach a class on Sunday afternoons, but I can meet you in the morning and show you how it works; it's easy. Mostly you just need to be here to open up, clean the bathroom once a day, and take money if someone wants to buy something."

"I'm sure I'll manage," I said, looking around at the art on the walls. "Which ones are yours?" I asked, and she nodded toward a small section on the back wall.

"You won't be very busy while you're here," Lillian said.

"Oh?"

"Things were really picking up before the war—people from all over were starting to hear about Laguna Beach and the artists down here, Hollywood folks too—but things changed over the past few years. No one's been thinking about buying art. It would have been impossible for a lot of artists like myself to make it if Hanson hadn't helped us out."

"It hasn't improved, now that the war's over?"

"Not yet, but we're hoping the pageant will help with that."

"Oh, yes, the pageant. Hanson asked me to go with you to the next meeting. He'd like me to attend in his place."

"You can't really replace him," she said with a laugh. "He's on the board, but no one will complain about an extra pair of hands. We certainly have a lot of work to do."

"What is it exactly, the Pageant of the Masters?"

"We take famous paintings by the masters, everyone from Leonardo da Vinci to Jean-François Millet, and we re-create them, life size, with Laguna locals literally posing in the paintings as the figures are in the originals."

I couldn't quite picture what she was describing.

"You have to see it to understand it. All the big artists in town get involved. They paint the backgrounds to look like exact replicas, and they work all kinds of magic with lighting and shadows, makeup and costumes, to make the people look as if they're part of the painting—it's really quite something to see."

I nodded.

"It runs for a few weeks each summer. This will be the first one since forty-one. It didn't run during the war, obviously. Too much lighting. Thank God that's all over and we can start to get back to normal life," she said.

"The whole town is buzzing with news of the pageant starting up again. If it's done right, it's going to bring a lot of people to town this summer, which will be good for everyone—the artists, the restaurants, the hotels."

"I'd love to see it," I said.

"Oh, you'll see it all right, it's all anyone will be talking about for the next six months leading up to the show in August. The next meeting is Sunday evening. Why don't you meet me after your shift, and we can walk over together. Meet me outside Tres Gai Café at five thirty after my class."

"I'll be there," I said. This job with Hanson was really turning out to be a jack-of-all-trades scenario, but it paid well, it came with housing, and I supposed filling in for Hanson at the pageant would be a good chance to meet people.

I put my hands in my pockets and looked around the gallery. "Where are Mr. Radcliff's paintings?"

She gave me a look as if I'd said something absurd. "Hanson Radcliff doesn't show here. He gives us a few little plein airs now and then, his warm-up sketches mostly—those sell immediately, and it helps us pay for the upkeep of the gallery. He does it as a favor to us. He's very generous. But we're unknowns, just getting off the ground, grateful to have a place to show our work. Hanson Radcliff is in the big galleries in town."

I nodded, feeling foolish for not knowing more about him.

"Go into the Laguna Beach Art Association—that's where you'll see the big shots around here: Edgar Payne, Frank Cuprien, Anna Hills, George Gardner Symons, and your boss."

"I will, thanks," I said as I headed toward the door. "I'll see you Sunday then."

ON MY WAY TOWARD TOWN, I SAW THE HOTEL AND THOUGHT OF Jimmy. He'd been so kind to me, so generous and encouraging. If he hadn't talked me into going back to Hanson's studio that day, who knows where I'd be now. I had the sudden urge to see him and let him know how grateful I was.

I walked through the lobby to the bar and caught him wiping down tables in the back, whistling.

"Jimmy," I said, popping my head into the empty room. "I hope I'm not disturbing you."

He stood tall and smiled when he saw me. "Not at all," he said, setting down his rag and walking behind the bar to wash his hands. "It's always great to see you—in fact, I've missed our late-night rendezvous."

"Jimmy!" I said, looking around to see if anyone had overheard.

"Oh, no, I'm sorry," he said, suddenly embarrassed, his ears beginning to turn pink. "I meant the sandwiches." He started pointing to the beach where we had sat most nights watching the waves and eating his often-unusual creations. "When you met me for sandwiches after my shift."

"I know what you meant," I said, trying to reassure him. "It's fine."

"I'm sorry, I didn't mean to embarrass you," he said quietly as he leaned over the bar toward me. "It's just that I always enjoy your company and I've been quite lost without it these past few days." I felt my body temperature rise, a quickening of my pulse. Surprised to have such a physical reaction to his words, I looked away from him. I'd had those childish pangs of lust before, but this was different, deeper somehow, and yet I knew I wasn't willing or ready to act on those feelings, not after everything that had transpired with Bobby.

"Actually," I said, quickly changing the subject, "that's why I'm here. I wanted to thank you."

"Thank me for what?"

"For all that you've done for me," I said quietly, nodding toward the booth that had served as my sleeping nook for the past few weeks.

"Oh, you don't need to do that, it was my pleasure."

"I'd like to," I said. "Now that I have a place where I can cook, I'd like to invite you to dinner, to repay the favor. When are you free?"

He smiled. "How about Thursday evening? I have the night off."

"Perfect. Now, don't get your hopes up, it won't be fancy. I haven't got much, but it'll be something."

"Something sounds just fine with me."

❧

I HEADED STRAIGHT FROM THE HOTEL TO THE ART ASSOCIATION gallery. It was a large, impressive building, and when I first walked in,

I wasn't sure what to do. I felt a pair of eyes on me from the corner of the room—a smartly dressed man sitting in a chair, pretending to read.

"Let me know if you have any questions about the art," he said.

I nodded and whispered, "Thank you," too intimidated by the grandeur of it all to say more.

Here the canvases were much bigger than in the Co-Op, bigger than anything I'd seen in Hanson's studio too. One took up an entire wall, lots of vacant space surrounding it. Light shone on the paintings, picking up each brushstroke.

I walked through the gallery, marveling at all the beautiful scenes of the coast, the mountains, the streets, a single bird on a rock rising out of the ocean, all bright and bold. I searched each one for a signature, an illegible scribble on the bottom right corner. And then in the center, I saw a painting taller than me, a bird's-eye view of an ocean cove, vibrant blue, the cliffs around it yellow, the palm trees deep burgundy. I don't know how, but I knew it was his. I moved in closer and sure enough, a messy "H. Radcliff" was painted in the lower right. As I stood there soaking up the colors, the atmosphere, the tranquility, a voice spoke quietly behind me.

"Striking, isn't it? Hanson Radcliff, one of the most well-known of all the Southern California impressionist artists, and noted for his spectacular seascapes. He's also helped Laguna Beach thrive as an artists' community by mentoring many newer, younger artists."

He spoke in a soft, yet commanding way, and I almost forgot there was a real person behind me. I turned to look at him, but he was staring straight ahead at the painting, as if seeing it for the first time.

"His style is borrowed from the French impressionists," he continued, "focusing on the effects of light, a bright and colorful palette, and the loose application of paint to capture a passing moment in time."

"It's beautiful," I said. "It makes you wonder how he was able to paint the whole thing before the sun went down."

"Indeed," he said.

"How much does it cost?" I wondered in a whisper, shocked at myself for asking out loud.

"Oh." He snorted a little as if I'd just asked a ridiculous question. "This is a Hanson Radcliff. He's sold paintings at the Stendahl Gallery in Pasadena." He spoke as if that might mean something to me. Then he paused, and I wondered if he was going to ignore my question, except now I really wanted to know.

"This one, my dear, this one is going for twenty-five hundred dollars." He smirked and gave the painting a nod before he turned and walked away.

I watched the back of his suit until he reached his spot in the corner, then I turned back to the painting, shocked. You could buy a small house for that kind of money. This man, Hanson Radcliff, was not at all what he seemed.

Stunned by the revelation that my boss was apparently very rich and very famous, I walked toward Penny's store in a daze. I wandered the aisles, completely forgetting what I'd come in for until someone called out to me from the register.

"What can I help you with, miss?" He was just a boy, thirteen or fourteen tops.

"Well." I tried to get my mind back to the dinner for Jimmy. "I don't have any pans, and I'm having a friend over for dinner tomorrow evening."

"What are you cooking, miss?"

"Good question," I said.

"Meat? Casserole?"

"Meat," I said. "I'll cook him a nice steak, he probably hasn't had one of those for a while."

"Right this way, miss." The boy led me to an aisle with cast-iron skillets. "We have a few to choose from," he said, and started listing the properties of each, the varying sizes, but I just couldn't get myself to focus. Twenty-five hundred dollars for a single painting. How many had he painted in his lifetime? How many had he sold? He could be rich beyond my wildest dreams. His house was large and right on the cliff overlooking the ocean, and his art was undoubtedly beautiful, so I'd been aware that he was successful and had talent, but it just hadn't crossed my mind that he was so well-known and accomplished.

"That one's fine," I said, pointing to the one the boy currently had in his hand.

"This one?" he said.

"Yes, yes, that will work."

"You've got it, miss," he said, walking it to the cash register, wrapping it in a sheet of newspaper, and setting it on the counter between us.

"That'll be four seventy-five."

I opened my purse and looked at the coins inside. I hadn't been to the bank to deposit my check yet. "I'm sorry, how much did you say?"

"Four dollars and seventy-five cents." Then he added, "It's a Griswold."

"Right," I said, assuming that meant something. I looked at him and then back down to my purse. I couldn't believe a pan could be so pricey. I still had to buy the food and a bottle of wine. There were other things I'd need too, but they'd just have to wait.

When I'd received word of Bobby Watson's death, I started sending most of my paycheck from the factory to his family in Wichita. At first, I justified that it was to cover the costs of the funeral, but then I continued. I had to do something to assuage my terrible guilt. I set a little money aside each week to buy food, and I saved a little for emergencies, but everything else I sealed in an envelope and mailed to his mother. It felt like a necessary punishment, something I'd be reminded of daily as I clocked in to work each morning and clocked out each night. I wanted to remember how cruel and selfish I'd been. I felt almost as if I myself had killed him, not just broken his heart. I kept it going right up until the day I left the factory. At least I'd been paid now, but I still needed to be frugal. I handed over the money and carried the heavy skillet home under my arm.

"JEEPERS, LOOK AT THIS PLACE!" JIMMY SAID, STANDING AT MY FRONT door, which opened right into the living room, his head almost touching the top of the doorframe. "You're really cooking with gas now!"

"I know, I can't believe my luck," I said. "It was filled with stuff Mr. Radcliff didn't want when I first set my eyes on it, but now that I've cleared it out, it's really quite lovely."

I'd set the table and, in the center, placed a jar of fresh-picked lavender from outside. I wore a light cotton dress; Jimmy looked dashing in a pale blue shirt, navy slacks, and polished shoes, and he held a cardboard box in his arms.

"What's this?" I asked, walking over to take a peek.

"Just some things that were going to waste at the hotel. I thought you might need some of them for your new place." He set the box down on the sofa and took out a set of four white plates and three bowls. "They replace these all the time, for the tiniest chip or crack in the glaze." Next he took out a set of white sheets. "There's a small tear at the bottom, but you could probably repair it; they toss them out for the smallest things."

"This is so thoughtful." The sheets Hanson had on the bed looked worse for wear even after I'd washed them and hung them out to dry, and the plates would be a welcome addition to the two mismatched ones, found in the cupboard, on which I'd planned to serve Jimmy's steak.

"I could hardly show up empty-handed."

"Honestly, I have too much to thank you for! I wouldn't have been able to take the job without a place to stay, and I never would have plucked up the courage to . . . well, you know."

"Be his muse?"

I shook my head. "Something like that." I took the box to the kitchen.

"So," he said, settling into the sofa after pouring us each a glass of wine and picking up a piece of the bread and cheese I'd placed on the table. "How are you liking this town so far?"

I smiled. "Well, I've been swimming every morning in the ocean. Something I never thought I'd hear myself say."

"A bit cold, isn't it?"

"I'm getting used to it." Although I'd started swimming to pass the time after leaving the hotel before I was needed at Hanson's, since moving into the new place, I kept waking up early. "I like the routine of it. I think that's why I enjoyed working on the airplanes so much. It was tedious work, but I liked the strict regimen of it all."

"It's great what you girls did here at home, you really stepped up."

"We just wanted to help, and to be fair, it paid well. I can't imagine what it was like for you."

"What did you work on?" Jimmy asked, immediately turning the conversation back to me.

"Bombers, SBD Dauntless. I felt nervous at first working on them, thinking of the young men who'd be flying inside them, but then I got the hang of it, and I stopped thinking of them that way. Did you ever fly?"

He shook his head. "I was in tanks."

"Tanks?"

He nodded and gave me that friendly dimpled smile of his, but he didn't say more. He got up and walked to the kitchen and came back with the wine bottle in his hand, even though we didn't need a refill yet.

"What's this," he said, picking up the tarnished silver lighter from the counter. He flipped it open and struck the flint wheel with his thumb, but there was no flame. "It's an old one, needs some naphtha."

"I found it with Hanson's things, it looked like it might be special. Turn it over, it's inscribed."

He rubbed his thumb over the swirling engraved letters, trying to wipe away the tarnish. "Yours truly, Bella Rose," he read out loud.

"Must have been his wife."

"No, his wife was Mary Jane Lewis," he said. "There's a photograph of the two of them in the hotel at some party when they were a lot younger."

"I wonder who Bella Rose was."

Jimmy laughed. "Probably one of many."

He set the lighter back on the counter, and I made a note to return it to Hanson on Monday.

"So, you think you'll stay on at the hotel for a while?" I asked as he sat back down next to me.

"Oh sure, for as long as they'll have me, though I've heard rumors of some financial troubles. But I don't let that bother me, I take it one day at a time." He hadn't seemed to want to discuss his own involvement in the war, but now that we'd left that conversation behind, he was back to his easygoing self again. "Yeah, I want to learn as much as I can. I'll work anywhere they want me in that hotel. I'm going to open up my own little restaurant one day, a bar and restaurant right on the beach. I'm going to serve the best steaks and seafood, have an outdoor oyster bar, and I'm going to create my very own cocktail menu."

I pictured him running his own establishment, overseeing the whole operation, and it seemed so right, so fitting. I smiled. "That sounds real nice, Jimmy."

"Doesn't it? Right here in Laguna Beach."

"I'd be your first customer. Speaking of steaks, I've got a good-sized one for the two of us and I need to put it in the pan."

Jimmy insisted on helping, and he cooked it just right while I made up a salad on one of the new plates. "I'm afraid this is all I've got to go with it," I said, showing him the salad and realizing now—when I saw his tall stature again in real life—that it might not be enough food to fill him up.

"This is the perfect accompaniment," Jimmy said, holding up his glass.

We sat at the table, shared the steak, and were on our last sip of wine when he became strangely quiet, then reached across the table and put one of his hands on mine. It might have been the first time we'd ever touched, except for an accidental brushing of the hand in passing, and my whole body came alive, as if I'd been waiting a lifetime to know what his hand would feel like on mine.

"I like you, Hazel, I really do," he said, looking at me.

"Jimmy," I said in a whisper, my voice quivering slightly, a nervousness clenching my throat.

"I wanted to tell you, Hazel," he said, very serious all of a sudden.

"Please." I stopped him before he could go any further. "Don't say any more." I had made such a wretched mistake with Bobby. I never wanted to hurt someone like that again. I wasn't ready to let someone in, and I didn't know if I ever would be.

"Hazel, you don't even know what I'm going to say. Give a man a chance," he said, a half smile forming despite my discouragement.

"I do, I think I do." I was sure he was going to ask me to be his girl, I was absolutely sure from the way he was looking at me, from the way he kept his hand on mine. If he said those words, I didn't know if I'd be able to turn him down. But I couldn't tell him about Bobby and what I'd done; he'd think I was terrible. And I couldn't not tell him either, not if I was to be truly honest with him. It wouldn't be right.

"Hazel," he said, a little more firmly now, jolting me out of my thoughts. "I just want to say, I haven't had the chance to tell you, or maybe I have but have chosen not to, but, well, I have a girl back home."

"Oh." I felt my face flush with embarrassment, and I hoped to heavens it wasn't showing. "I didn't know, but that's lovely." I stayed sitting as long as I could bear it but then got up to clear our plates, trying to hide the redness that I was sure had taken over my neck and face at making assumptions about what he was going to say.

"Her name's Jeanene, and she's finishing up school, beauty school actually," he said. "She's going to come meet me here when she's all done."

"Move here?" I could barely get the words out. "That's so nice. Something to look forward to." I turned back to him, smiling, as I placed the plates in the sink, to let him know that I was completely happy about this news. Beauty school. She was probably a knockout.

"She's real nice, I think the two of you are really going to get along."

"I'm sure we will." The thought of meeting her made my stomach twist, and it did nothing to make my blushing go away. My God, I was all ready to turn him down if he'd asked me to be more than a friend to him, yet this news had shocked me to the core.

"When do you think she'll come?" I said, trying to sound as breezy as possible.

"This summer, I think," he said. "Maybe."

"She's going to love it here," I said.

He nodded, his smile pinched. "I hope so."

CHAPTER 14

LILLIAN WAS RIGHT. BY THE TIME FIVE O'CLOCK ROLLED AROUND
on Sunday, only two people had walked through the doors of the gallery, and they hadn't stayed longer than five minutes. One other couple
stopped and looked in the window but moved on just as quickly. I turned
off the lights, locked the door, looked around to make sure I'd done everything on the list she'd left me, then walked toward town. I turned left
and strolled slowly along Forest Avenue, where eucalyptus trees shaded
the pavement from the afternoon sun.

In a shop window, a mannequin dressed in a peach bathing suit
with velvet panels caught my attention. It was a beautiful suit with
a short, fitted skirt. A woman appeared next to the mannequin and
smiled, then beckoned me in. I smiled back and shook my head, but
she didn't relent.

She opened the door and popped her head outside. "It would look divine on you," she said. "Come on in and take a look."

"I'm sure it's very lovely . . ."

The woman took me by the elbow and pulled me into the shop. I stood
at the door and looked around. Pictures of beautiful women wearing the
latest bathing suit fashions lined the walls. Bathing suits of all varieties,
one-pieces and two-pieces, hung like art on display. There were sunglasses, hats, and summer sandals.

"That's a beauty, the one you had your eye on," the woman said. "But
with your figure, you could wear a two-piece, halter style."

I shook my head.

"Oh yes." She held one up. "It ties around the neck and just shows the tiniest little bit of midriff—above the navel, of course. Some people need the boning in the stomach region, but not you."

I admired it, touching the white and red flowers climbing up one side of the bottoms and continuing onto the top.

"I do like it," I said. "It's just that, well, I've just started a new job and I'm trying to save, at least until I see a few more paydays."

"Ah, I see," she said. "Here in town?"

"Yes. I work for an artist."

She raised her eyebrows, waiting for more.

"Hanson Radcliff."

"Oh." Her eyes widened. "Well do come back when you can."

I quickly moved on, but not before glancing back at the sign above the door: MISS DEBUTANTE READY-TO-WEAR. Maybe next month, I thought, maybe I would go back and buy myself that bathing suit.

I passed two more art galleries, a men's store called Surf & Saddle that promised "Dude's Duds and Western Gifts," and another store offering an odd combination of handmade lamps, art, and tropical fish, before I reached Tres Gai, a busy patio café where I met Lillian.

"So do you get paid for helping with this show?" I asked as we walked down the canyon road toward the site of the show.

"No," Lillian said with a laugh. "It's mostly volunteers. I sure don't get paid. I think some of the artists in charge get a little bit of money for their trouble, but not enough to write home about." When we arrived, she pointed out some of the features. "This whole area is called the Irvine Bowl because it's so perfectly carved out of the hillside, and the natural acoustics are spectacular for a show like this. The part that we're walking through now, this is where the Festival of Arts will be, where local artists get to show and sell their work before and after the main event."

"What's the main event?" I asked.

"The Pageant of the Masters! The patrons coming for the pageant arrive early, drink wine, and admire the art—this was all started to enable poor artists to be able to eat, you know, and honestly it works. People are so enamored with the pageant, the grand spectacle of it, the little snippets they learn about the artist, and the overall atmosphere that it just puts them in the mood to buy art."

"Will your work be here?"

"Our little gallery gets a booth, thanks to your boss, Mr. Radcliff, so we each get to display one painting."

"Which one will you show?"

"Oh, I don't know yet, I've been agonizing over it."

After we walked through the place where the booths would be set up, the space opened up to a large seating area and stage, a backdrop, and a sort of barnlike roof where it looked as if lights might be installed. It was much bigger than I had imagined, and it looked as if it would seat some two hundred people at least.

A group of about thirty people were sitting in chairs in the middle of it all.

"Come on," Lillian whispered as we approached. "We're a few minutes late."

We sat in two chairs at the back and listened as an older gentleman talked to the group. "The biggest problem we've got on our hands is the damage done by leaving this place alone for the last four years."

"That's John Fredericks, this year's director. He mostly points out the problems and asks people to fix them. He's quite strict, but he gets the job done," Lillian whispered.

"As you can see, we've had vandals on the grounds, prop damage, costume damage," he continued.

"That's right." A woman with frizzy graying hair stood up. "Most of the costumes are damp and mildewed on account of not having seen the light of day for the last several years. We'll have to scrap a lot of them and search for new materials, but don't worry, I'll sort it out."

"Gladys Moynahan, she's in charge of costumes," Lillian whispered.

"But I cannot start costuming until someone decides on the final program."

The whole group groaned, and three men stood up—one older gentleman around Hanson's age, another a little younger, tall and skinny, and a third with his back to me—all of them attempting to speak at once, each one getting louder, trying to shout over the other, to the point where I couldn't understand a thing.

"That's enough," Mr. Fredericks said loudly. "Sit down, all of you. I put you three in charge of programming because I thought, as some of

the best-known artists in town, you'd come together and create a wonderful collection of respected paintings that would move the audience,
something that would speak to the sensibility of our times, but you can't
seem to decide on a damn thing and it's not getting us anywhere. We
can't finish casting the show until you make up your minds, and Mrs.
Moynahan can't make the costumes."

"Will I still be Judas?" a man called out. I immediately recognized the
loud voice of the town greeter—same red shirt and long beard.

"Yes, Eiler," Mr. Fredericks said. "You will still be Judas in *The Last
Supper,* as you have been in years past, and probably always will be."

I smiled—he had the perfect beard for the part.

Mr. Fredericks turned back to the three men who'd been arguing. "I'll
give you until the end of the week to come up with a program we can all
agree on. Otherwise I'll make the decisions myself."

When they all spoke up again, Mr. Fredericks silenced them with a
menacing "That's final," and they sat back down—except the one with
his back to me stood up again, just as quickly.

"I just want to say that unlike these so-called patriots"—he pointed to
the two other men—"I do not condone a German artist showing at the
pageant." He turned to the group, and when he did I almost gasped—it
was the man who'd walked in on me at Hanson's house while I was wearing nothing but a skimpy bathrobe, the man I'd pulled a knife on.

"There are plenty of American artists to choose from," he continued.
"I don't know why on earth we would feature a Nazi."

Mr. Fredericks shot him a glare. "You've been warned, Edgar." He
took an audible breath, waited for him to sit down again, then resumed
the meeting. "I am trying to track down Anatole Robbins, who so kindly
donated his own cosmetics and team of makeup artists for the show in
the past. I'm hoping he wasn't injured overseas, so if anyone hears anything, let me know. The magic he has done with makeup for our shows
has made the paintings more realistic than we could have dreamed. He
took this show from an amateur act to a first-class event, and he does it
out of the kindness of his heart, so if anyone knows how to reach him,
do let me know, and if I have to drive up to Hollywood and start knocking on doors to find him, I'll do it." He clasped his hands together. "Is
there any other news to be discussed?"

"We have a new volunteer," Lillian said, standing next to me. "Hazel," she said, then she leaned down and whispered, "What's your last name?"

"Francis."

"Hazel Francis," she said. "She's here on behalf of Hanson Radcliff."

I nodded and waved, feeling myself blush when all eyes turned to me, including Edgar's. "Mr. Radcliff couldn't make it due to his busy schedule, but he asked me to give you this." I passed the envelope forward. "And I'm here to offer to help wherever you might need me."

A few people in the crowd groaned, and I sensed their displeasure with my boss's minimal involvement in the show.

"Why do we even include him if he doesn't show his face?" someone said. When I realized it was Edgar who'd spoken, it surprised me. Weren't they friends?

"Hanson always comes through in the end," Mr. Fredericks said, tucking the envelope in his pocket, trying to calm everyone down. "He's generous in other ways. We're happy to have you, Hazel, we can definitely use the help. Now," he continued, "Floyd here is going to give everyone a tour of the grounds and show us where the lumber will be delivered and how we can help set up the booths for the festival."

"That's right." A man in overalls stood and addressed the volunteers. "We'll be delivering the lumber in two weeks and assembling the booths every night that week starting at six P.M. I'll have tools, so whoever can make it just bring your strength and work boots."

Everyone began gathering up their things.

"Floyd owns the lumberyard in town, and he gets his team to help build and take down the artist booths as well as building the sets. He's very kind and helpful around here," Lillian said. "Those others, though, fighting at the meeting every single week, they're a whole other story." She shook her head and then caught up with some other women from the meeting.

I followed along, feeling a little out of place—these were mostly artists here, volunteering their time in order to improve their chances of being seen, and I felt a bit silly trying to fill in for a man who, as it turned out, didn't have everyone on his side. I had hung back a little as we walked toward the area where Lillian had told me the booths would be set up, when I felt a hand on my shoulder and jumped.

"Well, hello there." It was Edgar Berg. "We meet again."

"Indeed."

"It's nice to see you," he said. "I almost didn't recognize you with your clothes on."

I shot him a glare, furious that he would make such a statement around all these people I'd just met, running the risk of ruining my reputation with his offhand remarks. I shook his hand free from my shoulder and picked up my pace.

"I apologize," he said, catching up with me. "I was joking, but in poor taste. I didn't mean to embarrass you. Please forgive me."

I hadn't liked this man the first time I met him, and I didn't like him now, but I wasn't going to give him the satisfaction of knowing that he got under my skin.

"I'll have you know that it was you who walked in on me unannounced," I said. "So if anyone should be embarrassed, it should be you."

"I am," he said, lowering his head in an exaggerated manner. "I am quite used to embarrassing myself."

"Yes," I said. "After tonight's performance, I can see that."

"Touché," he said, pleased with himself. "You don't know what kind of politics are involved with putting on this show; it's quite amusing, actually. Too many cooks in the kitchen, as they say. But we're thrilled you're helping out. You're a lot easier on the eyes than your old boss."

CHAPTER 15

IT WAS A CRISP MARCH MORNING WHEN WE PACKED UP HANSON'S gear and hiked into the hills east of town. Hanson insisted that he carry his collapsible easel, the paint box, his stool, and a couple of small canvases, and that I only carry the bag with lunch, but ten minutes in, he was puffing like a bull, his pipe hanging from his mouth, and he finally relented, letting me sling the easel on my back.

"Where would you like me?" I asked when we finally got to a spot he was satisfied with.

"Probably in the shade so you don't burn that skin of yours."

I unrolled the blanket we'd brought and smoothed it out under a cluster of tall straggly trees, removing rocks and a few branches from beneath it so I wouldn't have to adjust once I got into position. Though I still didn't enjoy posing, taking items of clothing off for a man to stare at and analyze my partially naked body, I was determined to get better at it. After seeing how stiff I looked in those early sketches, now that I'd practiced in front of the mirror a few more times, I was curious to see if it would make a difference, if I'd be easier to paint now that I'd seen what certain positions felt like, but by the time I was ready he had already set up his easel and stool and was facing the opposite direction.

"Is this all right?" I asked. "I could sit or stand."

He turned back to me, perplexed, took a puff of his pipe, and then returned to his canvas, chuckling. "Why would I go to the effort of hiking up to the top of this godforsaken hill if I wanted to paint a lady? I'm in the mood for the land today, young Hazel, the land." He laughed. It was starting to feel as though sometimes he just wanted me around for company. I didn't mind—he was quite an interesting person to spend time with—but I knew for certain that keeping him company was not going to make me indispensable. I wanted to be doing something purposeful, a job that only I could do, so that he'd have to keep me on.

"I can't very well eat lunch up here all alone," he said as if he could hear my inner conflict and was mocking it. "I could get eaten by wolves while happily biting into my cheese sandwich and no one would ever know. I'd be gone without a trace, forgotten." He laughed again, coughing some, then getting back to his canvas, blocking in the shapes of the trees and hills ahead of him.

"We can't take that risk," I said, slumping down on the blanket. I'd worn trousers and a light short-sleeve sweater, and I tried to sit ladylike on the blanket, but the thought of sitting and waiting for hours, possibly all day, even if I didn't have to pose, made me fidget.

"How do you even know where to start?" I asked. "You've got this whole view in front of you, how do you know what's important and what's not?"

"First you look around and decide what you want to paint."

I looked out to the view we were facing—a sandy path narrowed in front of us then gave way to a dramatic drop, hills contouring and curving for miles. Above dry patches of green, orange, and brown, the sky was striped with thin wispy clouds, and a small triangle of ocean was visible in the distance.

"You don't try to capture it all; you decide on one section, something that's interesting to you, and you put a frame around it in your mind." He made a square with his forefingers and thumbs and held it out in front of him. "You decide what your focal point is going to be, and then you break it down into manageable steps."

How could you possibly decide on just one piece? I thought. It was all so vast, overwhelming, beautiful. I made a square the way he had, and it helped, if only I could keep it there, blocking out the rest from view, focusing on what was important. I moved it around and settled on a thick-leaved rose-shaped cactus in the foreground, green at the center, red-tinged at the edges. Beyond, the curve of the hillside and the flash of blue sky.

He picked up his paintbrush again and went back to his canvas. "Then you break it down into the big shapes—the sky, a large rectangle perhaps, and then you draw in the rest, loosely."

I watched him paint, dipping his paintbrush into a small jar of oil and mixing it with colors on his palette. "You look for the darkest areas and paint those in first. Then you move into your mid-tones and highlights." An hour went by, maybe more. It didn't look like much at first, but soon it began to take shape, and it was fascinating to watch him turn a blank canvas into the very view before my eyes.

I thought about the fact that I was getting paid for this, for doing nothing, and it bothered me. I wanted to be useful. "Is there anything else I should be doing?" I asked.

He shook his head. "Saving me from wolves, that's all."

"Are you hungry yet?" I asked, opening the picnic basket where we'd packed lunch. I took out the sandwich wrapped in parchment paper and handed it to him, then remembered the lighter that had been sitting on my kitchen counter for weeks.

"Oh, I keep forgetting to give this to you." I reached into my pocket and pulled out the lighter. "I found this in some of your things," I said, holding it up. He squinted in the afternoon sun. "From Bella Rose," I added.

He placed his sandwich back on the paper and slowly took the lighter from my hand. "Where did you get this?" he asked quietly.

"In the apartment, a box in the back of the closet. It seemed as if it might be important, or valuable."

He looked at it for a moment, then shoved in into his pocket. He picked up his paintbrush and set it down again. "Have you been speaking to that woman too?" His demeanor had changed; he was accusatory and cold.

"No," I said. "Which woman are you talking about? Bella Rose?"

He shot me a look. "Don't get smart with me," he said, a flash of anger in his eyes.

"I'm sorry," I stammered, taken aback by his abrupt manner. He started to pack up his things, wiping his paintbrush on an old rag and shoving it in the paint box. "We don't have to leave. I mean, if you're ready we can, but . . ." I glanced at his painting: it wasn't finished, and the paint glistened wet in the sun.

"Pack it up." He motioned to the picnic basket and blanket.

Loaded up like a mule, he began to hike back down the trail, stopping briefly to find his flask in his pocket and take a swig. Hurriedly, I packed up the rest of the things and tried to catch up. I followed along a few paces behind him for a good ten minutes then jogged a little so I could close the gap between us.

We strode in silence for a while except for Hanson's huffing and mumbling under his breath.

"I've upset you and I'm sorry," I said, finally. "Whatever it is I did . . ."

"Almost forty years," he interrupted. "And still I can't do a goddamned thing without it being shoved back in my face."

He picked up his pace even more, and I had to trot along to keep up with his long strides. "I'm so sorry," I said. "But if I did or said anything to offend . . ."

"Don't play ignorant with me," he spat, giving me a sideways glance, a look of anger that sent a surprising ripple of fear through me. We'd hiked an hour deep into the hills behind the town, and I suddenly felt queasy at the thought of being alone out here with him. We'd fallen into a rhythm over the past month and a half of work, if you could call it that, a fairly consistent habit of being around each other, and that had given me a false sense that I knew him. But now, with this eruption of anger, and that look he just gave me, I feared I didn't know him at all.

"My past has got nothing to do with you."

"Mr. Radcliff," I said, feeling the need to return to formalities, "I assure you I didn't mean to. You had said to throw things out, and I was worried the lighter was of some importance, or had some sentimental value."

"There you go again. Sentimental." He spat on the dusty ground. "Where are you from?" He stopped suddenly and turned to face me. I almost tripped in my attempt to stop from the fast pace I'd been keeping up.

"Most recently I lived in Los Angeles."

"Kansas, isn't it? That's right. Unbelievable." He took another long swig from his flask. "Well, old news travels far. Those good-for-nothing journalists, trying to make a story of a sick woman and pin it on me." He shoved his flask back in his pocket. "You'd better watch what you do, young lady, because these things can follow you your whole damned life. Doesn't matter how much money you make, how much people respect you, what you do for your community, for art, for whatever, it will follow you, and then, when you're old, and it's all almost over and you think maybe the world has moved on, forgotten, some little kid from Kansas will show up on your doorstep, and she'll be just like everyone else. Guilt, it's a relentless pig." He marched on again, and this time I stood for a moment in disbelief, trying to absorb the fact that I was somehow to blame for his terrible change in mood.

"I don't know what you're talking about," I cried out, but either he chose to ignore me or he was already out of earshot.

I was damp with perspiration by the time I reached the bottom of the trail. He was sitting on the hood of his car smoking and coughing intermittently. It had crossed my mind that he might have even left without me, he'd seemed so enraged, but thankfully he waited. Though he seemed to have calmed a little, we still didn't exchange a word on the drive back to his place. We unloaded his things from his car into the studio, and then I stood around outside, awkwardly, waiting for some direction.

"That's it for today," he said, more weary now than angry, as if I'd been such a burden that I'd exhausted him.

"Yes, sir," I said. "What time should I arrive tomorrow?" I asked, cautiously.

He shook his head but didn't make eye contact. I couldn't lose this job. I had to do something, say something to make it right, but I didn't even know what I'd done wrong in the first place.

"Go on," he said, flicking his hand at me, brushing me off his property. "I don't need you tomorrow, or the next day. Go on home." With that he closed the front door and left me on his driveway.

I SAT ON THE FLOOR OF MY LIVING ROOM AND TRIED TO THINK WHAT to do. I wanted to walk down to the hotel and talk it out with Jimmy—I knew that would help calm my mind, that just getting it off my chest and hearing what he had to say would help—but I also knew I shouldn't. I couldn't keep confiding in him like that. I had to create some space between us now that I knew he had a girlfriend back home. But I felt panicked. Hanson had set me up with a place to stay, in addition to giving me a job I had absolutely no experience in, and I'd gone and ruined it.

Desperate to find a way to make it right, I considered walking back up to his house that very evening and explaining myself. But as soon as I had the thought, I knew it would just make things worse. Hanson needed time to cool off. Besides, what was there to explain? I thought. I didn't even know what I'd done wrong.

I looked at the clock mounted above the table in the kitchen—it was almost six, but my stomach was in knots, and I couldn't eat. They'd be starting to build those exhibition booths for the art festival soon, and I found myself craving the work. I imagined putting on my leather gloves and helping heave cumbersome wooden posts into place, hammering in nails to secure them. I wanted to focus on something necessary; I wanted to be somewhere I was needed. Suddenly energized, I pulled my overalls and work boots from the back of the closet and put them on. I dug out my gloves and bandana, pushed them into my back pocket, and ran down the steps. I walked through town at a quick pace, eager now, determined, not only to keep myself busy and to stop myself from imposing on Jimmy or Hanson, but to actually build something and be a part in getting this show running again.

As soon as I approached the entrance, the sound of hammering echoed through the space. Someone was shouting orders. I followed the noise and found a small group of men being directed by Floyd from the lumberyard. They worked in teams of two or three and carried the large wooden beams from a pile near the road, across an overgrown lawn with picnic tables peeking out from the long grass and weeds, and over to the cleared dirt space. Floyd was in the clearing making sure that each booth location was clearly marked with chalk.

"Everything's all measured out," he called to someone. "Just get the lumber in the right places first. We'll start constructing once it's all in place." He stood for a moment and watched the scene unfold. Men were working together, and he nodded his head slightly. I took his momentary pause as an opportunity.

"Hello, Floyd? I'm new here, and I came to lend a pair of hands, help put the booths together, as you requested."

He gave me a perplexed look as if he weren't quite sure what to make of me. "What did you say your name was?"

"Hazel," I said. "Hazel Francis. I work for Hanson Radcliff." I took my hand out of my leather gloves, which I'd already put on as I approached the workers, and I held it out to shake his. He took it and gave it a gentle shake, though he seemed uncertain if he should.

"Well, hi there, Hazel, thanks for coming on out, but I don't know if this is the right kind of work for a lady."

"Oh, I'm quite capable," I said, half expecting this. "You see, during the war, I . . ." I was about to explain that this was exactly the kind of work this lady was most comfortable with, when an all-too-familiar voice was suddenly far too close for my liking.

"Well, look at you, dressing the part. That is adorable." It was Edgar. "What are you doing here?"

"Miss Francis here says she'd like to help build the booths," Floyd said, which sent Edgar into a deep chuckle.

I stared at him, not amused.

"Have you any idea how heavy these pillars are?" Edgar asked, straightening up. "Look at me. I'm sweating like a pig, and I've only carried one, with two other men aiding me."

"You might need to improve your exercise regimen," I snapped. "I hear the daily dozen is quite effective at building muscle for even the most lethargic men."

"All right, all right," Floyd said. "Edgar, the crew need you to bring the next lot over." He nodded to where a couple of men were struggling to transport a particularly long post across the lawn.

"Gotcha," he said, saluting Floyd and winking at me. "Just don't let this one mess up her nails. She's a model for Hanson Radcliff, we don't want to get on his wrong side." He chuckled again as he strode off toward the pile of lumber.

"I do appreciate you comin' out to help, Miss Francis, but maybe Edgar's right. It's hard work even for my men, and you're probably better suited to the costume department. I know Mrs. Moynahan would be grateful for the help. Everything got damp and ruined . . ."

"Yes. But, you see, I'm actually better suited to hard labor, work often given to men. I worked at the airplane factory during the war. I know how to use a hammer, nails, rivets, rivet gun. My father—" Mentioning my father out loud after all this time sounded strange. "My father," I managed to go on, "was a train engineer and taught me a lot growing up." I was sure he would have, if he'd had the chance.

He nodded. "I certainly believe you'd be up to the task, but I'm not sure it'll sit well with the rest of the crew." He looked over at the team of men working, and I followed his gaze, but all I could pay attention to was Edgar, who barely seemed to lay a finger on the wooden beam being carried—mostly by two other men in work pants and sweat-stained shirts.

"I'd probably be more useful than some of the men you've got working here, or at least one of them."

He shrugged and squeezed his lips together, as if he couldn't argue with me on that one. "All the same, I think it would be a better fit if you helped out in costume. Gladys is probably in the storage room right this very minute, just walk all the way to the back there." He pointed. "Before you get to the stage and seating area, turn right. Costume is third door back."

I WALKED TOWARD A LARGE, RIPPED, AND FADED POSTER MOUNTED above the entrance to the seating area. It pictured a statuesque woman with a crown, wearing a long gown, looking out over orange groves with the mountains in the background, and it read PAGEANT OF THE MASTERS AND THE FESTIVAL OF ARTS, LAGUNA BEACH, ORANGE CO, CALIFORNIA 1941. It was still up from the last show before the war.

Gladys Moynahan was bent over double with her head in a trunk of what appeared to be costumes.

"Mrs. Moynahan? Hello, Mrs. Moynahan."

She was digging out swaths of fabric and throwing them behind her in the tiny, closet-like space. Finally, she stood up, her back to me, and rubbed the palm of her hand up and down her spine.

"Mrs. Moynahan?" I tried again.

"Jesus, Mary, and Joseph," she yelped, spinning around. "Child, you gave me a start!"

"I'm so sorry. I didn't mean to alarm you." She looked crazed, her frizzy chin-length hair wild, her face still flushed from being upside down. "Floyd said you might need a hand in the costume department."

"Oh, could I ever?" She wiped a hand across her perspiring brow and sat down on an old trunk, visibly relieved. "Oh, bless you, I could use a hundred hands to help with this mess, but I'll take whatever I can get." She pushed some clothes off a small upright box and patted it.

"Here, take a seat, let's have a little break and a cup of hot chocolate before we dive in, shall we?" She reached down, picked up a flask off the ground, unscrewed it, and poured a steaming chocolate milk into two cups. "Here you go, love," she said, handing one to me.

I smiled, took a sip, then pulled it away, quickly feeling the milk burn my tongue.

"Steady on, there," she said. "It's hot, boiled on the stove just before I got here. Let it cool." She blew on hers and leaned back against the wall, pleased, it seemed, to have an excuse to rest for a moment. "So, what sparks your interest in the costume department?" she asked.

"Well." I sighed, not wanting to disappoint the lady. "Truth is, I did offer to help build the booths."

"Ah," she said, as if everything suddenly made sense: my outfit, my shoes, the bandana.

"But they didn't want a woman doing a man's job."

She gave a few sympathetic nods. "They can be a stubborn lot." I thought we might continue the conversation, that she might sympathize with the way we women were treated as if we were incapable of anything unless it involved dressing someone or nursing a child. But she was focused on the task at hand. "Well, I think we're getting closer to having a final decision on the paintings we'll be presenting this year." She smiled and lifted a large book from a pile on the floor. "There are going to be a total of sixty-four pictures presented in three separate programs during the twelve performance nights. That's twenty-one pictures each night."

"They don't just do the same show every day?"

She shook her head. "No, that's not the way we do it. Many folks will buy tickets to see all three presentations just so they can see the complete sixty-four pictures. It's a lot of work when you think each picture, along with the people holding still in it, is only displayed for ninety seconds, but it's well worth it when you see the final result. Magnificent." She smiled and looked up to the ceiling of the small space we were crammed into as if she were picturing the whole thing right there and then.

"So, you have to dress a lot more people, then."

"One hundred and seventy-five Lagunians will be posing in this year's paintings—unless they change their minds about the program again—but here's what we've got so far." She opened the book on her lap and took out a newspaper clipping tucked into the book. It was a photograph of six marines raising the American flag atop a mountain in the Pacific right at the end of the war. I'd seen the image in the Sunday paper, and it had been reprinted in lots of magazines and papers since.

"*Raising the Flag on Iwo Jima*," Mrs. Moynahan said solemnly. "In the past we've focused on the old masters, but everyone seems to agree that this photograph is especially powerful and relevant. We'll have to find six strapping fellas to cast in that one."

She placed the photograph back into the book and turned to a page marked with a strip of paper. "This one's *The Birth of the Flag*, by Henry Mosler, another patriotic one."

The painting was of four women dressed in floor-length, corseted dresses and cloth bonnets, sewing the first flag.

"We'll need a lot of fabric for this one, four dresses and a flag," she said. "Old is best though, tablecloths, curtains, you don't want anything too new looking."

She continued showing me various pictures, many of which I'd never heard of: *Indian by Firelight*, by E. Irving Couse; *The Mill-Girl*, by William Strang. Others were well known, such as the sculpture *The Discus Thrower*, by Myron, for which the young man portraying it would need to have not an inch of fat on his body, and a lot of muscles. I wondered if someone of that stature lived in Laguna Beach. And then, *The Last Supper*, by Leonardo da Vinci.

"We always finish with *The Last Supper*," Mrs. Moynahan said, a look of pride on her face. "Though we'll have to find a few new disciples this year—the two young men who played Peter and Matthew didn't make it back home." She made the sign of the cross and closed her eyes for a brief moment. Then she stood up and screwed the lid back on her flask of hot chocolate.

"Come on then, let me show you what we have that's salvageable."

CHAPTER 16

WHEN THURSDAY FINALLY ARRIVED, I SHOWED UP AT HANSON'S STU-
dio and acted as if nothing had happened, and Hanson gave me that same
courtesy. It was 10 A.M. and he was dressed, alert, and ready to go, which
I took as a good sign. I hadn't enraged him so much that he'd spent the
past few days drinking, that much I could tell. But his cough was bad, a
hacking that sounded as if he'd smoked too many cigarettes.

"Can I make you a tea?" I asked as he clipped a large sheet of paper
onto his easel. "Tea and honey will help with your cough."

"No." He swatted away the idea. "It's just a tickle," he said, hacking
again. "It'll go away. Nothing a touch of bourbon won't fix. But you can
brew some for yourself."

"Thank you," I said, heading into the house as he waved me on.

When I returned carrying two cups of tea, I noticed the flask, lid flipped
open, on the table next to him. "See," he said, smiling. "I'm cured." I raised
an eyebrow. "Let's get moving, someone's coming to pick up paintings
for the exhibit in San Francisco this afternoon, so I want to sketch this
morning." He nodded to a stool he'd positioned in the middle of the room.

"What are we working on today?" I asked.

"Profile," he said. "Draped—a light robe is fine."

"All right." After changing in the bathroom, I returned to the studio,
sat down, and faced the wall.

"Toward the windows," he said. "I want to catch the light."

After Hanson's eruption on the hike, I'd made an effort to look more
presentable than usual and arrive promptly. I'd kept my morning swim

brief, and when I returned from the beach, I styled my hair, smooth and sleek and off my neck. I powdered my nose and put Vaseline on top of my red lipstick. All the while, I worried that these steps were merely the things I could control in an otherwise chaotic situation that mystified me. I asked myself whether I'd become too relaxed lately, growing accustomed to the easygoing ways of this little beach town, but I doubted that was the likely cause for his anger. I sometimes felt like nothing more than an old man's companion, and if that was the case, his finding my company offensive had to be avoided. But I'd been hired as a model, and I would try anything to protect my job.

An hour into the sitting I was relatively comfortable and didn't feel my usual restlessness. I'd learned to still my thoughts and my body when I had the desire to make an adjustment or scratch an itch, but this was a particularly easy pose to keep, so I allowed my mind to wander. I faced south toward the window, remaining completely still, watching the tree branches sway gently in the breeze outside, thinking about the art festival and how I'd been turned away from the "men's" work.

Mrs. Moynahan had charged me with finding fabric. She was going to be busy with repairing and renovating the few costumes that she'd saved from previous years and tasked me with starting a donation drive to collect new materials so we could piece together new gowns, dresses, and accessories for the various figures who would be represented in the show. She mentioned a visit to a Salvation Army store in another town some thirty miles away, but, in the meantime, she suggested knocking on doors and asking for donations of old curtains, tablecloths, bedspreads, anything that could be cut up and repurposed. It reminded me of the metal drives I used to take part in with the girls from the factory—making the neighborhood rounds, gathering up old pots and pans, tin cans, and even metal toys. As I was reminiscing about my factory days, I saw a young woman, about my age, her hands cupped around her face, staring right at me through the studio window.

"Oh my," I said, startled. "There's someone here." I wrapped my arms around myself, feeling exposed in my thin robe.

"Keep still, woman," Hanson said.

"Sorry." I stiffened again, trying to go back to my original position. "But I think she wants to come in."

Hanson seemed unbothered by this, as if he refused to allow an uninvited visitor to disrupt his work. I could hear the charcoal still moving across the page—shading, I presumed, short, quick strokes. But this woman wasn't going away. I watched her move across the window, peeking in, not seeing what she was looking for and trying another spot; then she walked to the door. She didn't knock; she tried the handle, seemed surprised when it was unlocked, and walked right in.

"Well, there you are!" she said. "Mr. Hanson Radcliff himself, hard at work." She fixed her gaze in his direction despite the fact that I was the one in her line of vision, positioned in the center of the room barely clothed, while he was half-hidden behind the easel. She wore a gorgeous white belted dress that draped from her slender figure and could have come right from the fashion houses in Paris, a large-brimmed white hat, and green peep-toe sandals.

She couldn't have been more than twenty-five, but she had the confidence of a woman well-acquainted with the ways of the world. She glanced at me for a second but then focused her attention back on Hanson.

He set his charcoal down, stepped out from behind the easel, and shot me a steely glare, as if this interruption were somehow my fault.

"Scarlett May Rose," she said boldly, marching toward him with her hand outstretched. "I believe you've been avoiding me."

Until now I'd tried to stay in position, watching the action by moving only my eyes, but I had to turn my head. Hanson grumbled loudly and stared at this young woman. I wouldn't have blamed him if he were captivated by her appearance—she was striking and somehow familiar—but from what I'd heard, Hanson had seen his fair share of beautiful women in his lifetime, and he was clearly annoyed.

"So, Mr. Radcliff, or should I call you Hanson, *have* you been avoiding me?"

"I don't know what you're talking about," he snapped, jolting himself out of his momentary silence and busying himself.

"Well, surely you've received my letters," she said. "My many, many letters."

Hanson took the paper off the easel, slid it onto his desk, then put his charcoals in a box next to it. "As I said, I don't know what you're talking about. You may be forgetting there's been a war on; priorities have gone to more important issues than some Hollywood dolly chasing down an old man."

"Oh, so you do remember me," she said with a smile. "It's lovely to finally meet you in person after hearing so much about you." She put her hand out toward him, and reluctantly he shook it. Then she turned to me. "I'm sorry to interrupt your session. It seems that Mr. Radcliff does in fact enjoy painting women, he's just shy about painting me."

"It's quite all right," I said.

"And what's your name?" she asked.

"I'm Hazel Francis, Mr. Radcliff's assistant."

"I can see that." She smiled and raised her eyebrows, and I felt myself blush. I had to admit—most assistants didn't pose for their bosses.

"Lovely to meet you, Miss Francis." She turned back to Hanson. "Well, I can see you're busy, but I just wanted to pop by and meet you in person and let you know that I'll be in town for a few days. I'm staying at that hotel by the beach, so you know where you can find me." She turned on her heel and walked toward the door. "Have a lovely day," she said, her fingers resting on the handle. "I'm sure I'll be seeing you again."

The rest of the afternoon, Hanson was in a foul mood. He finished the bourbon in his flask and filled it up two more times. He went into the storage room and banged around in there for a while and then lined up some canvases that were to be collected that day for an exhibit. He was clumsy and preoccupied, knocking over paintings as he went.

"Leave it," he barked, when I tried to help. I backed away, not liking this side of him, the same fiery mood I'd seen when we'd hiked into the hills the day that I showed him the lighter. I was more than relieved when the gentlemen arrived to transport his artwork.

～

THOUGH I WAS CURIOUS, I DIDN'T ASK HANSON ABOUT SCARLETT May Rose that day or the next. I wondered about her visit and why she'd been writing him letters, letters that he had apparently ignored completely. When I finished work the next afternoon, I walked through town and was about to head home, but when I neared the hotel, I felt a sudden pang of loneliness.

I hadn't seen Jimmy since the dinner when he'd told me about his lady friend back home, but I felt petty about avoiding him. Did his romantic involvement have to mean we couldn't be friends? Since I was the one it troubled, perhaps I could be the one to accept things as they were.

He was on the beach at the back of the hotel before his evening shift. Lounge chairs were all arranged, fresh towels rolled up and ready for hotel guests to go for a late-day dip in the ocean. He was combing the sand with the rake when he looked up at me, gave me a nod, but kept on with what he was doing.

"Are you busy?" I asked.

"My shift's about to start."

It was tense between us, and I suddenly wished I hadn't come.

"You haven't been coming around," he said.

"I know, work has been keeping me occupied." I considered telling him about the Pageant of the Masters, or the terrible hike to the hills with Hanson, or that Scarlett woman showing up at his door. Instead, I said nothing.

He kept on raking the sand, head down. He seemed aloof or embarrassed, I wasn't sure which. I cursed myself for inviting him to dinner—if I hadn't done that, he wouldn't have felt the need to tell me about his girl. Now I'd ruined everything.

"There's going to be a bonfire on the beach this weekend, some friends from the VA are organizing it."

"Is that allowed?" I asked, so used to the ban on lights and fires and anything that would draw attention to our vulnerable shores.

"It is now," he said. "Anyway, it's on Sunday," he said, resting the rake up against the wall. He hadn't actually invited me, or suggested I come along; he was merely stating a fact that there would be people at the beach on Sunday staring at a fire. I could neither accept nor reject an invitation that hadn't actually been spoken, so I once again said nothing, the silence between us growing more and more awkward as the moments passed.

"Hanson's been a real bear," I blurted out, trying to force us back into our usual banter. "I showed him that lighter that I'd found, and he went into a rage."

Jimmy looked up and raised his eyebrows; he also seemed relieved to have something to talk about.

"He was furious. I didn't work for three days after." I was contemplating telling him about the young woman who came to the studio that day. I thought if we could do this again, chat about the goings-on in the little town the way we used to, then it would be all right for me to make an appearance at the bonfire. The ice would be broken, things wouldn't be strained.

But a waiter called out from the hotel window. "Jimmy, you've got a customer waiting."

"Be right there!"

"I'll leave you to it," I said.

He gave me a smile, shoved his hands in his pockets, and walked quickly back inside.

Making my way out through the lobby, cringing at how quickly things had changed between us, from fast friends to near strangers in such a short time, I noticed someone causing a fuss at the front desk.

"I've made it very clear that I want a full view of the ocean—not a half view, not a quarter view, a full view," a woman announced loudly. "And if my things can't be moved into a room with a full view, then I'll have to find other arrangements. I hear the Hotel Del Camino has very well-appointed accommodations."

As I moved closer toward the main door of the hotel and caught a glimpse through the swarm of hotel staff scuttling around her, I realized it was Scarlett Rose. She looked right at me. I put my head down and kept on walking.

"Hazel," she called out. "Hazel Francis, is that you?"

I really didn't want to get involved in the commotion but glanced back when I reached the door.

"Wait a second," she said. "Wait."

She almost skipped over to me. She looked fabulous again, this time in high-waisted navy sailor pants with eight white buttons, a white rope belt, and a short-sleeve blouse. Women were being told that it was our patriotic duty to return to wearing skirts and dresses, now that the war was over, so when I saw another woman rebel with trousers, as I often did myself, I appreciated it.

"What are you doing here? Fancy a drink? I've got to give these goons a chance to move me to a decent room. There's a great beach bar out back."

I thought of Jimmy and didn't want to bother him again, but I was curious about who this young woman was, and why she seemed to get Hanson so riled up.

"How about we try someplace else," I said.

"Lead the way."

I took her to Café Las Ondas on the boardwalk, where outdoor seating looked onto all the beachgoers.

"Stunning!" she said, once we were seated and the waiter had taken our order for two sidecars. The sun was setting, and the ocean was reflecting the orange sky above.

"So, what brings you to town?" I asked.

"Hanson Radcliff brings me to town," she said. "Didn't I make that clear yesterday? I mean, make no mistake, I adore this little place, it's delightful, but I travel to a lot of beautiful places, and it usually takes more than just a pretty coastline to get me there."

"Like what?" I asked.

"Well, on set for a film or a casting call, something like that." She took a cigarette out and offered one to me.

"No thanks," I said. "I don't smoke."

She lit it, took a long, dramatic inhalation, and exhaled the smoke, even more dramatically, up into the sky.

"You don't recognize me from the pictures?" she asked.

There was something familiar about her, but I couldn't place it—maybe I had seen a picture with her in it and didn't recall. "I'm sorry," I said.

"That's all right. I can't exactly blame you. I've had a few small roles, that's all. I was on contract with MGM and cast for the leading role in a big picture just before the attack on Pearl Harbor. It was going to be my big break, and then this stupid war went and ruined everything."

"Oh, I'm sorry, that's some tough luck."

"That's an understatement. I was devastated. My film was dropped like a hot potato. Almost overnight, Hollywood started putting all their effort into war movies—building air-raid shelters on movie lots, and, of course, later, half of the stars shipped out overseas." She fanned the smoke away from her face and stubbed the cigarette out, not even half-smoked.

"I can't stand these things," she said. "I'm trying to get the hang of them, but the taste is quite repulsive."

"Things must be picking up again now, though, surely," I said.

"For some, but I'm old news. I was the next glamour girl in forty-one; five years later they're on to someone new." She rolled her eyes and perked up only a little when the waiter approached. "Oh goody, here come our quenchers." She clinked her glass against mine and took a sip. "That's why I'm here, that's why I want Hanson to paint me. I've been asking him for the better part of a year."

"Why's it so important that Hanson paint you? There must be a hundred artists who would jump at the chance, people who specialize in that kind of thing. Portraiture, not plein air," I said, trying out some of my newfound vocabulary.

"Ah." She smiled a condescending smile. "You don't know about it, do you?"

"Know about what?"

"I'll spare you all the details, but Hanson used to work for my grandmother, Isabella Rose. He was her personal artist."

"Isabella Rose?" I asked. "As in the actress Isabella Rose?"

"That's right," she said.

"Your grandmother was Isabella Rose from *Daddy's Girl, The Sunshine Song,* and *The Good House*?"

"Those and more," she said, a smug look on her face.

"Oh my. No wonder you're so . . ." I suddenly couldn't think of the right word to encompass all that she was: brazen, confident, familiar, gorgeous.

"So what?" she asked, smiling, waiting for a compliment.

"Well, so pretty and almost famous yourself," I said.

"Oh, I am famous." She took a generous sip of her drink and waved down the waiter for another round. "Just not famous for my own acting career, rather famous for my dead grandmother. And now that the movie studios are overlooking me, I need to give them a reason to take a second look."

I nodded. I couldn't believe I was sitting having drinks, watching the sunset with the granddaughter of Isabella Rose, and that Hanson had known her. "What's Hanson got to do with all that?"

"He did a painting of my grandmother that . . ." She looked out to the horizon as if choosing her words carefully. "Let's just say it garnered a lot of attention. A lot. People are still talking about it decades later, even though no one's ever seen it. Some people don't like him for what he did, especially some in my family, but I think if he painted me, you know, a very provocative portrait like the one he did of her, then the press would be all over it. Everyone would be talking about Hanson Radcliff's return to portraiture—if you can even call it that—and all eyes would be back on me, where they should be." She sat up tall and pushed out her chest. I admired her bravado.

Things were starting to make sense. If she'd been hounding him for weeks, months, a year even, as she said, and he was finally starting to consider the idea, then it could be that he'd wanted a model to practice on after all these years of painting landscapes. And there was that secret room in his house with all the nudes. I knew he didn't owe me an explanation about his interest in figure drawing, but I was certainly curious.

"I can almost see the wheels turning in your head," Scarlett said.

"He never told me about her," I said.

"Well, he has his reasons, I'm sure."

"I suppose so. You know, I found a lighter that your grandmother may have given him a long time ago," I said. "It was engraved with her name on it. He got quite agitated when I showed it to him."

"Oh." She shook her head. "I imagine it's quite painful for him to relive it all."

Painful? I frowned; I clearly didn't have the full story.

"Well, cheers to a new friendship," Scarlett said, raising her glass. "You know, Hazel, I can already see we're going to be the very best of friends."

CHAPTER 17

AFTER WORKING MY SHIFT AT THE GALLERY THAT WEEKEND, I WALKED toward town to meet Lillian for another pageant meeting. Farther down the beach, past the hotel and away from the young couples arm in arm on the boardwalk, I saw the glow of the bonfire and a small crowd of people around it. It was Sunday, and I'd been thinking about that bonfire ever since Jimmy mentioned it, wondering if I should casually walk by. Jimmy was probably one of those silhouetted figures standing around the edge of the fire. From a distance it looked magical—I'd never seen such a thing on the sand, with the waves of the ocean just a few feet away. My chest tightened with yearning as I realized how much I wanted to forget the pageant meeting altogether and mingle with this crowd, with Jimmy, instead, but I forced myself to keep walking. I'd already embarrassed myself by inviting him to dinner, then I'd shown up at his work. I didn't want to appear desperate by leaping at the news that he'd be there, since I wasn't even sure he wanted me to come. I had to respect his situation. Likely, he'd only mentioned the bonfire because he needed something to say, or worse, because he felt sorry for me.

That thought helped me pick up my pace. I crossed Coast Boulevard and turned left up Forest Avenue. Approaching the store where I'd seen the bathing suit, I stopped and paused momentarily, then walked right in.

"You came back," the shop attendant said.

"Yes," I said. "I'm ready to try on the bathing suit in the window."

This seemed to please her, and I felt a sudden surge of determination, as if this bathing suit was going to put to rest all my worries, or at least take my mind off Jimmy.

"We still have the two-piece I mentioned, which would look exquisite." She lifted it off a rack and held it up. "Would you like to try this one too?"

"Yes," I said. "If I may."

"Beach fashions are far more intriguing now," she went on as she led me into the dressing room and pulled a curtain closed. "And with the right figure, anyone can wear these new bathing suits without any fear of discomfort or immodesty."

I slipped off the dress I'd been wearing all day and pulled on the bottoms first, then the top. It was daring and glamorous. I turned, admiring the modern style from all angles, my midriff showing slightly, and the way it fit me just right. It looked like something Scarlett Rose would wear.

"These fashions are very much in the mode nowadays," the woman continued, as I walked out of the dressing room, bathing suit in hand.

I didn't need to try the other one; this one was perfect. "I'll take it," I said.

"Oh." She seemed rather shocked that she didn't have to do more to convince me to purchase it. "Wonderful."

She took her time folding the suit neatly, wrapping it with paper, and placing it in an equally beautiful box.

"Oh, I don't need that," I said, thinking about showing up at the volunteer meeting with all those artists, carrying an elaborately dressed box. "I'll just place it in my satchel."

I waited for her to tell me how much I owed, realizing I hadn't so much as glanced at the price tag.

"That will be twelve ninety-five," she said.

I swallowed hard, thinking of what I could buy for twelve dollars and ninety-five cents, but Hanson had paid me for two weeks of work, and now I needed a little something to lift my spirits. I left the store, pleased with my purchase, and saw Lillian waiting for me on the corner.

The next morning, when I swam in the ocean, I felt different, improved, somehow, wearing this luxurious two-piece suit. Knowing that it was more expensive than any item of clothing I had ever owned gave me a surge of confidence. I might have spent way too much on an overpriced bathing suit, but for that moment I felt rich. I seemed to swim with more grace. My legs propelled me forward with more power than they had before. I felt longer and leaner and more desirable. I wasn't going to be that poor girl from Kansas anymore, I wasn't going to be the girl without any family to speak of. I was going to make something of myself, and if not in the airplane factory, where I could have done good work if given the chance to stay on, then here in Laguna Beach, as an artist's assistant and model, if that was my only option. I was going to live up to my decision to succeed, to make a decent living wage, and not have to rely on anyone else. I would make this job with Hanson work, make myself indispensable to him, so that he couldn't send me on my way, no matter what missteps I took along the way.

As Hanson set up his blank canvas later that morning, and I arranged myself for a sitting, I dared myself to find a way to bring up Scarlett's visit. Despite his nagging cough, he seemed well rested and at ease. A few days had passed since she had intruded on his sketch session at the studio, so I hoped it wouldn't strike a nerve.

"So is the young woman from Hollywood . . ." I began, but he stopped me.

"I knew it, I just knew you were going to come in here today asking questions." He put his hand up. "We're not going to waste our time with that."

"I apologize," I said quickly, but then added, as innocently as possible, "but did you know she's the famous Isabella Rose's granddaughter?" Spending time with Scarlett had emboldened me, since I knew slightly more than he realized.

He looked at me, surprised, but he didn't lash out.

"You, arrange yourself," he said. "Have your back to me." He walked out of the studio and into the house and it must have been a good ten minutes before he returned. I recalled how Scarlett had used the word "painful" when we'd talked about Isabella, and I wondered if I had upset him with my question. Eventually, he joined me in the studio and sat behind his easel.

"My father didn't approve of my artistic ambition," Hanson said finally as I sat with my back to him, the shawl dropped to my waist, my head turned to the left, looking over my shoulder. "I left home when I was sixteen."

I was surprised by this remark. "What about your mother?" I asked.

"Don't move," he barked. I should have let him talk. I heard him get up, walk across the room, and pour himself a drink. It wasn't yet noon.

"She died when I was young. I don't remember her." Another long pause and footsteps back across the room. "I studied briefly at the Chicago Art Institute, but I ran out of money fast, so mostly I taught myself and traveled west. When I got to Los Angeles I worked as a commercial artist painting billboards. I'd stay up on that scaffolding for hours after my work was done, and I'd sketch or paint whatever I could see. The best views you could ask for. That's where I learned to do landscapes. Lift your chin."

I did as he asked.

"Too much—slight tilt to the left."

I dropped it slightly and tilted, feeling a strain on the back of my neck; this was going to be an uncomfortable one to hold.

"I met her, the young woman's grandmother, Isabella, at an exhibit that I stumbled into."

I couldn't believe my ears. Hanson had brought her up himself! I froze no matter the strain—willing him to continue.

"An opening night. I shouldn't have even been there, but I was trying to learn what I could, meet a few people in the art world, so I'd read the papers for gallery openings. I'd try to talk to people without getting myself kicked out. And she just took a liking to me. I mean, my God, I was in my twenties at the time, and she was twenty years older, but she was a fascinating woman. She asked to see my work, invited me to her house, a mansion on the beach in Santa Monica. I went the next day and never left; she gave me my own room, a studio to paint in, a beach at my doorstep, and a pool to swim in. She gave me a job as her artist." He slurred his speech slightly as he said that last word. "It was more than anything any young kid like me could ever have imagined."

I couldn't help turning to look at him. It all sounded like something out of a movie—a wealthy older woman, famous actress, in fact, takes in a young, handsome artist. Did he take her to bed? I wondered. Hanson didn't notice my staring at him; he was back at the bottle of bourbon, refreshing his glass.

"Except the only thing she wanted me to paint was her, from every conceivable angle, her and her dog," he said with a laugh. "She paid me well, and I accompanied her to every party in Los Angeles and beyond. I got to know her, really know her. Her passions, her insecurities, her desires. I began to fall in love." He paused; I was back in position and did everything in my power not to move again, hoping he would go on. "But after a while it became a little dull. She wanted glamour and beauty only, she wouldn't let me capture her truth, her natural self. And, boy, was she beautiful, especially when she wasn't all done up. But she had her demands. She wanted me to make her feel young again. And I gave her what she wanted."

I felt myself blush. So, he was bedding her, and painting her, and getting paid for it. I didn't hear any movement, no brushstrokes, no pencil on paper. I waited and waited until eventually he continued to paint. He didn't say any more, just resumed his work. I sat that way for another hour or so until finally he gave me leave.

"Get dressed," he mumbled. "We're done for today."

I wrapped the shawl around me and stood up, but he'd already left the room, the bottle of bourbon empty on the table.

CHAPTER 18

IT WAS A PERFECT SPRING DAY WHEN I EMERGED FROM THE WAVES at my usual location in the cove. The sky was clear blue with no marine layer or fog, as there often was, blocking the early morning sun. As I walked toward my towel, I spotted Edgar sitting nearby on a folding chair, drawing in his sketchbook.

"What are you doing here?" I asked, as nicely as I could manage.

I peeked into his sketch pad as I grabbed the towel and shook off the sand. He was drawing Pelican Rock, a boulder formation that poked out of the water during low tide and became a gathering spot for pelicans.

"Though this location might seem fairly private at this time of day, it is actually a public beach," he said, finally looking up from his work and fixing his eyes on me. "Wow, you're quite a dish in that suit."

I wrapped the towel around me.

"Um, thank you. So," I moved on quickly, "what brings you out so early?"

"It's the best time of day to sketch: it's empty, it's clear, it's got that magical feeling to it. Quite magnificent," he said, looking out to the ocean then fixing his gaze back on me. "I do like that suit, it's very becoming, the two-piece style—though I also liked your previous choice too."

"What?"

"I'm joking," he said. "We already know I make the most unappealing jokes, I offend people everywhere I go."

I wrung the water out of my hair then wrapped my arms around my torso. Had he seen me swim with no bathing suit? I'd been sure I was always alone.

"You should sit for me sometime in my studio," he said. "In all your natural beauty." He let those words sink in for a moment. "I would pay, of course."

"I didn't know you did portraiture."

"I don't generally, then again neither does Hanson, yet he seems quite taken with the idea."

"I can't. I'm very busy with Hanson and involved in the pageant now too, as you know."

"You must have a few spare hours, in the evening, perhaps."

"Hanson keeps odd hours, and part of the arrangement is that I'm available when he needs me," I said. "And there's the gallery," I said quickly, remembering that I had agreed to work on Sundays.

"It's your choice," he said.

I would never pose for this man, I told myself, he irritated me immensely. And yet some small part of me was intrigued. Hanson had asked me to pose only one body part at a time—legs, arms, ankles, shoulders, back—and that was just fine, preferable actually. Yet I wondered how it would feel to fully disrobe and pose, to allow myself to relax into a position and be looked at, studied, re-created in the eyes of someone else. I wondered if I could do it, and what the result would be. I didn't want my anxieties to come across in the artwork. Could I ever be so bold as to follow Scarlett's provocative example?

"Well, let me know if some time in your busy schedule opens up," he said.

I busied myself by finding my beach clothes, which I rushed to put on over my swimsuit.

"Edgar," I said, changing the subject yet again. "By any chance, are you familiar with a painting that Hanson did of the actress Isabella Rose many years ago?"

His face broke into a knowing smile, and he nodded slowly. "Of course, who isn't?"

"Oh, so you've heard of it then."

"Heard of it? It follows him around like a ghost."

"What does exactly?"

"The story."

"But what story? I seem to be getting bits and pieces of information, and I'm a little confused."

"I don't want to be the one to flap my lips about Hanson; he's a good friend of mine, always has been," he said, putting his pencil back to his paper and looking out again to the rock.

"I wouldn't want you to tell me anything private that I shouldn't know, but I'm curious about what happened between them. I mean, he told me he was her personal artist, but there seems to have been some beef between them or something like that, because . . ." I stopped here, unsure what more I could safely say.

"Some beef?" He laughed. "It was a little more than a beef, Hazel. He basically killed the woman."

"What?"

Edgar put his hands up. "Look, it's really not my story to tell."

"What do you mean he basically killed her? What happened between them?"

"There was a lot of speculation. The newspapers were all over it apparently, they still harass him. That's why he stays home most of the time, or sits at the hotel bar in the same corner spot. It was some bad luck, what can I say?"

"Edgar, please, you're being so vague. Tell me what you know, I beg you." At that, Edgar's lips curled up at the edges.

"I don't like to make a lady beg," he said.

"Please, Edgar, you're alarming me."

"Not here," he said, turning back to his notebook. "Come by the studio sometime and I'll tell you what I know."

I PACED THE APARTMENT. IT WAS SO TINY, IT TOOK ME BARELY FIVE steps to pace from one side of the living room to the other, but I did it anyway, over and over again. He "basically" killed a woman? What did that mean? Hanson Radcliff, the famous artist whose paintings sold for thousands of dollars, the famous artist whom I'd accompanied into the canyon and into the hills, alone, whom I'd sat for in a studio half-naked

for hours at a time, with no one else around—he was somehow involved in
the death of the celebrated Isabella Rose? How could this be? He *basically
killed the woman*—those were Edgar's exact words, I reminded myself.
That could mean any number of things, and when I'd pressed for more,
he refused to divulge anything in public. "Basically" didn't mean he'd
killed her. If he had, he would be in jail. Everyone would have known
her name, she was one of the first and most famous silent film stars before the talkies started, and it sounded as if whatever happened between
them was common knowledge, so there'd be no way he'd walk free if
he'd done something so terrible. Hanson might have a temper, and he
certainly drank too much, but deep down he had a kind heart, a forgiving heart. He could have fired me the minute he realized I'd made myself at home in his house while he was away. I simply didn't believe he
was capable of something so awful, but I didn't understand why Edgar
would say such a thing if it wasn't true.

Hanson was on his hands and knees in the studio when I walked
through the door later than usual. My hair was still damp from the ocean,
pulled back and pinned away from my face in haste. I couldn't warm
up after my dip that day, or it may have been the news I'd received that
morning that gave me a chill. I'd worn my wide-legged trousers because
they gave me a sense of power and assurance that I needed right now.

"Ah, Hazel." Hanson looked over his shoulder at me. "You're just in
time, give me a hand, would you?"

I set my purse down on the counter and walked over. He had a hammer in one hand and a set of blunt pliers in the other as he leaned his
body over a wooden frame of stretcher bars. I felt myself stiffen at the
sight of him, weapon in hand.

"How was it?" he asked.

"How was what?"

"Your morning swim."

"How did you know I went for a swim?"

"Because your hair is wet, and you told me you always swim before
reporting to work."

"Oh, yes." I laughed nervously. "I suppose I've told you that before."

He gave me a look. "Are you quite all right? Did you get knocked
sideways by one of those waves?"

"I'm fine," I said. "A little tired, that's all." That was the truth. Or rather, I was feeling exhausted and overwhelmed by the new information Edgar had imparted.

Hanson hammered a nail into the side of the large wooden frame, securing the ragged edge of a roll of canvas to it, then he tapped several more nails into place.

"Pull this tight, would you?" He handed me the roll of canvas. "Tighter," he said. "The damp air here makes the canvas sag over time, so I like it to be as tight as possible to start." I pulled it toward me, putting all my effort into it. "That's it. Hold it right there." He climbed over the frame to the other side, where I was, and secured the nails. I looked at his fingers tight around the handle of the hammer, his dry, wrinkled skin. What had those hands done, what secrets did they hold?

"Okay, back up now," he said as he turned the canvas around and fastened it to the other two sides of the frame. I watched him from a few feet away now and wondered what he might have looked like as a young man. He was tall, almost six feet, but had he been strong and muscular then, or slim as he was now? I was sure he'd been handsome, you could tell—the bones were there, the eyes, and I'd heard tales that he had been a ladies' man. But how? Who would overlook a notorious past?

"Am I sitting today?" I asked, after he was done stretching two more canvases.

"No, I'm meeting Berg this afternoon; apparently he found a good location in the canyon that he swears I haven't seen before. I doubt it, since I've covered every inch of that canyon ten times over by myself, but I'll humor him, since it's fun to watch him play the fool."

I prayed that Edgar wouldn't tell Hanson that I'd been asking questions about his past.

"Is there anything you'd like me to do while you're gone?" I asked, hoping he'd dismiss me early. I couldn't be in such close proximity to him and appear calm until I knew more.

"Well, since you've asked, could you gesso the canvases I just stretched?"

"Could I what?"

"Prime them. You have to prime them with gesso or rabbit glue before you can paint on them, to seal the base layer, otherwise the paint is absorbed by the canvas. Here." He handed me a broad, dull palette knife.

"You can slap it on all over with this and smooth it out with a big brush."
He walked to his stash of paintbrushes and pulled out the largest one.
"It needs to be uniformly smooth all over."

"All right," I said, taking the palette knife from his hand.

"You think you can handle it?" he asked.

"Of course," I said.

After he left, I did as he asked. I painted the canvases with the thick
white primer and left them to dry in the studio. Afterward, I went into
the house to wash my hands and wondered once more about the room
at the top of the staircase. All those paintings of women, locked away in
that little room—maybe Isabella Rose was among them.

CHAPTER 19

I OPENED THE WOODEN DOOR OF THE WAGON AND CLIMBED INTO the back seat alongside the basket I'd packed for lunch.

"Am I your chauffeur now?" Hanson said when he came out of his house, leaning into the car and handing me one more box. As he straightened up, he coughed into a handkerchief. "Good God," he said, hacking one more time. "My lungs aren't what they used to be."

"I can make you a warm drink before we hit the road," I said. "Or we could make a stop at the pharmacy."

"I'm fine." He waved me away, coughing again.

"Are you sure? Those F and F cough lozenges are quite good and don't taste horrible anymore; they came out with honey flavor."

"I said I'm all right."

I reached back, trying to shove the box he'd given me into the third row of seats, but it was already full. "I don't think this is going to fit."

"Put that on the seat you're sitting on and get your rear into the front seat where you belong," he said, opening the door for me and bowing dramatically as if he were a doorman. He then laughed and shook his head. He was in a good mood, poking fun and generally quite cheerful, but I was still on edge, startled if he looked at me the wrong way, jumpy if he got too close. I tried to shake off the uneasiness caused by Edgar's story and enjoy this overnight trip.

His Ford Deluxe, or the woody wagon as he called it, was a real beauty. It had a polished black hood and black canvas roof, wood-paneled doors and interior. I had my headscarf wrapped around my hair and slipped on my round, white-framed sunglasses when I climbed into the passenger seat. On the few previous occasions I'd had the pleasure of riding in it, the car made me feel like a movie star, as if we were going someplace special, even if it was only through town to pick up art supplies. But today we really were going someplace special: we were traveling to Los Angeles to the Museum of History, Science, and Art in Exposition Park for the very first G.I. Art Exhibit, which Hanson had helped curate. He was a member of the California Art Club, and they had collaborated with the Veterans Administration to showcase budding G.I. artists.

Hanson sat in the driver's seat and turned the engine a few times before it sputtered to life. We pulled out of his driveway and turned left onto Coast Boulevard. The engine ran coolly, and I looked out the window at the little town I'd grown so fond of, wondering how long I'd get to stay. It had only been four months, but it felt as if I was starting to settle in. That sense of belonging somewhere took time, but I'd been yearning for it for as long as I could remember.

Despite starting to feel comfortable here, I still couldn't shake that anxious feeling in the pit of my stomach, and I was fixated on what Edgar had told me. *He basically killed the woman.* What did that mean? I could ask Hanson, I supposed. We had a good two hours ahead of us; we were trapped in a car together, and I could ask him anything and he couldn't barge out of the room and pour himself a drink. But he could get angry, and I didn't want that all weekend, especially since he was in relatively good spirits now. But mostly, if I was being truthful with myself, I was a little scared to find out what Edgar meant. Had there been an accident, had there been a fight, had alcohol been involved? If I was to keep on working for Hanson, I eventually needed to know the truth.

"Ah, it feels good, doesn't it?" Hanson said, rolling the window down a few inches and jolting me out of my thoughts. "Out on the open road." We drove along the coast, out of Laguna and through neighboring towns. "I was right down there on that beach"—he tapped at the window—"years and years ago, the day Duke Kahanamoku and his famous Hollywood friends and surfers saved eight lives from a fishing boat."

"Duke who?" I asked.

"The surfing legend. You've never heard of him?"

I shook my head.

"That day, huge walls of water were curling in from the horizon, crashing right on the shore. No one had any right to be out there. Duke and his friends had their boards lying around them on the beach but even they weren't going in. And then we all saw a charter fishing boat out there, the *Thelma*, she was called, and she was obviously trying to find her way to safer waters, but she was losing her battle. Everyone on the beach had been watching those monstrous green waves for some fine entertainment, but we all got to our feet and went to the water's edge when we saw the boat. The rails were crowded with fishermen, and then *boom*." He slapped his hand on the steering wheel and made me jump. "One of those waves curled down on the vessel, water exploded everywhere."

"What happened?" I asked, gripped by his story.

"Before the next mammoth of a wave came, we could see that *Thelma* had capsized and thrown those fishermen overboard in that wild sea. Next thing you knew, Duke had his board under his arm and was running toward them."

"With his surfboard?"

"Most men would have got themselves killed out there, but he hit the water hard and paddled into towering breakers. I thought they were going to annihilate him, we all did—the surfing legend of the world was going to wash up right in front of our eyes, and we couldn't do a damn thing about it. Next thing you know, he was coming back toward the beach with a couple of fishermen clinging to his board, wet and heavy in their clothes. He pulled them to shore, we all ran to them, got them on their stomachs, coughing up seawater, and Duke, he went straight back in, a few of his surfer friends taking their boards and joining him. They kept coming back, dropping off one or two people, coughing and gasping for air, then they went back out there."

"What a hero," I said.

"That is the truth. Of the twenty-nine people on the boat that day, seventeen died, but twelve survived. Duke single-handedly saved eight of them."

"Tragic, but incredible that he saved all those lives," I said.

"Indeed." He shifted into third gear and stretched back into the leather seat.

He was chatting today, friendly. He was really quite enjoyable to be around when he was like this, telling stories of his more youthful days.

"You know, I'd painted the ocean probably a hundred times by then. I was young and eager, trying to make a way for myself as an artist here in Laguna, an artist of nature, of truth and beauty, I thought." He smiled, as if amused by his youthful zeal. "But I was an amateur, not just in technique but in life. What did I know? When I think back on those seascapes, they were flat, dead, emotionless. It wasn't until that day when Duke saved those people that I began to understand the ocean, her power, her rage, how she could act that way one morning and be perfectly calm the following day. Tranquil and kind and generous one minute, a killer the next."

His hands gripped the cream leather steering wheel a little tighter, and I glanced at them. I wondered if he was still talking about the ocean, or something else entirely. The thought chilled me.

"Anyway," he continued. "After that, I really saw things differently. I became infatuated with the waves, the colors, the movement. I was out there every single morning when the sun was rising. I finally painted some of what I saw that day, those green combers curling down on a lone surfer like the Niagara Falls."

"It's all so vivid," I said. It was easy to see that the experience had influenced him deeply.

"Well, yes. To truly create, you have to feel something, you have to see something that was already there in a new, a different way. You can paint or write or sculpt or draw 'til the cows come home, but until you have something inside of you that warms you, that burns almost, sends your heart racing, it won't mean anything."

I nodded, wanting to understand, feeling on the verge of grasping it, though feeling just a few feet away from being able to reach out and touch what he described.

"You have to find something that you're passionate about, something that drives you to do crazy things, something that keeps you up at night, and only then will you have the fire in you to be any good."

"That makes sense, I think," I said. "But what do you do if you don't have that feeling? Surely you can't feel that way every time you sit down in front of a new canvas."

"Ha, you're right." He reached over and took my forearm, squeezed it. "You've stumbled upon the impossible task of all artists, all creators. We can't possibly feel moved every time, so we just keep going, keep doing what we do, and we wait for the next time, and it will happen again. But as for that warm feeling, that burning sensation, that's what bourbon is for. Bourbon and sex."

He laughed and put his hand back on the steering wheel.

"So, do you still have it?"

"Have what?"

"The painting of the surfer in the ocean?" I asked.

He laughed. "No, I gave it to Duke. I tracked him down and gave it to him. He didn't know who I was, I was a nobody then, but he liked it, and he started commissioning me to paint more for him. In fact, he was really the one who helped me become known, after Isabella." He sighed, and I waited for him to say more—maybe he was about to share more about what happened with Isabella Rose. "Ridiculous, isn't it. He was the hero, I was just some chucklehead sitting on the beach watching, and he ended up being responsible for my early success, at least in my seascapes."

"You had talent, it sounds as if people recognized that."

He shrugged and didn't say more.

"I'd love to see some of your early work," I said. "Your ocean paintings or . . ." I hesitated for a second then went on. "Or any of your earlier work—landscapes from when you worked on the billboards, or even . . ." I debated for a second. "One of your early portraits of Isabella."

Before I even finished my sentence, he was shaking his head. "No, it's gone, it's all gone."

"But surely you have some early work, hidden away somewhere." I tried to say it as casually as possible—after all, at his studio that week he'd revealed to me some bits and pieces about his past—but he was shaking his head now.

"I said no." His tone had shifted abruptly, and I tensed. The air in the car suddenly felt stifling. I had done exactly what I'd told myself I wouldn't do. He opened the window a few more inches and the noise of the rushing air put an end to the conversation.

AN HOUR OR SO LATER, WHEN WE PULLED UP TO THE BILTMORE HO-tel, I was struck by its grandeur. Two bellhops in matching flat hats and button-studded jackets came to either side of the car and opened our doors. Hanson stepped out and began walking up the steps to the lobby, leaving the car and all our belongings behind. I tried to keep up.

"What about our bags?" I said, walking quickly at his side.

"They'll bring them up," he said, and sure enough he was right. When I checked, they were opening the back doors of the wagon and unload-ing our belongings onto a gold trolley.

"Mr. Radcliff." A sharply tailored man greeted him at the door. "We are honored that you have chosen to stay with us at the Biltmore Hotel."

Hanson nodded and kept walking.

"I'm Mr. Colligan, the manager here, and it will be my pleasure to ensure you're settled in your room and to get anything you might need to make your stay more comfortable." He reached his arm out toward the front desk, but Hanson walked past him through the lobby—opulent and rich looking with a vaulted ceiling, two huge bronze chandeliers, a carved marble fountain, and a sweeping double staircase. I felt tiny looking around in awe at the huge cathedral-like space, while Hanson marched on ahead.

"The lobby's decorated in the Moorish Revival style; we have frescoes by John Smeraldi, who's also known for his work in the Vatican and the White House," Mr. Colligan said quickly, noting Hanson's eagerness to get to his room. "The ceiling here is painted with twenty-four-carat gold accents," he said as a side note to me, as I was clearly more interested in hearing what he had to say.

He stopped for a split second for us to appreciate the décor but then had to jog a few steps to keep up with Hanson, still charging ahead.

"As I'm sure you know well, Mr. Radcliff, the Biltmore is proud to be known as the Host of the Coast. With 1,612 rooms, we are the largest hotel west of Chicago and home of the Motion Picture Arts and Sciences Oscars. The rooms are this way, Mr. Radcliff; you'll be in tower two."

"I know where I'm going," Hanson said gruffly.

I felt sorry for poor Mr. Colligan, who was desperately trying to impress us.

"If you so please"—he nodded to me—"the Biltmore Bowl nightclub will be providing wonderful entertainment over the next few days. When it was built, it was the world's largest nightclub."

"I've heard the nightclub is really sharp," I said, fibbing a little. I didn't know a thing about it, but this man was really determined to deliver his welcome speech, and I didn't want him to feel dismissed.

"Joe Reichman and His Orchestra are playing tonight, hope you brought your dancing shoes." He winked. "During the war we operated as a rest and recovery facility, but as you can see"—he looked around proudly, as if he owned the place—"we have returned to our former glory now."

"I've got it from here," Hanson said, stepping into the elevator cab.

"Will there be anything else that I can help you with at the present moment?" Mr. Colligan asked. I wanted to ask Hanson the same thing. I regretted pushing the topic of his earlier work and setting him off into one of his silent moods, and I wished I could take it back and ask him exactly what was needed of me for the weekend, but I knew better than to ask questions now.

"Show the girl to her room," Hanson said, pressing a few coins into the man's hand.

"Of course, and please don't hesitate to call on me if there's anything I can do."

But before he could finish, Hanson pulled the door closed, not giving the elevator operator a chance to get to it, leaving us standing in the hallway.

"Off we go, then," Mr. Colligan said. If he'd been offended by Hanson's roughness, he certainly didn't let it show. "Must be quite something to work for Mr. Hanson, what a talented artist he is."

"It's quite something," I said.

We walked on to what seemed to be the other side of the hotel entirely to reach my accommodation for the weekend.

"Is this the staff quarters?" I asked, noticing the drab hallways and dimmer lights on this end of the building.

"No, not at all, but these smaller, more affordable rooms are often booked for staff of our guests."

After my suitcase was delivered to my room, I unpacked a few things, hung up my dress for the art show, and dug out the calling card Scarlett Rose had given me when I met her in Laguna. She had specifically asked—no, she made me promise to call on her if I found myself in Los Angeles, and I had slipped the card into my suitcase just in case. I had so many more questions for her about her grandmother after Edgar's comment, and until I received instructions from Hanson, I had nothing but time on my hands. It would infuriate Hanson if he found out I was poking around again, though, so I set it down, took out my makeup bag, put some rouge on my lips and powder on my nose. Who did I think I was, anyway, thinking I could call on the granddaughter of a famous screen actress, when the famous artist I worked for had all but prohibited it?

But then the receiver was in my hand. I doubted she'd even answer. I gave the operator the exchange, and before I had a chance to change my mind, a man's voice answered.

"I'd like to speak with Miss Scarlett if she's available," I said.

"She's not, I'm afraid," he said, rather sternly.

"Oh, of course, I'm sure she's very busy." I waited but heard nothing; he didn't even ask for my name. "Could you please let her know that Hazel Francis called, and I'm staying at the Biltmore Hotel?"

"Very well," the man's voice answered. I doubted the message would reach her.

I sat down on the bed, all dolled up, but with nowhere to go.

CHAPTER 20

THAT AFTERNOON I TOOK A LONG STROLL AROUND THE GARDENS across the street from the hotel and found myself approaching a large, modern-looking building—the Los Angeles Central Library. I walked up the steps and into the building, looking up at the vast domed ceiling, intricately painted in cool tones of blue, green, and violet, with a starburst in the center, and arches on all four sides.

"May I assist you?" a gentleman asked.

"Oh, I was just admiring the architecture."

"Beautiful, isn't it?"

"Very," I said, suddenly unsure if it was open to the public.

"Are you looking for titles or research? Books are on this floor, but for articles, periodicals, that type of thing, you'll take the stairs." He pointed to an impressive staircase.

I nodded. "Okay, I'll take the stairs," I said, thinking my stroll into the library should appear intentional.

"Enjoy your visit," he said, starting to walk ahead of me toward the staircase himself, "and let me or one of the other librarians know if you need any help."

"Actually," I said, catching up with him. "You mentioned articles and periodicals. Do you keep old newspapers on file here at the library?"

"Of course; we have a print index, and many articles are archived."

Suddenly my interest was piqued. "So, you might have actual articles about a specific person or happening in the news from a while back, maybe forty years ago."

"I'm sure we do. Which publication are you looking for?"

"I don't know exactly," I said.

"What date are you looking for, you could start there."

"I don't know that either," I said, feeling rather foolish for starting this conversation on a whim, without any of the right information. "I only know the subject matter."

"And that is?" he questioned.

I hesitated, unsure if I should say, but he didn't know me or who I worked for. "It's about a famous actress who died. Isabella Rose."

"Oh yes, of course," he said.

"I'm interested in articles around the time of her death, the circumstances, that kind of thing."

"There was an artist involved, if I recall," he said casually. "Famous now, I believe." I must have gasped audibly, because he turned to look at me. "I could be wrong, maybe I'm thinking of another actress."

"No, no," I stammered. "I think you're correct." I couldn't believe this was common knowledge about the man I worked for, and that I had been so ignorant about it up until now. "Hanson Radcliff," I said quietly.

"Ah yes, a scandal of some kind?"

"So, you have information on this?" I suddenly felt close to finding out the truth about Hanson's past, too close. "Newspaper clippings, perhaps?"

"Very likely," he said. "But it will require some searching, and we're closing soon. Can you come back tomorrow?"

Tomorrow was the art show, and though I wasn't sure of my responsibilities with Hanson, I knew I'd have to make myself available to him.

"All right," I said. "I'll come back."

⟡

I WALKED INTO THE HOTEL DISTRACTED AND WAS JOLTED WHEN I heard a woman's voice call out.

"There she is, Miss Hazel Francis." When I turned and looked, it was Scarlett lounging in a large leather chair, looking as if she'd walked right off a Hollywood movie set.

"Scarlett," I said in a hushed tone, hurrying toward her, trying to quiet her before she called my name again. I immediately thought of Hanson's reaction if he were to walk through the lobby at that very moment. "What are you doing here?"

"Well, you invited me, didn't you?"

"Yes, yes, I called, so nice to see you again," I said, sitting down in the seat next to her.

"I was thrilled to hear from you, Hazel," she said, taking my hand in hers. I didn't quite know what to think. Why on earth would she be thrilled to hear from me? "I haven't eaten since last night and I'm ravenous. Should we get some chow? I know a great little place around here."

Pleased to be leaving the lobby of the hotel, I followed Scarlett out to her car and driver.

"Take us to that little Mexican café I like," she said to her driver, "La Golondrina." She turned to me excitedly. "Have you ever eaten Mexican food?" I shook my head. "Don't worry, I hadn't either, until I went to Acapulco earlier this year." She looked at me, her eyes wide, waiting for a reaction.

"Acapulco," I said. "Wowsers."

"It was a gas, a party-all-day-every-day kind of place—rubbing shoulders with the glitterati. I was even invited on Errol Flynn's yacht."

The car pulled up outside a small brick building with an outdoor patio. Inside, there were bright paintings on the walls, glass lamps hanging from the wood-beamed ceiling, and each table had a vibrant, colorful tablecloth.

"Here is perfect," Scarlett said after looking around and finding what she considered the ideal table: inside but with a good view of the patio. I sat down opposite her and tried to hide my smile. Here I was in Los Angeles, with Scarlett Rose—and she was treating me as if I were some sort of long-lost friend.

"We'd like two tequila cocktails," she called out to a waiter, "and some of your delicious avocado guacamole and a few of your handmade tortillas." She said it with a flourish and a slight accent. "Oh, and some of those sauces you do. Salsaaa," she said, drawing out the word. I felt as if she was showing off a little, but I found it endearing and all very exciting.

When our cocktails arrived, Scarlett raised hers to mine. "Cheers," she said. "To new adventures." I took a sip of the pink drink served in a long-stemmed glass and almost spit it out.

"Whoa," I said, putting my hand to my mouth. "What is that?"

"Tequila!" She laughed. "It's made from cactus. You don't like it?"

"It's strong," I said, trying it again, but more judiciously this time. "It's unlike anything I've tasted before, but it's growing on me."

"Well," she said, rubbing her hands together. "Do you have some news for me?"

"News?" What news would I possibly have for her? I thought of the librarian, and how he might uncover the story of what happened between Hanson and Scarlett's grandmother some forty years ago, but that wouldn't be news to her.

"News from your boss, Mr. Radcliff?"

I shook my head, confused—could it be, I wondered, that she was trying, as I was, to find more information about this incident? "I'm sorry, I don't know what you mean?"

"Isn't that why you called on me?"

I stared at her blankly.

"Hazel." She bounced up and down on her chair a little as if I were being coy and keeping something from her. "Has he agreed to paint me or not?"

"Oh," I said, with the sudden, sinking realization that this had been a big misunderstanding. The only reason she'd visited me at the Biltmore was because she thought I'd persuaded Hanson to allow her to pose for him. "Oh, Scarlett, I'm sorry, but no, he hasn't, at least not as far as I know."

"What?" She looked utterly disappointed. "Didn't you try to persuade him?"

"I tried to talk to him about your grandmother."

"Oh, for goodness' sake," she said, exasperated. "Who cares about that, it's old news."

I wanted to crawl under the table. To think that just moments ago I'd been marveling that someone like Scarlett wanted to spend time with me, a nobody from Kansas. What a cockeyed idea. I realized now that she had interest in me only because I was a way to get to Hanson.

"I'm terribly sorry if that's why you came," I said, feeling ridiculous, as if I'd lured her under false pretenses.

She sighed and took another sip of her cocktail. "No, it's not the only reason I came. I happen to like you, Hazel Francis, but I was certainly hoping for a positive outcome with your cantankerous boss. I really think it would catch the attention of the studios, especially after everything." What exactly did she mean by *everything*? Before I could chime in, she continued on. "I suppose I can't force him to paint me, but it sure would be swell if he changed his mind." She swirled what was left of her drink and knocked it back. "That darn war, I would have been the talk of Hollywood if that war hadn't come along and ruined things."

I nodded and wondered momentarily if Hanson might be looking for me, but then Scarlett put her hand in the air and made a circle with her fingers. "Another round, señor," she said dramatically. I cringed slightly at the thought of another one of those drinks—mine was still full—but I didn't object.

"Everything changed with the war," I said, trying to relate somehow. "I never could have imagined I'd end up building airplanes—or guessed I'd like it so much."

She scrunched up her nose. "Ugh," she said with a scowl. "Sounds awful. You couldn't have got me working on airplanes if you paid me all the money in the world."

I laughed.

"I did my part, though," she added. "I went on several war bond tours—the studios made us since we weren't filming. I was never the main attraction—the stars were people like Dotty, Bette, Marlene, and Hedy—but they wanted as many pretty young things as possible hanging around, persuading people to give up some of their salaries as loans to the government. We made stops at factories too, asking the workers to hand over their hard-earned money. Hey, maybe we crossed paths."

I smiled, but if I'd crossed paths with Scarlett Rose before, I would have remembered.

"It was all worth it though," she went on. "We just hoped that if we could raise a lot of money, it would help end the war as fast as possible. We gave out kisses, signed photographs, anything that would help end the stupid thing and let our movies get made again."

"That's great, Scarlett," I said. "Really, it is."

"I worked one night a week at the Hollywood Canteen too. We'd go entertain the troops, serve them food, dance with them, take their minds off things. Bette was the ringleader, believe it or not." She stopped and looked at me, as if to be sure I was following along. "Bette Davis."

"Oh!"

"And John Garfield, they gave us our marching orders: 'Dance with the boys, get the boys a drink if they want one, listen to the boys, nod sympathetically but don't ask them too many questions, don't gawk at the boys with injuries, don't stare at the spot where they got their leg shot off or their face mangled, or their finger missing.'"

I shook my head and took a steady drink of my tequila concoction. I'd seen those boys too, who came back injured, and I hadn't known where to look either. "It's heartbreaking to think about," I said, hoping she might not dwell on it further.

"But wait, here's the best part!" Scarlett went on, shifting gears. "Bette gave us our rotation in the kitchen. 'I washed the last hundred cups,' she said to me one day, 'it's your turn to wash the next hundred.' Ha! Bette Davis telling me to wash dishes!"

"Really? Wow!" Scarlett might be grandstanding, but I loved picturing her toe-to-toe with Bette Davis.

"Yeah, well." She shook her head. "I wanted my picture to get made. And I was disappointed as hell when I saw all those young fellas getting shipped out—all those handsome faces. I just wanted us to win, and have it be over."

She looked wistfully into the distance, and I did too, before changing the subject. The drinks were making me warm and a little looser by now.

"Scarlett, may I ask you a question?"

"Ask away!" she said, perking up again.

"How did your grandmother die? I mean, what happened with Hanson?"

She rolled her eyes and took a cigarette out of her jeweled cigarette case.

"I'm sorry to bring up such an upsetting topic," I said.

"What's upsetting, Hazel," she said sternly, "is that she's all anyone wants to talk about. Imagine if you were trying to make a life for yourself, you know, really make something of yourself, and all anyone could do was talk about a long-gone relative you'd never even met. It's exhausting!" She lit her cigarette and immediately started waving the smoke out of her face. "I think it's awful what she did. Luckily my mother had already met my father by then, so she wasn't alone, and she inherited her fortune, so she wasn't broke, but my mother might have had a very different future. She told me that when she was a kid she had hopes of becoming an actress too, but after what happened with Isabella, she wanted nothing to do with show business." It was strange to hear her refer to her own grandmother by her first name, but I supposed since she'd never met her, she saw her as everyone else did, a once-famous actress who died young.

"But what did she do exactly?"

"Oh, Hazel, honestly, I didn't come here to talk about her! Haven't I made that clear to you yet?" She was getting quite frustrated with me now. "That's what I liked about you, Hazel, you seemed so naive, so unassuming, and not caught up in all that Hollywood gossip. But maybe you're just like the rest."

"Oh no, I'm not, truly, I don't know a thing about Hollywood, except for loving the pictures. I was just curious because of Hanson, and I work with him, that's all, but you're quite right, it's not my business. I shouldn't be peppering you with questions. I'm sorry."

Scarlett pouted a little, but then I sensed her smile was coming back, and she was moving on from her little tantrum. "Just promise me one thing," she said.

I nodded.

"Promise me you'll work on Hanson, see if you can get him to agree to paint my portrait. It would be so good for me and my career, and for him too. And what's good for him is good for you, I'm sure of it."

"I'll see what I can do, Scarlett. If I can persuade him, you'll be the first to know."

CHAPTER 21

I SAT ON THE LIBRARY STEPS THE NEXT MORNING WAITING FOR IT to open at nine o'clock. There was no message from Hanson, so I gave myself until ten to be back at the hotel, at which point I could help him with anything he needed for the art show, if he needed me at all. When the doors opened, I hurried upstairs to the research desk I'd been directed to the previous day. A nameplate at the empty desk read ALFRED H. LANE. Not having the slightest idea where to start, I waited patiently until the gentleman I'd met yesterday emerged with a stack of books in his arms, which he unloaded onto his desk.

"Mr. Lane?" I asked.

"Why yes, hello."

"I came in yesterday inquiring about some periodicals."

"I recall, Isabella Rose was the actress you're researching."

I nodded.

"Is this for a project? University perhaps?" he asked.

I shook my head, wishing I had that as an excuse. "It's just for my own knowledge," I said, as vaguely as possible.

"Very well." He took a thick leather-bound book down from a shelf behind him and scanned its pages. "And the date was?"

"I'm not sure," I said as he continued to scan the pages. "Around thirty or forty years ago, perhaps."

"I see she died in 1910," he said, pointing to the page, then closing the book. "This way."

I followed him down a long corridor, his shoes making a soft scuffing noise as he walked ahead of me. He took me into a room that was completely lined, floor to ceiling, with large books.

"These are all of our archived articles." He pulled a ladder toward him and climbed up to a secondary shelf, then up to a third. "Here we go," he said eventually. "It'll all be in here." He made his way back down, book open in one hand. "This is right around the time of her death." I followed alongside him, eager to see the pages he was turning, until we reached a table in the middle of the room. He continued to turn the pages, one after another. He shook his head, closed it, went back to the shelves, and returned with a different book.

"Ah, this is probably what you're looking for," he said. "Plenty of clippings here to keep you going for a while." I glanced up at the large clock on the wall; it was already 9:20. "Let me know if you need anything else," he said and walked back down the hall to his desk.

Headline after headline from different papers announced the actress's death:

Los Angeles, Calif.—May 14, 1910. ISABELLA ROSE, AMERICAN ACTRESS, FOUND DEAD AT AGE 45 IN SANTA MONICA HOME

Los Angeles, Calif.—May 15, 1910. AMERICA MOURNS ONE OF ITS MOST LOVED STARS. ARTIST FRIEND QUESTIONED BY POLICE

Los Angeles, Calif.—May 16, 1910. ARTIST HANSON RADCLIFF FLED THE ACTRESS'S HOME AT THE TIME OF HER DEATH

Santa Monica, Calif.—May 17, 1910. NOTE FOUND AT SCENE OF BELOVED STAR'S DEATH
Isabella Rose, the actress best known for her performances in *Daddy's Girl* and *The Sunshine Song,* left a note by her side suggesting she had wearied of life and wanted to end it. The note read, "My youth and beauty have left me and without them I cannot go on." Isabella Rose is survived by her daughter, Katherine, age 20.

Los Angeles, Calif.—May 18, 1910. SEARCH IS ON FOR HANSON RADCLIFF IN CONNECTION TO DEATH OF ISABELLA ROSE

Los Angeles, Calif.—May 18, 1910. FORMER HOUSEKEEPER AND FRIEND CLAIMS ISABELLA ROSE WAS DISTRAUGHT, BETRAYED BY ARTIST FRIEND HANSON RADCLIFF

Floretta Mae Milman of Spokane, Washington, claims her former employer, Isabella Rose, called her distraught and inconsolable the night she died. Milman reportedly expressed concern that Hanson Radcliff, artist and former companion to Rose, may have further information and should be investigated for any role he may have played in Isabella Rose's untimely death.

Santa Monica, Calif.—May 20, 1910. ARTIST ACCUSED OF THEFT AND UNDER INVESTIGATION IN DEATH OF ISABELLA ROSE

Hollywood, Calif.—May 26, 1910. INQUEST INTO STAR'S DEATH BLAMES "SELF-OVERDOSAGE OF SLEEPING TABLETS"

I ran my hand down the page and read on.

"Self-overdosage of sleeping tablets" is the verdict returned today by the Los Angeles Coroner following the death of actress Isabella Rose, 45, who was found in the bathroom of her home in Santa Monica on Saturday. He described the 5.2 milligrams of barbiturate in her blood level as "extremely" high and believes she took up to 12 tablets at once. Cause of death: quinalbarbitone poisoning.

Police did not reveal further details except to say they are investigating whether there is any evidence of coercion in the self-poisoning.

This was awful and terrifying! What had I got myself into? I couldn't believe I'd let this man paint me, that I'd been alone with him for hours at a time. I wanted to leave, not read any more, but there was so much more to see. Such a tragedy, and the mention of her fading beauty, that she would find that reason enough to kill herself, made the whole thing even more bleak. I flicked the pages: the articles repeated similar information, and then, a few weeks later, she was barely mentioned—a Hollywood star, an aging darling who apparently refused to age any further, gone from public interest barely a month following her death.

"Mr. Lane," I said as I approached his desk once more. "I'm sorry to bother you again, but might there be any articles with photos that show Isabella Rose prior to . . . I mean, any mention of her companion, the artist? Mr. Radcliff. A bit earlier, a story about them together?"

He nodded. "We could go back to an earlier date." He turned to the bookshelf with the leather-bound books, opened one, turned its pages, set it down, and took out another, then another. I kept glancing up at the clock, watching the minutes tick by, hoping Hanson wasn't looking for me. He wasn't an early riser, no matter what the occasion, and I knew I had another twenty-five minutes until ten o'clock, but this time the task was taking Mr. Lane longer.

"I'm looking for a mention of them in the index from a few years prior," he said. "It's not necessarily going to be front-page news." He looked and looked, took out another bound book.

I wondered if I should offer to help. *Many hands make light work,* my mother always said when I helped fold the laundry she took in—to make extra money after my father died. But when I looked down, my hands were trembling.

"Ah, here we go." Mr. Lane seemed excited. "A photo caption." He walked briskly back down the corridor to the room with the books of newspaper archives, and I almost trotted along to keep up, pleased with his newfound sense of urgency.

"What did you find?" I asked, excited now at the prospect of getting closer to the truth.

"A theater gala." He looked pleased with himself. He climbed the ladder again—much higher this time—and came down, opening another book, tapping the page.

The picture was unmistakably Hanson in his twenties, with a full head of dark hair, arm in arm with a gorgeous, smiling woman in a long, dazzling gown. It was Isabella Rose. It seemed extraordinary how some women just stood out like that, as if they were born to be a star. Scarlett had the same quality, I thought, a charisma that filled any room. I leaned in to examine the picture of Hanson. He was good-looking as a young man, almost with a film-star quality himself. He looked as if he might be enjoying himself, walking arm in arm with Isabella Rose, adoring fans in the background reaching out to touch her.

Los Angeles, Calif.—September 12, 1909. ISABELLA ROSE ARRIVES
AT THE HYMAN THEATRE
Isabella Rose, 44, and her companion attend the opening night at
the Hyman Theatre in Los Angeles. Hanson Radcliff, 24, an artist
who resides at the Rose compound as "artist-in-residence," frequently
accompanies the actress to the theatre, screenings, and Hollywood
soirées.

There were more images, each time Hanson dressed in an evening
suit or black dinner jacket with swallowtail and white waistcoat, and
each time he looked happy but more reserved than she did, shy perhaps. I couldn't quite put my finger on the expression he wore at these
outings—maybe it was simply that he knew to let her shine. He was
so much younger than she was. I found myself desperately curious to
know more about Hanson as a young man. It was as if finding out more
about him would somehow tell me something about myself. It was an
absurd thought, I recognized that as soon as it crossed my mind, but I
felt it, nonetheless.

One other image showed them on the beach, in what appeared to
be a staged photograph. She was posing for Hanson while he painted
her. The composition looked arranged, as if they'd specifically asked a
photographer to capture the moment, and I thought they probably had.
Knowing the current state of Hanson's messy house and studio, I couldn't
picture him painting like that now. Everything around them was neat,
organized, and orchestrated. But perhaps that was how he used to be—
not messy and disorganized, chaotic, and often drunk.

Mr. Lane was up the ladder again reaching for another book.

"Here's something you might find interesting," he said, setting it down
on the table. "I have to get back to my desk, but if you need anything else,
you know where to find me."

Los Angeles, Calif.—March 23, 1918. SUICIDE ARTIST HANSON
RADCLIFF MAKES HUGE SALE
Hanson Radcliff, artist once associated with deceased film star Isabella Rose, has sold a painting of the Southern California coastline for
an astounding $750 to a private collector in Pasadena. This is the first

painting by the artist to be sold at auction. Mr. Radcliff was at one time considered a "person of interest" in the investigation of evidence surrounding Rose's death, due to overdose, eight years ago. He was known to be painting her around the time of her death. The artist fled Los Angeles and now resides in Laguna Beach, California, a haven for artists, where he focuses solely on land and seascapes. His final painting of Isabella Rose was never recovered.

I closed the book and placed my hands on top, as if willing it to remain that way. Suicide artist? It was a sickening name. It made Hanson sound like a murderer. My stomach twisted, but I had to find out what happened. Were charges brought against him, or was he cleared of suspicion? I started turning the pages again, searching for more information, but I was in the wrong year now. I was about to ask Mr. Lane for more help when I realized the time. I stood quickly, feeling suddenly light-headed. I bolted from the room, rushed down the stairs and out of the library, and just about ran back to the hotel, those words, "suicide artist," repeating themselves in my head.

Rushing through the lobby, I wanted to go to my room, to freshen my face, which I imagined looked ashen, to scrub my hands, scrub all evidence of that article off my skin, to change my clothes, something, but it was already 10:20, well past when I'd planned to be back at the hotel and report to Hanson, so I headed directly to the elevator that would take me to his room.

"Miss Francis," someone called. "Excuse me, Miss Francis." With one hand on the elevator gate, I turned to see Mr. Colligan. "If you're looking for Mr. Radcliff, he left a good forty-five minutes ago."

"What do you mean he left?"

"Yes, he took his car to the art show, just shy of an hour ago—he insisted on driving himself."

I looked at him, shocked. He had paid for me to stay at the Biltmore Hotel and expected me to assist him at the show, and I'd instead been snooping into his private life at the library. I felt terrible.

"All right," I said. "Please let him know upon his return that I am waiting for him in my room."

I sat on the bed in my room feeling like a disobedient child—with that horrible waiting feeling when you know you're going to get in trouble, but you don't know yet what the punishment will be. I wanted to be a good employee, a good assistant, or model, or whatever I was to Hanson, but I was so distracted lately by the news of his past, and now with some facts on hand, I felt even more distressed. Restless, I returned to the lobby.

"Would you like me to arrange for a car to take you to the museum?" Mr. Colligan asked.

I thought about it for a moment. Hanson would be angry with me either way, but there was no point sitting around the hotel wondering.

"Yes, please," I said. "Thank you."

A CROWD OF ABOUT A HUNDRED PEOPLE GATHERED AT THE MUSEUM. There were men in uniform and others in suits and ties, women dressed up in frocks and hats. On the walls were various styles of art: illustrations depicting battle scenes, comics showing conversations between men in trenches, a close-up of a man's bare feet—white, cold-looking—in the dirt alongside a pair of heavy boots. I searched the room for Hanson and passed by another section of the room—the art here was oil on canvas, flashes of red and orange, sharp angles, black and angry. A man in uniform sat in a wheelchair in front of the paintings with a blanket where his legs should have been. A woman stood by his side with her hand on his shoulder. There were rosettes on a few of the pieces of art—first, second, and third place—giving me the sense that the judging had already been done, and the ceremony was wrapping up. A clock on the wall showed it was nearing noon. Finally, I spotted Hanson's tweed sport coat and the thick white hair that he'd uncharacteristically tamed.

"Mr. Radcliff," I said, approaching him, knowing he hated it when I called him that but feeling it was more appropriate in a formal setting.

He gave me a disapproving glance then turned away.

"I'm sorry I wasn't in my room earlier; I went for a walk to the library. I had no idea the show was starting so early." I glanced at the drink in his hand, and then back to his face. It wasn't even midday, and he already had that look about him. "Is there anything I can do, now that I'm here, anything to assist you?"

He put his whiskey to his lips and tipped his head back, then he handed me the glass.

"Another whiskey."

I stood still for a moment; only one or two other people had a glass in their hands, and theirs were champagne flutes, drinks more appropriate for the time of day, but I got him his whiskey anyway.

"I wish you wouldn't," I said quietly, as I handed it to him, shocked that I'd actually said it out loud and bracing for a rebuttal. But he looked at me and shrugged.

"What can I say? This town makes me want to drink."

CHAPTER 22

BY THE TIME WE WERE BACK AT THE HOTEL, HAD PACKED UP OUR bags, and were ready to head back to Laguna, Hanson was slurring his words.

"Come on then," he said, picking up the car keys, then dropping them on the floor. "Better get on the road so we're back before dark."

I bent down, picked up the keys to his wagon, and held them in my hand. "I'll drive us back," I said.

"You?" He swiped at my hand to grab the keys.

"I'm a very good driver." My mother had always hated driving, and as soon as I was old enough, and probably before, I was the one to drive us around town. Hanson seemed to contemplate the idea for a moment. "You could relax, take in the scenery," I said, hoping I'd manage to convince him. But instead, he burst into a laughing fit, as if this were the most ridiculous thing he'd ever heard. The laughing turned into coughing, and when he managed to control himself, he wiped a tear from the corner of his eye, picked up his leather satchel and threw it over his shoulder, walked to the car, and got in the driver's seat.

I opened the glove box, took out a worn-out map, and unfolded it in front of me.

"I know where I'm going," Hanson said with a scowl, reaching over and trying to pull the map from my hands. I moved it out of his reach before he had a chance to tear the thing. "I spent many years in Los Angeles," he said, placing his right hand back on the gearshift and stepping on the gas.

"I did too," I said, though I'd never driven there.

He looked at me, a moment too long for someone who should be keeping his eyes on the road. I stared straight ahead in the hopes that he'd follow my lead.

"I used to live in Santa Monica," he said after a while. "In a big old house by the water. Beautiful house. Wide, open beaches."

I knew he was talking about Isabella Rose's mansion; he'd mentioned it before.

"Gardens, fountains, a swimming pool that looked out to the ocean." He slipped his hand into his breast pocket and took out his flask, then unscrewed the cap with one hand. The car swerved, he crossed the yellow line, and I reached over and grabbed the wheel, getting the wagon back into its lane.

Calmly he took a swig from his flask and offered it to me.

"No, thank you," I said sternly.

"What's the matter with you," he asked. "You don't like the old man driving you around town?"

"Not like this," I said. I didn't care if he knew I was scared.

"Oh, come on, lighten up."

"Harbor Parkway looks like the most direct route," I said.

"We'll take the coast," he insisted, pushing his back against the seat, as if settling in for a long ride. I ran my finger across the map from the hotel to Ocean. It was going to add at least forty-five minutes to our journey. We didn't talk until I saw the coastline up ahead.

"Ah, there she is, that beast," he said as we came over the hill and the ocean rose up in front of us. He rolled his window down, letting the cool air rush in.

He reached across my lap, as if to open that window too.

"I can do it," I said quickly before he swerved again.

"Better than the city streets, isn't it?" he said, putting his foot down on the accelerator. "So much more freedom when you're near the sea." He drove with one hand on the wheel, taking the curves too fast. There were fewer cars on the road, but outside my window there was a narrow sidewalk and a thin patch of greenery before a sharp drop to the ocean.

"Take it easy," I said, my hand gripping the door handle.

He was accelerating, and I saw an infuriating smile in the corners of his mouth; he seemed to enjoy the swaying back and forth, the winding road, but I felt sick, and the words from those news articles were swirling in my head. Hanson Radcliff, Suicide Artist.

He swigged from the flask again and drove dangerously close to my side of the road. He picked up speed as we headed downhill. I looked over at the shuddering speedometer as he took the last curve before a gas station at just over fifty. A hot red Cadillac pulled out of the station and onto the road in front of us, but Hanson didn't slow down. I glanced at him to look for recognition—his old face now close to the steering wheel, eyes squinting, he was leaning forward as if he couldn't quite see what was ahead.

"Car!" I yelled, the Cadillac maybe forty feet ahead of us. "Hanson, the Cadillac!" He swerved to the left into the oncoming traffic, and there was an eruption of horns as cars jerked left and right, out of our way. A screeching and squealing of rubber, shredding from the tires—theirs or ours, I couldn't tell. I braced myself for impact, tensed my shoulders, and squeezed my eyes shut. We swerved back onto our side of the road—the red Cadillac was cruising farther on ahead now—and I allowed myself a second to breathe.

"Jesus Christ, Hanson, you almost killed us," I said, but he was gripping the wheel, his body leaning toward me, trying to gain control.

"Hanson!" I screamed. We hadn't crashed into oncoming traffic, but the car was skidding sideways now. He'd overcompensated and lost control. We were veering toward the sidewalk, where a woman was walking, holding a young boy's hand. Her eyes locked with mine, and she seemed to freeze as I grabbed the wheel and turned in the opposite direction—but the car didn't react. I threw one arm over my face and the other, instinctively, reached out to shield Hanson. A violent thud and a crunch sent my head toward the window, then my body was flung in the opposite direction, crashing into him. I stayed where I was, every muscle tight, bracing for more, and then I jolted upright. The woman, the boy. Steam was everywhere; a blue metal contraption was wedged inside my broken window. A mailbox had taken the impact. I tried to open the door, but it wouldn't budge. Hanson was slumped against his door, murmuring.

There was a trickle of blood running over his eye and down his cheek. "My God. Hanson?"

"I'm all right," he mumbled, not opening his eyes. I didn't dare move him, but I had to get out of the car. I climbed into the back seat, forced the door open, and stumbled to the sidewalk. The woman was there, several feet from where our car crashed, her arms wrapped around the boy, who was crying into her thighs.

"Are you hurt?" I raced toward her and, without thinking, knelt down, took the boy by the shoulders, and turned him toward me, so I could see for myself.

"Get your hands off my child," she screamed, "you reckless fool!"

I backed away. "I'm so sorry. I just wanted to be sure, but you're all right? I'm so sorry." I put my hands up. "I'm so, so sorry."

I rushed back to the car. It was badly dented on my side but not destroyed. My hands shook as I tried to open the driver's side door, and when I did, Hanson almost fell out. He was heavy and weary as I helped him out of the vehicle. "Can you walk?" I asked. He nodded and stumbled around the back of the car to the sidewalk, where he sat back down again.

"I'm going to call the police," I said.

"No, no." He shook his head. "No, please."

"We need to get you to a hospital."

"No." He put his head in his hands. "It will be all over the papers. I can't face it, I can't."

I looked around, where people were already standing, watching.

"Can you move the car?" he asked. "Get it off the main street?" It seemed to take every ounce of energy for him to make this request. I didn't know what to do. This was his fault: he'd been drinking all morning, he'd insisted on driving, he'd put me and others on the road in danger. But looking at him now, he looked so old, so weak, blood dripping down his face onto his clothes. There was a small gash on his forehead. I left him on the sidewalk and got in the car, turned the engine, but the car was jammed and wouldn't budge. I got out again, walked around to where the mailbox was lodged in the door, kicked the car, then did it again. There was no way I could do this alone. I looked up at the small crowd forming.

"Give me a hand, will you?" I said to a few of the men who'd stopped their cars on the side of the road. "We're blocking traffic."

A few nodded and walked over, and they grouped together and shoved the car, leaning their backs against the rear side, pushing it away from the mailbox.

"Miss, you got to get in and give it some gas," one of them said.

I ran around to the driver's seat again, turned the engine, and looked back to them.

"Ready, set, go," he yelled.

I gave it some gas, but the tires just spun while the engine revved.

"Again," someone called out, while they pushed.

I hit the accelerator, just spinning, but then a slight movement, a jolt.

"Again."

I hit the gas once more, and this time it moved, a terrible crunching sound, as the door dislodged itself from the mailbox, and the car lurched forward. Someone gave the wagon a tap to say we could go. Hanson looked pitiful, still sitting on the edge of the road, but I had half a mind to drive off and leave him there. That wouldn't do anyone any good, though. I needed to get the car off the main road and away from the accident if we had any shot at saving his reputation. So, I got out again, tugged him up, and walked him to the car.

"I'll do the driving this time."

He didn't protest.

I opened the back door, and he let me help him inside, where he slunk down in the seat.

"We have to get you to a hospital."

He looked terrible, but he shook his head.

"You need medical attention. You're in pain."

He shrugged. "Nothing I can't handle."

I leaned out the window and beckoned to one of the gentlemen who'd helped me dislodge the car. "Is there a hospital around here?" I asked. "A doctor, someone who could see him?"

"There's a hospital that way," one man said, pointing in the opposite direction from where we'd been heading. "If you get to the airport you've gone too far."

"Thank you," I said.

We drove slowly, in silence, my hands trembling. Something from the right side of the car was scraping the road as we drove—the passenger side had been badly damaged. We wouldn't get far in this state. I gripped the wheel harder, hoping my hands would calm down, but the farther we moved away from the accident, the more it began to sink in. He could have killed us. He could have killed that mother and her young child. Rage boiled up inside of me. My mind went to my father and the train accident, how fast things could change, how abruptly things could end.

"I don't want to go to that hospital," Hanson grumbled.

"Well, I didn't want to get in the car with you in the first place!" I shot back at him. "But I didn't have much of a choice, did I?"

A look of shock or shame crossed his face in the rearview mirror, but I didn't care if I'd offended him.

"You always have a choice," he said, looking out the window.

Wolfe's Pharmacy was on a corner lot with large, vertical lettering that read DRUGS, ICE CREAM, TELEPHONE.

"Stop here, can you?" Hanson asked, tapping the window.

I was about to hit the brakes, give in to his demands, and try to fix him up myself, but one quick glance at his wound reminded me that he needed more than a tin of Cloverine Salve and some adhesive bandages. It could get infected; he likely needed stitches. I kept my foot on the pedal.

He groaned when I pulled into the parking lot of the general hospital.

"This is my choice," I said. "To make sure you're taken care of."

When we checked in, the young nurse looked concerned. "What happened here?"

"We had a car accident," I said, glancing at Hanson, who shuffled off and found himself a seat in the corner of the waiting room.

"Are you injured?" she asked.

"No, I'm fine, but Mr. Radcliff needs immediate attention."

Her eyes widened, and she looked from me to him. "Is it Mr. Radcliff, the artist?" she asked in a whisper.

"Yes, Hanson Radcliff," I said in a hushed tone. "But he would appreciate your discretion."

"Of course, of course." She nodded.

"No one was injured except for Mr. Radcliff himself," I said. "It was my fault, I lost control."

As I said that and took the blame for what he had done, I wondered why. To protect him and his reputation? But why? He hadn't cared about me. "I'll make sure the doctor sees him right away."

⌐

THE TELEPHONE BOOTH WAS LOCATED JUST OUTSIDE THE FRONT OF the hospital. I opened the door and stepped inside.

"Connect me to Hotel Laguna, please."

I didn't want to get Jimmy in trouble for receiving a phone call at the hotel in the middle of the day, but I didn't know anyone else to call. The car was damaged, Hanson was in the hospital, I had to let someone know. Someone who would care.

"I'm sorry to bother you, Jimmy, but Hanson, he crashed his wagon," I said when he was on the line.

"Holy mackerel, Hazel, are you all right?"

"I'm fine. He's got a good cut on his head, and the car's in bad shape. I don't think we can drive it home."

"I'll pick you up," he said. "I can borrow my buddy's car."

"Thank you, but the doctor says he needs stitches and should be observed overnight after his head wound."

"All right," he said. "I'm working the long shift tomorrow, but I can ask if someone else can cover. Though Russ is out till Wednesday."

"Don't worry, we'll figure something out."

While the accident had me shaken up, those newspaper articles were still spinning around and around in my head, making everything worse. I suddenly felt desperate to share what was on my mind.

"Hey, Jimmy?" Without waiting, I blurted out what I'd read about Isabella's death. "They implied that he was to blame!" I added, to make sure he understood.

Jimmy hesitated. "You can't make someone commit suicide. Try not to get carried away."

"I know that, but he was investigated for being involved somehow."

Why did men so often think they knew better than women? Even Jimmy. I wasn't getting carried away. If Hanson had just let me drive, instead of insisting on having things his way, I wouldn't have had to call Jimmy in the first place.

"I don't know, Hazel, you can be accused of murder, you can be accused of theft, but you can't be accused of making someone kill herself," he insisted in a hushed tone.

"I'm just telling you what it said, how it sounded, that the family seemed to think it was his fault. It's making me feel really uneasy."

The line went quiet, and I thought for a moment of how I'd fallen right back into treating Jimmy as if he were my confidant, but the silence on the end of the line made me see my presumption. I hadn't realized the circumstances when we first met, but we weren't doing that anymore, confessing our feelings, our fears—he was holding that space for someone else. Not me.

"Sorry," I said, suddenly self-conscious. "I know you're at work."

"Maybe you should quit if his past bothers you so much."

I sighed. "I can't. I need this job, and I need the apartment."

"Listen, Hazel, I've got to go, my shift starts in a few minutes, but it sounds to me like you need to ask him outright what happened."

I shook my head, but he was right. I had to find out the truth from Hanson one way or another.

AFTER AN HOUR OR SO, THE NURSE TOOK ME BACK TO VISIT HIM. His head was bandaged up and he had his eyes closed, and he was leaning back, propped on pillows. I quietly sat down on a chair next to the bed, but as soon as he heard me, he opened his eyes.

"There she is," he said, almost cheerily. "They stitched me up, eight of them, said I would have had a nice scar and possible infection if I hadn't come in, so I suppose I should thank you."

"You're welcome." I smiled.

"Pass me my satchel, would you?" he asked. He pulled out some dollars. "My head's throbbing. Run to the store and pick me up some liquor, would you? Brown if they have it, whiskey, bourbon, but I'll take whatever they've got. It's painful as hell."

"You're in a hospital, Hanson. Surely they gave you something for the pain."

"Not enough." He waved the bills at me.

"I don't think it's a good idea," I said. "It was liquor that got you in this mess to begin with."

His expression changed; the cheerfulness was gone. "I'm not asking you, Hazel, I'm telling you."

I glared at him. He had almost killed us both, yet he still wanted to drink. It was a sickness.

"You still work for me, don't you?"

I snatched the money from his hands and walked out of his room to the sorry-looking car.

I drove back the way we came, metal scraping on the asphalt. On the same stretch of road, I'd seen a sign for Michael's Wine & Liquor. I stopped there and bought him some bourbon and put it in the car, then I continued on to the pharmacy. At the counter I ordered a hot Ovaltine. I stared into the steam curling up from the cup. I was still mad as hell about the accident, about the drinking, but mostly I was furious with myself. I was weak; I did whatever people told me to do. I got in the car with a drunk. I left the hospital to buy him more liquor. I showed up for work each day for a man with a sordid past, a man who might or might not have been responsible for a woman's death. Jimmy was right. I had to confront him about Isabella Rose if I was to keep on working for him, and if he wanted his liquor, then he was going to have to start talking.

CHAPTER 23

I SAT IN A CHAIR ON THE FAR SIDE OF HIS HOSPITAL BED NEXT TO the window, so we could conceal the bottle, wrapped in a paper bag in my lap. I put his change on the table next to him.

"Pour some in the cup, would you?" he asked, nodding to the hospital's empty water cup by his bed.

"Not yet," I said, wishing I could take a nip myself to calm my nerves. I was very aware that after confronting him like this, I could be out of a job and without a place to live.

He looked surprised.

"When we were at the Biltmore, I met with Scarlett Rose," I said. "And then I went to the Los Angeles Central Library and looked up some newspaper articles."

At that, he sat up a little and reached for the cup. I kept hold of the bottle. "They implied that you were involved somehow, in the . . ." I didn't know which word to use: death, suicide, murder? "They implied that you might have been involved in the unfortunate passing of the actress." I was stumbling on my own words. "Of Isabella Rose. They referred to you as the 'suicide artist.'"

There. I'd said it. I waited for some reaction, some denial, or rage, something, anything.

He said nothing, did nothing, just looked straight ahead. I wondered if he'd even heard me. I wished I had something else to reveal, some other detail that could shock him into responding, but I'd just laid out all my cards. I had nothing else.

"I believe that I deserve to know the truth," I said, almost in a whisper.

He gave a little snort and managed to sit up a little straighter. "What you deserve, Miss Francis, is money paid for hours worked. You are a model and sometimes assistant, you do a fine job, require instruction, but it's tolerable, you're on time, you're available when I need you, all part of the agreement when I hired you." He looked at me straight on now. He was clear, concise, and sure of himself. "But," he said, "that young actress has come poking around and has begun toying with you to get to me. She's provoking you, and she's raised questions in your mind that seem to have caused you some trouble, and I don't want trouble. I am old. I want calm, I want peace."

He closed his eyes and let his head fall back. I waited and waited. He wanted peace. Did he mean right now, was he going to sleep? He groaned a little, a snore perhaps. I wondered if I'd done the wrong thing by agreeing to the liquor. Maybe I should get the doctor. I sat tight, and then he erupted in a coughing fit.

"Oh, my head," he said between coughs. He reached for the bottle, and I poured him one small sip.

"There were paintings of her all over her house, you see, installed in almost every room," he said. "They were stacked up in closets, under beds; she had one of her workers build a unit in her garage where they could be carefully covered and stored. Most of them were mine, and after a while I was glad that most of them were hidden away like that. You see, art, it can't be good if it isn't true, if it's created on demand, without feeling, impulse, or pain entwined with the brushstrokes. If you create something that you know isn't true at its essence, it makes you feel wretched; you loathe yourself. It makes you feel worthless, it makes you want to rip the canvas to shreds with a sharp knife, or carve the eyes out of a portrait with a palette knife."

He looked at me as if I might somehow be able to comprehend, but all I felt was a chill from the violence of it all.

"Then one day after we'd been 'ringing the bells,' as she called it . . ." He looked at me to be sure I was following. I wasn't. "Sex. Listen, it was pennies from heaven, easy money, and she was beautiful, attentive. Hell, I'd been young and willing to do anything to make it. As time passed, I saw it differently—the work, the art. I wanted to paint what I saw."

I nodded, shocked by his candor and eager for him to continue with the story.

"Anyway, she lay completely relaxed and draped on the bed. The sun shone through the window and lit her golden skin, imperfect in the most beautiful way that only natural light can do. The shadows, the rise and fall of her flesh, her hair strewn about, black with gray glinting through. I just about ran to my studio and brought my easel and canvas in. 'Don't move,' I told her. 'The light, it's divine, stunning.'" I remember she looked up at me and smiled and then laid her head back down. She dozed off for a couple of hours, one leg hanging off the bed, and I stood there and sketched and painted. She was always so poised, so precise, she had a desperate need to appear perfect, but for those few hours she was natural, relaxed, herself."

I pictured him as a young artist, eager to capture her beauty, eager to prove himself. I understood that desire.

"I don't know if I was in love with her in the traditional sense, or maybe I was, but, in that moment, I was in love with the vision of her, so vulnerable. I captured her happy, in bloom, I know I did. The light began to change, so, before she woke, I took the painting back to my studio, next to the bedroom she'd given to me. I worked all night and well into the early morning hours. I didn't want to sleep for fear that I'd lose sight of the way the light had danced on her body, I feared it would be gone from my mind, but, at some point, my eyes began to blur. I had to stop, take a break, before I ruined the one thing, the only true thing of beauty I'd ever created. I sat in the corner of the room, looking at it, and I allowed myself to rest my eyes. When I woke up, she was standing there, dressed for the day, absolutely furious."

"Why?" I asked.

"She hated it. She thought it was hideous and unflattering, vulgar and offensive. I hadn't finished, and I never would have allowed her to see it before I'd completed it, but more than that, I couldn't understand her repulsion at something that I saw as so utterly beautiful, so real, so true."

"Such a shame," I said.

"She was a beautiful woman, but she looked ugly when in a rage. She screamed at me, *How dare you depict me that way. Destroy it immediately, or I will destroy it for you.* I told her I wouldn't, I told her it was the first time I'd painted her in such an honest and feminine way, but she wouldn't have it. She picked up a knife from my paint box and held it to the canvas. She said, *Destroy it, or I will destroy you.*" He snorted, almost a laugh. "Then she threw the knife on the floor and started out of my room. She said, *When you're done, dress and meet me by the pool for breakfast.*"

"What did you do?" I almost didn't want to know. Had he been so upset that he'd struck her? It was an awful thought, and I regretted it immediately.

"She stormed out of my studio, and I knew it was over. I couldn't go back to painting her the way she wanted to be seen. I felt like a fraud for doing it all those times. I threw my things in my bag, stuffed as many paintbrushes and paints as I could in my satchel, picked up the painting, and walked right out of her back door and onto the beach. The painting was still wet; I carried it above my head, holding only the wooden bars that stretched the canvas, and I walked south until I couldn't walk any more. I barely had anything with me; she'd paid for everything—from the clothes on my back to the food that I ate, the roof over my head and all the supplies I needed to paint. I had nowhere to go, so I took breaks then just kept on walking. Around Long Beach, someone told me about an artist colony in Laguna, that I'd get there eventually if I kept heading south. At some point I hopped on a train, and then I walked some more."

He rubbed the spot on his bandage where his wound was and reached for the empty cup. He shouldn't drink more, but I wanted him to keep talking, so I obliged with a splash, and he knocked it back again.

"Did she try to find you?" I asked.

"After I reached Laguna Beach and tracked down a place to live— there were a few well-known artists who opened their doors to other artists, allowed them to sleep there, to create; they wanted to build a community—I finished the painting there. A few days later, it was all over the news, she'd killed herself."

I brought my hands to my mouth. "How tragic."

"Indeed." He took a deep breath that shuddered. "It was my fault," he whispered. "The papers said she left a note, and it was obvious she blamed it on the painting, on my portrayal of her. Apparently, she'd called a friend and told her as much. In my eyes she'd always been beautiful, she'd been youthful even then, but I'd shown her as I saw her. To me it felt freeing, but to her it was like murder.

"The papers were all over me—they'd chase me down, ask me questions. I don't even know what I said. I took to the bottle, it was the only way I could get through the days. I'm sure I divulged too much about the episode once I reached Laguna and met other artists, probably while inebriated. That just fueled the lingering gossip. The reporters wouldn't leave me alone. I was horrified."

He put his head in his hands and rubbed his eyes. "Our love wasn't the kind of love you see in the pictures, that you read about in books. But she took care of me, and I think I took care of her. I cherished her. She was too old for me, of course she was—my God, she could have been my mother—but I was young and impressionable, and she was so sophisticated. She gave me the gift of time and space to create. Nothing is more valuable than that. I thought I was capturing her essence; I didn't mean harm.

"I was so blind drunk most of the time after that. I had to numb the pain, the guilt, the remorse. I'd sit out on the cliffs and paint the ocean, the rocks, the fauna, and I'd sell them to whoever wanted them, then I'd sit at the bar, and I'd drink until I'd spent the money I'd earned, then I'd do it again and again and again."

Hanson reached over and took the bottle from my hands. I couldn't believe he was going to drink more so soon, but instead, he offered it to me, and I obliged, the smoky liquid momentarily soothing me.

"What happened to the painting?"

"I had to hide it. The press were desperate to get their hands on it and splash it all over the papers, but I couldn't let that happen, not back then."

I sipped a bit more bourbon. "But you said it was beautiful and honest."

"It was. I wish she could have seen it again, really seen it. I spent a lot of time at the hotel bar," he went on. "The way I remember it, I brought the painting into the hotel, and the manager back then let me hide it there. I couldn't keep it at my studio; everyone knew where I lived by then."

"And it's still there?" I asked.

"No. I've looked for it, but I was pretty far gone that first year after her death. Maybe we didn't hide it there, maybe we did, maybe it was stolen.

Maybe I destroyed it. Maybe someone else did. I suppose I'll never know, but I wish I'd had the courage to set my eyes on it one more time before it disappeared. I would've liked to know if it was the way I remembered it, a thing of beauty, or if it was as egregious as she thought."

The nurse approached the room, and I pushed the bottle under the bed. "He should get some rest," she said.

The nurse flattened his pillow, and he lay back for sleep. "Thanks for the company," he said, settling in.

"In the morning we'll check his wound again and make sure he's fit to be discharged. We can set up a cot for you in another room if you'd like."

I glanced at the clock on the wall. It was just past seven.

"Thank you," I said.

I BARELY SLEPT AT ALL, SO WHEN I PEEKED INTO HANSON'S ROOM early that morning, I was surprised to find it was bustling with people. A nurse was changing Hanson's bandage, while the doctor and his assistant asked him a battery of questions.

"Are you being discharged?" I asked.

"They want an X-ray," Hanson said.

"Of your head?"

"A chest X-ray." A young doctor turned to me. "Are you his daughter?"

"No, I work for him."

"It's all right," Hanson said. "This girl here knows all there is to know—she might as well know what's in my medical files too."

"He's been coughing all night," the doctor said matter-of-factly. "And he's complaining of pain in his chest. We need to see the lungs to rule out tuberculosis."

"It's not tuberculosis, for God's sake, I hurt my ribs in the accident." He looked my way and must have noted my concern. "Don't worry, I'll be fine." But he was wheezing and started coughing before he added, "I'll be back in a jiffy." He waved me away.

"Actually," the young doctor said. "We could be a while, we'll be running some tests."

"When will he be ready to leave?" I asked.

"It depends on the results, but certainly not until this afternoon."

"I'll be back in a little while then," I said. "I'm going to get some fresh air."

WHEN I RETURNED A FEW HOURS LATER, HE WAS SLEEPING IN BED, propped up with pillows, an untouched tray of bland-looking lunch on the side table. With his face relaxed and his body dressed in hospital clothes, he suddenly looked terribly old. I sat in the chair by his bed and waited.

After a while, the doctor from that morning returned with a chart, roused him, and checked his blood pressure.

"Well, Mr. Radcliff, fortunately, we were able to rule out tuberculosis."

"I told you I was just fine," he said groggily, pushing himself up on his elbows and coughing as he did so.

"However, it appears you are suffering from pulmonary emphysema." Hanson looked up.

"It's the most common chronic disease of the lungs," the doctor said gently, "more frequent than TB or lung cancer, but it is grave." He helped Hanson to a full sitting position and placed his stethoscope on his back and then his chest. He pulled up a chair on the other side of Hanson's bed.

"Never heard of it," Hanson said.

"Emphysema is the enlargement of the lung or lungs due to loss of elasticity. In your case both lungs are affected. Have you suffered from chronic bronchitis for some time?"

Hanson shrugged, and the doctor looked to me.

"I don't know his medical history," I said. "But, Hanson, you've been coughing quite severely from the day I met you." I looked back to the doctor.

"I don't know what I've got or haven't got, I haven't been to see a doctor in twenty, thirty years. I usually medicate myself with a stiff drink, and it does the trick."

The doctor sighed. "That will most definitely lead to cirrhosis of the liver, but the lungs are our primary concern at this time. If your bronchitis had been treated early, we might have had a fighting chance." He sighed again, and as he did, it felt as if the air left the room. I glanced at

Hanson, and I could tell he was trying not to react. He looked out the window and then to me.

"How's my wagon?" he asked.

I stared at him. This was serious. The doctor was sitting; he had sighed heavily. This was not good news. I, for one, had questions running through my head: What did this mean, how could we treat it, could we treat it, was this life-threatening, and if so, how long did he have to live? As these questions ran through my mind, I panicked. He could be a real beast at times, but I was starting to learn how to deal with him; in fact, I'd become very attached, especially now after he'd revealed the full story about Isabella Rose. He'd trusted me, given me a chance. I was learning so much and settling in. I suddenly couldn't imagine my days without Hanson in my life.

"We'll need to keep you in a few more hours, run some pulmonary functioning tests using a respirometer. And we'll need to discuss ongoing treatment—there's some talk of inhalation therapy, but it hasn't proved to be all that helpful in slowing progression."

I looked to Hanson again, and it was as if he couldn't hear a thing the doctor was saying.

"My wagon?" he said again. "How bad is it?"

"It's in bad shape," I said. "It needs work. It won't make it all the way home in its current state."

"Mr. Radcliff," the doctor said firmly, standing now. "I know this is alarming news, but it needs to be taken seriously. There are things you can do to aid yourself, to reduce the impulse to cough, to make yourself more comfortable. But we just don't know how long your lungs will endure—six months perhaps, maybe more, maybe less. I'll give you the name of a doctor closer to home, but you will need to follow up."

"How are the stitches?" Hanson asked the doctor, raising his eyebrows up and down and showing him the side of his forehead.

"They should heal quite nicely," he said. "The nurse will be in soon." And with that, he left the room.

"Well, if the wagon isn't in good shape, then how the heck are we going to get home?"

I shook my head; clearly Hanson was refusing to acknowledge the severity of his situation.

"It'll need to go to a mechanic, or a car repair shop, but I imagine it'll take several days, or a week."

"I'm not waiting that long," he erupted. "I'm getting out of here today, and that's final." He started to cough as his frustration rose.

"Be calm, Hanson, please. I'll sort something out." He looked at me, nodding; he suddenly looked frightened, as if he had to escape. "I will get us out of here today," I said, patting his hand. "I promise."

Back in the phone booth outside the hospital, I picked up the receiver. I imagined Jimmy getting word of another phone call at the hotel. Another personal call, from someone who shouldn't be all that personal to begin with. This was my burden, not his. I tried to think of anyone else Hanson might have mentioned that I could call, but my mind was suddenly blank. He was famous—how could I not think of a single person who would come to his rescue? And then I recalled the small black, leather-bound address book he always kept in his jacket pocket. I walked back to the hospital room and found him curled on his side, snoring. His tweed sport coat was hanging on the back of the chair, so I reached into the inside pocket and retrieved it.

It felt strangely personal to flip through the tiny pages listing the names, addresses, and phone numbers of his acquaintances. Some entries were crossed out. Had they fallen out of favor, I wondered, had they moved, died? I turned the pages looking for a name I recognized, and then I saw Edgar Berg, his address and phone number listed next to his name.

"Hello, Edgar," I said once the operator had put the call through. "It's Hazel. I'm with Hanson in Los Angeles. He was involved in an accident. His car is worse for wear, and we won't be able to drive it all the way back to Laguna Beach."

"Is he alive?" he asked.

"Yes, of course he's alive, but he needed stitches, so we're at the hospital, and they've discovered that he's actually very sick."

"Well, we all knew that."

"The reason I'm calling is that I know you are dear friends, and he could use your help. Could you pick us up? This evening, as soon as possible. He's very eager to be back home in his own bed."

"Is he going to make it?" I took a deep breath; he was asking all the wrong questions and none of the right ones. "I just mean, how bad is he?"

"Bad enough that I'm calling you and asking for your help, Edgar. Can you pick us up or not?"

"Of course, I can. I was supposed to be at the pageant tonight, painting the booths we constructed, but a drive up the coast sounds a lot more relaxing."

"Thank you," I said. I gave him the address and hung up the receiver, shaking off a nagging feeling of regret at involving Edgar at all, but I had to get us home one way or another, and Edgar was the only friend of Hanson's I knew.

Next, I inquired about the closest car repair shop in town and made plans to drop off the wagon as soon as Edgar arrived so that, finally, we could head back home.

"WHY IN GOD'S NAME WOULD YOU CALL THAT MAN, OF ALL PEOPLE?" Hanson growled when I told him of the plans.

"Because he's your friend?" I offered.

He closed his eyes and rubbed his forehead.

"Well, who would you have liked me to call?" I asked, bewildered that all my arrangements were unappreciated.

He didn't respond, just shooed me away.

"It's a valid question, Hanson. When we get home, you'll need to call your family."

"Ha," he scoffed.

"I really think it would be wise. I can help if you like. I can inform them of your health situation and perhaps arrange for someone to take care of you."

"What family?" he asked, staring at me straight on, as if he actually didn't know the answer to that question.

"I don't know what family you have, you'd have to tell me."

"I don't want anyone to know what that doctor said, do you understand?"

"But you will need to see a doctor closer to home."

"I'm not seeing a doctor, and the news of my health doesn't leave this room, do you hear me?"

I nodded slightly.

"And we certainly will not discuss it with Edgar."

His eyes pierced mine with intensity, and I wondered if he could tell that I'd already mentioned it.

"Not a word, or you'll be out on your ear."

"But, Hanson—"

"No," he said. "One word and our arrangement is over."

"All right," I said. "I won't say a word."

CHAPTER 24

IT WAS PAST EIGHT O'CLOCK WHEN EDGAR FINALLY SHOWED UP AT the hospital, and at such a late hour, I had to negotiate Hanson's discharge with the staff. Fortunately, the car repair shop allowed me to leave the car after hours, parked outside, so they could begin work the next day.

Hanson had dressed and insisted on sitting in the waiting room rather than his room for the last few hours, and I knew it was because he didn't want to be perceived to be ill.

"Edgar, my good man." Hanson stood and slapped his friend on the back. "Good of you to collect us, the wagon wasn't going to make it far at all."

"That beauty," Edgar said. "What a shame."

"I know, damned shame—her paint is scratched up and the front fender is dragging on the ground. But we'll get her back in tip-top shape."

Hanson was minimizing the whole thing as I trailed behind the two of them, carrying his discharge papers.

The entire ride back, they didn't mention anything further about the accident, the bandage on Hanson's head, or, thank God, his illness. It was as if none of it had happened. When we arrived in Laguna Beach, I could tell that Hanson was exhausted, but he tried to keep the façade going.

"Want to come in for a drink?" Hanson asked Edgar, though it was the last thing he needed.

"No, no, next time. I'll drop the girl back home."

Edgar waited in the car while I helped Hanson take some of his belongings into the house. Once inside, he all but collapsed into a large velvet chair in the living room. I turned down his bedsheets, poured him a glass of water, and placed it by his bed.

"I'll be back to check on you in the morning, then," I said.

"Oh, I'm fine," he said. "I'll be right as rain by the morning."

I nodded, though we both knew there was little truth to that.

"THANK YOU," I SAID TO EDGAR WHEN I CLIMBED INTO THE FRONT seat of his car. And I meant it. He'd given up a good four hours of his time to collect us, follow me in his car to the repair shop, and then drive us back to Laguna.

"Not a problem," Edgar said as he pulled out of Hanson's driveway and turned left onto Coast Boulevard. "I enjoy that drive. I used to do it quite a lot during the war years."

"Really?"

"I used to drive up to some of the aviation plants a lot for work."

"Are you kidding me? I was at Douglas for four years. I started out on the production line as a riveter," I said. "What kind of work did you do?"

"Nose art," he said.

"Nose art? You mean on the fuselage?"

"That's right," he said. "I traveled around all over the place, sometimes to the desert where they were training, but often to Douglas in Long Beach."

I turned toward him in the seat, suddenly fascinated.

"So, they didn't draft you?" I asked, thinking he must be in his early forties and would have been eligible.

"I have a hearing problem in my left ear, I was born with it. But I still managed to do my part. A lot of military men were barracked here at the hotel in town, and at El Toro, not too far from here, and they recruited some of us artists to paint the planes."

He'd just gone up tenfold in my estimation. I rarely got to see the planes fully assembled and had seen nose art only in pictures in the papers, never up close. "What kind of thing did you paint?"

"Pinups mostly, replicas of some of the greats: Alberto Vargas, Gil

Elvgren, Rolf Armstrong. But also simpler things, like cartoons, shark teeth, dragon teeth—the Japs were terrified of sharks." He grinned. "Sometimes they just wanted a steady hand to paint numbers and letters, but of course the pinup girls were the most fun. I've got some pictures of my work back at my studio, would you like to take a look?"

"I'd love to."

He hit the brakes and made a sudden turn. "Sorry," he said. "I live up this way."

"Oh," I said. "You mean now?"

"No time like the present," he said.

It must have been at least ten o'clock, and I was exhausted and in desperate need of a soak in the bathtub after all I'd been through these past few days. But I didn't want to quell his enthusiasm. And, to be honest, I was excited to be around the airplanes again, even if it was only in pictures.

His studio was smaller than Hanson's, but pristine, almost like a public gallery of his work, each piece hung at what appeared to be the right height, complementary to its neighboring pieces. He had his plein air art clustered together neatly on one wall—canyons, seascapes, eucalyptus groves—and framed images of his aircraft work on another. An easel was set up in a corner of the room, and while it was more pleasant to be in there—the pungent smell of oil and turpentine didn't dominate, and I didn't have to wonder if I might sit or stand on a splotch of wet paint—it didn't have that well-worked-in feel that Hanson's had.

"Fancy a splash?" Edgar asked, opening a cupboard to reveal a full bar.

"Oh, no, thank you."

He shrugged and poured himself a drink. He took off his jacket and unbuttoned the top button of his shirt, then he ran his hands through his hair, which released it from the perpetual hold the pomade seemed to have on it, and let it fall more softly around his face. He looked better in his own environment, as if being around his own art, his own décor, somehow suited him and allowed him to relax. He walked over to me with a second glass in his hand. "You've had a long day, you deserve it."

"A long couple of days actually," I said, taking it from him. "All right, just a splash, then. Thank you." I took a sip. "Oh my, that's strong!"

"It's just gin." He walked back to his bar, popped a bottle, and freshened mine with tonic, more what I was accustomed to.

I approached one of the paintings mounted on the wall. "I see you like to paint nature, like Hanson," I said, noting familiar scenes of the coast, bold colors contrasted against pastels.

"Hardly," he said, sounding slightly offended. "We're very different: he has a more abrupt style, mine's more subdued. I focus on the small details, the subtle elements of nature."

"Oh, yes, of course," I said, feeling idiotic for having tried to speak about art to the artist himself, and also surprised that he would not want to be compared to Hanson. "I really don't know much about art."

"Don't worry," he said, softening, "you'll learn. You're surrounding yourself with some of the greats, and that's the best thing you can do." He put his hand on my back and led me over to the wall at the back of the studio where he had framed photographs of his aircraft art.

"This one here might be my favorite." It was a photograph of Edgar standing on a ladder next to an almost life-size painting of a topless woman, one arm held across her chest, one long leg stepping forward, wearing nothing but a bikini bottom. She had a tiny waist and gleaming skin, a huge smile, and long, full hair falling about her shoulders. The words "Little Gem" were painted around her.

The painting was glamorous and unlike any of his other work, but the crude sensuality of it all made me blush. I knew pinup art was risqué and often exaggerated the figure's womanliness, but I hadn't considered how it would all feel at this time of night, alone with a man I barely knew, looking at images of beautiful women embracing their femininity in all its glory. I took another long sip of my drink and realized I'd almost finished it in a couple of nervous gulps. "You did this?" I asked.

"Me and another fella. The paintings weren't technically approved, but some of the generals would commission us to come in and paint them, and I suppose the higher-ups turned a blind eye. They said it was a morale booster to have your plane come in with a beautiful woman on the nose. These men knew that they could be shot down and killed on every flight they took; I think it must have helped to know a gorgeous gal was right there with you."

The thought of planes getting shot down, young pilots and crew strapped inside who shouldn't have been there in the first place, it all made me nauseated. I turned to the next one, a smiling blonde in a skimpy two-piece swimsuit with voluptuous breasts, her hair flying freely behind her as she straddled a bomb that appeared to be falling through fluffy clouds. For a split second, I envied her—her beauty, yes, but more than that I envied the lustiness he had captured. I could see in his depiction how comfortable the girl felt showing herself off, no bashfulness, no cowering, no shame, just a good-looking gal enjoying her beauty. I wished I could have that same sense of confidence.

Edgar took the empty glass from my hand and returned with a full one. I considered declining again but took it anyway. I shouldn't have been there, at night, I should have come the next day, in daylight, a more respectable time, but I was glad to see his work. Even the sight of the glass nose of the plane reminded me of the pride I'd felt standing in a football stadium–sized room, filled with row upon row of glass domes, with women, just like me, next to each one, polishing the glass. I recalled the bright lights from up above, reflected on those domes like stars in the sky.

Edgar noticed me looking at another image.

"Ah yes, this is Sweet LaRhonda." He sighed happily. "She's a stunner, isn't she? We copied most of these from the well-known pinup artists— we didn't have time to get models to sit for us, so it wasn't as creative as you might think, but it was a heck of a lot more fun than sitting in those muddy trenches."

I nodded, though I didn't like hearing him speak so lightly.

"Those boys certainly needed something to cheer them up, give them hope," I said. My mind was on Bobby—the hope he'd needed, that I'd taken away.

I suddenly remembered how some of the girls would scratch their names into the interior of a plane, somewhere discreet. Sometimes they'd write the boys a love note and hide it under the seat, or jam it into a corner seam, reveling in the thought of reaching someone far away and bringing a little light to their day. I thought of Rusty, who liked to write not-so-innocent things in the hopes of warming up some boy's sleeping bag. She even wrote her address on a tiny piece of paper, which found its way into a soldier's hands, and they started a steamy correspondence. She told us she was doing it for her country.

"I could paint you like that, you know," Edgar said, coming up close to me.

"Like that?" I laughed, feeling my cheeks blush.

"Or however you like," he said. "I offered it once before, but you turned me down, remember."

"I remember," I said. "I don't have the looks or the proportions to be a pinup girl."

"I don't think you realize your own beauty," he said, stepping toward me, his face close to mine.

I quickly turned my head, taking interest in another image, not allowing the drinks to cloud my judgment. Just days ago, I had really disliked this man: his entitlement, his arrogance, his laziness at the pageant, his cockiness toward me. But today he had shown me a different side, a more likable, more charming side that I hadn't seen before. It may have just been the gin, but after witnessing how decent he'd been when picking up Hanson and me, and now learning about his connection to the aircraft plants, I had to admit, I was liking him a little better.

"I would be inspired," he said, "if I had the opportunity to paint you. It's all we want as artists: a moment, an object, a person, a vision that makes you want to drop everything and take your brush to canvas." He looked at me as if I were just as beautiful as those gorgeous pinup girls, and I swallowed my urge to laugh, then I thought of Hanson seeing Isabella that way.

"I don't think so," I said finally. He dropped his head in disappointment, as if he thought I might have agreed to it at that very moment.

"Edgar," I said, making my way toward a small navy two-seater on the far side of the room and taking a seat, "when I saw you at the beach a few weeks ago, you said you'd tell me more about the Isabella Rose incident if I stopped by your studio. And, here I am."

He grinned and walked toward me. "What is it you'd like to know?"

"I was curious if you knew anything about that painting. Whatever happened to it, do you know?"

He laughed and sat down close to me. "If I knew that, I'd never have to work again."

"Why?"

"It would be worth a fortune. People have been talking about that painting for years and years, there have been articles written about it. Can you imagine how much it would be worth?"

I shook my head; since it had been painted so long ago, I hadn't considered its value before, only its value to Hanson.

"And," Edgar went on, "imagine what it would be worth once he's gone."

"Edgar!" I said, shocked that he would voice such a thought.

"I'm not wishing ill on him, Hazel, I'm just saying it's likely worth a pretty penny, that painting."

"If it still exists," I said.

"Oh, it's still around."

"What makes you say that?" I asked.

"Because it's worth so damn much. The only person who wanted it gone was Isabella Rose, and she's dead, so what does she care now?"

"It sounds as if it was his one true masterpiece, and it's been weighing on him all these years. I think that's why he is the way he is."

"A drunk?"

"He's not a drunk," I instinctively defended him. "But I do think he drinks to drown out those thoughts, the idea that his painting could have contributed to her death."

"Maybe he was responsible, maybe he wasn't, we'll never know."

"But if he could see it again, to see that it really was as beautiful as he remembered it, he might be able to put his mind at rest."

Edgar shrugged. "I don't know, maybe. Why do you care so much about it?"

"I care for him. He's troubled, but he's a good person."

"He's hard to care for sometimes," Edgar said.

"We all are," I said.

Edgar was at the back wall again, admiring his artwork.

"I'm going to try to find out what happened to that painting, so he can see it again, so he can assuage all the guilt he suffers," I said, quietly, more to myself than to Edgar.

"Good luck with that," he said, laughing lightly.

"Someone, somewhere, has to know what happened to it," I said.

Suddenly, it was all I could think about. Hanson might only have a few months left to live, a year at most, the doctor seemed to suggest. He'd been good to me, he'd given me a chance, a place I could call home, and he'd forgiven my own lapses. He was good to the people of this town, and many of them didn't even know it. I suddenly felt compelled to help him.

"It's late," I said, making my excuses. "I should head home. But thank you, for the drink and for showing me your work."

"I'll drive you," he said.

"No," I said. "You stay, I need the fresh air."

CHAPTER 25

AT A LITTLE PAST FIVE IN THE MORNING, I LAY IN BED THINKING about the painting. Finally wide awake, I got up, pulled on a thick sweater and trousers, and walked across the street, down Cliff Drive to the pathway that led past the Victor Hugo Inn and its flower beds, resting in the moonlight, and down to the beach. It was still cool and dark out when I left the house, but by the time I reached the sand, the sky was already turning from darkness to a deep, glowing blue, and soon it transformed again to a hazy, gray dawn.

A couple of young men carried their surfboards down to the water's edge. Near Pelican Rock, one surfer swam to shore to retrieve a board that had washed up without him. Another man fished at the water's edge while his dog ran along the beach, then back again, with an occasional bark at dozing seagulls. It was all so peaceful and purposeful, and I felt bonded somehow to the other few who had chosen to forgo sleep for the calm, lucky spirit that the ocean offered us, as if only we were in on the secret.

If I were to help Hanson find the painting, where would I even start? He'd already searched the hotel. If it had really been stolen, the police could get involved, but then I thought back to Hanson's recounting of booze-impaired memories that were hazy at best about a painting that went missing some thirty-six years ago. A detective would laugh at me and tell me not to waste his time.

Later, on my way to check on Hanson, I stopped into Walter Mc-Quinn's Ice Cream Parlor, nodded at the guy behind the counter in the white paper hat, and headed to the telephone booth. I didn't expect to speak to Scarlett directly, so I was surprised when she answered the telephone, so much that I almost forgot what to say.

"Who is it?" she asked, then sighed.

"It's Hazel, Hazel Francis, Mr. Radcliff's . . ."

"I know who you are, but why on earth are you putting a call through at this ungodly hour of the morning?"

"I'm sorry if I woke you." I checked the clock mounted on the wall with a Coca-Cola in the center. It was almost 10 a.m.

She sighed again. "You didn't, I'm having the whole house redecorated, finally, now that we're allowed to buy things again. Anyway, today, the curtains are being replaced, so I've got a house full of people taking the old ones down. It's quite exhausting."

"I'm going to be in Los Angeles next week," I said. "I have to collect Hanson's car from the repair shop."

"Do you have news from him?" she asked, her voice tilting with excitement.

"Not yet, but I am still trying, and I might have more success if you can help me with something."

"All right, I can meet you on Friday," she said.

"Wonderful." I didn't know what information I might be able to glean from Scarlett about the painting—after all, she'd made it very clear on numerous occasions that she did not want to talk about her late grandmother—but I had to start somewhere. "And say, Scarlett—what are you going to do with those old curtains that you're taking down?"

The operator began to speak, and I was out of change.

"Could I have them?" I said quickly. "If they are going to waste. I'll explain later."

"Hazel, that is the strangest—" And then the line went dead.

∿

WHEN I ARRIVED AT HANSON'S HOUSE, HE WAS SITTING IN THE WELL-worn armchair that I'd left him in the night before. He looked tired and disheveled, but he had changed his clothes, so I had reason to hope he hadn't slept there. He perked up a little when he saw me.

"Coffee?" he asked, starting to get up, though I didn't smell the usual rich aroma from a freshly brewed pot.

"I'll get it," I said, and he sank back into his chair.

"How are you feeling today?" I asked, as I poured the water in the pan to boil, then spooned the coffee grinds into the jug.

"Just fine," he said. "I told you I'd be right as rain."

"We should change the bandage," I said, looking over at him. The idea seemed to exhaust him even more. "But we'll have coffee first."

I poured the water into the jug, and after ten minutes or so I strained it into the metal coffeepot. It was comforting to know that he needed me and relied on me to show up each day.

"I was thinking about what you told me," I said, pulling up a chair from the dining room. "Yesterday at the hospital, about Isabella."

He nodded, and I sensed that something had shifted between us. Now that he'd told me the truth about his past, he didn't seem as defensive, or maybe it was just that he was too tired to put up a fight.

"Are you really not interested in painting Scarlett?" I asked. "She thinks it would be good for her acting career if she was painted by the very man who'd captured either her grandmother's beauty or her deterioration—depending on one's opinion amid the scandal."

"I assumed it was something like that. And no, I don't want to do it."

I nodded. I certainly wasn't going to push him. I didn't blame him for not wanting to be part of this young woman's publicity scheme. I wouldn't want to do it either.

"But then I'm curious, if she's been asking you to paint her for some time, and you have no intention of doing it, why did you hire me as a model, when the paintings that you do most are landscape?"

He looked out the window. "I have to admit, when she started in with those letters several months back, I was intrigued. I've been fascinated with portraiture ever since I painted Isabella all those years ago, but I didn't want to return to that kind of art, not publicly anyway."

I thought about the room I'd found at the top of the staircase, full of half-finished paintings of women.

"I turned to landscapes and seascapes because it was harmless. I couldn't hurt someone with landscapes. So, I escaped into nature, I found refuge in it, away from everything and everyone else. I could paint here in

Laguna for a lifetime, and there'd still be more rocks, sea, hills, and canyons beyond the hills that I hadn't covered."

"I thought you told Edgar that you'd seen it all," I said, smiling.

"Edgar is a competitive swab, and someone has to keep him on his toes."

I poured Hanson more coffee.

"Where else can you drive through the winding road of the canyon, each curve giving you a new vista of those giant crags and sloping hillsides, dotted with wildflowers and greenery . . ." It felt as if he might drift off into a dream, but he began again, "Only to leave the canyon behind and come upon the view that broadens to the breaking surf of the Pacific Ocean?" He looked at me, eyes wide, excited by what he could see, while sitting in his own living room. "Nowhere," he said. "Nowhere else. So I lived in this world of nature and beauty, and I stayed away from portraiture. And the landscapes and seascapes sold. They sold very well."

"So then why return to figures now?"

"Because even when something is this beautiful and plentiful, and Mother Nature spoils you, there's always that other thing that tugs at you. Your other love. I've tried over the years to paint figures, but it's too hard without the figures in front of you. I've sat at cafés, at the bar, I've painted my housekeeper while she worked. I've painted from memory. I've never asked someone to sit for me, formally. I was afraid to, and it's damned frustrating. So, I suppose Scarlett's letters reminded me how much time had passed, how little time might be left."

I reached out and put my hand on his. His skin felt thin and cool over his knuckles. He took his other hand and put it on top of mine.

"You're a good kid," he said. "I'm glad we found each other."

CHAPTER 26

I'D TAKEN THE TRAIN FROM EL TORO TO UNION STATION, A TAXICAB to the car repair shop, and then driven Hanson's good-as-new wagon to Scarlett's house in Beverly Hills. Hanson hadn't laughed this time when I said I would drive it back to Laguna. Instead, he seemed sincerely grateful. When I pulled into Scarlett's driveway, she burst out the front door to greet me.

"You must come in and see the new décor," she said, jumping up and down with excitement.

"Is this all yours?" I asked, in awe of the dramatic winding driveway that had led me up to an enormous house with a wraparound balcony.

"Sure is." She spread her arms wide, and I took in the perfectly manicured lawn, the flower beds, and the primped and pruned trees and bushes. This had to cost a small fortune.

"Everything was so old-fashioned before," Scarlett said. "Inside was dark and dingy, all damask silk divans and matching curtains, my mother's choice." Scarlett seemed as if she'd been shot out of a cannon, overly eager to show me around. "Now everything's pink," she said, taking my hand and pulling me into the house.

In the entranceway the open eyes of a large white bear rug stared up at me from the ground, its white teeth bared.

"Oh my," I said, stepping back.

"Isn't that the most delightful rug," Scarlett said. "Drives my dog, Bugsy, absolutely mad, but I think he's wonderful. I've named him Roar."

To our right was a formal dining room with a huge table and twelve chairs. Without even entering the room, I could see that crystal dripped from every surface—candelabras on the table, a chandelier dangling from the ceiling, and decanters on a cabinet against the wall.

"Come upstairs first." She skipped up the stairs and opened the door to her bedroom, and sure enough, it was as pink as could be, with flowers stenciled on the walls. A large bed with a mirrored headboard and a dark green velvet bedspread was the centerpiece, with a gold chandelier hanging above it. "Isn't it fabulous!"

"It certainly is," I said. It did look like the perfect home for a glamour girl like Scarlett, and I got the sense that she was trying to create a movie star world for herself right there within her own walls. She showed me the pink living room, her dressing room, and even the pink bathrooms, all pristine and freshly decorated.

"Did you keep the old curtains, by any chance?" I asked.

"I did," she said, pulling a stack of folded gold, silver, lilac, and peach embroidered curtains out from a closet and dropping them at my feet, a puff of dust erupting into the stream of sunlight that shone through the enormous windows. "You can have my old bedspreads too," she said, her face scrunched in disgust as she emerged with another pile of fabric in multiple colors. "Though I don't know why you'd want them."

"They're perfect," I said.

"You need to ask your boss for a pay raise if you need these old things."

"It's not for me, it's for the Pageant of the Masters."

"What on earth is that?"

"The town is putting on a big art show this summer—they re-create famous paintings with real people, and they need old fabrics like this for costumes."

"Ooh, theater? Do they need actors?"

"It's called living art, and they enlist locals from Laguna Beach. The town greeter is Judas in *The Last Supper*. But no, they don't act, they pose; they have to sit very still while the painting is on display. Hanson's involved, well, reluctantly."

"Sitting still? It sounds very dull."

"Apparently it's exciting when it all comes together. I've never seen it myself."

"If Hanson's involved, I do hope you'll tell him that I'm donating all of this very expensive fabric."

"I'll make sure he knows."

"Champagne?" Scarlett asked, walking to the kitchen.

"No, thank you, I have to drive all the way back to Laguna tonight," I said.

"You can stay here. I have five guest bedrooms that never get used."

"That's so kind of you," I said, and it really was, and who would have thought a few months ago that I'd be asked to spend the night with a Hollywood starlet, or, rather, the granddaughter of a star.

"But we'd have such fun," she said, pouting.

"I would love to stay, Scarlett, but I have to get back to check on Hanson," I said, then quickly corrected myself, not wanting to reveal anything about his injury or illness. "To return his car, he needs it early tomorrow. Speaking of Hanson, I was thinking about your request for him to paint you."

"Go on," she said. I had her attention now.

"Perhaps he'd be more inclined to paint you if he could see the painting again, the one he did of your grandmother."

"Why would he want to see it? Didn't it ruin his reputation?"

"I wouldn't say it's ruined. He's Hanson Radcliff."

"I thought he didn't want anything to do with that old painting. I'm hoping he might want a second chance to prove himself, by painting me."

"I'm not sure he needs to prove himself to anyone," I said, feeling protective. "He's lived an incredible life, he's remarkably accomplished." She rolled her eyes and poured herself a glass of champagne. "If it was possible to find the painting, and if he could see it again, I think he might be inspired to paint you." I didn't know if there was an ounce of truth to that, but it was my only hope of getting Scarlett to reveal if she had any information about the painting. "Do you think anyone in your family knows its whereabouts?"

She considered this for a moment and seemed to take her time putting the champagne back in the ice bucket.

"Should I show you the swimming pool?"

"Scarlett."

"It's in the shape of a giant heart," she said, sauntering out toward her backyard.

"If you do know something about the painting, please tell me. In addition to possibly helping your cause, it would really be of great importance to Hanson if he could see it one more time."

"One more time?"

"Or again, I mean if he could see it again, it would help reassure him about what happened all those years ago."

"Oh." Scarlett shook her head. Her demeanor had suddenly changed; she was acting coy. "I really can't say. My family wouldn't permit me."

"So, you do know where it is?" I asked, wondering at her change in manner but hopeful nonetheless. "Or you know who has it?"

"This way," she said, holding the door open for me. "It's a pool of love, isn't it something?"

The swimming pool looked ridiculous, actually—how could anyone swim laps in a shape like that? And however extravagant, it was the last thing I wanted to talk about.

"Scarlett, if you want me to help you, then you need to tell me what you know about the painting. It's the only way I'd be able to convince Hanson to paint you."

"Fine," she said, feigning exasperation. "We have it."

"You have the painting? Of Isabella Rose?"

"Yes."

"Where?"

"I can't say."

"Well, who has it, and how did they get it? Hanson said he left her house with it, and then he thinks it might have been stolen."

"We are within our rights to keep that painting in our family's possession; it is of my grandmother, after all."

"So, are you suggesting that someone from your family found it and took it back?"

She turned her back to me and dipped her toe in the pool. "It's lovely and warm."

"Do you think you might be able to retrieve the painting and bring it to Hanson's studio, even if only for a few hours?" She shrugged and took a sip of her champagne. Her disinterest in the whole thing was infuriating. She might not have any idea how important this painting was to Hanson, but I did, and I was the only one who knew that we didn't have much time left.

"Is that a yes, or a no?" I insisted.

"I can't transport that enormous painting all by myself down to Laguna Beach, it's impossible."

Hanson had made it sound smaller when he described leaving Isabella's house and carrying it all the way to Laguna Beach, but maybe I had that wrong. Or she was exaggerating.

"I could help you," I said.

"Let's go for a dip," Scarlett coaxed. "Late afternoons are the best time for a swim."

"I can't."

"I have a whole collection of bathing suits, some I've never even worn."

"I really must start back. I've never driven his car at night before, so I want to take it slow and leave before dark."

"Please stay longer, it's no fun to swim alone."

I didn't understand why she was clinging to me.

"Hanson's expecting me." I turned to leave. "But thank you so much for the fabric, it will all be greatly appreciated. And if you do find out more about that painting, please do let me know."

I loaded the fabric into the back of Hanson's wagon as she stood on the steps to her house, watching me. I glanced back and smiled, feeling a surprising wave of sadness for her. Despite all her money, a fabulous house, a swimming pool, a driver, and access to anything she wanted, I realized now that what she was truly desperate for was a friend. I would have stayed if it hadn't been for Hanson's delicate state—his injury as well as his illness—and I wished I could have explained that to her.

"I'll see you again soon, hopefully!" I called out before climbing into the driver's seat.

"Wait." She jogged down the steps toward me. "Hazel, wait."

I rolled down the window.

"Tell Hanson that if he paints me, then I'll show him the painting."

I sighed. I knew Hanson well enough to know he would never agree to bribery.

"That's the only way," she said.

IT WAS DARK WHEN I REACHED HANSON'S HOUSE, AND I COULD HEAR him coughing inside as soon as I got out of the car. He was sitting at the kitchen table in his pajamas and robe, wielding a brush, a small canvas before him.

"It's good to see you hard at work," I said, walking to his side to see the painting—a narrow tower shot up out of a rocky sandstone ledge on the beach, all the way up to the top of a cliff. It had a few small, unevenly shaped lookout windows sporadically spaced on the way up. "Is that a lighthouse?"

"No, an enclosed staircase at Victoria Beach, right down the street." He tipped his head toward the window as if I might be able to look out and see it. "I'm doing a few quick sketches for the gallery. It helps them out."

"That's very kind. Lillian mentioned that you do that sometimes. It's impressive that you can paint it without seeing it in real life."

"I've painted it so many times I can see it in my head. A rich senator built the tower about twenty years ago, so he could have easy access from his house on the cliff down to the beach below. It's pretty; people like to buy paintings of it and take them home."

"I'd love to see it," I said.

He coughed again, and it didn't ease up. "We'll go," he managed, during a brief reprieve, "this week maybe."

I went to the kitchen and poured him a glass of water, but it was some time before he could stop coughing and take a sip.

"How are you feeling?" I asked.

"How do you think I'm feeling?" he said, agitated. "There's nothing that makes a man feel old and gone like someone asking him all the godforsaken time how he's feeling. My head's pounding where the stitches are, and every time I cough it feels like the stitches are going to rip open.

My lungs are on fire. That's how I feel most days, so there you go, you don't need to ask anymore."

"Understood," I said.

"You have the wagon, I assume?"

"Yes, she looks good as new, and she's a beauty to drive."

"Good," he said. "Thank you for going up there."

It might have been the first time Hanson had ever actually thanked me. "I've never driven such a nice car," I said, then hesitated. "I saw Scarlett while I was in Los Angeles."

I watched for a response, but he kept on painting.

"She has a lovely house."

Still nothing.

"She said she knows where the painting is."

I didn't want him to fly into a rage and set him off coughing again, and shockingly he didn't. Instead, he leaned in close to the canvas and squinted to paint the shingles on the cone-shaped roof of the tower.

"I'm talking about the painting you did of Isabella Rose all those years ago. She said she has it."

He snorted a little but kept on.

"Hanson, are you hearing what I'm saying? Scarlett has your painting."

"She doesn't have it," he said, dabbing his brush on his palette and adding some burnt umber to the pool of paint he was working with.

"What do you mean? She said someone in her family has it, and she would be able to gain access to it, if . . ."

He sighed and set his paintbrush down. "If what?"

"If you agreed to paint her."

"I'm not going to be coerced into doing something by some wannabe little starlet. Why are you digging around like this?" He shook his head. "I've told you not to do that. And anyway, she's lying, she doesn't have it. I left Isabella's house with that painting in my hands."

"But you said yourself you lost track of it. Maybe they took it back."

"Took it back?" He raised an eyebrow. "It was always mine."

"I mean stole it, someone in her family could have stolen it from you."

"Unlikely," he said, genuinely unmoved by the idea that it could be in Scarlett's possession.

"You said you wanted to see it again." A surge of desperation ran through me. The possibility that it could be so close sparked an urgent need to get my hands on it. I wanted to see for myself if it was really as disturbing as Isabella Rose claimed, or if Hanson was justified in his portrayal. I suddenly had the strange but definite feeling that if he could just see it, it would save him.

He wiped his brush on a rag. "I don't want you meddling in old news. This has followed me around my entire life."

I knew deep down that Hanson would never give in to painting Scarlett—not now, especially after the way she was handling things—but part of me hoped I was wrong. Part of me at least hoped that he'd be energized by the idea that it was within reach, that it might give him something to wish for.

"How big was it, anyway?" I asked.

He looked puzzled.

"The painting, how large was the canvas?"

He held his hands out in front of him and made a rectangle that was about three feet by four feet. Not small, but not unmanageable the way Scarlett had suggested. Certainly not impossible for her to carry. I sat down in one of the kitchen chairs, defeated. Maybe she was lying after all.

CHAPTER 27

THE SIDEWALK WAS LIT ONLY BY THE MOON AND A FEW SPORADIC streetlights. I hadn't talked to Jimmy since I'd called from the hospital, and I knew his shift would be over soon. I didn't want to make a habit of stopping by at his place of work anymore, but he deserved to know that Hanson was back home. When I reached the hotel, I walked around the side of the building, down the stairs that led from the boardwalk to the beach, and sure enough he was there, beach chairs already lined up against the back wall of the hotel. He was raking the sand and forming a flat surface under the light of the moon. I watched him for a moment, the sleeves of his white shirt rolled up, a soft glow coming from the windows of the hotel.

"Hazel," he said, looking up. "It's good to see you."

I waved and walked over.

"And perfect timing. I haven't had dinner yet." He motioned to a paper bag on a beach chair. "Join me?"

"Oh no, I'm not hungry," I lied, not wanting to take his food from him again. It had seemed fine before, but now it seemed too personal. "But I'll sit with you."

"It's meatballs in tomato sauce and cheese," he said, grinning. "Might be my best yet."

I laughed. "You enjoy it." Things felt almost normal between us, and I was grateful.

"How's Hanson?" he asked, settling into a chair next to me.

"Well, he's home, and . . ." I wasn't sure how much I could share.

"That bad, huh?" He looked concerned. "He hasn't been to the bar these past few days. I should visit him. Maybe take him a cocktail to cheer him up."

"A drink is probably the last thing he needs, but I'm sure he'd be happy to see you. The cut on his head is healing, but he's . . ." I hesitated again. "You should go and see him. Sooner rather than later."

"What does that mean?"

"Nothing, just that he was injured, and you know he's not a young man. He doesn't seem to have much family to care for him."

"He's got you."

"I do care for him, very much. But it's not the same as family."

"Don't worry, I'll go."

While Jimmy ate, I told him about visiting Scarlett, her claim to have the painting, and Hanson's apparent disinterest, but he seemed confused by the whole thing.

"Why do you want to find it so badly if Hanson doesn't even want to see it?"

"Because he does want to see it, he told me when he was in the hospital, and it sounds as if it's valuable, so it's likely to surface at some point. How awful would it be if everyone else got to see it and make their opinions on it known, but he missed his chance."

"Hanson's the kind of man who will live forever," Jimmy said, passing me a bottle of Coca-Cola that he'd already opened.

I took a sip. "No one lives forever, but his legacy will, and it should be a good one. Besides, he does so much good for this town, and he shouldn't be haunted by another person's opinion of a painting he did many years ago."

"Where's all this coming from, Hazel? You're so melancholy all of a sudden."

"Oh, I don't know, I suppose the accident scared me a little. It could have been much worse." I wished I could be honest with Jimmy about Hanson's health, but I'd promised to keep it quiet, and I'd already said too much to Edgar. I had to keep my word.

"Anyway," I said, forcing a smile. "How are you? How's work?"

"It's fine, fine." He shook his head and scrunched the paper bag from his sandwich into a tight ball. "Well, a little worrisome, honestly," he said. "I've been hearing talk about the hotel, apparently the financial trouble has worsened."

"But it looks great, the rooms are lovely, the food is delicious."

He shrugged. "It hasn't really picked up the way they thought it would after the war, they haven't been filling the rooms, and there are rumors that it could close down if they don't start making a profit again."

"No," I said. "You can't let that happen."

"There's not a whole lot I can do," he said, bristling in a way I hadn't seen before. "I'm just the bartender."

"You're not *just* the bartender," I insisted, leaning toward him in my enthusiasm. "You're part of this place. When you greet people at the bar, they feel like they're having a drink in someone's living room. You're friendly, you're interested in what people have to say, and you make people feel welcome."

He looked at me in surprise.

I should have been embarrassed at gushing about him, but I meant it. He was so kind and genuine, so charming. "You can make anyone feel special, even a stranger, the way you did with me that first day we met."

Our eyes connected, and we stayed that way for several long seconds.

"Hazel," he said, his eyes searching mine. He inched toward me ever so slightly before abruptly leaning back in his chair, turning his head away.

"That's nice of you to say," he said. "But when it comes to this hotel business, it's got a whole lot more to do with making money than with someone being nice to them."

I wanted to say more, to assure him that everything would be okay, but I was trembling from the moment that had just passed between us—his face so close to mine that I could feel the warmth of his breath. I had to get away from him before one of us did something we'd regret, so I made my excuses and left.

⚐

I PULLED UP NEXT TO THE CAFÉ WHERE I USUALLY MET LILLIAN TO go to the meeting for the pageant. She didn't see me at first and stood on the sidewalk looking around.

"Lillian," I called out. "I'm over here."

"Well, this is quite something!" she said, her mouth agape, admiring the car.

"It's Hanson's," I said as she climbed in the passenger seat. "I borrowed it so I could deliver some fabric to Mrs. Moynahan."

"You must be getting along rather well with Hanson Radcliff, if he's letting you borrow his car."

"It's only for a few hours," I said, but she was right—Hanson and I were getting along quite well.

"Tonight, everyone's going to be in their assigned groups," Lillian said. "I believe you're in costume."

"Yes." I sighed. "What are you assigned to?"

"I'm helping paint the backgrounds of the paintings in the show," she said, rubbing her hands together. "It's a huge job to take these paintings that are often small and replicate them on a life-size canvas, we have to be careful to get the proportions right, map them out first, but I'm really happy to be doing it."

I felt a pang of envy at hearing that Lillian had a role in such an important part of the event, while I was going to be stuck sorting through old fabrics, but I reminded myself that I didn't have the kind of skills or experience she had.

When I pulled into the parking lot, I saw an unmistakable and incredibly overdressed figure standing under the banner.

"What is she doing here?" I said.

"Whoever it is, it looks like she's about four months early for opening night."

Scarlett started waving madly as soon as she saw me. "Hazel, I've been waiting for you!"

"Why? Is everything all right?"

"Of course, it is! Why wouldn't it be?"

"I don't know, you're just here, at the pageant. Why are you here?"

"Well, that's a nice welcome." She forced a laugh. "I remembered that you said you were going to donate those curtains and bedspreads tonight at your little meeting, and I had a sudden thought that I should be there, to donate them. They are from my house, after all."

"Oh yes, of course, thank you, but you really didn't need to drive all this way. I would have let Mrs. Moynahan know that they were from you."

"First of all, I didn't drive, Henry did." She nodded to a black car parked nearby with her chauffeur standing by its side. "And secondly, who's Mrs. Moynahan?" Scarlett asked.

"She's in charge of costumes."

"Oh, I don't care about her, I want to make sure Hanson appreciates it."

"He will appreciate it, I promise you," I said, as convincingly as possible. "Come on, help me carry this, will you?"

We walked back toward Hanson's car, and I handed Scarlett half of the fabrics, which were surprisingly heavy. She looked at me with disgust. "Do you have any idea how much dust must have collected on these horrible things?" She passed them back to me and snapped her fingers. In seconds her driver was in front of us. "Carry these, Henry. Follow Hazel, she knows where to go." She trailed behind us in very high heels.

Mrs. Moynahan was thrilled. She carefully unfolded each item and examined it for size and suitability, discussing where each piece could be used.

"We can make a gorgeous dress for one of the girls in *The Birth of the Flag*," she said, looking up at me. "Henry Mosler, remember?" She reached for a book and quickly turned to the page of the painting.

As soon as I saw it, I recognized the painting—three women in full-length gowns, stitching and embroidering the very first American flag. I took the book from her and showed it to Scarlett.

"And this will be perfect for the cardinal's attire in *The Cardinal's Portrait*." Mrs. Moynahan held up the reddish-peach-colored curtains from Scarlett's dining room. I turned to another marked page in the book and showed her the painting by Toby Rosenthal—a humorous scene of a cardinal who'd fallen asleep while having his portrait painted. Scarlett looked uninterested and bored.

"We'll need some dull, brown fabric for the monk's hooded tunic," Mrs. Moynahan said, and as she did, Scarlett sighed loudly.

"Why don't I show you around the grounds?" I said quickly, not wanting Scarlett's mood to dampen Mrs. Moynahan's excitement and enthusiasm.

"Thank God," Scarlett said, when we were out of the closet and back out in the open. "I thought I was going to die of boredom in there."

"She just wanted to show you what your donation will be used for. Aren't you glad that those old fabrics that you were just going to throw away will have a second life?"

"Honestly, I couldn't give two hoots. Now where is Hanson anyway? I was hoping for a chance to chat with him about, you know, what we discussed the other day." She grinned and nudged her shoulder against mine.

I stepped aside, taking a bit of pleasure in dashing her hopes. "Hanson's not coming to this meeting, that's what he has me for. I attend the meetings on his behalf."

Scarlett frowned. "He's not coming? Well, then, why on earth am I here?"

"I have no idea," I said.

"What a waste of my time," she said with a scowl.

"And about *what we discussed*," I said. "Do you have any more information you can share about the painting?"

She shrugged and grinned as if this was some kind of game.

"Do you really have that painting, Scarlett, or was that just a ruse?"

This time she looked at me with surprise, and I could tell from the expression on her face that I'd caught her off guard, that she hadn't quite decided if she should tell me the truth or lie. I shook my head and walked on ahead.

"Hazel," she called out, following quickly behind me. "Fine, I don't have it, you're right. I got carried away."

"Why would you lie about that? This is important."

"It's important to me too," she said, trotting along to keep up, in the heels that I could only imagine were getting stuck in the dirt as we walked. "There's no need to be sore with me!" She suddenly stopped in her tracks. "I want what I want, and I'm going to do whatever it takes to get it."

"Well, then you're going to have to do that on your own," I said. "I can't help you anymore."

I turned back in the direction that we'd come from and headed to the costume closet.

Later that evening, after what felt like hours sorting through fabrics,

I walked back to Hanson's car and heard a high-pitched laugh coming from across the dirt lot. It was foggy out, and I couldn't make out the figures right away, but I recognized the laugh. Scarlett's driver hadn't left and was still parked in the same spot, and when I looked again, I saw Edgar holding his car door open for Scarlett to climb in.

CHAPTER 28

"JIMMY," I SAID, SURPRISED TO FIND HIM SITTING WITH HANSON at his kitchen table the following week, with a plate of pastries in front of them and two steaming cups of coffee. I looked from one to the other and suddenly felt anxious—I was happy that Jimmy was visiting Hanson, as he'd said he would, I just hadn't expected him to be there at the same time as me.

I'd spent so many hours with each of them separately but never together. "More coffee?" I asked, as if I were still waiting tables at the diner back home. They both glanced at their full cups and shook their heads. "Should I come back later, then? When you're done with your visit?"

Jimmy cocked his head as if to ask why I was acting strange, but I looked away. Even if I could answer him, I wouldn't know what to say. It was almost as if I didn't want Hanson to know that Jimmy and I had a friendship beyond the bar of the hotel. And on top of that, I hadn't been able to stop thinking about that moment between us behind the hotel.

"No need to leave on my account," Jimmy said finally. "I have to get back soon anyway, to get ready for the lunchtime crowd."

I took a coffee cup down from the cabinet to give myself something to do. "May I?" I turned to Hanson before I poured myself a cup—an unnecessary formality; it was usually the first thing I did when I arrived, and I never asked permission.

"By all means," he said. And then he looked from me to Jimmy and back again. "Turns out Jimmy knows all about our little accident," Hanson said, raising his eyebrows.

"Yes, well, I called him from the hospital, before I knew you'd have to stay an extra day. He very kindly offered to pick us up," I said.

"But then you called Edgar Berg instead," he said, with disdain.

"Jimmy had to work, and I had to get us home somehow," I said quietly.

"Well, we're back now in one piece, the wagon is good as new, and I am too." He chuckled, which set off a coughing fit. "Almost."

Jimmy stood and gave Hanson a pat on the back. "You should talk to a doctor about that cough," he said. "It doesn't sound so good."

I looked to Hanson, but he didn't meet my eyes.

"I'll be fine in a couple of days."

"Good, because I'm saving your seat at the bar."

"Good man, good man," Hanson said.

"I'll be off, then." Jimmy took his coffee cup to the kitchen. "Will I see you tonight, Hazel?"

"Oh." I blushed, not wanting Hanson to get the wrong idea. "I don't know, probably not, I'm sure we have a lot to do today, full day."

Jimmy shrugged. "You know where I'll be if you change your mind. Take care, Hanson. Oh, and Hazel?" Jimmy nodded toward the door. "Can I have a word?"

I walked outside, unprepared to explain myself for acting so awkward.

"Sorry, I don't know why . . ." I stammered. "I mean, I just didn't expect to see you . . ."

But Jimmy had other things on his mind. "Actually, I wanted to tell you that, um, remember I told you about Jeanene?"

I swallowed, but my throat suddenly felt dry as sticks. I nodded and tried to smile. "Yeah, sure, I remember."

"Well, she's coming for a visit."

"A visit? Oh, that's great news." My voice was annoyingly high-pitched all of a sudden.

"She's on summer break from beauty school, so she's taking the train. It's going to take several days, but she'll be getting in at the end of the week. She wants to see what Laguna Beach is all about. She's never seen the Pacific Ocean, can you believe it?"

Of course, I could. I hadn't seen it either until recently.

"I'd love for you to meet her, and I was thinking, maybe if you've got time, you could show her around a little, take her to some of the shops. I can't take any time off, not with the way work is right now. I don't want to give them any reason to let me go."

"Oh, right." There was nothing in the world that I wanted to do less than spend time with Jimmy's girl. The idea of it made me want to vomit.

"Just for an hour or so." He looked at the ground and seemed almost as pained as me to be talking about this.

"Sure," I said, quickly, just wanting the conversation to be over. "Happy to help. I'd better get inside."

"Gotcha," Jimmy said. "Thanks, Hazel." He gave me a soft but awkward punch in the arm, as if we were old chums from school.

Back in the house, there was an uncomfortable silence between Hanson and me. I picked up a stray envelope and put it with another few sheets of paper on the countertop. I placed the pan on the stove, even though there was plenty of coffee left.

"You like that fella, don't you?" Hanson said finally.

"What would give you that idea? I know him from the hotel, that's all, from the hotel where you sent me that very first night I was in Laguna for our interview."

"I know which hotel it is. When I'm in better shape I am at that bar for a drink or two most nights of the week. I'm just saying there's something between the two of you, I can see it. And when I see something, I see something; for better or worse, I see truth."

"Well, I hate to be the one to tell you, Hanson, that in this case you're wrong. Jimmy has a lady friend back home. She's going to move here to be with him."

"Maybe so, maybe so, but I'm telling you what I see, and there's something there, between the two of you, no doubt about that."

I was about to make up a list of all the reasons why Jimmy and I would never be attracted to each other, but thankfully Hanson saved me from myself.

"So," he said. "Next week how about we go to Victoria Beach?"

"Yes!" I clapped my hands together, relieved to change the subject.

"Good. You want to see the tower, and it's lazy of me, painting it from memory. We'll go early and catch the morning light."

"I would love that!"

Hanson's cough sounded worse than usual that day. He had spells where he just couldn't stop, and I suggested, again, that we call the doctor who had been recommended at the hospital, but he wouldn't have it. By lunchtime he was exhausted. I fixed him something to eat, but he left it on the kitchen counter and said he'd eat later. He wanted to sleep, and he gave me the rest of the day off.

I didn't know what to do with myself. I wanted to be busy, to not think about Jimmy's lady friend visiting in a few days, or how I had inexplicably agreed to show her around town. I wanted a distraction. I'd already been swimming, Hanson didn't need me, Lillian didn't work in the gallery on Fridays, my lead on Hanson's missing painting had come to a dead end, and I certainly wasn't going to visit the hotel. Aimlessly walking back toward town, I found myself at Edgar's street and turned onto it. I knocked, but there was no response, and just as I was about to leave, he answered, slightly disheveled.

"Hazel." He ran his hands through his loose, wavy hair. "I'm sorry, I wasn't expecting anyone." He was wearing a thin sweater and crumpled trousers, rolled at the ankles. He looked better this way, less slick, more natural, rugged, but he seemed embarrassed by his appearance. "You've caught me looking rather a mess."

"It's very artist-like, but if I'm catching you at a bad time . . ."

"No, no, not at all, I was just finishing up for the day actually. I've been in the studio since early this morning, haven't seen the light of day."

"I was just heading home from Hanson's and wondered if you might like to take a walk with me."

He looked at me thoughtfully and smiled. "I would like that," he said, as if that were the nicest thing anyone had ever said to him.

We walked down to the boardwalk, past the old dance hall, toward the beach. As we walked, his hand brushed mine, and I wondered for a minute if he might grab it. In that moment I wouldn't have minded if he had. Maybe it was a reaction to Jimmy's news, but I started wishing I didn't feel the need to push everyone away all the time. I still hadn't fully decided what I thought of Edgar—sometimes he was charming

and fun, other times he could be offensive and crass—but I was thinking about the look he'd given me at the door. He'd shown interest in me
a couple of times, and each time I'd brushed him off as if I were somehow superior. He was older than I was by about twenty years if I were to
guess, but he had a youthfulness, a playfulness that seemed to keep him
young. "You Are My Sunshine" flowed from a radio in one of the shops
on the boardwalk.

"Do you like Jimmie Davis?" I asked.

"Sure. I love music. Over there, that used to be Cabrillo's dance hall,
a fantastic place. Judy Garland and Mickey Rooney both danced the
night away in that hall, and word has it Rooney even played a set on the
drums once."

"What happened to it?" I asked, looking back. The name CABRILLO
BALLROOM was still painted in black letters above the arched doorway.

"They turned it into a bowling alley, but they still have a small dance
floor and a band that comes in and plays on Friday nights," he said. "Do
you dance?"

"Of course," I said. "Well, a little. When I first started working at
the factory, the girls and I used to go dancing at the USO almost every
night we had off. I stopped after I got promoted—there was no time for
that anymore—and the more responsibility I had, the less I felt good
about those late nights. I learned a few steps in those early days, though.
How about you?"

He grinned. "Why don't you let me show you sometime?"

"How about Friday?"

It was bold of me, a bit saucy even, but I wasn't going to wait around
being nothing but a tour guide for a bartender's girlfriend. I was going
to go out and have my own fun with whomever I pleased. And besides,
if Edgar was good enough for Scarlett, then surely he was good enough
for me.

We walked along the sand and up the winding pathway to the cliff
top, past the Victor Hugo Inn and across Coast Boulevard.

"This is me," I said when we reached the gallery. "I live up there." I
pointed to the building behind the gallery.

"May I walk you to your door?" he asked.

I hesitated, then nodded.

Upstairs, as I opened the door, he stopped and looked at me. I felt my pulse quicken just a little, slightly panicky, as I wondered if he was going to try to kiss me.

"This was an unexpected but lovely visit," he said, brushing a strand of hair from my face, then picking up my hand and bringing it to his lips. "I'll see you Friday then."

As I closed the door behind me and heard his footsteps going down the stairs, I felt relieved. I stood with my back to the door, just as surprised by our encounter as he was. I drew a bath and climbed in. This, I told myself, this is exactly the kind of distraction I need.

CHAPTER 29

ON FRIDAY, EDGAR PICKED ME UP AT SEVEN. I DRESSED IN A WHITE flowing skirt that hit just at my knees, the only dancing skirt I had, and the same one I'd worn when I kicked up my heels in Los Angeles. I wore it with a fitted short-sleeve sweater with three buttons down the front. I pinned my hair, prettied up my face, and answered the door. He was all dressed up again; I almost wished I'd told him not to slick his hair back like that.

He took me to dinner first at Don Manchester's Brazil, halfway down the hill from Victor Hugo's. A sign on the door read MEXICAN FOOD, STEAKS, SEAFOOD, AND AN OUTDOOR OYSTER BAR.

"Have you ever tried oysters?" Edgar asked, taking my arm and leading me to a patio that overlooked the ocean.

"No, I have not," I said, a little repulsed by the idea.

"Well, tonight's the night!"

He ordered half a dozen oysters and a Moscow mule for each of us that arrived in a copper cup.

"Cheers," I said, tapping my cup against his and shivering slightly in the ocean air.

"Maybe we should have ordered you a hot toddy."

"I'll warm up." I took a sip. "Edgar, you know how I told you I wanted to try to find that painting for Hanson?"

"I remember," he said.

"Do you have any idea how I would go about doing that? I thought I had a lead from Scarlett, Isabella Rose's granddaughter."

"She's a firecracker that one," he said, and his eyes lit up at the thought of her.

I could still see Scarlett stepping into his car. Had they spent time together after that evening? I quickly moved the conversation along. "Anyway, turns out she doesn't know any more about the painting's whereabouts than the rest of us. She wasn't being truthful with me. But, is there some kind of lost art retrieval agency, a museum or an association perhaps, that might be interested in helping locate it?"

He shrugged, then chuckled. "If art was stolen from a gallery or such, then the police would get involved, but I don't think that painting was ever stolen. I think Hanson has it in his possession."

"Why would you think that? He's told me specifically that he wishes he could find it."

"Are you sure? Those were his exact words?"

"Yes, I mean . . . exact words? I don't recall, but he certainly has expressed a wish to see it again. If he knew where it was, why would he want to find it?"

"I don't know," he said. "I don't think Hanson is always as forthright as you believe him to be." He took a gulp of his drink, and I did the same. "I think he's waiting for the right moment to unveil it."

"That's absurd."

"Is it? He's getting older, his health is fading. He was once one of the best-known artists in California, and certainly one of the highest paid. Now, he's producing less, newer artists are taking the spotlight, he's falling into the shadows. He doesn't like that."

"That's not the impression I get from him," I said, but I wondered if there could be any truth to that.

"You haven't known him as long as I have. He has that painting hidden away somewhere."

I shook my head but considered that for a moment. "He does have that room at the top of the stairs, kind of hidden away," I said, almost to myself. "I once—" But looking up and seeing Edgar's eyes on me, I felt abashed at my indiscretion and worried he'd know I'd been snooping. "I only peeked inside once, when I first started working for him—just some paintings, portraits, nudes."

"Really." He leaned in closer, his interest piqued.

"I mean, I'm sure every artist as prolific as Hanson has a room where they keep some of their older work." I had to learn to keep my mouth shut. "I'm sure you do too."

"Of course, my garage is stacked full of canvases, early paintings mostly, plenty I should paint over."

"These were sketches mostly, not much to look at." I tried to backpedal.

Edgar sat back, and the waitress brought a silver platter with six oysters sitting on ice chips. He clasped his hands together. "Spectacular!"

All I could see were slimy-looking globs in a half shell that I couldn't imagine actually putting into my mouth.

"Don't chew it, just tilt your head back, let it slide off the shell, into your mouth, and down your throat, like this." He demonstrated and finished with an "Ahhhh. Tastes just like the ocean."

I picked one up. I wanted to believe that I could be more adventurous than the scared, inexperienced girl from Kansas I used to be. I wanted to taste the ocean, I loved the ocean. I threw my head back, slid the mucus-like sea creature into my mouth, and, as it touched the back of my throat, I gagged. It sat in my mouth, the soft, slippery form getting warm on my tongue.

"Swallow it," Edgar said, laughing. "Just swallow it, it's a delicacy."

Somehow, I managed to do as he said, and I quickly washed it down with the remains of my Moscow mule.

"Edgar!" I said. "That did not taste like the ocean."

"Come on," he said. "Live a little, try another. You just have to get used to the brininess of it."

I shook my head. "You can have the rest, I'll stick with my cocktail."

Afterward, we ate Mexican food. I was even able to pronounce a few of the menu items correctly, thanks to my dinner at La Golondrina with Scarlett. I ordered quesadillas, guacamole, and tortillas, making the "ya" sound instead of "la," which made me feel very worldly. Later we went to the bowling alley, but the band wasn't going on until at least ten, and Edgar seemed eager to dance.

"There might be music playing at the hotel."

"No," I said, a little too fast. It was nearing nine thirty, Jimmy's shift would be over soon, and he'd said that Jeanene would be in town at the end of the week. We hadn't spoken again since our conversation at Hanson's house, but I wanted to avoid that run-in for as long as possible. "I've been there so many times already," I said. "Why don't you show me someplace new?"

"Fine. Let's go to Big Jim's Broiler—they've got two bars and a dance floor, nightly music, we can jive there."

"That sounds perfect."

Sure enough, there was a band playing, and after he bought us a round of drinks, he was eager to show me his moves. It had been a while since I'd danced, but when they started in on "In the Mood," my feet started tapping, Edgar was snapping his fingers, and I was pretty sure it would all come back to me. He took the drink from my hands, set it down, and pulled me out on the dance floor. He drew me close to him for a few basic steps and then without any warning he spun me out, pulled me back in, did a fancy under-the-arm switch-back move, and a low spinning maneuver, before pulling me close to him again.

"Edgar," I said with a laugh, embarrassed by his sudden display. "I don't know that I'm ready for all that."

"Sure you are!" He spun me around six or seven times, then gave me a breather with the gentle basic one, two, backstep to get my bearings, before doing the same thing again. He was a good dancer, that was for sure, and a strong lead, which meant that even if I didn't know all the fancy footwork, he was turning me in all the right directions, so it was hard to go wrong. After a while I started to let loose and really allow him to lead. The music seemed to get louder, the saxophones and trumpets carrying the rhythm, and I began to forget about everyone else in the joint. Soon I was warm and starting to perspire, but I didn't care. Edgar seemed to be having a swell time too. As I loosened up, he got more and more creative.

"Ready for this?" he said, and without waiting for a response, he spun me around, then got down on his knees and fanned up my skirt as I turned; he then jumped up, took me into a close embrace, lunged back out, then picked me up, swung me around his torso, and threw me over his shoulder. I'd seen those moves before but had never attempted them.

Shocked and stunned, I, thankfully, landed on my feet just as the song came to an end, and Edgar was grinning from ear to ear.

"I wasn't expecting that," I said, feeling as if I'd been thrown around like a rag doll. "Let's take a break."

"You got it," he said, taking my hand and leading me off the dance floor. I was dizzy, and it took me a few minutes to get my bearings and walk in a straight line, but when I did I almost gasped. Jimmy was standing at the edge of the dance floor with a stunning redhead at his side. She was tall and slim, almost as tall as Jimmy. She had chilling blue eyes and the perfect shade of rouge painted on her full, rounded lips. I froze, then wiped the sweat from my forehead and attempted to smooth out my hair, which must have looked like a disheveled mess after that spectacle on the dance floor.

"Jimmy," I said as Edgar led us right next to them, still holding my hand.

Jimmy had a look of surprise on his face. "Wow, I didn't know you could dance like that."

"Neither did I."

"Oh, I'd like you to meet Jeanene, I've told her all about you."

I released my hand from Edgar's and extended it. "So nice to meet you," I said, but she was already hugging me.

"The pleasure is mine. All I've met here so far are Jimmy's VA friends, so I'm very glad to finally meet a woman. This is my older brother, Mike." She nodded to a young man standing next to her, who I hadn't realized was with them. "Having him as my chaperone was the only way my parents allowed me to come all this way to visit," she said. "Since we're not engaged to be married." Then she smiled and revealed a perfect set of pearly white teeth. "Not yet anyway." She wrapped her arms around Jimmy's torso and squeezed.

Jimmy and Edgar shook hands, but Jimmy couldn't seem to wipe the look of surprise off his face, and that irked me.

"What are you two doing here?" he asked.

"Same as you, I suppose," I said. "Dancing the night away." I tried to sound cheerful and easygoing, but it came out sounding sarcastic.

"Oh, I can't cut a rug like that," Jeanene said. "I'm all limbs, they get in the way."

I looked down at her long legs—they seemed to go on for miles.

"Another round?" Edgar was asking Jimmy and Jeanene too, but I couldn't bear to stand there and talk with them another minute.

"Sure," I said, linking my arm in Edgar's. "I'll come with you." I shoved him a little to get him moving toward the bar.

"Wait." Jeanene stopped me. "Jimmy said you offered to take me shopping tomorrow when he's working the lunch shift."

"Oh, right," I said, glancing up at Jimmy. He pinched his lips together into a straight line. If I refused now, it would look as if I was jealous or bitter or something that I didn't want to be. "Sure thing," I said. "I'll meet you at the hotel around eleven."

I don't even know what Edgar ordered next, but I knocked it back as fast as I could and he ordered another.

"You were thirsty," Edgar said.

"Must have been that oyster. Hey, let's finish these and get back out on the dance floor," I said, placing my hand on his shoulder, hoping Jimmy could see me flirting. "You didn't tell me you were such a cloud walker."

"You didn't tell me you were this much fun!"

Maybe it was the cocktails or the fact that Jimmy was standing there watching with that gorgeous girl by his side, or maybe it was both, but I let Edgar throw me around that dance floor any which way he pleased. We spun, flipped, and swung around, and we just about bent over backward at one point. I glanced over in Jimmy's direction a couple of times and made sure to show him I was having a grand old time. We stayed for four, five, maybe even six songs and finally, when I looked their way again, they were gone. I slowed my pace to be sure they weren't anywhere to be seen.

"Let's take a little breather, should we?" I asked, pulling him to one of the stools on the side. Edgar got real close to me and slipped his arms around my neck, but when I sat down, I felt dizzy. I expected my head to stop spinning, but it didn't. My skin was damp after all that dancing, and while I had been burning up just moments earlier, a chill suddenly came over me.

"Oh, gosh," I said, standing up.

"Are you all right, Hazel? You've gone awfully white," Edgar said.

"No, not really. I feel a little funny." I tried to take a few steps toward the door and Edgar followed behind me. "Oh no," I said, putting a hand to my mouth. "I think I'm going to be sick."

I staggered outside just in time to vomit all over my white dancing skirt.

Horrified and embarrassed, I asked Edgar to take me home immediately. I took off my clothes and dumped them in the bathtub, crawled into bed, pulled the covers up to my chin, and fell fast asleep.

CHAPTER 30

I HADN'T PUT UP ANY CURTAINS IN MY BEDROOM—I LIKED THE SUN to stream in and rouse me gently for my early morning swim. But after that awful night with Edgar, I deeply regretted that decision. My head felt as if it were splitting open. A bitter, sour taste was in my mouth, and when I sat up to drink some water, a wave of nausea rippled through me.

"Oh God," I groaned, slumping back down into my pillow. I lay there for a few more hours, unable to sleep or wake, and finally I got up to check the time. It was only nine, and I was expected at the hotel to meet Jeanene in two hours. Not sure what else I could do to cure my headache, I forced myself out of the house, walked down to the beach, and dove into the ocean.

It helped. Momentarily, at least. The shock of cold made me forget about my pounding head and churning stomach, it made me forget about making a fool of myself, dancing like a madwoman with Edgar, just so that Jimmy could see, and what? Be jealous? While he had an almost six-foot-tall stunner at his side? I hoped it would make me forget how I'd thrown myself at Edgar in an effort to show Jimmy I wasn't interested in him. I tried to forget how this was the same childish behavior that had got me involved with Bobby Watson. My God, it had been four years, and I hadn't learned a thing.

I dove under a wave and then another. I crossed my legs and curled myself into a ball, letting myself sink to the bottom, feeling the jolt of another wave crashing over me. I was far enough below the breaking wave for it to toss me around a little, but gently—a tumble, not a fall. One more, I thought, I can hold my breath for one more. I waited, but it didn't come, and I couldn't hold my breath any longer. I uncurled my legs and pushed myself up to the surface, but as I did, the wave I'd been waiting for crashed down on me, just as I was gasping for air. It swirled me around and tossed me sideways; my face scraped against the ocean floor. When I managed to get my feet to the ground and my head above water, I gasped for air and realized that the bottom of my swimsuit had been ripped off my body. I looked about in the water, frantically groping under the surface, but there was nothing. I dove back in, searching for it, but it was gone.

The sun was out, and the beach was getting crowded with families and young couples setting up their blankets for a day of summer sunshine. It must have been past ten o'clock now, and on a Saturday no less. My head throbbed, and the side of my face stung badly. I wanted to cry, but what good would that do? Salty tears in a vast and salty ocean. No one would notice, no one would care. All anyone was going to see was my humiliation as I emerged from the waves half-naked.

I made my way toward the shore, one hand over the front of me and one hand over my rear. I kept my legs bent for as long as I could, trying to keep hidden by the water, but soon I had to make a run for it. People stared; a kid laughed and said, "Mommy, look!" I kept my head down and ran for my towel, wrapped it around myself, and kept on running up to my house. Once inside, I slammed the door closed and locked it.

I ran a bath, looked in the mirror, and saw a wide red scrape that ran down the right side of my face from the bottom of my eye all the way to my lip and across the tip of my nose. It was not an attractive graze; it wasn't symmetrical and couldn't be mistaken for a shadow or a contour in my cheek. It was two inches wide, hideous, and gritted with sand. I just wanted to stay home until this scrape and the humiliation healed over, but that was simply not possible.

"HAZEL," JEANENE SAID, WAVING AT ME AS I WALKED INTO THE lobby of the hotel, my oversized white-rimmed sunglasses covering half my face. "What happened to you? Did you fall on your face on that dance floor? He sure was spinning you faster than a top."

I shook my head and pretended to laugh. "A little accident at the beach this morning, that's all."

"It looks painful. Does it hurt?" She reached out to touch it, and I swatted her hand away.

"Yes, it hurts!"

She dropped her hands down by her sides but got her face really close to mine to inspect it further. "I'd offer to cover it up with some Max Factor Pan-Cake, I'm good at that kind of thing, but I think you've got to let it heal first," she said. "It looks kind of oozy."

"I'm aware," I said, taking a Kleenex out of my pocket and dabbing it.

"Maybe if we give you some lips it will be a distraction?" she offered, but I shook my head. She turned her pretty, hunter's bow smile downward into a frown that didn't suit her. "Poor you," she said.

"I'll survive."

We walked out of the hotel toward Forest Avenue. Eiler Larsen waved at us enthusiastically as he always did, looking particularly energized. "Good morning," he bellowed. Jeanene jumped and grabbed hold of my arm.

"Good morning," I called back. "How are you today?"

"Excellent," he boomed.

"Let's cross over before he comes any closer," said Jeanene, pulling me toward the street.

"That's just Eiler. He greets people, it's what he does, waves at all the pedestrians and motorists coming into Laguna. He's harmless."

"Doesn't look harmless."

He pointed his cane right at Jeanene and stared at her. "Smile, young lady, you look wonderful when you smile."

She hurried us across the street.

I took her to Scouller's, a clothing store that I had a feeling might be her cup of tea, even though I really knew nothing about her, and I'd never been into the store myself. A sign in the window read LAGUNA'S STYLE HEADQUARTERS FOR DISCRIMINATING WOMEN.

We walked around the store rather aimlessly; she picked up the sleeve of a blouse, then dropped it, doing the same to a jacket, touching the buttons of a dress.

"Where's your brother?" I asked, thinking this might be less painful with someone else tagging along.

"He went fishing."

"You didn't want to go with him?"

Jeanene looked at me and scrunched up her face. "Surely you're joking!"

I shrugged.

"How long have you lived here?" she asked.

"A little over six months," I said.

"Wow, that seems like a long time to spend in a town like this."

"Six months isn't a long time, I'm just getting settled."

"You're staying here? Like for good?" She looked startled.

"As long as they'll have me, I suppose."

She walked toward the door, and the bell rang as we left. "Don't you get bored in this tiny town? I mean, what do you do all day long?"

"I work for an artist, and when I'm not doing that, I volunteer for an art show that's happening this summer."

I walked her along South Coast Boulevard past Mary Maxwell's House—famous for its caramel pecan pie, though I imagined Jeanene had never eaten a bite of pecan pie in her life. We passed Peck's Barbershop, the Sandwich Mill, the Seaside Gallery, one of the pottery shops. I walked slowly, thinking she'd look around and let me know if she wanted to go inside any of these places, but she didn't even look in the windows.

"It's quaint, but I would go crazy if I lived here. I'm going to live in a big city. New York City, to be precise."

"Really?" Did she not know about Jimmy's dream to open a restaurant on the beach?

"Yes, I live in Queens now with my parents and two sisters, just outside Manhattan. I've lived there all my life, but I've always known I wanted to move to the big city. I'm going to be a makeup artist to the stars. I'm going to learn to cut hair too, so I can do it all."

"Does Jimmy know?" I asked as we turned up Forest Avenue and continued on past the hardware store, Lee's Café, and the studio shops that showcased local art.

"Sure, he does. And I might open my own beauty salon one day, just like that." She pointed to the Aloha Beauty Salon across the street. "But bigger and more glamorous and in the heart of NYC," she said proudly.

"That'd be something." I had to admire the way she knew exactly what she wanted to do. I stopped walking for a minute, since she didn't really seem to have much interest in looking in any of the stores I was taking her to. "Is there something you want to see in particular?" I asked. I was exhausted, my head was still pounding, and I didn't feel like parading her around town if she didn't even want to be there. "The Patio Shops are up that way, gifts and such . . ."

"Jimmy told me I had to buy myself a bathing suit since he has plans to take me to the beach while I'm here, but I have to be honest, there is no way he's going to get me in that ocean. I really don't like the way that sand feels on my feet, and who even knows what lurks under that dark surface. No thank you, it is not for me."

She seemed unenchanted by everything our little town had to offer, she had no interest in living here, and either Jimmy knew that or they hadn't discussed it at all. But I had no desire to get involved in any miscommunication. "Well, if Jimmy says you need a swimsuit, you should go to Miss Debutante."

I took her back down Forest toward the bathing suit store where I'd bought my two-piece, and Jeanene talked the whole time. She would make the perfect hairdresser with that kind of chatter.

"I mean, don't get me wrong, I understand why Jimmy didn't want to go back home after he got discharged. His father isn't the nicest man in town."

"How so?"

"He used to kick Jimmy around, and his little brother, too," she said in a whisper. "Everyone knew about it. I've never seen a young man sign up for the marines so fast as how Jimmy did. He was out of that house quicker than you can say 'dixie.'"

"I had no idea." I felt sick thinking of Jimmy—tall, handsome, caring— being beaten by his own father. What kind of man would do such a thing?

"His dad's a real jerk, so I understand why Jimmy wants to get away from Queens, but New York City is the perfect place to start over. He'd never even have to go back home, except to see my family, but that's different. He could be a bartender at any of those big New York establishments."

"I guess."

"I just gotta work on him a little, that's all, he'll come around."

We walked into Miss Debutante's, and the saleslady didn't recognize me, as covered up and scraped as I was.

"Good afternoon, ladies," she said. "What can I help you find?"

"I'm lookin' for a swimsuit, a pretty one, one for lounging, not actually swimming."

"With a figure like yours, slim, long legs, and a long torso, you simply must try one of our new two-piece swimsuit styles. They are absolutely à la mode."

I felt as if I were having déjà vu. She had said almost the exact same thing to me. I glanced at myself in the hanging mirror and lifted my glasses to check on my wound. It was red and raw. I looked from myself to Jeanene and felt like an ogre—my face disfigured, my skin gray from the previous night, my height like that of an elf next to her.

"How about this one," the shop lady said, holding up the exact same swimsuit that I'd bought. "It's very popular."

"No," I said abruptly. "Not that one." Jeanene looked at me, surprised. "You need more color to complement your skin tone." I looked around and grabbed the first one I saw, a plain blue one-piece with thick straps and a skirt. "This one. No one's wearing the two-pieces around here, they're considered a bit gauche."

The shop lady reared her head and huffed at me.

"Blue's not really my color," said Jeanene.

"It will look great on you." I couldn't stand the thought of her prancing around the beach, my beach, in my bathing suit, a bathing suit that I now owned only half of. Lounging around in it next to Jimmy, looking gorgeous. I just couldn't bear it. "Also, I heard that the bottoms of those two-pieces can fall right off," I added, desperate to deter her from buying it but unwilling to share my humiliation of that morning.

"Weren't you in here a few months back?" the lady asked.

"Me?" I hesitated. "I don't think so." I put my sunglasses back on.

"Yes, I remember you, at first you liked another suit, but this one with these flowers up the side, this very one stole your heart." She held up the one I'd just told Jeanene not to buy. "And then you came back after you'd been paid." The lady seemed proud of herself for remembering the whole thing in such great detail. "You were working for the artist, Mr. Radcliff if I'm not mistaken. And you'd been waiting for your first paycheck."

"Maybe," I said. "I don't recall." The scrape on my face started pulsating, as if all the blood rushing to my cheeks in humiliation had decided to gather in my wound instead.

"This one?" Jeanene asked, pointing to the bathing suit in the lady's hands. "You bought this one?"

"I um, I don't really remember, it was a while ago."

"But you'd remember if you have the suit or not, surely."

I shrugged; I didn't know what else to say.

"You just didn't want me to have it." She looked hurt. "Why? What do you care? I'm going back home next week, what does it matter to you?"

I looked at her, speechless. I didn't want her to go back to Jimmy and tell him I'd been petty and unhelpful. "I just, it might look a bit silly if we both wear the same swimsuit," I said. It was absurd, I was absurd. I didn't even have the bottom half of the suit anymore. I *was* petty and unhelpful.

"So you want me to get that one?" She looked at the blue one in disgust. On second glance it was definitely more suited for an older lady, much older. "You know, I thought it was a bit funny Jimmy being so friendly with a girl, but now I see it. You're jealous of me, you don't want me wearing this suit and wearing it better than you."

"No," I said, horrified that things had gone so wrong. And that she had me pegged just right. "No, that's not it at all."

"You know what?" she said to the shop lady. "I will take the two-piece."

The lady carefully wrapped the bathing suit in tissue paper, laying it gently in a box. Next, she wrapped it all in an elaborate red bow. The whole thing seemed to unfold in slow motion. What could I do, what could I say to turn this around so Jeanene wouldn't go back to Jimmy and tell him I'd been so terrible?

Before I could think of a thing to say, Jeanene turned to me.

"Thanks for showing me around," she said tightly. "But I can find my own way back from here."

꩜

THE NEXT MORNING, I DRESSED, DABBED MAKEUP AROUND MY SCRAPE, but not on it, as Jeanene had suggested. I slipped on a long yellow summer dress, my big sunglasses, and a sun hat. From a distance I didn't look too bad. I walked up to Glenneyre Street and toward Edgar's studio, feeling the warmth of the sun on my shoulders. The first thing I needed to do, and maybe the easiest thing, was to apologize to him for ruining his Friday night. I'd tell him it was the oyster that did it—that, and the spinning on the dance floor. I wouldn't mention the fact that I knocked back far too many cocktails way too quickly. I walked around the back of the house to his studio and saw just the top of his head through the window. He appeared to be standing at his easel, painting. I didn't want to startle him with a loud knock, so I opened the door quietly and peeked inside. He was painting, as I'd thought, but he was talking to someone too, and when I looked across the room to see who it was, I gasped out loud. It was Scarlett Rose lying sprawled on a mattress completely naked.

In my haste I accidentally knocked over a tripod standing by the door, surprising everyone.

"I'm so sorry, terribly sorry," I sputtered. "But Scarlett. Edgar. What on earth are you doing?" I quickly walked over to Scarlett, picked up some clothing that was strewn on the floor, and flung it on top of her. "Are you all right?"

Edgar approached me, paintbrush in hand. "What are you doing here? And why in heaven's name did you make such a clatter? Can't you see I'm in session?"

"In session?"

"Yes, in session."

"What kind of session?"

"A portrait session! My God, what happened to your face?"

"None of your business."

"Goodness, Hazel, you of all people shouldn't be so flabbergasted to see a model sitting for a portrait. It's not as if you haven't taken your clothes off before."

I looked to Scarlett, horrified. Why would he be painting her?

"Join me," Scarlett chirped, rolling onto her back and kicking her legs up in the air, her ample breasts splaying about her before she scooped them up and held them in place on her chest. She let her head fall off the end of the mattress, her blond hair cascading onto the floor. "I'm

Edgar's pinup girl," she said in a seductive tone. "You should see his work, he's a master with the brush." She winked at him, and I was sure now that they'd slept together.

I was furious. Edgar had taken me on a date just days earlier, and here was Scarlett, lying naked in his studio and having a grand old time. I wasn't jealous, I wasn't even attracted to Edgar if I was truthful with myself, but I couldn't help but feel betrayed by everyone I had come to know in this town, everyone except Hanson.

"I'll leave you to it," I said, walking to the door. "I didn't realize you two were so intimately acquainted. But I can see now, you're perfect for each other!"

I walked back home dumbfounded. Edgar and Scarlett? Two selfish peas in a pod. I thought I'd been making friends, starting to become part of this community, but all of a sudden it seemed that the only person I could really trust was Hanson, and his health seemed to be getting worse by the day. He wouldn't let me call the doctor, and he wouldn't do anything to help himself. Without him, I would be lost here. I couldn't think about that. Everything seemed to be going wrong, but the one thing I could try to focus on was his painting. If I could just get that painting for Hanson, at least I'd be doing one thing right.

I'd have to work fast. I didn't know how much time we had left.

CHAPTER 31

THAT EVENING I SHOWED UP TO THE PAGEANT MEETING DUTIFULLY but reluctantly. While Lillian joined the artists, painting more of the backgrounds of the featured paintings, and a group of men built the scaffolding and sets that would allow the figures in the artwork to climb into place and be held in position, I headed straight back to the costume closet and helped Mrs. Moynahan iron and sew the fabric together. She was using the remaining part of Scarlett's velvet bedspread for the skirt of the woman in a painting called *Charity*, by William-Adolphe Bouguereau. Mrs. Moynahan had dyed the fabric using beet juice to turn it a deeper shade of burgundy and accurately depict the skirt. In the painting, a young woman was sitting on a marble step caring for and protecting five young children. The young woman's bare breasts were covered by a sleeping child in her left arm, and on her right two others—one who might have been nursing as a third child climbed at her side. Two more toddlers rested by her feet. The description under the picture in Mrs. Moynahan's book said she was giving them nurturing, sustenance, and knowledge.

At the end of the evening, when I was very ready to go home, climb into bed, and sleep like a log, a bell rang, and Mrs. Moynahan set down her work.

"Emergency meeting," she said. "Mr. Fredericks must have something he needs to say."

I followed her out to the meeting area. So much for avoiding people tonight, I thought, as I stood in the back, trying not to draw attention.

"Good evening, all," Mr. Fredericks said, and the chatter died down. "It's late. I need everyone to listen up!" he said. "As you know, opening night is just a month away, and things are going quite well, thanks to your long hours of patient work." He paused. "It takes tireless effort to produce this magnificent spectacle, so, to those of you whose labors allow our friends, neighbors, and visitors to witness the return of another inspiring Pageant of the Masters—well done."

Everyone clapped, but he started speaking again before the applause died down as if he had a lot to get to. "We've received a generous donation from a local artist who wishes to remain unnamed, and it will go a long way in helping to get this show back to the high-quality production we're accustomed to."

I wondered if the donation was from Hanson, and if so, why he wouldn't want to be acknowledged.

"But, we have a few casting issues, and I think we can all agree that last-minute changes can be troublesome, so I'll need some help here." He frowned and looked at his watch—perhaps he knew we all wanted to go home. "Some of you may have heard the wonderful news, that our very own house lawyer and pageant treasurer, John Solomon, is going to be a grandfather. His daughter Caroline is expecting her first child. Congratulations, John. But that means she cannot be cast in her role as the, the young woman, front and center, in Abbott Thayer's painting." He looked down as if he really didn't want to say the rest. "*A Virgin.*"

Several people laughed.

"Ain't that the truth," someone called out.

Mr. Fredericks's face grew red with indignation. "That's enough, quiet down! Caroline has expressed a wish to remain in the pageant, and she will appear as the young peasant woman in *Song of the Lark,* by Jules Breton." He turned to the volunteers. "Mrs. Moynahan, please fit her for that blue apron"—his hands circled the air around his own portly belly—"full over the stomach."

Mrs. Moynahan nodded.

"Any more jokers out there?" He seemed to dare the group.

No one spoke.

"That's more like it. Now, we need a new Virgin!"

The volunteers erupted, until Mr. Fredericks banged on the music stand in front of him.

"I bet Hazel would do it," a man's voice called out from the front of the group. I recognized it immediately as Edgar's—no doubt to make me pay for walking in on him and Scarlett and speaking so harshly. "Hazel Francis, Mr. Radcliff's assistant, she'd be a perfect Virgin."

People started to murmur and look around, while I shut my eyes and tried to recover from what I knew was an insult. When I looked up, almost all eyes fell on me. With all the whispering, I immediately remembered the scrape on my face. At least it was good for something.

"I can't," I blurted out, suddenly thrilled about my hideous excuse not to get involved. "I'm so sorry, I would have loved to, but I had a bit of a fall this weekend and scratched up my face."

"Oh, what a shame," Mr. Fredericks said. "But that will be gone in a few days, a week at most, surely."

"Yes, yes," people muttered. "Be healed up in no time," and, "Put a bit of salve on it, that's all."

"All in favor, then?" Mr. Fredericks asked, and everyone, after getting a good look at me, much to my humiliation, said, "Aye."

"One final hiccup, and then we can all go home," Mr. Fredericks went on. "Bob MacPherson's son, who's been our Greek figure in various forms and statues in past years, told me he's put on a little weight after returning home from serving our country, he said he's been rather enjoying his mother's cooking, God bless." He looked around in challenge, but the group was quiet this time.

"He will appear instead as the monk in *The Cardinal's Portrait*. Mrs. Moynahan says the robe can be quite forgiving. So, we're looking for an athletic fellow for *The Discus Thrower*, by Myron."

Everyone talked amongst themselves.

"Mr. Robbins's makeup team can accentuate the muscular detail, but we do need to have a good starting point."

"What about that dishy young fellow who works behind the bar at the hotel?" called a blowsy older woman—Doreen. "He's a handsome devil. I'll bet he's got the goods underneath. Every time Alfie and I sit at the bar for a cocktail I can't take my eyes off him."

I immediately felt myself blush, as if everyone in attendance could somehow read my innermost feelings, but of course no one could have known any of that, or how I'd humiliated myself in the last twenty-four hours.

"Would you mind asking him, Doreen?" Mr. Fredericks said. "Next time you and Alfie are there?"

A sudden pang of urgency hit me—I should ask him, I knew him far better than this Doreen lady, and it would give me an excuse to try to smooth things over. But maybe it was too late for that after the disastrous shopping trip with Jeanene; maybe it would be better to just stay out of Jimmy's way for a while. Besides, Doreen was already jumping at the chance.

"It would be my absolute pleasure," she said, breathlessly.

I had to wonder if he'd actually say yes.

CHAPTER 32

WE LEFT EARLY ON MONDAY MORNING—WELL, AT NINE, WHICH WAS early by Hanson's standards—and we took it easy walking down his street, turning onto Victoria Drive, and descending the stairs that led to Victoria Beach. Hanson commented on my face, understandably, since it actually looked worse by now, starting to dry up and scab slightly, turning a reddish-brown color.

"You didn't have to go and get a gash on your face to make me feel better about mine," he'd said when I arrived. "Though it does, a little."

He wasn't wearing the bandage anymore. His wound was healing nicely, although I wondered if it would leave a scar.

"I had a run-in with a wave that was bigger than me," I said.

He nodded. "I've told you about that ocean, she can be a real beast when she wants to be. We won't be profiling the right side of your face for a couple of weeks. Having said that, it would make for an interesting study."

"Don't say that, it's hideous!"

"The colors are actually quite complex," he said, but I turned my face away from him to stop him from examining it any further.

I carried the small easel and his paint box, and he insisted on carrying the canvas, his leather knapsack, and a parasol. At the bottom of the stairs, we turned right, and when I saw the tower jutting out from the rocky cliff and shooting straight up into a cloudless blue sky on an otherwise secluded beach, I felt quite overcome with emotion. It was magical, like something out of a fairy tale.

The tower and the steep cliff wall were the exact same color, and while they stood apart by a few feet at the bottom, they connected on the way up, and it really did look as if they were part of each other, as if the tower belonged to the natural coastline. At the top, by the peak, a gnarled and twisted tree hung off the bluff as if daring fate, and near the tower's base was the low circular wall Hanson had told me about—a large pool capturing ocean water at high tide and forming a shallow swimming haven, protected from the waves.

Hanson was wheezing as he found a rock to sit on some distance from the tower, then set up his easel.

"Can people get inside and climb that staircase?" I asked, trying to take his mind off the difficulty he was having catching his breath.

"You'd have to ask the new owner of the house. The senator who had it built moved away; the new owner calls this his pirate tower. He dresses up when kids come around and hides coins between the rocks at the base, tells them it's treasure. He's a character."

"Seems like there're a few of those in this town."

"Keeps it interesting." He adjusted the easel to fit the canvas, pulling out the wooden legs to the right height. "So," he said, taking out his glass jars of linseed oil and turpentine and balancing them on the flat part of a neighboring rock. "What do you want to do next?"

"You mean after this?" I asked, surprised. He was usually the one to make our plans for the day, and I expected him to be quite tired after he'd painted for a few hours.

He took his time before he responded, opening up his paint box, taking out a pencil, looking out to the view ahead of him, squinting to see where he would start.

"You're quite capable as my assistant, but I'm not going to be around forever. So, what do you want to do next, with your life?"

I laughed nervously. "I'm doing what I want to do."

"Do you want to get married? Do you want to be a mother?" He looked at me. "Most young women want that, you know. Do you want to keep on working?"

"I love to work." I answered quickly, as if I were suddenly back in his studio being interviewed.

"This is not about me, this is about you. I'm asking what you want for yourself." He held my gaze, forcing me to think about this, to respond.

Yes, I wanted to fall in love. Yes, I wanted a family, children, but I didn't know if that was in my cards. I'd had my chance and thrown that away with disastrous consequences. How would I know real love from lust, desire from curiosity, friendship from romance? How would I not ruin it, and hurt someone in the process?

"I'd like to get married someday," I said. "But I also love to work, and if I could have had my way, I would have kept on working in that airplane factory."

"Really?" he said, not convinced.

"Why does that surprise you?"

"I just don't see the appeal of putting those big old machines up in the air where they don't belong."

"It wasn't the airplanes, necessarily," I said. "I thought it was . . . I thought maybe I wanted to become an engineer or even a pilot, but I realize now that it was being part of something, a community, feeling I was doing some good in the world, however small and menial it might have been at times. There were risks and responsibilities; I had to do it to the best of my ability, and I did. And then it was gone—the teamwork, the friendships, the mission, it was all over so abruptly." I thought about the events of the weekend that had just passed. I'd been building a community here, and it too felt as if it were slipping through my fingers.

He began to sketch out the tower on the right side of his canvas, the cliff reaching out to meet it at the top. "I have some regrets in my life," he said. "I walked away from Isabella because I was too pigheaded to stay and prove to her that she mattered, had something to live for. I was too young and stupid to guess what the painting meant to her. I could have stayed, helped her see her own true beauty, her own worth. Her mind was confused, warped sometimes, from all the things she heard on those movie sets, constantly comparing herself to others, the new crop of young girls coming through the studios. She started taking those pills and wasn't thinking straight. She thought she was washed up. But she wasn't. She had a lot of life left in her that didn't have to do with looks either. She might have found peace within herself if I hadn't just up and left her when she threatened my art."

"You can't keep blaming yourself for this," I said.

"And then, years later, I let my wife walk away because I was too proud, and often too drunk, to go after her and beg her to stay. I would have liked to have some children. I probably wouldn't have been a very good father, so maybe it's for the best."

"That's not true, Hanson," I said. I actually thought he would have been a good father if he'd had the chance.

"I don't want you to live your life full of regrets."

I wanted to tell him I already had my fair share of regrets, that I too felt responsible for another person's death, that my selfishness had broken Bobby's heart at his most vulnerable time, a time when he was seeing atrocities I could only begin to imagine. But instead, something else came pouring out.

"I don't remember my father," I said. "Life before he died seems like a made-up fairy tale that my mother told me to help me fall asleep at night. I only remember him as a photograph, a single faded photograph we had in a frame in my mother's room. I'm scared that one day I won't remember my mother either, that she'll become a distant memory too." I was scared about Hanson dying, but I couldn't say that. I hadn't known him long, but he gave purpose to my life. I looked forward to our days together. Without him I'd be lost and alone all over again. Out of nowhere, I began to cry.

"Come, child, come here." Hanson lifted himself off the rock and pulled me to my feet. He put his arms around me and held me. I felt his bones through his shirt, his spine down his back, and I realized for the first time just how frail he really was. The tears kept coming, fiercely now.

"I didn't really have anyone to show me how things should be," I said, muffled, into his shoulder. "And I went and made a mess of things."

"There, there," he said, and I just sobbed harder. It was as if I had been saving up all my tears for this very moment: tears for my father, tears for my mother, tears for Bobby Watson, tears for Hanson, maybe even tears for Jimmy. All of it flowed out of me.

"I'm sorry," I said, but he just held me, patting my back until at last the sobbing subsided. "I don't know where that all came from."

"No need for apologies," he said. "Sometimes it gets to be too much, this life we live, and you've just got to let yourself go."

$\sim\!\!\!\!\lambda$

A FEW HOURS LATER, WHEN HANSON HAD DONE AS MUCH PAINTING as he could manage that day, I helped him pack up his things.

"If you're so fond of those airplanes, you should visit the airfield," he said, loading his knapsack as we prepared to leave the beach.

"What airfield?"

"On the bluffs, a little farther north, not too far from here." He pointed in that direction. "Pancho Barnes was what she called herself. A wealthy young bird—tough and fearless—dressed more like a man than a woman, looked like one too actually." He stared off into the distance as if he were picturing her. "She worked as a stunt pilot in Hollywood at some point, if my memory doesn't fail me, and a test pilot for Lockheed, I believe."

"She sounds fascinating," I said, though I wondered what he was getting at. I closed up his easel and tucked it under my arm.

"She had a big old party house here in Laguna and built an airstrip all her own, just for her and her pilot friends to fly into. Went broke, sold her house, and moved to the Mojave Desert. The whole airstrip is abandoned now. Still, thought you might be interested."

"I had no idea Laguna Beach had its own airstrip!"

"Used to," he said. "Maybe I'll take you sometime."

We walked toward the steps and a thought came to me. "What if we did a sitting at that airstrip?"

He looked at me, surprised. "It's all overgrown now," he said, beginning to mull it over, "but might make for an unusual background."

"What if," I said, suddenly excited by the idea, "you painted me in my overalls, boots, and headscarf—the gear I wore at the factory?" I smiled.

"That would be something," he said. "It would look good with your scar too." He laughed. "Tough girl just like Pancho."

"It's not a scar, it's a scrape," I said, putting my hand to my cheek. "It'll be gone in a few days."

"We'd better be quick then." He grinned.

"I can picture it now," I said, clasping my hands together. "They used to hang posters all around the locker rooms and lunchrooms at the factory, encouraging us not to give up, telling us to persevere, that we could do this hard manual labor. I remember one of a woman showing off her muscles, revealing just how strong she was." I held up my arm and flexed for Hanson's amusement—it made us both laugh. "With those wild, bold colors that you use, and your quick brushstrokes—I can see it all in my mind. It would be thrilling."

Hanson laughed. "You know, I think I can see it too. Go on then, make a plan, you'll be in charge that day."

I smiled as we walked toward the staircase, envisioning what he would create, thinking it was exactly how I'd want to be captured—confident, comfortable in my own skin, and content right here in a place I never would have expected to end up.

Hanson put his hands on his knees and took a deep breath, which set him off coughing again. He stood for a moment at the bottom of the stairs and looked up. He seemed to know it would take a herculean effort to climb them.

"Maybe we should sit for a minute." I gestured toward a bench at the bottom of the stairs, hoping he'd take a rest, but he waved his hand and started climbing, stopping every few steps to cough—hacking and holding on to his rib cage.

"I'm fine, I'm fine," he kept saying, swatting me away, as I tried to take his knapsack from him.

We'd just made all those lovely plans, and it made me so happy to think of them, but I made a silent vow to deter him from excursions like this in the future. This was too much for him; he needed to slow down. It was good enough that the two of us had imagined what we could have done.

By the time we reached his house, I could tell he was ready to lie down. We turned in to his driveway, and I saw that his front door was wide open. No one ever used the front door.

"Did you leave that door open this morning?" I asked.

"No. Why would I?"

"Wait here," I said, noticing he was wheezing again from the last steep walk up Victoria Drive. "I'll go inside and check."

I walked through the front door and looked around. "Hello?" I looked

in the kitchen, in the living room, in the dining room. "Anyone there?"
Hanson had followed me in. "Why don't you sit for a minute, Hanson."
But he ignored me. "Nothing looks out of place," I said. "Maybe the
wind blew it open."

"What wind?" Hanson said.

It was a perfectly still, warm, sunny day.

"Hello, is anyone there?" I said more sternly this time as I checked
in the bedroom, the bathroom, down the hall. And then I saw the door
at the top of those little stairs, violently broken open. The wood on the
doorframe was damaged and split, as if someone had taken a crowbar
to it—someone who didn't know firsthand that all it needed was a good
shove to get unjammed.

"Oh my God, Hanson, I think you've been robbed."

"Jesus," he said, panting, pushing past me to get up the stairs.

"This is terrible," I said, though all I could think was that I'd told Edgar about the little room at the top of the stairs at our dinner on Friday
night. It was too much of a coincidence not to be connected.

Hanson started going through the stacks and stacks of canvases that
lined the room. He opened the drawers of the desk. He looked around
the walls. It was a small room, no more than ten feet by twelve, almost
every square inch of it covered with a sketch or a painting. Nothing looked
broken or out of place, at least to my eye.

"Is anything missing?"

"Hell if I know." He coughed again, then put his hands on his knees.
"I need to sit down."

I pulled out the wooden chair from behind the desk.

"Not here," he said. "In my room."

I helped him down the narrow staircase, walking ahead of him, worried he'd fall or faint. I felt shocked, stunned that someone could have
broken in and been looking around, helping themselves, when this was
Hanson's house, his personal belongings, and he was already weak. It
must have been an even greater and more unwelcome shock to him. As
we walked down the hallway, he put his arm around my shoulder, and I
led him to his room. He sat down on his bed, pale and quiet.

"Water, please, Hazel," he whispered.

I rushed back with a glass, and as he brought his hand up, it was shaking. I put the glass to his lips, and he rested his hand on it; the full weight of the glass seemed too much for him to hold.

"I'm going to lie down now," he said, weakly.

"Yes." I helped him take off his shoes, and I moved the pillow closer to him as he laid his head down. I pulled the blanket over him and stood for a minute.

"Anything I can get for you? Anything I should do?" But Hanson had already closed his eyes and his breath had slowed. He needed to rest.

***

I STOOD IN THE KITCHEN, MY MIND RACING. HAD EDGAR BROKEN into Hanson's house to look for the missing painting? Had he found it? Had he taken it? He'd made reference to the fact that it would be valuable, very valuable. It was possible that he would hold on to it and sell it later. He'd also claimed Hanson might reveal it at some point to bring attention to himself again in the waning years of his life—a ridiculous notion. That was the last thing Hanson would want to do; he was more comfortable in the shadows. But if Edgar truly believed that, he might attempt to find it, steal it, keep it from Hanson so that Edgar wouldn't be eclipsed. They were both big names in the art world—not only in Laguna, but in all of Southern California, in the whole country, it seemed. Hearing the way they spoke of each other, they seemed more like rivals than friends.

And then there was Scarlett. She was now involved with Edgar, in one way or another, I wasn't sure quite how involved. But I had told her that if she had the painting in her possession, Hanson might be willing to paint her. She knew I didn't have it; she didn't have it. Maybe she and Edgar concocted this scheme together. The idea made me sick, the two of them scheming against an old man who could barely hold a glass to his lips, who was so shaken by intruders breaking into his private room of paintings that his body shut down, and all he could do was sleep.

Furious, I began to pace. If they had that painting, if it had been here all along as Edgar suspected, and they'd taken it from him, that was theft. I would call the police. I would get them both arrested. How would Scarlett like being written up in the paper as an accomplice to a burglary of an old man, a dying man? I should call the police right now, whether it was Edgar's doing or not—someone needed to be held accountable.

But Hanson was still asleep. I crept into his room to check on him. He was sleeping soundly. I didn't want to wake him, and I shouldn't do anything without his permission; this was his house. I sat in the kitchen feeling useless for a long while, and finally I tiptoed past his bedroom, along the hall, and up the tiny staircase, back into the tiny secret room.

Maybe the painting had been in here all along and Hanson hadn't wanted anyone to know. Maybe that's why he never told me about it. I started to look at the paintings more closely. When I'd first been in this room, I'd known nothing about the tragedy with Isabella Rose or how it had haunted Hanson for all those years. I looked at the paintings with more compassion now, trying to see the women through his eyes. They weren't vulgar or crass as I had seen some of them that first time, they were real. Most were not posed at all, just a moment captured. I kept looking, taking one out and studying it, really taking it all in, trying to feel what each woman felt in that moment. One had a feeling of happiness, exuberance as she embraced the world around her; she was relaxed, at peace. Could that be the painting? I wondered. Could that be Isabella Rose? I picked it up; it was small. I looked closely but it didn't look like her. I had seen her face in the movies, at the library, and this wasn't it.

I took out another then another, spreading them out on the floor all around me. I was so engrossed that I almost forgot Hanson was asleep in his room below. When I heard footsteps coming up the narrow staircase, it was too late to put everything away.

"What the hell are you doing?" he boomed.

"I was just looking."

"Well don't. This room is off-limits, it's not open to the public as people clearly think it is. I'm entitled to have some privacy, you know."

"Of course, I'm so sorry, I didn't mean to . . ."

"Let's call it a night," he said.

"But what about the burglary? Aren't you going to call the police?"

"What are they going to do?"

"They could help find the intruder?"

"I doubt that, and whoever broke in has probably got what they were looking for and got out of town. It's too late now."

"Hanson," I said. "I think I might know who broke in, and I might be responsible."

"What are you talking about?"

"A while ago, before I really had a chance to get to know you, I'd only just started working for you, and, well, I found this room when you were on one of your painting excursions."

He frowned.

"And then I accidentally mentioned it to Edgar last Friday night."

"Jesus." He shook his head. "Why would you do that?"

"I didn't mean to, it sort of slipped out." I cringed recalling that night. Why hadn't I kept my mouth shut? Loose lips sink ships. I knew that.

"I'm sick of this, I'm sick of all the prying. I can't take it anymore. Just get out," he bellowed, pointing to the door. "Please."

I jumped up off the floor where I'd been sitting and started collecting the paintings around me.

"Leave it, will you!" he snapped. "I've had enough. I've had enough of other people in my house, going through my things. Get out of this room and get out of my house, and don't come back."

"I'm sorry, I really am." My voice was shaking.

"I need the rest of the week to take care of some things," he said, his back to me. "Next week, if I need you, I'll let you know."

I stood for a second, not knowing what to do or say, and then I backed out of his house, stunned, and walked slowly toward town.

CHAPTER 33

FOR THE NEXT WEEK I KEPT MY HEAD DOWN. I HELPED OUT A LOT in the costume closet and avoided people as best I could. The scrape on my face dried up and had almost gone away by Sunday.

That night Mrs. Moynahan was doing a costume fitting for everyone in the show, so I arrived early to help her get organized.

"Let's get your fitting out of the way first before everyone gets here," she said eagerly. "I'm going to need your help getting the cast dressed and pinned and ready to go."

"All right," I said.

"And you're going to love what I've whipped up for you."

For *A Virgin*, I was to pose in the center, striding forward with my left leg, holding the hands of two young children, maybe six and seven years old. According to Mrs. Moynahan's art volumes, where she'd bookmarked all the paintings in that year's show, Abbott Handerson Thayer's own children had been the models for his painting. I was to stand in for the central figure, originally based on the Greek goddess of flowers, Flora—portrayed by his daughter Mary. Mrs. Moynahan said that as the painting evolved, Thayer had decided she should instead represent Nike, the Greek goddess of victory. It was a dramatic and beautiful painting, clouds rising up behind her like wings against an otherwise clear blue sky. I wasn't sure how the title became "A Virgin," but now that I'd accepted that I'd been volunteered for the part, I was actually quite pleased to portray her. She had a calm confidence about her, a certainty that I admired.

Mrs. Moynahan flipped through her rack of costumes and took out a long, mustard-yellow chiton-like dress that wrapped around me, fastened at the shoulders, and tied at the waist. It was somewhat stiff, almost as if the fabric had been glued in place.

"Joan of Arc wore it a few years back. I dug it out, adjusted it, dyed it with cabbage and yellow lentils, and here you have it," she said.

I took it from her. It did have a hint of cabbage smell to it. But when I turned it around, I saw it was only half a dress.

"There's no back to it!"

"Don't worry about that, the audience is only going to see the front of you. You'll be wearing clothes underneath."

I put my arms through the sleeves of the gown, and she pulled it tight around my waist, with strings she'd attached, like a corset.

"You're slimmer than before," she said.

I wasn't surprised. I'd hardly eaten in the past week, I was too upset about everything that had transpired and worried about Hanson's health deteriorating without me there to help.

Soon people started coming in for their fittings, and I realized just how much work went into bringing all of this artwork to life. We had a long white dress for *Lady Hamilton at the Spinning Wheel,* by George Romney, and the blue apron, brown skirt, and white blouse for a pregnant Caroline in *Song of the Lark.* Floyd and his wife came in for Grant Wood's *American Gothic*—a print apron for her, overalls and a black suit jacket for him. Our Christ needed two fittings: first for *Christ and the Rich Young Ruler* by Heinrich Hofmann, and again for *The Last Supper.* We worked our way down the complete list—twenty-one pictures, and this was just for the first program, with two more to follow.

By ten thirty, I was sure we were almost done. If anyone missed their fitting, they'd have to come back another day. But as we were packing up, we had one more knock on the closet door.

"I was told to come here tonight for a fitting, or something." I heard his familiar voice as Mrs. Moynahan opened the door. "I just finished work, so it was the earliest I could get here."

Jimmy looked nervous, but not all that surprised to see me, and he squeezed into the space between us.

"Hi there, Hazel," he said.

"You must be the bartender from the hotel," Mrs. Moynahan said. "You really didn't need to come down here, though. There's nothing much for us to fit on you, unless you want to try on your loincloth." She chuckled.

"Oh," he said, his cheeks turning pink.

"No need for that," I said, quickly trying to put everyone at ease.

"I'm only joking," Mrs. Moynahan said. "I'll have something for you in time for the show, but since it's such a small costume, I've been focusing on the more intricate ones. It's makeup who needs to meet with you more than costume. They're not here tonight, but they will be later this week, and they're going to want to see you. They're going to have to paint your whole body white, and your hair, to simulate marble."

She picked up one of her books and turned the pages until she found the right spot. "The Discus Thrower," she said, showing it to him. "He is quite the athlete."

Jimmy whistled. "I think I'm going to be a big disappointment."

"Oh, don't you worry about a thing. Anatole Robbins and his makeup team are miracle workers. They have thirty-five shades of foundation to enhance those muscles you've got under there. That and the stage lights, it's a science."

Jimmy excused himself and left, visibly taken aback at what he'd agreed to, and I packed up my things to head home. Jeanene had left almost a full week ago, but I hadn't seen Jimmy since that awful night of dancing at Big Jim's. He didn't know about Edgar or Scarlett or the break-in at Hanson's. I wondered with dread if Jeanene had told him about the bathing suit incident, or if she'd worn the two-piece to the beach, or jumped into the ocean for a dip after all. I tried not to let myself think about it. It wasn't my business what she wore, or what they did, or what they talked about, but I couldn't help myself.

"Thanks for all your help tonight, love," Mrs. Moynahan said, giving me a squeeze. "I couldn't have done it without you."

"You're very welcome," I said. "I enjoy it." And there was some truth to that. Sure, I would have liked to be out there building and painting and getting dirt under my fingernails, but there was a lot of satisfaction and creativity involved in bringing the visions together. In some ways, it felt like one of the most important jobs of all.

I walked through the grounds, fairly dark now, and toward Laguna

Canyon. Only a few workers were left. I usually walked home with Lillian, but she would be long gone. When I reached the street, I saw Jimmy standing under the streetlight.

"Can I walk you home?" he asked.

"I don't know, Jimmy, it's late." I put my hands in my pockets and kept walking.

But he jogged along to keep up. "All the more reason for me to walk you home," he reasoned.

"Well, I suppose," I said. "If you're walking in the same direction."

We strode along in silence for a while. I had so much I wanted to say, but none of it seemed right. Not now. So I didn't say anything. I was glad he was walking with me; it was comforting to have him by my side in the darkness on that stretch of Canyon Road. All the shops and cafés in town had closed long ago.

"There's something I need to tell you," he said finally.

"You don't, Jimmy, you don't have to tell me anything. There are things I could tell you too, but we should just let sleeping dogs lie, don't you think?" There was no value in bringing up the disagreement I'd had with Jeanene, or explaining why I'd been out dancing with Edgar, or anything else for that matter. That gorgeous girl of his couldn't stand me by now and had probably convinced him to pack up his bags and move back east, and why wouldn't he? Especially since there were rumors about the hotel closing down. But he didn't need to explain all that to me. I didn't want to hear it.

"It's about Jeanene," he said.

"I know. Just leave it, Jimmy." I couldn't stomach what he was about to tell me, his apologies for being in love with her, his looks of pity because he probably knew, clear as day, that I had feelings for him. That was a conversation I simply couldn't have. Not now, not ever.

"Hazel, I just want to explain."

"You don't have to," I said, firmly now. "I'm not interested."

I turned right when we reached Coast Boulevard, and he stood at the corner.

"So that's it?" he called out to me. "That's all you're going to say?"

"Yes, Jimmy," I said. "That's it." And I walked on up the street toward my house, forcing myself not to turn back.

CHAPTER 34

IT HAD BEEN A WEEK SINCE I'D BEEN TO HANSON'S HOUSE, AND IT
had pained me to stay away. He'd told me not to come back and that he'd
let me know if he needed me. *If* he needed me. I understood that he was
angry, but I wasn't going to stay away any longer. I'd walk in there and
tell him how sorry I was. He'd forgive me, he had to.

When I knocked, no one answered, and when I tried to turn the handle, it was locked. It was never locked in the morning—usually I walked
right in—but after the burglary, it made sense.

"Hanson," I called out, knocking harder now. "Hanson, are you in
there?"

I walked to the front of the house, to the door he never used, and
knocked. His car was in the driveway, so it didn't seem likely he'd have
gone out of town, though I supposed anything was possible, especially
if he was feeling betrayed by me, by Edgar. Maybe he just wanted to get
away for a few days. But to where, and with whom?

A tall wooden gate at the side of the house led around to the backyard and patio. I'd be able to see through the patio's glass doors if anyone was home, but the side gate was also locked. No one ever went that
way. I held on to the post on the left, then hiked my leg up onto the center rail of the gate. Pulling myself up, I could see over the pickets. The
gate wobbled a little, and I wondered if it was going to hold my weight.
I laid my stomach and chest on the top wooden rail and swung my legs
over one at a time, jumping down and landing intact. There was a stone
footpath somewhere beneath my feet, but the whole side passage was

overgrown and wild. I shoved through branches and tendrils and made my way to the back of the house.

When I looked through the glass, it definitely seemed as though Hanson had been home. Plates and cups were piled on the kitchen counter, a sweater that I didn't remember seeing was thrown on a chair. But there was no sight of him. I knocked on the glass door and then slid it open. I waited a moment. He'd been angry at me for doing exactly this, snooping around, entering places I wasn't supposed to be, interfering. But he hadn't been well when I left him, and he'd refused the doctor's visit. I was the only one taking care of him, and then he'd banished me.

"Hanson," I called out, quietly at first. "Mr. Radcliff?" Then, more assertively, "Hanson! I'm coming in, I just want to make sure you're all right." I stood inside the door and listened. It was silent except for a low rumbling, like a cat purring, and then a glass breaking. I hurried to his bedroom, and there he was, lying on top of the sheets, pale, eyes bloodshot and watering, a hand on his chest.

"Oh my God, Hanson." I dropped to my knees at the side of his bed and put my hand on his. He was wheezing badly, but he managed a smile.

"I'm going to call the doctor, we need to get you to a hospital," I said, desperate.

He shook his head and patted my hand, then looked me in the eyes. I blinked tears away. "What can I do?"

He nodded slightly and swallowed.

"Should I get you water?" I looked down at the broken glass on the floor and picked up the pieces. I wondered if he'd knocked it off the bedside table to alert me to his whereabouts.

He nodded.

"Water, all right, I'll get some, I'll be right back."

I ran to the kitchen, threw out the broken pieces of glass, and filled a new one. I raced back to the bedroom and his eyes were closed.

"Hanson?" They flickered open again. "I'm going to sit you up a little, so you can take a sip." I put one hand around the back of his head and slid the other behind his shoulder, but he was heavier than I expected. He couldn't help himself move into a sitting position. "All right," I said. "I'm going to slide another pillow under you, to raise you up a bit." He nodded.

When he was slightly more upright, I was able to ease him higher. It seemed like a heroic task for him to drink the water, and when he did, he started coughing. It sounded far worse than it had just a week earlier.

How had this happened—in a matter of days? It was a terrible turn for the worse. Whether he wanted me or not, if I had been here, caring for him, I might have forced him to see the doctor—at least made him more comfortable.

"When was the last time you ate? Should I make you some food, something easy to eat?"

He shook his head and waved his hand, as if to let me know that was the last thing he wanted. When he settled back onto the pillow, he looked me in the eyes again to make sure I was paying attention.

"Go to the hotel," he said in a slow, gravelly whisper. He closed his eyes and tried to breathe, but it wasn't coming easily. I waited, squeezing his hand, letting him know that I was ready to listen to whatever he wanted to say. "Victoria Beach," he said.

"All right," I said. "Anything you want, I'll do it. But Victoria Beach? What do you mean by that?" I racked my brain, not wanting him to speak any more than he had to. He'd been doing those sketches for the co-op gallery. He'd painted the tower when we were there that day. Had he taken it to the hotel? I didn't know exactly what I was supposed to do. I looked back to him, and his eyes were closed, his chest rising and falling.

"Hanson," I said in a whisper, but there was no response. His breathing seemed slightly easier in that moment, and I thought perhaps I shouldn't disturb him. I watched, transfixed for a few moments longer, then I backed slowly out of his room. Despite his protests, I called the doctor and asked that he come as soon as possible. Then I left by the front door and started running. I ran headlong down his driveway, down Coast Boulevard. People stared at me. I saw someone crank his head out the window of his car. I didn't care. Hanson shouldn't be alone. I kept on running fast all the way down to the hotel, through the lobby, and straight back to the bar. No one was there. I ran out the back, and another waiter was raking the sand.

"Where's Jimmy?" I cried, breathless.

"He's around somewhere, maybe in the cellar. Are you all right?"

"No! Where's the cellar?"

"This way." He dropped the rake and hurried to me, then led me to a narrow staircase. "Down there."

"Jimmy," I called, crashing into the dark and damp basement, filled with boxes and bottles.

He rose up quickly from where he was crouched and hit his head on the low ceiling.

"It's Hanson."

Jimmy dropped what he was doing, and we raced back up the stairs and into the bar.

"What is it? Tell me!"

"It's not good, Jimmy, he's really sick."

"What? I just saw him a week ago. He was coughing, but he—" Jimmy stopped his questions and frantically untied the black apron around his waist, throwing it behind the bar.

"It's worse, things are a lot worse now. I'm frightened."

"Russ!" he called to the guy outside. "I need you to cover for me."

He looked startled, but he nodded. "Will do."

I turned to Jimmy. "Hanson asked me to come to the hotel, something about Victoria Beach. We were there last week, he painted the tower. Did he bring it here?"

"I don't think so; he hasn't been here for weeks, at least not that I know of."

"What did he mean, then?"

"I don't know."

"We have to figure it out!" I started for the lobby, not knowing why.

"Wait, Hazel! Wait! There's a painting of Victoria Beach in one of the suites."

"That could be it," I said.

"It's not by Hanson though, they wouldn't hang an original Hanson Radcliff in a guest room. If they did, we'd all know about it."

"Can I see it?"

"There's someone in there, the Presidential Suite. A movie director, Tay Garnett," he said, as if I might recognize the name. "Rumor is, he's so depressed about all the fog rolling in each morning, delaying his shooting schedule, he hasn't left his room in four days, and he hasn't stopped drinking."

"When's he leaving?" I asked.

"Nobody knows, the whole crew was only supposed to be here a few days, but they have to stay 'til the fog clears and they can get the shot—or, until they can roll him out of there."

"We have to get in that room, and we have to get in there now. There's no time."

Jimmy looked tense.

"Give me a minute," he said, thinking something through before running off.

I waited in the bar and paced. How was Hanson—was he breathing, sleeping? Could this just be a bad patch? Could he come out of this? I should go to the pharmacy and ask for help. But I had to get back to him.

Jimmy returned to the bar fast, his hands in his pockets, and he nodded for me to follow him. We climbed the staff staircase to the top floor, and when we got out into the hallway, he looked around cautiously.

"I could get fired for this." He was taking a key out of his pocket as we raced to the Presidential Suite. He slid the key into the lock.

"Housekeeping," he called cheerfully, and I followed behind. The room stank like booze and cigarettes. A man lay facedown on the bed, but slowly looked up at us with one bleary eye half open. "Housekeeping," Jimmy repeated. "Just picking up used glasses and such, don't let us disturb you." The man, a middle-aged, red-faced souse, slammed his head back into the pillow and moments later began to snore.

Above the bed was a painting of the tower at Victoria Beach. It was beautiful. The sky was pink, and the fog hovered around the base of the tower like a cloud.

"There it is," I whispered. There was no signature, so Jimmy couldn't know, but it was a Hanson Radcliff, no doubt about it. I knew his style, his brushstrokes, his use of color, and this was one of his. Pressed against the side of the bed, I reached up toward it, leaning just inches above the sleeping drunkard. I barely managed to lift the framed painting from its hook on the wall. It was about four feet by three feet, heavy in its wooden frame.

Jimmy was rushing to my side, and I almost lost my balance under the weight of it.

"What are you doing?" Jimmy whispered sharply. He grabbed it and we backed away from the bed. "You can't take it down. What do you think you're going to do, walk it out of here, and no one will notice?"

"That's exactly what I'm going to do." I took it from him and carefully laid it down on the rug.

With my fingertips, I pried the canvas out of the heavy wooden frame and turned it over. If I could unfasten the staples holding the canvas to its interior frame, I could roll it up and sneak it out of there. I doubted the inebriated big shot would miss it, and I could bring it back later that day.

"I need a screwdriver . . ." I looked around to the desk. "Maybe a letter opener."

"Here," Jimmy said, handing me a bottle opener from his back pocket. Built into the handle was a corkscrew, but the metal was thinner at the other end.

I began wedging it under the staples, releasing them one by one.

"I'm going to lose my job, and you're going to get yourself arrested," Jimmy said.

"This is a Hanson Radcliff painting, the artist himself has requested it," I said. "But no one's going to know it's missing. It's only for a few hours, trust me."

Jimmy ran his hands through his hair. I had a few staples out, then two more.

Suddenly, I noticed something unusual—the frayed edge of the canvas on the back was thick, double layered somehow. I peeled one layer away from a corner and realized there were two canvases, one stretched tight over the other. I moved quickly now, removing the rest of the staples as fast as I possibly could without causing any damage. When I was done, I removed the wooden slats that the canvas was stretched on, placed them next to the frame, then tried to ease the two canvases apart. They were stuck, and I didn't want to force it, but after I gently moved my fingertip between the edges they separated, and when I lifted one canvas from the other, I couldn't quite believe my eyes.

There it was, the painting that had changed the course of Hanson's life, that had consumed my mind for so long. Isabella Rose.

Jimmy leaned closer, whispering, "Is that what you've been looking for?"

"He didn't want the tower one at all," I said. "He wanted me to find this. This whole time he said he didn't want to see it. He must have changed his mind."

Jimmy knelt by my side. "You must have changed his mind."

I turned it over, and on the back "Isabella" was scribbled in pencil in the corner. Beneath it, Hanson had signed his name.

Racing now, I placed the wooden stretcher bars onto the back of the Victoria Beach painting, and I pressed the staples into the tiny holes they had left in the canvas and the wooden frame. I pushed down on them, but they wouldn't go any further.

"We need a hammer," I said softly. "Hand me your shoe."

Jimmy pointed to the man asleep on the bed.

"He's sauced," I said. "He won't notice."

Jimmy sighed and removed his shoe. I used the heel to tap the staples back into place, then I put the painting back into the larger wooden frame and mounted it on the wall where we'd found it. I picked up the overturned portrait.

"What are you going to do with that?"

I looked around, and my eyes settled on a beach towel. I carefully rolled the canvas up, loosely, very loosely, hoping to God the paint wouldn't crack after all these years, then I draped the beach towel around it.

We eyed the sleeping man on the bed. He hadn't moved the whole time.

"I'll take the back way, you take the regular stairs," Jimmy said. "If anyone sees you, they'll think you're just a guest heading to the beach. I'll meet you one block up—Legion Street and Coast."

"All right, but hurry."

Out on the street, we ran up the hill to Hanson's. At one point I was out of breath and slowing us down, worried about not pressing on the canvas too hard. Jimmy turned and looked at me; he wasn't even breathing heavily.

"Go on ahead," I said. "Please, just get there."

He nodded and took off running. I was about five minutes behind him.

Inside, the house was quiet, and I had a terrible feeling I was too late, but when I reached Hanson's room, he looked much the same as he had before I'd left. Jimmy had pulled up a chair to the side of his bed and had his hand on Hanson's shoulder while he talked to him softly.

"Here," he said, standing, offering me his seat.

Hanson watched me as I took the beach towel off the canvas and care-fully unrolled it on the bed in front of him. He managed to push himself up onto his elbows, and he let out a soft cry.

"You knew where it was all along," I said.

He nodded slightly, not taking his eyes off the painting. He shifted his weight onto his left arm and reached out to touch it with his right, but that seemed too much for him.

"It's beautiful, Hanson, it's just as you described it. A masterpiece. Your masterpiece."

I looked over to him, and a single tear trickled down his hollowed cheek, then he let himself fall back onto the pillow.

"Thank you," he said in a whisper. He took my hand in his and squeezed it weakly. "It's for you," he said.

"No," I objected, but he'd closed his eyes, as if the sight of it was all the excitement he could manage in that moment.

Jimmy came to the door and mouthed, "Doctor."

"Now, Hanson," I said. "We've called the doctor, and he's almost here." I could hear his footsteps coming down the hall. "And I don't want any fussing this time." I patted his arm, and he sighed, but that started a coughing fit.

The doctor checked Hanson's lungs and chest and gave him mor-phine to keep him comfortable. He told us to call him if anything changed, and that if there was any family he wanted to see, now would be a good time.

When I asked Hanson if there was anyone he wanted me to contact for him, a family member, perhaps, or friends, he only had one strange request—Mr. Solomon, the treasurer at the pageant.

Within an hour, Mr. Solomon arrived, briefcase in hand, entered Hanson's room, and closed the door behind him. After fifteen minutes or so he emerged and gave me a peculiar look.

"Will you be staying to see to his needs?" he asked.

"Of course," I said. "I won't leave his side."

He nodded, seemingly satisfied, and left.

After Jimmy returned to the hotel, I sat in Hanson's room and quietly read to him as he drifted in and out of sleep. The morphine made him even more drowsy, as the doctor said it would. He couldn't eat and could only manage the smallest sips of water every now and then. I offered him a little bourbon, which I fed to him by teaspoon. And then, later, after I'd locked all the doors, placed an extra blanket over Hanson's legs to make sure he didn't get cold in the night, and placed a fresh glass of water by his bed, I returned to check on him one last time before I settled down for sleep on the sofa. With just one look, I knew.

"No," I cried and ran to him. His head was tilted to the side, his mouth slightly open, his hands on his chest. "Not yet, Hanson, please, not yet." There was so much more to say. He couldn't have left me yet. But the tears that fell from my eyes meant I knew it to be true. I touched his cheek, still warm, and realized how peaceful he looked in that moment, the tension between his brows relaxed.

Then I laid my head on his chest.

Hanson Radcliff was gone.

CHAPTER 35

THE FUNERAL ITSELF WAS SMALL AND INTIMATE—A NO-FUSS AFFAIR that seemed to be over too soon, not enough words spoken, praise, but somehow not enough. Though he'd seemed to ignore the fact that he was ill, Hanson had been planning for his death and had left detailed notes with Mr. Solomon regarding the ceremony and his affairs. Mr. Solomon, it turned out, was not only the treasurer for the pageant, he was also Hanson's lawyer. I tried to be helpful, but in many ways his directions were so clear that there was little for me to do.

"We should talk when all this is over," Mr. Solomon said to me a few days prior to the funeral.

I nodded. "Yes, of course," I said, but I knew what he was going to tell me. I was no longer working for Hanson Radcliff, and I would need to vacate his property and hand over the keys. I avoided him after that as much as I could, wanting to get through the next few days, and then I would think about what to do next.

The reception was held in the interior courtyard of the hotel, and every now and then, sun streamed in between patches of gray clouds that lingered overhead, threatening rain. Jimmy worked the outside bar near the fountain. Most of the volunteers from the pageant were there, as were all the artists from the co-op gallery and many other faces I recognized from around town.

When Lillian saw me through the crowd, she rushed to me and hugged me.

"I know he meant so much to you," she said.

"He did, and to you too. What will happen with the gallery now that he's gone?"

"Apparently he's set it up so that we can continue to work there. I'm not sure exactly of the arrangements, we're meeting with Mr. Solomon early next week. What about you?" she asked, her eyes filled with pity. She knew as I did that I lacked a skill or a trade to continue with, now that Hanson was gone. I was dispensable.

"Oh, I'll figure something out," I said, but I believed it was time, once again, for me to move on.

As I edged my way out of the courtyard and toward the exit, I caught a glimpse of Edgar all dressed up and smug with Scarlett on his arm. She looked fabulous as usual, even at a funeral—a fitted dress that flared below the knee and accentuated her tiny waist and full bosom, an unnecessary tiny black lace parasol tilted over her right shoulder. She barely knew Hanson, I thought; her display seemed too showy. I'd settled on a conservative dress with a discreet black bow at the neck and a small black netted fascinator.

"Oh, Hazel, sweetheart, we're both so devastated for your loss," Scarlett said, pulling Edgar along with her toward me.

"It's everyone's loss," I said.

"Say, Hazel, you were right about this town," she said. "It's just divine, so peaceful. I've decided to stay awhile."

"Stay?" I asked, shocked.

"Well, for now at least. I've moved in with Edgar, or rather I just haven't left," she said with a laugh.

I looked to Edgar, but he was surveying the crowd, as if intentionally avoiding eye contact. I didn't want to look at him either. If I did, I might erupt in a rage, accuse him of breaking into Hanson's house and contributing to his downfall. But I refused to do that, not here, not at Hanson's funeral.

"Well, I hope you'll be happy here," I said, and with that I walked away.

Back at the apartment, I stood in the living room and stared out the window. I had to think about the future. I could try to get a job in town. I could ask Lillian if they needed me to work in the gallery, but they didn't have the money to pay me, that was why they shared shifts. Without Hanson I was lost. Working for him, I'd felt needed, valuable, but without him, I felt like an interloper. I couldn't bear to think that soon Jeanene would either join Jimmy in Laguna or convince him to return to the East Coast. Edgar and Scarlett had each other. The pageant would open in a few weeks, but it would all be over by the end of the month.

I forced myself to accept things as they were. I'd go back to Los Angeles— it was familiar at least, and now that some time had passed, surely I could find work there. I packed my belongings in my suitcase. I took the mismatched plates and dishes that Jimmy had given me out of the cupboard and ran my finger around the rims. I might wrap them in the towels he'd brought with them—I'd need such items wherever I ended up next. But after bundling them up, I realized I wouldn't be able to carry everything. I put them back in the cupboard and placed the suitcase by the door.

It didn't feel right taking the painting with me. It belonged to Hanson, but he'd insisted that I keep it. If I left it here in the apartment, what would become of it? Would someone exploit it? Would it end up in Edgar's hands? Or Scarlett's? Would that even be so bad? I couldn't think. Everything had happened so fast, and now it was over.

I'd be rising early to catch the first train out of town, but I couldn't sleep. The rain had started as a light drizzle, but now it was drumming down on the roof, heavy and determined. I sat on the sofa and watched the outside world blur through the window.

If I hadn't felt so jealous and wretched about Jimmy starting a life with Jeanene, I wouldn't have thrown myself at Edgar the way I did. I never would have gone to dinner with him, and I wouldn't have shared that private information about Hanson's secret room, a room that in the end had no consequence. The painting wasn't even there, and yet Edgar's break-in had been one more thing that hurt Hanson—invading his privacy, a sweeping blow at a fragile time in his life when what he needed was care and love, not betrayal.

I'd left him to fend for himself, a whole week when I should have been at Hanson's side helping him, tending to him, calling the doctor. He would have fought me on it; he was angry with me, but he always fought me on things, was always mildly aggravated about one thing or another. It was his way, and I'd become quite accustomed to it. He'd had passion—when he believed in something he let it be known. I'd grown to admire that in him, not fear it. If only I'd held on to that thought when

he sent me away. I should have shown up for work just as I always did. If I
had been stronger, more determined, passionate about what I believed in
the way that he was, then Hanson might still be with us. If I hadn't sent
that letter to Bobby Watson when I did, then maybe he'd be with us too.

Everyone I had ever been close to was now gone—my father, then my
mother, Bobby, and now Hanson. Suddenly all the losses, all the hurt
and regret seemed to pile on top of one another, the weight of them all
heavy on my chest. I pressed my face against the window, tears running
down my cheeks, the rain streaking down the glass. I was alone again.
I was desperately alone.

At some point I grabbed my coat and an old umbrella and headed out
into the rain. I couldn't sit home all night long, wallowing, and there
was no point trying to sleep. I walked down toward the beach to see the
ocean at night one more time; she always had a way of calming me. It
must have been past midnight, and no one was out in this rain. When I
reached the boardwalk, I saw something peculiar on the sand, a silver,
shimmery layer that covered the whole lower part of the beach from the
water's edge and stretching several hundred feet down the coast. It was
as if the surface of the sand was alive. As I moved closer, I noticed someone in a yellow raincoat crouched down toward the shimmering sand.

"Excuse me," I called out, rushing toward him, but the rain seemed
to drown out my voice. "Excuse me," I said, louder this time.

An older man, in his late fifties or sixties, turned his head toward me.

And as I got closer, I saw hundreds, maybe thousands of silver fish
jumping and wriggling about on the moonlit sand.

"Oh my gosh," I said, startled and afraid for the stranded fish. "What
on earth is going on?"

"It's the grunion run," he said, laughing. "You've never seen it?"

"No! Why are all the fish out of water like this? Should we help them
get back?" I looked around at the thousands of fish and realized that
would be an impossible task.

"Heavens, no. Happens every year around this time, just after a full
moon. At high tide the grunions hurl themselves up onto the sand to
spawn."

"Why would they do that?"

"Just what they do. The females bury themselves in the sand to lay

their eggs, and the males wrap themselves around the females to fertil-
ize them."

"Won't they all die if they stay out of the water this long?"

"Just watch, once they've had their fun they dance right back into
the water."

I did as he said, and, sure enough, some were wriggling and writhing
and actually leaping their way back toward the tides.

"To be honest," the man went on, "they have a much better chance of
making it on a night like this." He grabbed a handful of the small slippery
fish and dropped them into a bucket at his side. "Most years, hundreds
of people would be running to the grunions, catching them with whatever they could—fishing nets, sink strainers, I've even seen someone come
down here and scoop the little buggers up with window screens. If it wasn't
such a downpour right now there'd be bonfires all along this beach, and
folks making a party out of it, cooking them up in some oil and cornmeal."

How cruel, I thought, watching the man as he scooped up more of
the silvery fish and dumped them into his bucket.

"Tonight's their lucky night. They won't be out here long, only lasts
half an hour or so before they all return to the ocean."

"What happens to the eggs?"

"They hatch in about two weeks or so and wash out with the sea when
it's high tide again."

"So they'll survive?"

"Yes," he said, chuckling. "Quite something, isn't it? A whole bunch
of new life starting right here on this beach, before our very eyes."

I watched for a while, mesmerized—the fish aglow, glittering in the
moonlight, flinging themselves about, the rain splashing off their skin
like sparks.

"I've never seen anything like it in my life," I said. "It's almost biblical."

The man in the yellow raincoat laughed and straightened up for a moment. "Yes," he said, "I suppose it is."

The spectacle continued for another ten or fifteen minutes, until the
last little grunion had made its way back to the ocean, and the beach was
just wet, slick sand, as if nothing had happened at all.

CHAPTER 36

THE NEXT MORNING, I WOKE EARLY, DRESSED, LOCKED THE DOOR behind me, and walked to the hotel before I could change my mind. I left a note for Jimmy at the front desk saying goodbye and asked him to give the apartment keys to Mr. Solomon. Next I took the bus from the Ocean Avenue stop to the train station. At 9 A.M. I boarded the train to Los Angeles Union Station and took a taxi to the only place I could think to go back to—Douglas Aircraft. I'd try one more time to find a position there. Maybe things had changed over the past six months; maybe they realized by now how useful we'd been, how they needed women back on the factory floor.

Thankfully, Mr. Lockhart seemed to recognize me when I knocked on his office door.

"I'm Hazel Francis," I said, helping him place me. "I worked for you during the war."

"Of course, I remember you, quick hands," he said, gesturing for me to take a seat.

I awkwardly shuffled farther into his office with my suitcase and the canvas rolled up in a cardboard box.

"Are you moving in?" he said, looking at my luggage.

"No," I said. "I'm traveling up from Laguna Beach and was wondering if there might be an opening at the factory."

"I see."

"I understand that many of the jobs were given back to the returning soldiers, but I wondered if perhaps anything might have changed."

"Not in production, that's for sure," he said.

"Oh no, of course not," I said, though I felt it was ridiculous—we'd done a fine job building those planes when they needed us, why not now?

"Those were special circumstances during the war, circumstances I hope we'll never go back to. Almost gave me a heart attack having to manage all those women walking around in godforsaken trousers." He nodded approvingly at my day dress and T-straps.

I forced a smile and silently questioned why I'd come back. In Laguna, I'd been free to dress how I wanted, live how I wanted; alone in a small apartment, I could do what I pleased—heck, I posed as an artist's model, and no one batted an eye in that town. Of course, there were some who wanted women in their "rightful" place—the costume department—not letting me do manual labor with the boys. I thought of Edgar and Floyd. But for the most part, Laguna had given me a sense of freedom and acceptance.

"There's a secretarial job in the blueprint department. The few women we have working here are dropping like flies, you know, on the nest."

I looked at him, perplexed.

"In the family way. Husbands are home, they're making up for lost time. You understand?"

"Completely," I said. "Well, not me. No husband, no prospects, just a young woman, looking for a job in an airplane factory."

"Shame," he said. "Bet it would make your parents proud to see you married off starting a family of your own."

"I'm sure there are other things that would have made them equally proud," I said. "Like working here and serving my country."

He grimaced. "It's not like that anymore, we're back to being just an airplane factory. What was it you said you did in Laguna Beach?"

"I was an assistant to an artist." He didn't need to know that I sat for him from time to time. That part of my job had become so infrequent toward the end, and it never turned out to be as revealing as I'd worried it might. "And I worked at an art show that will open this summer, in just a few weeks actually."

"So why did you leave?"

"He died." My eyes watered as I said it, then I continued, "My boss, Hanson Radcliff." I searched Mr. Lockhart's face for a glimmer of recognition at Hanson's name, but if there was any, he didn't let it show.

"Well, it's yours if you want it."

"I'm sorry?" I was suddenly lost in thought about Hanson, about Laguna Beach, about the show and opening night all happening without me.

"The job. Do you want it or not? Thirty-five cents an hour."

My eyes widened—it was so much less than it was when I'd worked there before.

"Like I said, those were special circumstances," he continued. "We're not at war anymore. I've got plenty of men willing to work, so take it or don't, it's up to you."

"I'll take it," I said. "Thank you."

I RENTED A ROOM NEAR THE FACTORY AND BEGAN WORKING THE following week. Work boots were not required—in fact, I was told to dress like a lady at all times. I wasn't even allowed on the factory floor. I had to enter and exit the blueprint office using an external staircase. The only other woman in the vicinity was with child and already showing slightly. She trained me for two days then left.

The work was mostly filing, dull and mundane, not exciting the way I remembered it, and the men who worked there either ignored me completely, or gave me a nod, or worse, a tap on the rear when I brought them their coffee. I suppose I'd expected the thrill to come back to me. I'd assumed that once I was surrounded by airplanes again, the din of drilling and hammering, that I'd be transported back to my days during the war when I had my first taste of possibility—but I just couldn't get excited. And the noise, if I wasn't actively involved in creating that din, it reverberated in my brain and gave me a relentless headache. At lunch, I sat in the break room alone, eating my sandwich, thinking of Jimmy and me sitting in lounge chairs at the back of the hotel under the stars, and Hanson making me poached eggs on toast, with fresh herbs from his garden.

The days went by, and I was never asked to work late. The evenings in my room dragged on and on. I'd lie on my bed and wonder how the plans for the pageant were coming along, wishing I could still help out. They'd be in the homestretch now, and I wished I could see it—the finished product, all coming together, the lights, the makeup, the costumes, the cast, all those locals I either knew or recognized, bringing the art to life. I thought about poor Mrs. Moynahan and how I'd left her with all that work to complete. I should have told her I was leaving, I should have explained why I couldn't stay instead of rushing off like that as if someone was chasing me out of town, when in fact it was my own fear of loneliness and disappointment that sent me running.

On the Monday of my second week, I sat on my bed and was flipping through the paper when my eye caught a small, two-inch column about Hanson. I grabbed the paper and began poring over every word. A good half of it was dedicated to the scandal surrounding Isabella Rose. It infuriated me. What about the contribution he'd made to his community throughout the years, how he'd been at the helm of the Art Association when it started, how he'd helped and nurtured new talent, giving them a space to create and thrive? What about his contributions to the pageant in the early years, and later his monetary donations to keep it going, bringing tourists and art lovers to Laguna Beach? None of that was mentioned. Just a comment about his paintings and how much they sold for. He was so much more. He was so much more than that to me.

I lifted the rectangular box with Hanson's painting onto the bed and unrolled the canvas in front of me. The way he had captured her body in a relaxed state, happy, blissful even—that was the beauty in it, like laughter, big and unrestrained and free. I wished someone could know me the way he'd known her. All the imperfections and the insecurities, all the mistakes and the broken parts.

It bothered me that speeches were given at the funeral, short articles were being written in newspapers, but no one knew the truth about the painting in front of me, no one had ever seen it.

Only Hanson, Isabella, and now me.

I suddenly sat up straighter, filled with certainty. It was too late for Isabella, it was too late for Hanson, but it wasn't too late for the rest of us. Hanson's painting was a lesson in regret, but it was also a lesson in love. It had to be shared. The truth, not the scandal.

It was getting dark out, but I sprang off the bed, shoved the few things I'd unpacked back into my case, rolled up the painting carefully, placed it back in the box, and walked out into the night.

It cost me a small fortune to take a taxi all the way from Los Angeles to Laguna Beach, but I couldn't wait until the morning for the next train. On the drive south, I looked out the window and thought through the consequences of my hasty actions. I'd somehow secured a job back at the factory, the place I always thought I wanted to be, and leaving like this after such a short time was going to cause me to lose my position just as fast as I'd managed to finagle it. But did it even matter? I'd expected my work at the factory to feel as it did before—meaningful, fulfilling, important—but it didn't. Things had changed. I'd changed. My heart was in Laguna. I had to get back to finish what I'd started.

>☂

I CAUGHT JIMMY JUST AS HE WAS ABOUT TO LOCK THE BACK DOORS of the bar and head inside for the night. In a moment of relief at seeing his familiar face, I ran to him and threw my arms around him.

"Hazel!" he said. "You're back." But then he stepped away, holding me at arm's length. "How could you leave like that, so abruptly? You didn't even say goodbye."

"I'm sorry," I said. "I didn't know how to."

"Everyone's been asking about you, and Mr. Solomon has been looking for you."

"Did you give him the key?"

"Yes, I did as you asked."

"Darn it," I said.

He stood there, looking annoyed. "What's that supposed to mean?"

"Do you think you could help me pick a lock?"

He looked away.

"Please," I said. "I'll tell you everything if you can just help me with this one thing."

>☂

IT DIDN'T TAKE LONG FOR JIMMY TO PICK THE LOCK TO HANSON'S apartment. I could tell that no one had been inside since I'd left it—the things I couldn't take with me were exactly as I'd left them. We went in, and I shut the door behind us. I lit a single candle and sat on the floor. I didn't want Mr. Solomon or anyone else to see lights on.

"What are we doing here, Hazel?"

"I need to stay here. Hanson wouldn't mind, just for a few nights."

"I've been worried about you," Jimmy said. "Everyone's wondering if you're still going to be in the show. They haven't found a replacement. Poor Mrs. Moynahan has been beside herself, with all the costume work and no help."

I'd felt terrible about Mrs. Moynahan but had completely forgotten about my role in *A Virgin*.

"I know, I know. I came back to help Mrs. Moynahan. I'll be in the painting on opening night, but they might have to find someone else after that. They'll have some time."

"What does that mean?"

"There's something I need to do, for Hanson, and I'm hoping you can help me."

I unrolled Hanson's painting and set it out in front of us.

"When Hanson saw this in his final moments, he was happy, wasn't he, relieved?"

Jimmy nodded. "He was. It was as if he could finally let go of that heavy burden."

"The painting was just as he remembered—he captured her essence and did it with love."

"Yes," Jimmy said. "You did the right thing by finding it and letting him see it again, you really did."

"I couldn't have done it without you," I said, quickly jumping to my feet. "The thing is, his entire adult life had been shrouded by guilt and uncertainty. Hanson's gone now, but if we don't do something, the scandal lives on and taints his memory."

"What can we do about it?"

I started pacing the tiny living room, too wound up to sit still. "I'm going to get his painting in the Pageant of the Masters."

"How? The show's opening in four days."

"I don't know, exactly, but I'm going to make sure that people know the truth—about Hanson and the painting."

Jimmy stood up. "You want to talk about a scandal? You said a suicide was blamed on this painting; you can't be sure it will be well received now. It's not just Laguna folks who come to see this show, they come from all over, some very well-heeled patrons."

"It's art," I said. "Surely they'll appreciate what Isabella couldn't see, blinded by fear."

Jimmy shrugged. "Even if you're right, you can't change the lineup now. You of all people know how much work goes into producing each and every image. The designers take weeks to create those sets—there're the background paintings, costumes, the actors, makeup, lighting, narration, and all the crew behind the scenes who change out each set." Jimmy folded his arms across his chest. "It's a nice idea, Hazel, but I don't think it's possible, and I doubt everyone is going to agree with you about adding it to the lineup. Not everyone knew him the way we did."

"Everyone won't have to agree; in fact, I am quite sure that if I ask permission it won't happen," I said. Hanson had taught me to live life free of regrets. It wasn't easy, I still had plenty of my own, but I was going to try to heed his advice. "Look, Jimmy, you're right, I know it sounds like a crazy idea. It might not work, but I'll never know if I don't at least give it my best shot."

THE NEXT MORNING, WEARING A BIG SUN HAT AND MY OVERSIZED sunglasses, with the rolled and boxed painting in my arms, I waited outside the co-op gallery to catch Lillian on her way in.

"We'll be open in half an hour," she said, as she unlocked the front door.

"Lillian," I said, lowering my sunglasses. "It's me, Hazel. Can I come in?"

She looked at me, rolled her eyes, then opened the door and let me in.

"You know I stood on the corner at the café waiting for you, twice, so we could walk up to the pageant together. It would have been nice if you'd told me you were leaving town."

"I'm very sorry," I said. "It was a last-minute decision, but you're right, there are several people I should have informed, and you're one of them."

"You're part of a big production. In a small town like this, people rely on you. You become a necessary part of the puzzle. You can't just up and leave and expect everyone to pick up the pieces."

"You're right. That's why I came back."

She raised an eyebrow.

I told her all about Hanson's painting, what he'd told me, where we found it. I even told her my suspicions about Edgar breaking into Hanson's house. Then I told her my plan to get it into the pageant as the final work of art.

"But the final image is always da Vinci's *Last Supper*."

"I'm hoping that this year there could be one more, to honor Hanson's legacy."

"You'd get my vote. He's done more for artists here than we could have ever dreamed of. But in such a short amount of time it's just not possible."

"I think we can do it if we have help and if we keep it quiet. I was going to ask you if you would consider being in charge of painting the background. Maybe you could ask the others here at the gallery to help out, discreetly of course."

"But opening night is in three days. Even if I could get everyone together, the paint won't be fully dry—oil paint takes time to dry completely."

"So it will still be wet, who cares?" I opened the box and unrolled Hanson's canvas.

Lillian gasped. "Look how he captured the light on her skin, and her hands, draping off the bed like that." Lillian studied it closely. "Hands are always the hardest to get right. And to think he was just a young man when he did this?"

I smiled, seeing Lillian's appreciation for Hanson's painting, confirming that I was doing the right thing.

"Who's going to pose in it? You?"

"No!" I said. "But I know someone who will be perfect."

CHAPTER 37

I DIDN'T TRUST EDGAR ONE BIT. I WASN'T SURE IF I COULD TRUST Scarlett either, but I would have to take my chances. After my visit with Lillian, I walked up to Edgar's house, and when I looked up from behind the bushes that lined his front yard, I thought I saw Scarlett in one of the windows. I considered throwing a small pebble at the window to get her attention, but I couldn't let Edgar hear me.

"Hello there, Hazel Francis, sleuthing around again, are you?" I almost jumped out of my skin when I heard Edgar's voice. He was walking up the street toward me, barefoot, with wet hair and a towel around his shoulders, apparently after a swim in the ocean. "I heard you skipped town."

"I didn't skip town," I snapped back at him. "I had business to attend to."

"Business? I thought your business had come to an end?" he said with a sneer. "You know it's never good to run off like that, just days after your wealthy boss dies. Rumors will start about what you took with you."

His tone was outrageous, considering what he had attempted. "I have only respect and admiration for Hanson. I would never take anything I wasn't supposed to, unlike some people I know."

"Oh, Hazel, always so prim. Relax a little. I think we can agree that we were both on the lookout for the same thing, for the same reason."

"My reasoning could never be the same as yours."

"What's going on out there?" Scarlett stuck her head out of the window. She had a white towel wrapped around her hair and a silk robe hanging precariously off her shoulder.

"I'm just chatting with Hazel," Edgar said. "Nothing to worry about."

"Actually, I came here hoping to find you, Scarlett," I said. "Can you meet me at the café on Forest in half an hour?"

"I can do that," she said.

"Great," I said, giving Edgar a piercing look as I walked away.

AT THE CAFÉ I TOOK A GREAT RISK BY TELLING SCARLETT MY IN-tentions and had to beg her not to reveal the plan to Edgar.

"I know it's not everything that you hoped for, and you weren't able to persuade Hanson to paint you, but I believe this might be the next best thing; in fact, it may be even better."

"What exactly do you have in mind?" She lowered her voice and leaned in.

"Well, as you know, all the paintings are reproduced; they fill the entire stage since the figures depicted are real people, so the designers and artists would re-create Hanson's painting, or at least the backdrop and bed, and you would pose on it, as Isabella."

Scarlett looked puzzled. "I just can't visualize how it will all work. Is this a tableau vivant?"

"Sort of, yes. I've never seen it myself, but my understanding is that the lighting and makeup trick your eyes into believing you're seeing a two-dimensional image. People come from all over the country to see it."

"I don't know," Scarlett said, twirling her straw. "Sounds a little pe-culiar. I'm more of a movie kinda gal."

"You'd be the star of the show, everyone would be talking about it. Isn't that what you wanted? It's the first Pageant of the Masters since the war started, so there's a lot of anticipation, and we're expecting a lot of press," I said, with fingers crossed that it would actually be the case. "The show can only feature Laguna locals, but seeing as you're staying with Edgar, it's within the rules."

Scarlett shrugged. "For now, I'm living with Edgar. I still have my LA house, of course."

"That's all right," I said. "Now, there are a couple of things that we must discuss. Firstly, as you know, your grandmother's portrait was in the nude; anything too revealing can be covered with a small strip of fabric and painted to match your skin tone, but for the most part you would be baring all."

Scarlett laughed. "God didn't give me this body for nothing! That's not what I'm worried about."

"Good." I clasped my hands together. "And secondly, you would not be able to breathe a word of this to Edgar."

She looked at me uncertainly.

"It would ruin everything. He would not want Hanson's painting featured in the show. He made it very clear to me on our—" I stopped. Scarlett probably had no idea that Edgar and I had been out for dinner and dancing just days before she rolled around naked in his studio. "He made it clear when we talked, that he did not want this painting to see the light of day because it would overshadow him as an artist; he didn't want the attention on Hanson. Even with Hanson gone, Edgar won't want him to be celebrated. I'm worried that if he finds out, he'll try to sabotage it."

Scarlett nodded slowly, seemingly untroubled about disappointing him. "I believe you. In fact, I know that's true. But how would we pull this off without Edgar knowing? He's one of the people running the show."

"We'll just have to keep it very hush-hush, and get help from as few people as possible. We'll play innocent and say we wanted it to be a surprise for him as much as for everyone else."

Scarlett smiled—reassessing me a bit, and thinking it over.

"It may cause some problems for you with Edgar after all is said and done," I admitted.

"Oh please, I know how to get his mind off anything and onto something else. I have complete power over that man," she said with a laugh. "And besides, if it really does get the attention of the press, then I'll be hitting Hollywood in no time."

I grinned back at her. "That's what I thought."

MY NEXT STOP WAS THE PAGEANT GROUNDS. I WANTED TO KEEP MY head down as much as possible and only interact with the people I absolutely needed to in order to make this plan work. I knew there would be a smaller group of volunteers working on the show in the middle of the day, Mrs. Moynahan being one of them.

Before knocking on the costume closet door, I braced myself to be yelled and cursed at for leaving the poor lady in the lurch, but, instead, when she opened it, her face erupted in a broad smile and then a laugh.

"Oh, bless you, sweet child, you came back." She took me into her arms and squeezed me tightly. "Bless you, I've been sitting here, shamefully using the Lord's name in vain, knowing there was no way that I could finish all this in time for opening night." She gestured to a clothes rack full of costumes that needed work. "I am so happy you've returned. Now, I think we can get it done!"

"I'm very sorry, please forgive me. I was distraught after Mr. Radcliff's death. I had to get away to think about what was important to me, and I realized it was Hanson and this community. But I'm back now, and I'm here to help you as much as you need me."

"Oh, praise the Lord himself," she said. "And you'll still be the Virgin, now that you're back?"

"Yes, Mrs. Moynahan." I laughed. "I'll still be the Virgin."

We sat and sewed, and she brought me up to date on all the things that needed to be done over the next few days. When she was done, I took a deep breath and confessed my plan to sneak Hanson's painting into the show.

She was quite taken aback and seemed unsure if we'd be able to make it work. "Shouldn't you ask Mr. Fredericks first?"

"I'm worried if I ask permission that it won't happen."

"I think you're right there," she said. "Once things are decided, he's really loath to change, even small details. But he will be furious if you go behind his back."

"I know," I said. "But it's a risk I have to take."

She nodded. "Well, hi-de-ho and blow my socks off!" she said, when I unveiled the painting for her.

"And this young film star knows she's going to be showing off more than her peepers?"

"Oh yes," I said. "She's rather excited about it. She's a real stunner and quite proud of her assets."

It may have tipped the scale for Mrs. Moynahan, seeing the storied painting for herself. "Well, I for one would like to see Hanson's painting celebrated, so I'll do anything I can to help. There's not much we can do for the young woman in the costume department, but I'll have a word with Mr. Robbins himself and I'll see to it that he personally does the makeup. Capturing the skin tones Mr. Radcliff used is going to be imperative to get this right. All those shadows on her body where the sun streams in—he'll have to replicate them just so. And I'll make sure he understands that this is top secret. Can I take the painting with me this afternoon to show it to Anatole?"

I hesitated, anxious about letting the painting out of my hands for more than a minute, but I knew he'd have to see the real thing in order to bring it to life.

"All right," I said. "But please don't let it out of your sight."

THAT EVENING I HAD TO REVEAL THE PLAN TO FLOYD IN ORDER TO get the set built, and thankfully he was also willing to help, excited, in fact, at the prospect of honoring Hanson at the pageant. Fortunately, the foreground of the Isabella painting was relatively simple, making the set design uncomplicated—simply a partial bed for Scarlett to lie on, and a desk in view on the right. Floyd made a plan to create a rectangular bed frame out of leftover lumber the following day, which he'd wrap with padding and cover with the last of Scarlett's donated bedspreads. The color would be wrong, so that too would need to be dyed, or maybe even painted after the backdrop was complete. But all in all, things seemed to be coming together, and I was beginning to believe we might actually be able to make this happen.

"We don't usually show the original artwork alongside the re-created paintings," Floyd said. "But since this painting has never been seen by the public before, I think we should display it in a frame downstage when the living picture is revealed. That way, since it's going to be the last artwork the audience sees, attendees can view it on their way out."

"That's a wonderful idea, but it's not framed, it's just a rolled-up canvas. It should be stretched and framed."

"Oh." Floyd's face dropped. "That needs to be done by a professional.

I can't have any of my men messing around with a valuable piece like this. And a professional framer takes weeks."

"When I found it, it was in a beautiful frame," I said.

"It was? Do you think you could retrieve it?"

It would be nice to have it back in its original frame, I thought, the one Hanson had likely made all those years ago. I recalled seizing it before—from above the bed in the hotel's Presidential Suite—and didn't relish the idea of another hair-raising attempt, and yet that would be the fastest option. "I don't know," I said. "But I can try."

On my way home that evening I left a note for Jimmy in a sealed envelope at the hotel's front desk, explaining the need for the frame, and asking if he might be willing to somehow retrieve it. If that toper of a director was still on the sauce, no one would notice it was gone. Perhaps the manager would even allow it, if Jimmy explained the reason. Afterward, I headed back to the apartment for some much-needed sleep.

THE FOLLOWING EVENING, AFTER EVERYONE ELSE HAD LEFT THE pageant grounds, I stayed up until the early hours of the morning with Lillian and the artists she'd recruited from the gallery to help her paint the twenty-by-fifty-foot backdrop that would be rolled into place after Scarlett was in position on the bed and the rest of the set had been moved onstage. The sun was coming up when the finished backdrop was finally hung up to dry.

With just one final day before the show opened to the public, I was feeling satisfied that the backdrop had been completed, the set was already arranged and hidden away, and Scarlett was on board. I spent the rest of the time with Mrs. Moynahan finalizing the costumes and praying that everything would go according to plan.

CHAPTER 38

ON THE MORNING OF OPENING DAY, I WOKE UP, DRESSED, AND RUSHED back to the pageant grounds. Mrs. Moynahan was already at her sewing machine, getting ready for a final run-through, which was to start at ten.

"Mr. Solomon's been looking for you," she said, and I wondered if he'd heard rumors about getting Hanson's painting into the show, or maybe he'd caught on to the fact that I'd been staying at Hanson's apartment and leaving it unlocked so I could come and go. Either way, I had to stay out of his way for the rest of the day to avoid slowing things down. "Oh, and Jimmy, the Discus Thrower, left this for you," Mrs. Moynahan said with a smirk, pointing to the framed painting of Victoria Beach, leaning up against the wall.

"He did it," I said, clasping my hands together.

"He was here early, just as I was arriving," she said. "Sweet fella. Sweet on you too, I'd say."

I shook my head and got right to work, carefully easing the Victoria Beach painting out of its frame and wrapping the Isabella canvas over it. The corners and edges, which had been hugging these wooden stretcher bars for almost forty years, fit right back into place, just as the painting had been when I found it in the hotel, except this time the paintings were switched and Isabella was facing out. When I was all done, I pressed the double canvas back into the frame, leaned it against the wall, and admired it once more. I couldn't believe we were actually going to do this, put Hanson's never-before-seen painting on display for all to see. I only wished he could be there to witness it.

The day's dress rehearsal was not without a few minor mishaps—no one could get the toddlers in William-Adolphe Bouguereau's *Charity* to hold still, despite the fact that they'd practiced it perfectly several times before, and Caroline, slated to appear in Jules Breton's *Song of the Lark,* was suffering from a bout of morning sickness, which she assured us would be much improved by the evening's performance. Jimmy, along with a couple of disciples in *The Last Supper,* didn't show up for their rehearsal call times, but that was to be expected—not everyone could make a daytime run-through. I was sure Jimmy had switched his evening shift at the bar for the daytime shift, so he'd be on time for the performance that night.

Scarlett sat in the back and watched the entire rehearsal, coming backstage a couple of times, at my suggestion, to see how the stage crew pulled the set together. The curtains would close on one picture and Stanley Newcomb, the narrator, would begin to speak about the next artist and painting for a minute or so. In that time, the next twenty-by-fifty-foot frame slid to the front of the stage, the set rolled into place behind it, the actors climbed into place, and, if necessary, strapped in for safety. The backdrop was the final layer in the tableau, and then the curtain opened, and the lights went on, creating the illusion of a two-dimensional painting for ninety seconds while the orchestra played—then the whole process would start over for the next image. There was no way for Scarlett to rehearse without giving away our plan, but hopefully she'd seen enough and would be able to follow directions and get into the right pose while the narration introduced Hanson's painting. I'd already written the narration to accompany Hanson's work, I just had to get the updated script into Stanley's hands.

The day was hectic. Between sneaking around and securing all the final plans for Hanson's painting to be displayed and helping Mrs. Moynahan complete the final costume details, I almost forgot that I myself would soon be needed in makeup for my part in the show. Mrs. Moynahan had taken a short break to run home and eat something, and I was just walking back to the costume room from backstage when Jimmy approached, looking pale.

"Everything all right?" I asked.

"Not really. The film crew got their shot," he said.

"What are you talking about?"

"Remember the director guy who was staying at the Presidential Suite? He checked out this morning before heading down for breakfast. The chambermaid noticed the painting was different, so they questioned him. He told them he vaguely remembered the kid behind the bar coming in his room a few weeks back. He must have meant the time when you and I were both in his room."

"Oh no! He barely opened his eyes that day."

"He opened one, and apparently that was enough. When you're a drunk, you never forget your bartender. The crazy thing is he wasn't even in the room when I snuck in early this morning and replaced Victoria Beach with a painting of Main Beach that I'd found in the storage room."

"What's going to happen now?"

"I'm fired unless the painting is back where it belongs by tonight."

"Oh God, Jimmy, I'm so sorry!" I put my hands to my face.

Floyd's suggestion that Hanson's original painting be displayed downstage from the replica had made sense. The famous artworks in the show would be familiar to the majority of the attendees, but no one had ever seen Hanson's Isabella portrait before; no one even knew if it still existed. Framing and displaying it helped provide its history as well as a means of comparison with the tableau. But Jimmy couldn't lose his job over this. And, if he wasn't planning to leave Laguna yet, getting fired from the hotel would only accelerate a move back to the East Coast with Jeanene. I couldn't bear the thought of that either, even if it was inevitable.

"Take it back to the hotel," I said. "You have to. Just put the Victoria Beach painting back in the room. I'll find another way to display the Isabella painting." But as I said this, Mrs. Moynahan was bounding toward us with a look of concern.

"What is it?" I asked. "Do you need me in costume?"

"I just got back to the closet and it's not there."

"What's not there?"

"The painting, it's gone. I returned it to the costume closet after I took it to makeup, and now it's gone."

My stomach dropped. I hadn't locked the closet door. I'd hurried out to talk to Floyd, just for a few minutes, about the color of the bedspread in Hanson's painting, after Mrs. Moynahan left for lunch. I'd been in such a hurry, I hadn't locked it. "This is my fault!"

"Why? Where could it be?" Mrs. Moynahan asked. "Who would take it?"

I shook my head. "I think I have an idea."

WE FOUND SCARLETT IN MAKEUP. SINCE HER ENTIRE BODY WOULD be on display, every shadow and brushstroke from the painting re-created on her skin, she was one of the first people called in. She was sitting on a table draped in a towel, having her feet and ankles painted by two makeup artists, while Anatole was working on her face, all of them referencing a photograph that Floyd had taken of the original painting.

"Scarlett," I said. "I have to ask you something."

The makeup artists looked at Jimmy, Mrs. Moynahan, and me, and could probably tell from the strain in our faces that it would be wise to take a five-minute break.

"Did you tell Edgar about the painting?" I asked.

Her face broke into a coy smile.

"Oh, dear God," I said.

"I only told him that I was going to be in the show. I couldn't help myself, I was just getting so excited after I saw the rehearsal."

"What painting did you say you'd be appearing in?"

"Well, once I'd spilled the beans about my being in the show, I didn't see the point in keeping the rest of it a secret, so I suppose I did tell him about Hanson's painting. But he promised not to say a word. Also, I didn't want him to be angry with me for showing off so much of my figure without telling him first."

I put my fingers to my temples and tried to think.

"But I wasn't going to let him stop me," she said, trying to reassure me. "If he said I couldn't do it, I would have done it anyway. I would never miss an opportunity like this because of him."

"Well, now there might not be an opportunity to display Hanson's painting, thanks to your good conscience."

"What? Why?" she said.

"Never mind," I said. "Where is he now?"

"I don't know, I haven't seen him for a few hours."

Back outside, Jimmy looked distraught.

"I'm so sorry, Jimmy," I said. "I never should have asked you to get that frame. It was too risky, and now both paintings are missing."

"It's not your fault."

"Yes, it is, and I don't know what Edgar's going to do now. If he doesn't want the Isabella painting to come to light, he could destroy it, he could sell it, he could hide it away again. No matter what happens with the pageant, I simply can't let any of those things happen."

"What should we do now?" Mrs. Moynahan asked.

"We have to find it. Can you locate the police chief, what's his name, Winslow?" I asked her. "Tell him we have a theft on our hands and it's urgent. He should be heading to costume soon anyway, since he's in the first tableau." She nodded. "And Jimmy, can you meet me up front in five minutes? If you see Edgar, don't let him out of your sight."

"Are you sure you know what you're doing?" Jimmy asked.

"Please trust me," I said. "I created this mess, I think I have a way to get us out of it."

He looked in my eyes and nodded.

"Jimmy, I feel terrible about all of this. I'll try to explain to your manager that this was my doing, I'll take all the blame."

Jimmy shook his head.

"The last thing I want to do," I whispered, "is give you a reason to leave."

"Hazel," he said, pulling me closer, but there was no time.

⤴

I STOOD ON CANYON ROAD, AT THE ENTRANCE TO THE PAGEANT, watching for anyone coming or going. It was already 4:45 P.M., and the show was to go on at seven. Chief Winslow and I both needed to go to makeup. In addition, I was supposed to be helping everyone into their costumes. Panic rose up in me as the minutes ticked by.

Finally, Jimmy walked up with the chief and we headed for his car.

"I've already filled Chief Winslow in," Jimmy said, opening the door for me as the chief got in the driver's seat.

"Good," I said, climbing into the back seat.

Chief Winslow was a dignified, taciturn man, with a small, raised scar below his eye. Looking straight ahead, he gave a brusque nod as I shut the door.

"We're going to 41 Catalina Street," I said, my eyes wide at the prospect.

"Edgar Berg?" Chief Winslow asked.

I nodded. "Yes, sir."

He looked at me in the rearview mirror. "I hope you're not wrong about this."

I hoped I wasn't either. As we turned onto Edgar's street and neared his house, my stomach tightened in a knot. What if it wasn't there? What if Edgar had already disposed of it? Or I was wrong, and it wasn't Edgar after all? I could be making an awful mess even worse.

When we pulled up to the house and Winslow opened the door, I jumped out.

"Damn it! Get back here," I heard the chief muttering, but I barged right into the studio.

"What are you doing here?" Edgar erupted, striding toward me until he slowed to a stop as the chief and Jimmy followed me through the door. His eyes flickered toward the corner of the room.

"I think you know what we're doing here, Ed," Chief Winslow said.

I looked over to where he'd glanced, and the painting was propped up on a workbench, in plain view, an open toolbox next to it.

"You didn't even bother to hide it!" I said, mystified.

Edgar's face was red with fury, and he marched over to the painting, a knife gripped in his fist.

"No!" I shouted.

But as I lunged for his arm, Jimmy was on him, and the knife went skittering across the floor. Edgar took a swing and missed. Jimmy swung right back, knocking him square on the jaw, then bounced back up, wiped his brow, and rolled up his sleeves, ready to go again if he had to.

"I've been wanting to do that for a while now," Jimmy said.

The chief stepped forward and lifted Edgar to his feet, then grabbed him by the elbow. "I hate to do this, Ed, but we're going to have to take you down to the station for some questioning." He looked out the window as a second police car pulled up. "Actually, Sergeant Moore will take you." He turned to Jimmy and me. "If we leave now, we might just make it."

"This is ridiculous. I was just keeping it safe," Edgar called, twisting around while the officer escorted him to the police car. "You know I'm basically running the show," he screeched.

We carefully placed the framed painting in the trunk of Chief Winslow's car, and Jimmy and I climbed into the back seat. "Don't worry," I said to Edgar, before I closed the door, "I think we can take it from here."

On the way back, we stopped briefly at the hotel, where Winslow explained to the manager that Jimmy's actions were warranted and necessary for the sake of the pageant. I wasn't sure that Jimmy was off the hook, but it was all we could do with the time we had left.

CHAPTER 39

THE SHOW BEGAN PROMPTLY AT 7 P.M. AND OPENED TO A FULL house. We'd arrived backstage just in time for the chief to get into his military uniform. He didn't need much in the way of makeup, since his face wouldn't be in view.

The narrator explained how the photographer, Joe Rosenthal, had captured the image of six marines raising the U.S. flag atop Mount Suribachi during the battle of Iwo Jima, in the final stages of the Pacific War. The audience gasped when the curtains opened to reveal the black-and-white scene of the men climbing on rubble to declare victory. Some people rose to their feet and applauded in what felt like a moment of gratitude for those who'd fought, sorrow for those we had lost, and hope for the future. It was the perfect image to open the show.

The toddlers in *Charity* froze in position for the entire ninety seconds that the curtains were open, with the promise of chocolate waiting for them stage left. The child propped up on a pillow in *The Doctor* by Sir Luke Fildes actually sneezed mid-pose, which only seemed to amuse and heighten the experience for the audience, reminding them for a moment that what they were looking at was actually a living tableau and not the two-dimensional paintings that the lights and makeup had tricked them into believing they saw. I felt a momentary thrill as I prepared to take my place in *A Virgin*, holding the hands of the two little girls at my sides. The curtains opened, and a peaceful calm came over me as I looked out to all those faces in the audience, many that I recognized and saw daily, as well as strangers who'd traveled from out

CHAPTER 39

THE SHOW BEGAN PROMPTLY AT 7 P.M. AND OPENED TO A FULL house. We'd arrived backstage just in time for the chief to get into his military uniform. He didn't need much in the way of makeup, since his face wouldn't be in view.

The narrator explained how the photographer, Joe Rosenthal, had captured the image of six marines raising the U.S. flag atop Mount Suribachi during the battle of Iwo Jima, in the final stages of the Pacific War. The audience gasped when the curtains opened to reveal the black-and-white scene of the men climbing on rubble to declare victory. Some people rose to their feet and applauded in what felt like a moment of gratitude for those who'd fought, sorrow for those we had lost, and hope for the future. It was the perfect image to open the show.

The toddlers in *Charity* froze in position for the entire ninety seconds that the curtains were open, with the promise of chocolate waiting for them stage left. The child propped up on a pillow in *The Doctor* by Sir Luke Fildes actually sneezed mid-pose, which only seemed to amuse and heighten the experience for the audience, reminding them for a moment that what they were looking at was actually a living tableau and not the two-dimensional paintings that the lights and makeup had tricked them into believing they saw. I felt a momentary thrill as I prepared to take my place in *A Virgin*, holding the hands of the two little girls at my sides. The curtains opened, and a peaceful calm came over me as I looked out to all those faces in the audience, many that I recognized and saw daily, as well as strangers who'd traveled from out

"This is ridiculous. I was just keeping it safe," Edga
around while the officer escorted him to the police ca
basically running the show," he screeched.

We carefully placed the framed painting in th
Winslow's car, and Jimmy and I climbed into the back
I said to Edgar, before I closed the door, "I think we ca

On the way back, we stopped briefly at the hot
explained to the manager that Jimmy's actions were
essary for the sake of the pageant. I wasn't sure tha
hook, but it was all we could do with the time we h

CHAPTER 39

THE SHOW BEGAN PROMPTLY AT 7 P.M. AND OPENED TO A FULL house. We'd arrived backstage just in time for the chief to get into his military uniform. He didn't need much in the way of makeup, since his face wouldn't be in view.

The narrator explained how the photographer, Joe Rosenthal, had captured the image of six marines raising the U.S. flag atop Mount Suribachi during the battle of Iwo Jima, in the final stages of the Pacific War. The audience gasped when the curtains opened to reveal the black-and-white scene of the men climbing on rubble to declare victory. Some people rose to their feet and applauded in what felt like a moment of gratitude for those who'd fought, sorrow for those we had lost, and hope for the future. It was the perfect image to open the show.

The toddlers in *Charity* froze in position for the entire ninety seconds that the curtains were open, with the promise of chocolate waiting for them stage left. The child propped up on a pillow in *The Doctor* by Sir Luke Fildes actually sneezed mid-pose, which only seemed to amuse and heighten the experience for the audience, reminding them for a moment that what they were looking at was actually a living tableau and not the two-dimensional paintings that the lights and makeup had tricked them into believing they saw. I felt a momentary thrill as I prepared to take my place in *A Virgin*, holding the hands of the two little girls at my sides. The curtains opened, and a peaceful calm came over me as I looked out to all those faces in the audience, many that I recognized and saw daily, as well as strangers who'd traveled from out

"This is ridiculous. I was just keeping it safe,"
around while the officer escorted him to the pol
basically running the show," he screeched.

We carefully placed the framed painting i
Winslow's car, and Jimmy and I climbed into the b
I said to Edgar, before I closed the door, "I think we

On the way back, we stopped briefly at the h
explained to the manager that Jimmy's actions we r
essary for the sake of the pageant. I wasn't sure t h
hook, but it was all we could do with the time we

CHAPTER 39

THE SHOW BEGAN PROMPTLY AT 7 P.M. AND OPENED TO A FULL house. We'd arrived backstage just in time for the chief to get into his military uniform. He didn't need much in the way of makeup, since his face wouldn't be in view.

The narrator explained how the photographer, Joe Rosenthal, had captured the image of six marines raising the U.S. flag atop Mount Suribachi during the battle of Iwo Jima, in the final stages of the Pacific War. The audience gasped when the curtains opened to reveal the black-and-white scene of the men climbing on rubble to declare victory. Some people rose to their feet and applauded in what felt like a moment of gratitude for those who'd fought, sorrow for those we had lost, and hope for the future. It was the perfect image to open the show.

The toddlers in *Charity* froze in position for the entire ninety seconds that the curtains were open, with the promise of chocolate waiting for them stage left. The child propped up on a pillow in *The Doctor* by Sir Luke Fildes actually sneezed mid-pose, which only seemed to amuse and heighten the experience for the audience, reminding them for a moment that what they were looking at was actually a living tableau and not the two-dimensional paintings that the lights and makeup had tricked them into believing they saw. I felt a momentary thrill as I prepared to take my place in *A Virgin,* holding the hands of the two little girls at my sides. The curtains opened, and a peaceful calm came over me as I looked out to all those faces in the audience, many that I recognized and saw daily, as well as strangers who'd traveled from out

"This is ridiculous. I was just keeping it safe," Edg
around while the officer escorted him to the police c
basically running the show," he screeched.

We carefully placed the framed painting in t
Winslow's car, and Jimmy and I climbed into the back
I said to Edgar, before I closed the door, "I think we ca

On the way back, we stopped briefly at the hot
explained to the manager that Jimmy's actions were
essary for the sake of the pageant. I wasn't sure tha
hook, but it was all we could do with the time we h

CHAPTER 40

THAT NIGHT, WE ALL CELEBRATED THE PAGEANT'S TRIUMPHANT return with champagne backstage. When Scarlett emerged from the dressing room, the thick makeup from her face and body gone and replaced with her glamorous red lips and long lashes, she was bombarded by the press and blissfully held court.

"Miss Francis." I heard Mr. Fredericks's stern voice and determined footsteps coming toward me.

"The evening would seem to have been quite a success," he said, and I began to smile at his approval—but it was premature. "However, you had absolutely no right to go behind my back with that stunt. I am the director of this show, and you are merely a volunteer, a first-time volunteer who, might I add, left your duties in the most critical time prior to opening night."

"I am so sorry," I said. "I really felt I had no other choice . . ."

"You could have come to me."

"I worried about Edgar trying to stop us, and I . . ."

"Never mind Edgar. In future you will run all things by me before orchestrating any of these types of antics." He looked over to the mass of reporters scrambling around Scarlett, their camera bulbs flashing, and I saw him try to hide a smile.

"In the future?" I asked.

"Yes, fortunately for you, we seem to have created quite a flurry of excitement, and I for one am quite pleased we could honor the late Hanson

Radcliff in such a meaningful way. But next year, we'll be finding someone else for the costume department."

I sighed and looked down.

"I'm hoping you'll take on the role of assistant director, and we can
work closely on mounting next year's show."

"Me?" I asked, shocked and honored.

"It doesn't pay." He hurried to disabuse me of any illusions about his
offer. "It's a strictly volunteer role, they all are, but it's a prestigious one."

"I would gladly accept, if I am still here in Laguna."

"Why wouldn't you be?"

"Well, I'm no longer employed here."

"Oh, you won't have any trouble with that, I'll make sure of it," he
said. "I think it's fair to say Mr. Radcliff would have been proud of what
you accomplished here tonight. Now, if you'll excuse me, I have the press
to attend to."

Finally, I was able to make my way over to Jimmy.

"You did it," he said, smudges of white still on his face and in his hair.

"We did it," I said.

He took my hand and pulled me into the wings away from the rest
of the cast and volunteers.

"Hazel, there's something I have to tell you, and I can't wait any longer."

Hope rose up in me, but alongside it, fear. If he said nothing, we could
go on for tonight, riding the thrill of the evening, pretending as if nothing would change.

"Jimmy—" I said.

But he took my hands in his. "I called things off with Jeanene. And
the reason is because I'm in love with someone else." He pulled me closer
to him. "I'm in love with you, Hazel Francis, I have been ever since I first
set eyes on you in the hotel bar. When I think of a future, I feel hope
because of you, and my dreams are bigger with you in them. After you
left Laguna and didn't tell anyone where you were going, not even me, I
was crushed. I couldn't stop thinking about you—the way you look, the
way you laugh, the way you think, your determination, your passion. I
couldn't imagine my life here without you in it."

A wave of relief washed over me, and I wanted to throw my arms around
him, but he continued. "I know I don't have much to offer. I'm just a bar-

tender, if they'll still have me, and I don't have a proper place to live, but I'll work all that out, I will. And I'll make a name for myself, I can promise you that. I'll make a life for us here." He paused. "If that's what you want."

"It is what I want!" I said, my eyes filling with tears. "*You* are exactly what I want."

He pulled me in tightly and kissed me. Finally, the urgency of his lips on mine, his arms around me—this was everything I'd been waiting for. Suddenly, all I wanted was for us to be alone. He took my hand, and it felt as if we might both break into a run to get off that stage, away from everyone else and into each other's arms. But someone called us back.

"Miss Francis." It was Mr. Solomon again. He could not have had worse timing. "Miss Francis, I have been trying to reach you. We have to talk."

"I know, and I'm sorry, Mr. Solomon," I said, my heart pounding. "I was planning to find you tomorrow. Can it please wait until then? It's been a really busy week and a very long day."

"It can't wait. It's extremely important. It's imperative that we speak. I require an audience with both of you, in fact."

Jimmy and I stopped and turned to him.

"It's about Hanson's final will. We can make an appointment to meet tomorrow and go over the details in my office, but you need to know his general intent regarding the hotel."

"What about it?" Jimmy asked.

"Hanson Radcliff was the sole owner of Hotel Laguna—"

"What?" I said. Jimmy looked just as shocked as I was. "No, he wasn't. He didn't own the hotel."

"He did. He's owned it for some fifteen or sixteen years, even during the two years when the government took it over for the military, but he wanted to remain anonymous. He bought it when the former owners were going to close it down, when they hit hard times. Anyway, for some reason, he's left the whole thing to the two of you, a partnership."

"No," I said. "That can't be right!"

Jimmy laughed. "He didn't want to lose his seat at the bar."

Mr. Solomon shrugged. "Something like that."

Thoughts of Hanson were flying through my head. His concerns, his questions that day at Victoria Beach. What he'd said about Jimmy and me. "Are you sure about this?" I asked.

"That's not all," Mr. Solomon continued. "He's also left the apartment to you, Hazel, and a significant amount of money."

I was dumbstruck.

"The gallery building will go to the co-op, plus the carrying costs for years to come. He's donating his house and studio to the city of Laguna Beach, to be used as a public studio by artists who need a place to work. He's leaving all of his artwork to the Laguna Beach Art Association, with the exception of Isabella, which, as I believe you know, he's left in your hands."

I stood there, shaking my head. Having come to know Hanson as I did, his shocking generosity made sense. It was wild, it was reckless, it was risky. It was kind.

He turned to Jimmy. "He told me he knew you were the right man for the job." Mr. Solomon shrugged his shoulders again, seemingly as baffled by all of this as we were.

"I don't quite know what to say, Mr. Solomon, except that—I want to ensure that the Isabella painting is safe. I don't want to risk it being stolen again, and yet it deserves to be seen. I've been thinking of calling the LA County Museum, or the Pasadena Art Institute, to ask if they'd be interested in putting it on display—or maybe an exhibition, if the Art Association would allow it."

"A retrospective perhaps," Mr. Solomon added. "That's a wonderful idea, very wise, and I'm happy to help. Come to my office in the morning, both of you, and we can go over the details."

Jimmy and I walked back toward the apartment hand in hand, stunned by every whirlwind event of the day, topped off by Hanson's gift. When we reached Coast Boulevard, we crossed over and looked out onto the beach, the ocean black, its surface glimmering in the moonlight.

"I think I need to put my feet in the water," I said.

We walked down to the sand and kicked off our shoes. When the cool water ran over my toes, I felt the usual calm it always brought.

◁

I WOKE IN THE EARLY HOURS OF THE MORNING IN THE TANGLED sheets of my bed, Jimmy sleeping peacefully by my side. For the first time since I'd arrived in Laguna Beach, I had no desire to jump out of bed and run to the ocean. That could wait. I gave in to the warmth of his smooth, tanned skin and I snuggled into him, perfectly content where I was. To think I'd arrived here with nothing and no one, and now I had everything I'd ever wanted right here in my arms.

For as long as I could remember I'd wanted to belong, to be part of something bigger than myself. By passing the hotel on to us, Hanson had placed the anchor of this community in our hands—a place where people came together to eat, drink, rest, celebrate, and even mourn.

And yet something tugged at my heart.

Jimmy stirred, then opened his eyes. "Good morning, beautiful," he said, kissing me.

He turned on his side and swept the hair from my face. "You look deep in thought. What's on your mind?"

"I keep thinking about the hotel," I said. "It's so incredibly unexpected and generous of Hanson to leave it to us. But I don't know how to run a hotel."

"But I do," he said, smiling. "Or at least I have some ideas. We have a lot to learn, but whatever we don't know, we'll figure out together. The managers and the staff can teach us. I know the hotel is struggling at the moment, but with time, it will be a success again." He lay back and put his hands behind his head. "After I was deployed, I used to dream of owning my own bar or restaurant. It's what kept me going through some terrible, awful times. But a hotel—it's more than I could have ever imagined."

I ran my hand over his strong chest, thinking of all that he'd seen overseas and hoping that someday he'd share that burden with me.

"I have some dreams too," I said.

Jimmy smiled. "Tell me."

"There's an abandoned airstrip up on the bluffs. Hanson told me about it. He said it was built by an aviation enthusiast, Pancho Barnes." I'd been reliving the conversation I had with Hanson at Victoria Beach as I lay awake that morning. "She moved to the desert, and it's fallen into disrepair. I'd like to use some of the money Hanson left us to get it up and running again. It would be good for business all around. Those Hollywood directors could fly in and out of here easily and come straight to the hotel. And maybe, just maybe, I'll even learn to fly one of those planes one day."

"I like the way you think." He kissed my bare shoulder. "Over these past few days, you proved to this whole town that you can do anything you put your mind to, anything at all."

I lay back on the pillow and smiled, thinking of those posters and pamphlets that encouraged us to keep going when we worked at the factory. YOU CAN DO IT, they read. YOU CAN DO IT.

"That's true," I said. "I really can."

I rested my head on Jimmy's chest, feeling the steady rhythm of his heartbeat, hearing the faint sound of waves crashing on the beach through the open window, and I knew in that moment that I'd found my way home.

AUTHOR'S NOTE

The very first Festival of Arts was held next to Hotel Laguna in 1932, the same year as the Los Angeles Olympic Games. Artists opened their studios and displayed their works in the hope that this would draw visitors from Los Angeles to Laguna Beach to discover new artists and buy art. The following year, local artist Lolita Perine had the idea for a living work of art and persuaded residents of Laguna Beach to dress in costume, sit behind an oversized frame, and re-create well-known works of art. Over the next few years, local developer and visionary Roy Ropp elevated the living–art program to a much higher quality, and he renamed it the "Pageant of the Masters." The show was held at various locations over the next seven years, and in 1941 the Irvine Bowl Recreation Park was named the pageant's permanent home. Record attendance and ticket sales created intense anticipation for the following year, but World War II halted the festival and the pageant for four years—the only other time in its ninety-year history that the show did not go on was 2020, due to the Covid pandemic. Ropp died in 1974 but is remembered as the "Father of the Pageant."

Today the Festival of Arts' Pageant of the Masters attracts more than a quarter of a million visitors each summer, has a pool of more than five hundred volunteers, and is known as one of the most unique productions in the world.

I've been lucky enough to glimpse behind the scenes at art shows in Laguna Beach and gain insight into the artist community that thrives there through my parents, both artists, who have displayed their work in galleries and art festivals in Laguna Beach. After college I moved into a tiny apartment behind a cooperative gallery called the Quorum where my parents used to exhibit their work. This little apartment and gallery is where I imagined Hazel living and working. And while the characters in this book are completely fictional, I was certainly inspired by the artists that were part of the California Impressionist movement.

Hotel Laguna had been closed for several years when I started work on this novel, and its future seemed uncertain. When it was renovated and reopened in 2021 I took it as a sign that this book was meant to be. For those who already know Laguna Beach well, you may have noticed references to businesses along the boardwalk at Main Beach that no longer exist. In 1968 the City of Laguna Beach purchased the one-thousand-foot-long oceanfront property for $3,135,000 and later demolished the buildings to allow for an unobstructed view of the Pacific Ocean. In 1974 this stretch of land, known as a "window to the sea," was dedicated as Main Beach Park.

Setting this novel in 1946, immediately following World War II, allowed me to acknowledge the role of women on the home front during the war, stepping up and thriving in positions previously reserved only for men. When I discovered that my husband's grandmother had worked as a "Rosie" in an LA airplane factory during the war, I was truly inspired to hear stories about her life from my mother-in-law. I also had the good fortune to connect with the American Rosie the Riveter Association, through which I was able to interview several "Rosies" both in person and on Zoom. While Hazel's story is not based on any one person, these firsthand stories of courage, strength, and determination were key to my understanding and appreciation of these amazing women.

The following books were also instrumental in helping me bring this story to life:

Art Colony: The Laguna Beach Art Association, 1918–1935 by Janet Blake and Deborah Epstein Solon
Images of America: Laguna Beach by Claire Marie Vogel
Images of America: Rosie the Riveter in Long Beach by Gerrie Schipske
Images of Aviation: Southern California's World War II Aircraft by Cory Graff and Patrick Devine
Our Mothers' War: American Women at Home and at the Front During World War II by Emily Yellin
Then & Now: Laguna Beach by Foster J. Eubank and Gene Felder

ACKNOWLEDGMENTS

I am so grateful for my wonderful team of publishing experts who have helped bring this book to life. Thank you to my editor, Leslie Gelbman, for believing in this book, for your invaluable editorial guidance, and for sharing your love of Laguna Beach with me. Thank you to the entire team at St. Martin's Press: Kejana Ayala, Hannah Tarro, Dori Weintraub, Erica Martirano, Brant Janeway, Grace Gay, Jonathan Bush, Nicola Ferguson, Gail Friedman, Ginny Perrin, and Lizz Blaise.

To my agent, Stephanie Kip Rostan, thank you for guiding me with your calming wisdom every step of the way, and huge thanks to the team at Levine Greenberg Rostan, especially Courtney Paganelli, Melissa Rowland, Cristela Henriquez, Miek Coccia, and Michael Nardullo.

I am truly grateful to librarian Nelda Stone at the Laguna Beach Public Library and Johanna Ellis from the Laguna Beach Historical Society. In the early days of 2020, when we were on lockdown and in-person research was impossible, they sent me articles and historical details that helped me tremendously, and later Nelda shared with me original programs and historical excerpts from the Pageant of the Masters, which inspired new plot twists that I hadn't expected.

Michele Pisa-Jones of the Orange County Chapter of the American Rosie the Riveter Association was instrumental in connecting me with "Rosies" around the country, specifically several women whom I was able to interview at the Emerald Court Senior Home. These firsthand stories were absolute treasures.

I could not have written *Hotel Laguna* without the weekly support of my trusted writing workshop friends Jennifer Belle, Donna Brodie, Barbara Miller, Meryl Branch-McTiernan, Sam Garonzik, and Steve

Reynolds. And I may not have finished this book without the kindness of fellow St. Martin's Press author Christi Clancy, who allowed me to write uninterrupted in her peaceful Palm Springs home.

Thanks also to my early readers Suzanna Filip, Elisa Moriconi, and Ginny Ray.

I'm indebted to the vast community of booksellers, librarians, book bloggers, bookstagrammers, TikTokers, and literature lovers who help spread the word and connect readers with authors. I am especially thankful to my beloved author friends Fiona Davis, Lynda Cohen Loigman, Jamie Brenner, Susie Orman Schnall, Amy Poeppel, and book influencer Suzy Leopold (aka The Thursday Authors).

I am of course forever grateful to my parents, Michael and Jayne Harrison, for their constant support and endless hours of babysitting.

And finally, my deepest gratitude to my husband, Greg Ray, and my sons, Christopher and Greyson, for putting up with having an author in the family, where anything they say or do can, and very likely will, be used in fiction.

Just One
of the Kids

Raising a Resilient Family
When One of Your Children
Has a Physical Disability

KAY HARRIS KRIEGSMAN, Ph.D., and
SARA PALMER, Ph.D.

The Johns Hopkins University Press

Baltimore

Note to the Reader: This book presents general guidelines, information, tips, and tools for raising a resilient family when one of your children has a physical disability. This book is not meant to substitute for advice or treatment from health care providers, educators, vocational counselors, or other professionals who work with your family. The services of a competent professional should be obtained whenever specific advice is needed.

© 2013 Kay Harris Kriegsman and Sara Palmer
All rights reserved. Published 2013
Printed in the United States of America on acid-free paper
9 8 7 6 5 4 3 2 1

The Johns Hopkins University Press
2715 North Charles Street
Baltimore, Maryland 21218-4363
www.press.jhu.edu

Library of Congress Cataloging-in-Publication Data

Kriegsman, Kay Harris.
   Just one of the kids : raising a resilient family when one of your children has a physical disability / Kay Harris Kriegsman, Ph.D., and Sara Palmer, Ph.D.
       pages cm
   Includes bibliographical references and index.
   ISBN 978-1-4214-0930-6 (hardcover : alk. paper) — ISBN 1-4214-0930-5 (hardcover : alk. paper) — ISBN 978-1-4214-0931-3 (pbk. : alk. paper) — ISBN 1-4214-0931-3 (pbk. : alk. paper) — ISBN 978-1-4214-0932-0 (electronic) — ISBN 1-4214-0932-1 (electronic)
   1. Children with disabilities—Family relationships. 2. Parents of children with disabilities.
I. Palmer, Sara. II. Title.
   HQ773.6.K75 2013
   649'.151—dc23   2012035771

A catalog record for this book is available from the British Library.

Special discounts are available for bulk purchases of this book. For more information, please contact Special Sales at 410-516-6936 or specialsales@press.jhu.edu.

The Johns Hopkins University Press uses environmentally friendly book materials, including recycled text paper that is composed of at least 30 percent post-consumer waste, whenever possible.

This book is dedicated to you, the families hailing from Vancouver to Massachusetts, Wisconsin to South Carolina, whose stories form the backbone of this book. Mothers and fathers, grandmothers and grandfathers, and brothers and sisters, both able-bodied and with physical disabilities, you talked with us face-to-face, by telephone, or via e-mail. You generously shared details of your emotional and family lives, describing the day-to-day challenges and rewards of being a family that includes a child who has a physical disability. You inspired us with your hopefulness and creativity in developing what you needed to forge ahead. This book could not have been written without you.

Contents

Preface

Why This Book?

Where do you go for information, encouragement, and advice when you have a child who has a physical disability? In our work with children and adults who have physical disabilities and with their parents and families, we discovered that there are many books and articles for parents raising children with cognitive or emotional disabilities. Few, however, address the needs of families that include a child who has a *physical* disability but is cognitively normal and emotionally healthy. The challenges these kids face overlap to some extent with the challenges of kids who have cognitive disabilities, but these children also have distinctly different challenges—and different capabilities. People who have *physical* disabilities have the mental and emotional capability to engage independently in adult activities, although they may need physical help to do so. People who have cognitive or emotional disabilities may not need physical help but may depend on parents (or others) for cognitive and emotional assistance on into adulthood.

At small local meetings, at national conferences on physical disability, and in our clinical practices, families of children who have a physical disability have expressed their need for information to help them raise their children successfully. They wanted guidance on how to create more inclusive families, in which each of their kids, whether or not they have disabilities, would be able to participate in social life, recreation, and education and be prepared for employment or other productive activities in adulthood. And they wanted to know how to access opportunities and resources, within and outside the family, to make this possible.

Our book aims to help parents and children achieve these goals. It is written specifically for and about parents of families that include a child who has a physical disability and one or more children who are able-bodied—mostly from the perspective of real parents, who volunteered to share their experiences with us. (One family whose story is featured in the book has a son who has a physical disability and no other children.) In writing this book, we did extensive interviews not only with the parents but also with grandparents and children, both able-bodied and with physical disabilities, from many families. We sifted through their experiences to identify the tools they developed and used, as well as the ones they were searching for in their quest to raise healthy, happy children prepared for successful adulthood. This book combines the wisdom of these families with our own personal and professional experience and the work of other disability experts to present a framework for raising resilient children. Included are many tips, tools, suggestions, and resources to help you raise *your* family. (Look for the ⚠, ☛, and T symbols throughout.)

The names of all people we interviewed have been changed to protect their privacy, and all names used in the family stories or elsewhere in the book are pseudonyms. Some people portrayed are composites of multiple people.

Why Us? Personal Perspectives

Kay always wondered as a child, "What's the big deal about having a physical disability?" She did the same things her brothers did, albeit from a sitting stance or using crutches and braces, after a bout with polio at age 7. They all played musical instruments, were active in 4-H, did assigned chores, helped care for two younger sisters born many years later, had the usual childhood fights, and bottle-fed the "bummer lambs," abandoned at birth by their mothers.

Although she had physical therapy, operations, and doctors' appointments, Kay was also just one of the kids and felt included and needed in the larger family scene. Disability was just one of a number of challenges her family faced, the chief one being economic upheaval, at times requiring both of her parents to work outside the home. While this was hard on the family, it had a positive side for Kay, as it took the focus off her disability and meant that she had to be a contributing member of the family. She washed dishes, set the table, and vacuumed while sitting on the floor.

Kay was not aware as a child how her disability affected her parents. While her family treated her like any other child, it wasn't always easy. Kay's mother still remembers that just after her daughter was airlifted from their small mountain town to a big-city hospital, the head of the hospital billing office was disdainful and made her feel incompetent because their family had no health insurance. Kay's brothers felt the effects of their sister's eight-month hospitalization. Like other children during the polio epidemics, in the first few weeks of Kay's illness her brothers were quarantined. They were angry with the landlord, who demanded the rent when their mother returned home from taking Kay to the distant hospital, so they showed the landlord what they thought of him, taking a knife and "decorating" the woodwork in the house. Their mother laughed and cried with pride in her sons' misguided protection of her, while wondering how she could ever pay for the repair.

When Kay returned home from the coddled atmosphere of the hospital, her family had new responsibilities to shoulder. Getting on with life meant adding new activities; for instance, Kay's mother had to do physical therapy exercises with her every day.

In the years following, Kay never heard from her family that she could *not* do something. If there were a student council meeting on the second floor of a building without an elevator, her family would find a way for her to attend; usually, her brothers "bumped" her up the steps in her wheelchair. It was expected that she would ask a boy to the Sadie Hawkins Day dance, go on 4-H trips, and drive a car at age 16. Although her family encouraged her to take risks, there were times when they weren't comfortable with what Kay herself was ready to do. Although Kay walked with crutches except through her high school's busy hallways (where she used a wheelchair), her family assumed that she would take her wheelchair to college for safety and to conserve her energy—and use it. She refused. The compromise was that the wheelchair took the ride over the Continental Divide to the university and then was safely stowed away in the basement of the dorm.

Kay's parents made a choice to see what *could be* rather than what *could have been*. Her parents must have been saddened when their little 7-year-old girl, who loved dancing and "running the hills" with her brothers, had to begin using double leg braces and crutches to walk. But they never conveyed a sense that they saw her as anything but an equal to her brothers and sisters, neither less nor more. They always chose to deal with "what is."

The acceptance and equal treatment by her family shaped Kay's attitudes about physical disability and her interest in helping other families raise hearty, independent-minded kids—whether or not they have a physical disability. You will see many of her experiences echoed in the stories of other families we interviewed for this book.

With the love and support of Will, her late husband, Kay returned to graduate school to work on her PhD in counseling while mothering Bill and Katie. For many years she codirected the HOW (Handicapped Is Only a Word) Conference, an annual event for teenagers who have physical disabilities, their parents, and their teen siblings. HOW emphasized opportunities for socialization, peer support, future planning, and fun. Kay's work with families—parents, children who have disabilities and their siblings, and some grandparents, as well—expanded from one-on-one sessions to small groups to large conventions. She published a book for teenagers who have physical disabilities, coauthored two books with Sara, and published articles on disability in professional journals and consumer magazines. She maintains a private psychology practice working with people, both able-bodied and who have disabilities, going through the normal ups and downs of life.

Sara grew up able-bodied in a family that was not directly affected by physical disability. Much of her experience with disability has come from her work as a rehabilitation psychologist, helping people who have disabilities and their partners and families cope with difficult circumstances and live more fulfilling lives.

Sara's course work for her PhD in clinical psychology included nothing about physical disability. But her husband was in medical school at the time, and he planned to specialize in physical medicine and rehabilitation. Through him, Sara was introduced to the field of rehabilitation psychology, met more people who had disabilities, and was inspired to explore this new career path. During her internship at the Seattle VA Hospital, Sara elected to spend three months on the inpatient rehabilitation unit, evaluating and treating people with spinal cord injuries, strokes, amputations, multiple sclerosis, and other disabilities. She found it refreshing to work with people who were generally mentally healthy but were coping with the emotional fallout from a life-changing accident or illness. Colleagues often asked her if it was depressing to work with people who had such "tragic" circumstances, but Sara felt uplifted by the strength and creativity she saw in her patients as they discovered ways to cope with their disabilities and reengage in life. She signed on for another three-month elective, and rehabilitation psychology has been the focus of her career ever since.

Over the years, Sara has worked in various hospitals and in private practice. She has worked with many teens and young adults who have disabilities and with their families, in addition to adults and seniors. She has written books about spinal cord injury and stroke for people who have these conditions and for their families. She has volunteered with disability organizations and been an educator and advocate within her profession for people who have disabilities. Sara has learned an enormous amount about living with a physical disability from her friendship and professional collaboration with Kay, spanning more than twenty-five years.

We hope this book will urge you on to claim the excitement and possibilities that exist in you and your family, finding the "aha" moment as you transition from feeling the "*burden*" of disability to the joy of *discovery*, when you begin to think, "What if we try it *this* way?"

In Appreciation

We have many to thank, beginning with Jackie Wehmueller, the most gracious, instructive, and supportive of editors, who guided us through two earlier books and helped us hone our voice in this one. Our appreciation for her wise counsel, soothing voice, honesty, and concern cannot be adequately put into words.

We thank Jeremy Horsefield, whose copyediting further improved the tone and readability of the manuscript.

We are grateful to Armetta Parker of United Cerebral Palsy, Charleene Frazier of the Spinal Cord Injury Network, Kevin Fang, Sherry Arvin of the Spina Bifida Association, the staff of the Osteogenesis Imperfecta Foundation, and the staff of the Arthritis Foundation, who put out the call to parents, siblings, and grandparents who wanted to be interviewed for the book. Their assistance was invaluable.

Finally, we thank our families, who are always there for us: Kay's mother, Elizabeth Harris; her siblings, John, Dick, Beth, and Sue Harris; and her children and grandchildren, Bill, Christy, and Kyle Kriegsman, and Katie, Jerry, Darby, Raymond, and Addy Peters; Sara's father, Irving Sarnoff; her brother, David Pepper Sarnoff, and his wife, Pepper Sarnoff; and her children, Josh Palmer and Eleanore Olszewski and Noah and Hana Palmer. Sara gives special thanks to her husband, Jeffrey B. Palmer, for his constant love, support, and patience; for his perspectives on parenting and disability; and for his insights on the art of writing.

Raising Children—Resilient and Ready for Adulthood

Kelsey and her husband are parents of an outgoing first grader who has spina bifida. The couple are best friends, confide in each other, and make joint decisions. By discussing their thoughts and ideas together, they help each other understand the advice of medical experts. They can support one another in pushing for more information when needed, and they can tap into each other's intuition when making decisions about their daughter's care. "At one point we felt that something wasn't right with her. We asked the doctor, and we were correct—our daughter needed surgery."

When Roberto's son Cory was 14, he was injured in a skateboarding accident and became paraplegic. Roberto was sad and upset—but not devastated—when this happened. Because Roberto's older sister has severe rheumatoid arthritis and lives a full life with a disability, he knew that Cory would still be able to reach many of his life goals—and embrace some new ones. When he returned to school after rehabilitation, Cory, formerly a soccer star, found a new role on the team—becoming the coach's assistant and co-strategizer.

Liz's daughter Janet was born with a disability. It broadened her view of the world. "It made me more knowledgeable. I had already crossed cultural barriers, coming from Scotland to Africa to the Midwest, with sabbaticals in far-flung corners of the earth." A divorced mother of two, Liz found that her daughter's disability required some special planning but did not prevent the family from traveling. Disability was just another part of their life equation. Janet, now an adult with a family of her own, shares her mother's passion for travel and adventure.

Kelsey, Roberto, and Liz raised their children—both able-bodied and those who have disabilities—to participate fully in life, not watch from the sidelines. They found ways to keep their kids healthy and safe—and to still include them in family activities, sports, travel, and other exciting life experiences. They prepared their children to handle life's challenges successfully and to become capable, independent adults. In short, they created *inclusive* families, building *resilience* in themselves and their children. And you can, too.

First of all, what is an inclusive family? It is a family that embraces every one of its members, including the child who happens to have a physical disability. Each person in the family is valued and respected as an individual and as part of the whole. His unique interests, talents, and aspirations are recognized and supported. Parents divide their attention fairly among all the children, and each child is loved, nurtured, and given what she needs to flourish. There may be times when the pressing needs of one family member are given more weight in the short run, but over the long run, the needs of everyone will be met. For instance, when Bobbi needs surgery to correct scoliosis or Elliot breaks his arm in a soccer game, their needs must get priority. But even in the midst of a crisis with one child, inclusive parents let each child know that they are loved and cared about. And after the crisis is resolved, an inclusive family returns to "normal" mode where every child's needs are given equal consideration. An inclusive family cultivates the sense of "I can do it!" in each child and strengthens their "rebound-ability," or resilience.

What, then, is a resilient family? Resilient families land on their feet no matter what challenges come their way. They go beyond merely surviving tough times: they adapt, rebound from stress, grow, and thrive. Parents in resilient families can meet their children's everyday needs, respond to unexpected setbacks, and anticipate challenges not yet on the horizon.

As psychologists with expertise in physical disability, we are particularly interested in the rebound-ability of families that include a child who has a physical disability. What are the keys to resiliency in these families?

Over the years, in our therapy practices and at national and local conferences, parents of kids who have physical disabilities have shared their stories with us. Their stories revealed their struggles and their successes and helped us begin to answer this question. To write this book, we also interviewed numerous parents, grandparents, and children in families that include a child who has a physical disability. Some families were more, and some less, resilient. Some had an easier and some a harder time including their child who has a physical disability in family life (and in life beyond the family). But each of these individuals inspired us with their love for their families, their tenacity in finding answers and resources, their openness to taking uncharted paths, and their generosity of spirit as they helped other families following in their wakes. And each of them taught us something about building resiliency.

Through a combination of these extensive family interviews, our own personal and professional experiences with disability, and concepts of resiliency outlined by other psychologists, we developed our own theoretical model for *creating an inclusive and resilient family when your child has a physical disability*. This model forms the backbone of the book.

Whether you are just starting out and "clueless" or a seasoned parent looking for a few new tips, this book aims to educate, support, and inspire you. The book explains the basic principles of inclusion and resilience, and it demonstrates the wide variety of styles and techniques that parents use to turn these principles into everyday practice. We hope this book also helps you become more resilient as a parent (and as a person), increases your confidence, and redefines what is "normal" for you and your children.

How Parents Create Resilient Families

The hallmarks of resilient families are *pragmatism* (being realistic, down-to-earth, practical), *belief* in your child, and *vision* (seeing long-term potentials and possibilities). This combination of characteristics builds a sense of security, self-confidence, and a taste for adventure in children. Parents anchor their children in reality by *solving practical problems* in the here and now. They encourage their children to develop their talents, abilities, and self-confidence, by *communicating positive expectations* and belief in their children's strengths. They prepare their children for the future by *sharing their vision* of their children as independent adults and giving them opportunities to learn the behaviors and skills they will need to take on adult roles.

Resilient Families = Pragmatism + Belief in Your Child
+ Vision of Child's Potential

$$\text{Resilient Children} \quad = \quad \text{Experience + Responsibility} \\ \text{+ Socialization + Risk Taking}$$

But sometimes, especially if one of your children has a physical disability, you can get so caught up in day-to-day practical problems or routines that you don't pay attention to what your children need to become capable adults. Many parents are highly capable in raising their children from infancy to early adolescence, only to have difficulty launching them into young adulthood because they haven't done the "prep work." Parents may find it scary to think about their children growing up, leaving home, and handling their own lives—and this is often true to a greater degree for their children who have physical disabilities. So, our model for raising resilient children emphasizes those aspects of life that parents need to structure for or with their children *throughout their childhoods*, in order to prepare them for life beyond the family when they become adults.

In our framework, there are four essential factors that prepare a child for life as a competent, independent, resilient adult:

1. participating in a variety of *experiences* that educate them about life;
2. assuming *responsibility* to build abilities and self-esteem;
3. having opportunities for *socialization* to help them form relationships with people outside the family; and
4. taking *risks* appropriate to their age to learn how to judge what is safe and what is not.

Competence in these four fundamentals is built on the foundation of an inclusive family—and developed in the context of each family's values and culture.

Experience

We learn about life by being a part of it, by *experiencing* it. Do you remember taking your toddler out to walk in the snow, to feel the cold and hear the crunch under her boots, or visiting the beach, where your child sifted the sand through her fingers and put a toe into the surf? Remember that first fall when the training wheels were removed from the bike? These memories or experiences become your child's "book of knowledge" about life. When snow or sand or falls from bicycles are mentioned, your child knows the feelings, sights, smells, and other sensations. This knowing becomes a link to other human beings and the experience of life.

Providing this shared experiential language is a vital part of raising a child. There are countless realms of experience to which you can expose your child, from physical to intellectual to social, from artistic to philosophical.

Creating music and artwork, for instance, can be an important experiential part of a child's life. It helps a child make a design or object that didn't exist before; not only does the child create something unique, but in the process he figures out how to solve a variety of problems and shares his experience with others.

When you have a child who has a physical disability, there are challenges in providing equal exposure to life experiences for that child and your able-bodied children. Parents work this out in a variety of ways. The O'Briens, for example, encourage involvement in all types of sports and give music lessons to all of their daughters, knowing how vitally these contribute to each girl's self-concept. Sean O'Brien coaches his younger daughters' ball games and spends equal time horseback riding with his oldest daughter, who has a disability. In another family, daughter Jamie likes modern dancing, so she takes lessons, while her sister Brittany, who uses a wheelchair, takes adaptive dancing classes for both able-bodied students and those who have physical disabilities. Myron, a teenager who uses an accessibility scooter, takes classes at the local culinary school, while his brother Les plays soccer. Each family chooses either the same or different activities so that their children can experience the worlds that call to them. Families who strive to be inclusive, with or without children who have physical disabilities, generally follow the "rule" that when a door is opened to one child, another (though not necessarily identical) door is opened for the other children.

Many parents also help their children who have disabilities to have physical and sensory experiences of the world that might be difficult for them to do on their own. One father, in order to allow his daughter, who uses double leg braces, to experience what it felt like to run, put her feet on his and then ran with her. Running felt so exhilarating for the little girl that she cried when her father was so tired that he had to stop. Years later the daughter saw a young woman running across campus, her hair blowing behind her, and thought, "I know what that feels like."

In his fictionalized autobiography, Christopher Nolan, an Irish writer who had cerebral palsy, wrote poetically about the physical and emotional impact of experiencing a cold stream for the first time while on a family vacation:

> Certain chores had to be done and then the family moved over to the mountain stream. They washed and splashed but as ever Joseph [Nolan] was there too. Nora [his mother] lifting him from his chair handed him to Matthew [his father]. Barefooted he was let splash, let feel the wild, surging, frantic flowing water, let stand on the hard, cold, rock floor, and curl his toes and see how white and graceful looked his feet under the spring-cool water.

Nolan's parents realized his need to be in the world and experience it as others did, feeling the pulsing stream and the hard rocks on the stream bed; they made these types of experiences, and many others, available to him.

Some parents feel that it is equally important to give able-bodied siblings some experience of the medical or rehabilitation world that is an integral part of the life of their child who has a disability. Their children's encounter with what their sibling does in physical therapy, medical treatments, or recovery from surgery is educational; it answers questions and demystifies what happens. Experience is a two-way street.

Technological wonders open up new worlds of possibilities for your able-bodied children and those who have physical disabilities to participate together in many experiences. The sports world is a great example. For Lance Bowers, competitive biking is made possible by a hand-powered bicycle. Sit-skis tethered to experienced able-bodied skiers allow people who have disabilities to enjoy the world of snow sports. Others enjoy adaptive horseback riding. And as the Fisher family discovered, many water sports enjoyed by able-bodied kids can also be adapted for those who have physical disabilities. Swimming, boating, kayaking, and canoeing are some of the possibilities. Add scuba diving to that list: at a national meeting teenagers with spina bifida (SB is the most common neural tube defect) were taught scuba basics and tried them out in the water. Talk about I-can-do-it faces rising from the depth of the pool!

Advances in accessible sports open doors to inclusive *family* activities, but perhaps more importantly, they open doors for children who have physical disabilities to participate with their *peers*, building bridges through this shared experience. Wheelchairs and braces fade into the background when a 10-year-old who happens to use a wheelchair sit-skis with the class jock.

Responsibility

All kids long to know they are valued and needed. They understand that others see them as reliable when they take on responsibilities that are appropriate to their age and ability levels. In years gone by children contributed to the family's survival and welfare by tending gardens or livestock, cooking, cleaning the home, caring for younger children, or making clothing. These chores gave children a sense of worth and were essential in building the skills they would need to assume adult roles in their own families. But at times this work was so strenuous and demanding that it left little time for them to play and be children. Even today, some parents assign so many chores to their offspring that their childhoods are stolen from them.

But in most of today's middle-class families, children's chores are much lighter—like loading the dishwasher or folding laundry. Yet the assignment of responsibilities is often a bone of contention between spouses, or between parents and children. In the families we interviewed, for example, some parents thought their children ought to be helping out more around the house, while their spouses felt that schoolwork, sports, other outside activities, and having some "down" time were more important than chores. In some families, academic achievement and participation in extracurricular activities take the place of home chores, becoming responsibilities for which children are held accountable. But in the long run, doing some work for the family's good builds each child's ability to be concerned and accountable to others. Think of all the things your kids could do using just a little of their time, such as setting/clearing the table, filling/emptying the dishwasher, sorting and running a load of laundry, cleaning the kitchen or bathroom, making a bed, putting dirty clothes in the hamper, feeding the cat, and so forth.

The prospect of deciding *how much* responsibility to give children at different ages, stages, and levels of abilities can create a quandary. You probably remember your mothers and fathers giving you a reasonable amount of responsibility to help with the family. Cindy, for instance, felt that her parents judged the amount well. She helped babysit her nieces and nephews, with gradual lessening of supervision. Eventually she took on jobs without oversight. She felt that this progression and the positive feedback about her babysitting prepared her for parenthood. Rose's mother encouraged her to build skills and self-confidence by teaching Rose to cook and make important decisions for herself, allowing her to take increasing responsibility as Rose seemed physically and mentally ready to accept it.

Some families easily find chores for their able-bodied children but are puzzled about how their child who has a disability can contribute. If you and your child are unable to find a way for him to do any of the chores mentioned above, what about having him keep the family calendar on the computer, answer the phone, read to or help a younger sibling with homework, or dig dandelions out of the family's lawn? You may assign chores, have the children volunteer for jobs from a list of options, or have them assign their own tasks. Jobs children volunteer for may surprise you because they may realize they can do more than you think they can.

Responsibility for self-care—grooming, choosing clothing, dressing, and gathering things needed for school—is taught early in many families. Your child may have added chores like bracing, physical exercises, or tak-

⚠ Sometimes children who have physical disabilities are inappropriately given the job of "family therapist," expected to act as the go-to person for siblings, or even parents, who have emotional problems. In a group of teenagers, a young girl who used a wheelchair said that when her parents were going through a tough time, her family assigned her the job of "keeping everyone happy"—and she was feeling like a failure. This is not an appropriate assignment for any child—or adult; no one can be responsible for the emotional life of another person.

ing medicines. One mother taught her son to catheterize himself at age 7 so that he would be able to go to sleepovers with his pals and take care of himself without her help.

Of course, whenever you assign home, school, self-care, or other duties to your children, you will need to follow up and make sure your children's responsibilities are duly carried out.

Socialization

Being social creatures, we are constantly building bridges to others. Some of us are very skillful at making social connections, and some not. Children's actual experiences of giving to and receiving from others help them build the social skills to begin and develop relationships, where they may find the common ground that leads to friendship.

We each have different degrees of the need to relate. Some of us are born extroverts, wanting to be around many people most of the time, while others are introverts, preferring a smaller group of friends and more time to be alone. Each social type can learn to hone his social abilities in the other direction; finding a middle ground between extroversion and introversion will often result in a more fulfilling social life. Remember that introverted children tend to feel fatigued when they have to put forth extra energy socializing with a large group of people, while those who are extroverts find it energizing to be part of a large group of people.

Understanding your children's social orientation allows you to support them in meeting their needs for social interaction. For instance, you can help your shy child by modeling social interactions, such as having her watch you make an introduction, or by letting her know that you sometimes feel shy or anxious, too. Share with her the skills you've developed to overcome that awkwardness. Make up some opening lines for her to memorize so that she'll have a quick initial hello, a handy tool to use when necessary. Let her know that she may need more alone time to re-stoke her social energy than her extroverted brother needs; her brother should know that the opposite is true for him—and that each preference is perfectly normal.

Parents set the tone for their children as they step out of the family and onto the broader stage, from neighborhood, to playgroups, to school. Your expectation that you and your children will accept others and, con-

> **T** *Spotlight technique.* Tell your child that when she feels that everyone is looking at her, she can, in her mind's eye, turn the spotlight on someone else. She can do this by showing her interest in that person, or asking a question about that person, thus turning the attention away from herself.

versely, that others will accept you and your children communicates your belief in your children and in the basic fairness of relationships. If you are anxious about how your child will be accepted into the larger community, your uncertainty can be easily "read" by your child.

To widen your children's social circles, you might take some time to think about what skills your child will need at the next step of his development. Socialization can be challenging for any child, whether she is outgoing and friendly or shy and retiring. Many children experience teasing, exclusion from groups or cliques, or rejection by their peers for any number of reasons. You can help your child by first listening and repeating back what she is telling you to make sure you are getting it right. Then express your appreciation for your child's feelings, validating them so that she knows you respect her. Assure her that, although it sometimes feels like it, she is not the only person to have faced this situation before. By relating how all relationships sometimes run into rocky terrain and by modeling appropriate assertiveness, you can help your child learn to speak up for herself. For instance, when Jenni was "boycotted" by her third-grade playmates, she sought out the new girl in the class to play with, making the new girl feel included. Jenni's mother wisely advised her to avoid making enemies with her old friends, telling her that they would respect her more if she didn't react in an angry or spiteful way. Her mother's careful guidance and support led to Jenni's eventual readmission into her old group of friends. At the same time, Jenni helped bring the new girl into the larger group. Jenni's mother negotiated this terrain wisely. By keeping your cool when your child is upset, you can teach her valuable lessons in navigating social interactions.

For a child who is "different," because of his ethnicity, being adopted, or having a physical disability, making friends and joining groups can have an added layer of difficulty: it's hard to get others to see him *as an individual*, not defined solely by his "difference." Since social evaluations by others begin at first sight, a child's clothing, hairstyle, accessories, or makeup "speak" first. It is helpful to most children to look like other kids in dress or hairstyle in order to be one of the gang. For children from other cultural backgrounds or who have physical disabilities it is even more important to have similarities in order to bridge the chasm between themselves and the mainstream. Your child can further narrow the gap with others by developing unique interests or a good sense of humor to draw attention to the ways he is like others, rather than different from them. Perhaps he is into teen adventure novels or the latest singing group; these shared interests can outweigh the disability in the eyes of his peers.

On the other hand, it can be empowering to help a child find a positive place for her disability or other difference within her overall self concept and personal identity. Adoptive parents of a child from a foreign country or different ethnicity can support his exploration of his cultural identity, even though it is not the parents'. For example, American parents can teach their adopted Chinese children about China or send them to "Chinese school." Similarly, parents can encourage their child who has a physical disability to think about how she wants to make disability part of her individual identity. For many children it will be desirable to see the disability as an important part of themselves—but not as the whole picture. It takes thought and some practice for children to accomplish this, to be able to say, "I am a girl who happens to have a physical disability; I am not a disabled girl."

Risk Taking

Each child's "first"—of whatever!—widens her horizons and informs her and the world of what she can do. But every "first time" has its risks, whether physical or psychological. In reality we take a risk every time we step out the front door, say hello to a stranger, or walk across an intersection. As your child moves toward more independence, he'll need to take more risks, something that is exciting and frightening at the same time.

You may feel a little nervous when the topic of risk taking by your children comes up. Yet risk taking is inherent in life. It helps define our limits, what we are able to do and what is beyond our physical or emotional capacities. It can also result in the achievement of something we thought ourselves incapable of doing.

Risk taking comes in many forms and levels. From that first wobbly step, when you wish you could build a wall of foam for your toddler to fall into—especially if he wears tiny leg braces—parents find themselves wanting to make each new step a safe one. Coming to the realization that each step makes the next easier and surer helps us lessen our protective stance bit by bit. That first scraped knee hurts you as much as your little one, but you learn to cleanse and bandage the wounds that follow with the knowledge that they *will* heal in time.

Do you remember the first time you saw your child in the limelight, perhaps as an elf in the kindergarten holiday program? Knowing he was a bit shy, did you want to coach him through the songs? And then you noticed he was enjoying the rhythm and melody and had quite forgotten there was an audience. Fast-forward to tying his tie for his high school prom; he was eager to be on his way—while you sat at home, worrying about the after-prom party.

Parents of children who have physical disabilities share concerns about the risks we've discussed. But you have additional questions about your child's physical and emotional safety. For many, the very idea of risk taking brings to mind hospitalizations, fractures, and long periods of recuperation, not to mention the pain of demeaning remarks others might make to their children when they take the plunge into new social situations.

Parents, by and large, tend to be more protective of their child who has a disability than the child's siblings are. Several years ago a father and son got into a discussion about the fact that the father, newly retired, was driving his 23-year-old daughter, who used a wheelchair, to work every day. His son encouraged the father to let his daughter take public transportation to work. "But what if it rains?" asked Dad. "Well, Dad, she'll get wet, just like I do." Dad was most concerned with making life easier for his daughter, while his son was distressed that his sister was not encouraged to take reasonable risks that would allow her to be more responsible for herself. Brother knew that his sister was capable of growth toward independence, while Dad wanted to shelter and protect his daughter. Parents are wise to listen to siblings' opinions about the abilities of their brother or sister who has a physical disability, as they are sometimes more accurate in their appraisal of what their sib is capable of doing, and they don't carry the guilt some parents do.

As physical risk taking poses the possibility of injury, it is a hot topic for most parents. Weighing what is to be gained against the potential for harm of any action is a daily task for all of us. Even a risk gone awry can turn into a good thing, becoming a way to "normalize." For instance, at summer camp, Herbie, in his double leg braces, was riding a horse when it suddenly shied, knocking Herbie off. Herbie was very proud when he returned to school with his arm in a cast; he now had something in common with the other guys in his class, several of whom had broken their arms doing sports activities.

Jalah, who has OI, had a busy mother who gave her lots of freedom to make decisions about what she could do. She wanted Jalah to feel "normal" so she allowed her to bike and roller-skate. Her physician told Jalah's mother to "let her be a kid," even if it meant having a few extra fractures. Jalah sees this freedom to try out the world as a valued gift from her mother. She has tried to hand down this freedom to her son, Jon, who also has OI.

Kelsey's parents also trusted her to make her own judgments about safety and risk. She gained confidence in herself as a result and learned to trust her instincts; this was a "gift" from her mother and father. Other parents note that the trust their parents placed in them as children was translated into trust in themselves when they became adults.

Physical disability is an add-on challenge for you and your child, making it more difficult to assign responsibilities for him and help him join social activities, take considered risks, and learn from common experiences. While everyone has to get around some obstacles in life, individuals who have physical disabilities face extra hurdles, such as stairs, lost time from school for operations or medical treatments, and negative attitudes of others that limit their participation in normal life activities. The rest of this book will show you how you can create resilience in all your children, including those who have a physical disability.

How This Book Will Help

So you have defined your goal: build an inclusive and resilient family. How do you do that? We will give you a broad perspective on families—yours and other's. Stand back for a moment to look at your challenge: preparing your children to become competent adults. Now that you have the foundation for the task ahead, the chapters that follow will take you from the moment you learn that one of your children has a physical disability, to coping day by day, and on to planning for your and your children's future. The perspectives and wisdom of real parents, grandparents, and siblings who may or may not have physical disabilities are included throughout the book.

Part I, "In the Beginning," explores how you learn about and cope with the new reality that your child has a physical disability. The focus of chapter 1, "Getting the News," is on hearing the words, at birth or later, that your child has "a problem," and dealing with the initial impact of a diagnosis of disability. It describes the spectrum of emotions—helplessness, sadness, anger, loneliness, and delayed bonding—that parents may experience and that grandparents and others close to them may also feel. Your first reactions to your child's disability and expectations for him or your family are explored. Out of this period of emotional tumult, parents discover strategies and inner resources that are helpful as they begin to take charge.

In chapter 2, "Coming Home," we look at adjusting to changes in the family routine when you have a child who has a physical disability, including changes in time and energy demands. In addition, emotional and attitude adjustments have to be made, and you'll need to learn how to deal with medical procedures and to communicate with rehabilitation professionals. During this process, you find that you are becoming an expert on your child's medical and disability-related issues and can become a partner with the professionals. As the process moves on, you will discover your family's "new normal."

Part II, "All in the Family," looks at the different perspectives of parents, siblings, and grandparents. Chapter 3, "Inclusive Parenting: Make It Work for You," emphasizes how you can reap the rewards of parenthood through creating your own unique family. The need for parents to build strong supportive relationships with their spouses or significant others, with extended family, and with the community is discussed. We explore how coping with your emotions and caring for yourself allow you to move on to the nitty-gritty issues of parenting, from time management skills to the expression of positive expectations for your child's success.

In chapter 4, "Brothers and Sisters: Siblings Sharing Family Life with Physical Disability in the Mix," the contributions and complexities of growing up with siblings, both able-bodied and those who have disabilities, are explored. By talking things through, sharing experiences, arguing, and helping each other, brothers and sisters build their "cope-abilities." Younger and older adults have found that their relationships with their siblings who may or may not have disabilities, in which so much was shared as they grew up, have a major influence on their values and beliefs, how they communicate, and how they support one another as adults.

Chapter 5, "Grandparents: Seeing through a New Lens," shows how grandparents can play a supportive role to their children and grandchildren when physical disability enters the picture. Depending on a grandparent's geographical proximity to his family and the extent of his resources, he can offer everything from emotional to physical to financial help. Grandparents can enrich the lives of their children and grandchildren, by being there for them and sharing their interests and talents. Many grandparents adapt to their new roles with renewed sense of purpose in life. Families point out that it is helpful to everyone if there are some boundaries between generations and a balance between emotional involvement and each generation's need to lead their individual lives.

In Part III, "Into the Wide World," the focus is on preparing your children for adulthood and yourself for life after parenting. In chapter 6, "Opening Doors to Inclusion," we discuss how to launch your children on the road to independence by giving them access to educational, vocational, and social opportunities and teaching them to manage their medical and physical needs, request accommodations in school and the workplace, and deal with the social barriers of stereotypes and negative attitudes. We explore the ways parents can balance dreams and reality to help their kids make plans for success in their future vocational and family lives, as well as how they can educate their kids who have physical disabilities about love, sexuality, and relationships, to prepare them for dating, intimacy, and marriage.

You'll see in chapter 7, "Letting One Dream Go to Let Another Grow," that as your children mature and begin to leave home, you'll find yourself moving on from on-the-job parent to empty nester. It begins with taking stock, gaining confidence, and trusting your instincts. By this stage you are balancing "I can do it!" with "Thanks for the hand!" and finding increased patience and tolerance in yourself. You may reconnect with your spouse or perhaps date again, plan a change of careers, return to work or enter retirement, spread your wings socially, investigate new hobbies or interests, or pursue a passion.

Interwoven between chapters are the stories of families striving to be inclusive. They represent a wide scope of family types with varying supports and challenges. Yet each is invested in the future of their children and has a strong belief in each child and in each parent. They share their unique experiences and perspectives on managing a family with both able-bodied children and children who have disabilities. They demonstrate the many ways that families can survive, cope, adapt, and thrive, while preparing their children for success in adulthood.

PART I

In the Beginning

pregnancy. Though I did know one of my twins was transverse in utero, all my doctors assured me it would be fine. When I found out he would be disabled for the rest of his life, I was devastated to say the least. For the first four days I was in the NICU with him I cried; I could barely speak to him over my tears because I was so distraught."

As the first grandchildren on both sides of the family, the twins were much anticipated. When Paul had to call his parents with the news about David, "it was hard to do. I made sure my Dad was home so I could tell my folks together." Paul couldn't answer many of their questions. His father flew out to be with them immediately, as did Casey's sister. The occasion of the twins' birth went from joyous to somber.

Grandmother Elizabeth had never been in a children's ward and found it wrenching to see David with a tracheostomy (breathing) tube. She often procrastinated, once not getting to the hospital until 11 p.m. But her son-in-law urged her to visit, and she understood how important her presence was to him and Casey.

David remained in the NICU for two months. Paul visited him at least once a day. He was still angry and filled with "ill will" toward the doctor who delivered his son and who he believed should have prevented David's injury. "I should have two healthy boys. It was depressing to see what the kids and their families were going through in the NICU. It was gut-wrenching."

Meanwhile, baby Andrew was thriving at home. Casey would "breast-feed him at home, pump extra for his next feeding, go to the hospital, feed and spend time with David, pump, and return home and do it all over again." She and Paul traded places so that while one was home the other was at the hospital.

Elizabeth had recently left her job with the understanding that she would return on an ad hoc basis in a few months. But when she learned about David's disability, she wanted to be available to help her family. Elizabeth's husband, on the other hand, believed that David would get better. "Why get upset about it?" he asked. She was frustrated by his denial of the serious issues David faced.

At first Elizabeth was unsure about her role. "I wanted to step in and do lots. Yet I didn't want to be interfering." While wanting to be respectful of Casey and Paul's role as parents, she soon jumped in to ask how she could help. She cooked, washed, fed the dog, dealt with everyday problems, and kept up normal routines, like decorating the Christmas tree while David was still in the hospital. She lived with Paul and Casey during this time, because her home was too far to commute.

When David left the NICU, he was sent by air ambulance to a rehabilitation hospital specializing in infants with SCI. After two weeks of intensive rehabilitation, he finally joined Andrew at home, where Elizabeth continued to help out. As a novice grandmother, it was "intimidating to care for someone with such elemental needs." But she soon learned how to provide David's daily care and familiarized herself with the full gamut of issues, from his medical and physical problems to the complexities of health care delivery and insurance. Elizabeth also became the second set of eyes and ears at medical appointments.

Paul lost his job two months after the twins' births, adding to the stress on the family. Casey recalls, "By the end of the year, we had no income and were having to pay for COBRA health insurance. I was forced to go back to work part-time." Their schedule centered on doctors' appointments, clinic visits, and daily home visits from therapists, nurses, and nutritionists. Looking back, Casey says she was on autopilot for the first two and a half years of her sons' lives. She thinks Elizabeth's help was their saving grace. "Her moral support, mom-education support (i.e., how do I do this?), and her help watching Andrew allowed my husband and me to be at the hospital together and to talk with the doctors." Paul agrees that extended family support is invaluable. "I would recommend that you live near your family. They are invested in you and your family and will help." Having a good relationship with each other was also important in helping Casey and Paul cope. "Luckily for us, my husband and I were fairly good at communication before all this happened. We were also dedicated to our family and knew we would do whatever it took to make David better. We continue to do that." Paul adds that many marriages can't survive "for better or worse" and says that couples have to work together. "You can't walk away and put the burden on a single parent." He likens parenting to a tag team, with success based on positive beliefs and creativity. Along with spouse and extended family support, Paul finds it essential to become involved in your community.

When the twins were 2½ years old, the Webers moved to another state where Paul found a new job, and as David stabilized, they settled into a routine. Paul's job gave them a steady income and good health insurance, so Casey could stay at home with the boys. This is when Casey "started falling apart" and Paul felt helpless. "There was nothing I could do to rectify this for her. I felt torn apart. I didn't know what to do or how to fix things. How could I get her over her depression?" Casey tried counseling and stress reduction classes. "They helped a little, but anti-depressant and anxiety meds helped the most by taking the edge off. I was then better able to organize myself, think, and relax."

Elizabeth, who'd "run on adrenaline" during David's early medical crises, had a period of emotional upheaval, when the boys were 6. "I had flashbacks to when the doctors walked in. It seemed to me they crawled along the walls and would have run away if they could. They did not want to deliver the news about David."

David's physical disability makes it challenging for the Webers to enjoy community and social activities. Playmates' homes have stairs and limited wheelchair accessibility. Playing fields and nature walks are often not wheelchair-friendly. Also, they need to prepare and bring supplies for David and time his bowel program to fit into their schedule. Everything has to be carefully thought out in advance; even the weather plays a role in their plans. During the summer, they can't go to amusement parks because the heat may cause David to have dysreflexia (a dangerous rise in blood pressure triggered by pain, temperature changes, or infection in people with SCI). For all hot-weather activities, they need to make sure there will be fans or air conditioning and cover from the sun. Some activities, such as scout hikes, are not possible for David; Paul says that when he thinks about what David is missing, "I want to sit and cry."

Nevertheless, Paul believes that life is to be lived, and the Webers—including David—participate actively in life as much as possible. "When you get past the 'woe is me' phase," says Paul, "you'll find that life has not stopped."

The Webers are major league baseball fans, like to go to movies, and take vacations. Both boys have flown with them several times to visit Paul's family. Because David's power wheelchair can be damaged during in-flight storage, they now take his manual chair when they fly—though this does limit his independence while they are visiting his grandparents.

Casey is the primary caregiver for the twins, but Paul is also involved with both boys and never hesitates to help with David's care. Casey's medical background is an asset in her role as hands-on care provider and "case manager" for David. She sets up appointments, orders equipment, gets supplies, and talks to insurance companies. "It's like a full-time job."

Casey and the boys have traveled to Washington, D.C., to increase awareness about paralysis and lobby their congressman to support related health care bills. When the twins were five, Elizabeth accompanied them on a trip. While Casey was at a meeting, Elizabeth took them sightseeing. At the Lincoln Memorial she sat on a bench while the boys chased pigeons. When they needed a taxi, the boys signaled the taxi like the doorman at the hotel did. "The boys have the expectation that the wheelchair will not deter them."

Elizabeth has lived through stressful times with the twins and feels closer to them because of it. She has gotten to know them well and finds them "delightful and normal. I love them to death." She takes them many places, making sure things can work for both of them. When the family was invited to a wedding reception, she checked the site out ahead of time and gave the manager a list of things needed to make it accessible for David. They were all done. "If no one had spoken up, nothing would have changed." Elizabeth also educates extended family and friends to make them aware of accessibility issues.

Elizabeth likes her children to tell her what they need. If she is overly involved, she wants them to let her know. She tries not to cross the line between help and interference. She encourages other grandparents, if they can, to put their lives on hold for a while in order to support their children and grandchildren in times of need.

The twins are close with each other. If he gets something for himself, Andrew automatically does the same for David. They do the normal things boys do; David likes to wrestle, using his upper body strength, and tries to trip his brother. Games and pretend play are important to them. They play Little League baseball, and Paul is one of their coaches. David pitches and has good coordination but poor strength; he gets to base in his wheelchair. He plays on two teams—one with his brother and one that is a special-needs team. Both boys belong to a Cub Scout den where Paul helps out.

Although not involved with organized religion before she had the twins, Casey wonders if it would provide good support for her family, especially David. Paul, though, has his doubts. He had a hard time "forgiving the Lord" after David's birth.

Casey feels that she is "definitely a different person today than I was prior to having a child who has a disability. The main portions of my personality remain; however, some things have changed for the better and some for the worse. One doctor told me several weeks after David was born, 'You can't let this change who you are.' I feel you can't help but have this change who you are. For the better, I feel I am more sympathetic or empathetic to others than I used to be. I do not take things for granted as I once did. I have used our experience with disability to be proactive and get involved in advocacy. For the worse, I am not as happy-go-lucky as I used to be. I worry. I get anxious. I get overwhelmed. I get angry. I get frustrated and exhausted from the excess care and attention David's disability entails. I feel at times like our life revolves around his needs. I have also realized I am more selfish than I thought I was."

Paul has high standards of behavior for both boys. His own upbringing shaped him to be a strict, no-nonsense dad. He doesn't like whining. He feels that kids in general "get off too easily" and insists that each of the boys has "to pull their weight." Paul and Casey are very clear, however, that Andrew is not responsible for taking care of David.

Casey feels strongly that as a parent you must meet every child's needs, but she finds that trying to keep things as equal as possible for the boys is a challenge. "The issue is how to balance the extra needs of an individual who has a disability with one who doesn't need as much assistance. They say the focus should not be on the individual who has the disability, but due to health and physical needs, it almost can't be helped. We try to incorporate it into our routine as much as we can." She wanted to spend one-on-one time with each child, "taking each twin on outings by himself." But she found that "the one-on-one time with the child who has a disability is to medical appointments, not fun activities. For the able-bodied child, the special time usually involves doing something fun. Plus, because they are the same age with the same interests, what I did with one was always something the other wanted to do. It always seemed unfair to leave one out. So my compromise is to always make time for something fun for the whole family to do together that focuses on our family as a whole unit." They do this by making play situations accessible so the boys have the same opportunities. If they can't adapt a situation, they don't do it. "We try to focus on what we can, not what we can't do."

But Casey also tries to take time each day just to sit with each twin, individually, and talk directly with him. "I was told early on, which I found useful, that it is not the amount of time you spend with each child, but the amount of quality time. It's not about going and doing, it's about paying attention to each of them and showing them both that I care about them, I love them, I respect them, I will always be there for them; they mean the world to me."

1

Getting the News

"We knew our baby had a hemorrhage, but I didn't expect the severity of what was to follow."

—SEAN

"When my daughter got sick and suddenly couldn't walk, the doctor was away and couldn't see her. She got weaker for two days, and then we found out it was polio. I was devastated. I didn't know anything about polio—and I was unhappy with myself that I was so remiss."

—CHARLOTTE

"Giving birth to a child who has a disability has pulled back a curtain on a whole new world."

—LIZ

"Being a parent is a journey to the unknown."

—PILI

Diagnosis: Hearing the Words

You can recall as if it were yesterday the moment you received the news that your child had a physical disability. You may have been pregnant, or just given birth, or your toddler or teen had just had an illness or accident. Hearing the words, noticing what was said or not said, feeling the physical sensations, and being aware of who was there and who was not are still clear in your memory even years after.

Hearing the Words before Birth

Lola remembers hearing the doctor say that her first baby's physical development was abnormal when she was seven months pregnant—and the subsequent torrent of her emotions. Her husband Philip received the news from Lola later that day. She was crying and upset, and he tried to reassure her. "I told her it would be the same, just different. I told her to go to her mother's; she was in shock."

Many parents recall their emotional turmoil when they heard the news that their babies would have spina bifida (SB), one of the disabilities more commonly diagnosed before birth through prenatal blood tests and ultrasound.

In the twenty-eighth week of her pregnancy, Priscilla Brandon hadn't felt her baby move and was sure something was wrong. Her obstetrician sent her for an ultrasound with state-of-the-art equipment. A number of hospital personnel congregated to observe the test, but no one said a word. Her husband Lee recalls that when they were later told that the baby might have SB, the doctor gave them the most "devastating worst-case scenarios. It was the worst day of my life." They were referred to a geneticist, whose news was equally bad. "Things are bleak," he said. "I have to prepare you; there may be brain damage." Priscilla cried for forty-five minutes after getting this news.

When she was five-and-a-half months pregnant, Kelsey learned through an ultrasound that her baby had SB. She remembers being offered the option of abortion and responding, "Absolutely not." At the same time, she felt that her "heart was broken. What did I do to cause or deserve this? Why me?"

Cindy discovered her baby's diagnosis of SB at her sixteen-week prenatal visit. While she knew people who were doing well with SB in her community, she says, "You never expect to have it happen to you." She had planned a celebration lunch with friends after the appointment but opted not to go. She chose not to tell people about the diagnosis; "I was still praying for a beautiful baby. I didn't want people to say, 'I'm so sad,' because I wanted this to be a happy time, and it was." Her husband had a harder time; after hearing the news, he was withdrawn and helpless, saying, "There is nothing I can do, I can't fix it." It was the only time Cindy had ever seen him cry.

Rose and her husband were thrilled when they became pregnant with their third child. They were shocked when they found out in Rose's fifth month of pregnancy that the child would have SB. Rose was depressed for a month. Her husband kept "his emotions close; he wouldn't talk about it. But he was stressed out."

When disability is discovered while the baby is still in utero, parents have some time to begin taking in the news, integrating the reality of disability into their physical and emotional preparations for becoming parents. They have time to learn about their child's disability, to develop some ideas of what life will be like, and to think about how they will include that child in their family life.

Priscilla and Lee, scared by the doctor's dire predictions for their baby's condition, decided to learn more about SB. Priscilla did research at their local college and found another specialist through the area's children's hospital. He explained to her that hydrocephalus associated with SB is treatable, and that brain damage can often be prevented. This information and the doctor's reassurance helped Priscilla and Lee develop a realistic, yet more optimistic, picture of what was to come. They began to experience some of the joyful anticipation that most parents feel.

Erica was six months pregnant when she and D. K. were told that their first child would be born with osteogenesis imperfecta (OI). They were both startled because the pregnancy had gone so well up to then. They went immediately into information-gathering mode, trying to learn as much as possible about OI and prepare for the birth. Erica admits that changing her expectations about her baby required some "psychological adjustment."

Hearing the Words at Birth or Later in Childhood

Whether your child's disability was discovered at birth or later in childhood, you never forget the moment you heard the words, "There is a problem with your baby." Parents naturally feel vulnerable when threatened with the possible loss or disability of their child. Hopes can be unwittingly inflated—or destroyed—by the first words you hear from a nurse or doctor about your child's diagnosis and prognosis. Jim remembers how the doctor told him, "Your son may be a vegetable so you should find a good place to put him." "All I could think of was . . . an artichoke," he says, recalling the surreal experience. His son is now a strapping teenager who uses a wheelchair.

Diane recalls that her daughter was diagnosed with OI when she was 1 year old. There had been some signs at birth, such as darker sclera, but she appeared to be developing normally. It was only after her first baby tooth came in "opalescent" that a series of medical tests confirmed OI. X-rays showed evidence that she had had multiple fractures at some time during infancy (characteristic of OI), of which the family was unaware. "My reaction was initial sadness, feelings of loss, but there really wasn't time to dwell on it for I had a 2½-year-old at home to take care of. Learning my child had a lifetime disease that would hurt her and had hurt her was difficult to swallow. Not knowing she had both ulnas and a femur fractured—and in hindsight, remembering that I was present when it had happened—caused terrible guilt. However, being an optimist, I keep looking at the glass as half full. . . . I had two miscarriages before Rochelle and in some way I think that may have prepared me to be strong mentally and physically."

When your child is diagnosed with a disability, you may ride a roller coaster of emotions—sadness, guilt, confusion, anger, frustration. You may mistrust the doctor and perhaps deny the diagnosis, or blindly trust whatever you're told. You may feel incredible weariness, or be energized by a desire to escape or do something to make it better. It is mentally and physically fatiguing. You may say to yourself, "This can't be happening," "This can't be real," or "It will be different tomorrow."

For parents who have never known anyone who has a physical disability, or whose image of disability has been shaped primarily by negative stereotypes or media portrayals, adjusting to the idea of having a child who has a disability may be particularly challenging, whereas parents who are more familiar with physical disability through personal experience, such as having a close friend or family member who has a disability, may find it easier to cope with the diagnosis. They can more readily envision a life for their child in which disability is just one part, not the whole story.

Parents who adopt children who have physical disabilities have *chosen* to incorporate disability into their family life. They tend to have a more positive view of disability, although they may not be aware at the time of adoption of all the issues they will encounter as parents. Still, the initial impact for them is different. Like parents who receive the diagnosis during pregnancy, they are better prepared and do not have to do the re-imaging of their child. The child they have is the one they want.

Rachel and Donald could not afford the high cost of private adoption, so they became foster parents to children who had disabilities and then adopted them—six altogether! They were well aware of the challenges they would confront as the parents of children who had a variety of disabilities. They planned their lives around their family, and Donald took early retirement to help carry the load at home.

Frequently, only limited information about the physical condition or medical history of an adoptee is available to adoptive parents. Although they know that their child has some type of disability, they may experience some emotional upheavals later on if their child has unexpected difficulties with health or development or his disability diagnosis comes into sharper focus over time.

Of course, almost all parents, whether biological or adoptive, experience—simultaneous with their uncomfortable feelings—feelings of love for their children and the joy, pride, and exhilaration that go with becoming a parent.

Ripple Effects of the News

When you throw a stone into a pond, you see concentric rings widening and spreading out around it. Like the ripples from that stone, the news about your child spreads from your immediate and extended family members, to your closest friends, to those not as close, and finally into your community. As parents, you feel the initial impact when the stone hits the pond. Your parents (your child's grandparents) feel the first ripple as they get the news from you and are filled with questions and concerns.

As soon as she knew her baby would be born with SB and hydrocephalus, Kathleen called her mother, Elsie, to tell her the news. Having no idea what the diagnosis meant or what to expect, Elsie was frightened. She wondered, would the baby live? How severe would it be?

Helen found out that her grandson would have SB when her daughter-in-law, Pili, was four months pregnant. "I was so sad. What's going to happen? A member of the family wanted Pili to have an abortion. I was so against that—but I was really scared for them."

Some grandparents absorb the impact more easily and are able to be supportive to their children right away.

When Joleen called her father to tell him his granddaughter had an as-yet-undiagnosed disability, he reassured her—and himself at the same

In the initial stages of dealing with your child's disability, choose one trusted family member to be a go-between for you and other family and friends. This will conserve energy for all the other demands and decisions coming your way.

time—that every child has "something." This baby girl might have a new kind of challenge, but they would find a way to handle it.

The next ring of ripples hits friends and then acquaintances as they get the news that your child has been diagnosed with a physical disability. Because friends are farther from the emotional center, they are often able to provide support, express concern and kindness, and help with reassuring visits, gifts of food, or perhaps babysitting for your other children. While Jada's son was in acute care following an automobile accident, her friend did research on the best rehabilitation centers for him to transfer to. She also told Jada about another family she knew who had gone through a similar situation and were willing to give Jada support.

But sometimes friends and family make assumptions about your feelings and needs—for instance, that you *must* be depressed, angry, or devastated—which may or may not be on the mark. This adds a layer of stress to the process of coping with the fact that disability is now part of your life. While you may not be devastated, you are probably using much of your energy to cope with your own feelings, to learn about your child's care needs, and to master the "medicalese" spoken in the hospital.

While it would be nice to have the wherewithal to respond to your friends' misconceptions about how you are actually affected by your child's disability, or to deal with *their* emotional distress, it is more important to reserve your energy for your child and your own needs. Later on, you will have the time and fortitude to answer your friends' questions, calm their anxiety, and correct their assumptions—if you choose.

Responding to the Reality
Initial Emotional Reactions

Parents of children who have physical disabilities experience a spectrum of emotional reactions, ranging from anguish to great happiness. They think about the disability in different ways, too—some see disaster, while others see opportunity. And many parents experience a yo-yoing of these feelings and thoughts, up one moment and down the next.

Helplessness

Many parents experience feelings of helplessness or inadequacy after their child is diagnosed with a disability. Paul recalls "going home to cry" when his son was diagnosed with quadriplegia soon after birth. Paul's grief was mixed with helplessness and frustration; he could neither control what was happening to his baby nor comfort his wife in her own grief. "There was nothing I could do to rectify this for her. I felt torn apart. I didn't know what to do or how to fix things."

Andrea, whose son's rare disorder required multiple surgeries during the first weeks of life, had a similar experience: "I felt completely helpless. My baby was in pain and my husband was so sad, and I couldn't do anything about it."

Debbie, another new mother, didn't know anything about her child's disability. She felt inadequate and blamed herself, because she "missed the signs" and because there was nothing she could do to make it better.

Loneliness

Parents frequently experience loneliness while coping with the initial diagnosis of a child's disability and the intense demands on their time and energy. One parent describes it "like a dark tunnel with little light and you just try to pick your steps carefully and take the right turns to get to the light at the other end. It is frightening." You may feel separate and alone. You may not have a confidante to whom you can turn for support, or you may be hesitant to "burden" your mate with your own feelings of vulnerability or fear. Sometimes old friends are awkward or unresponsive, not knowing how to be supportive. It feels like they desert you in your time of crisis.

Anger

Some parents experience anger in reaction to their child's diagnosis of disability. You may feel anger toward the medical staff, your spouse, God, or yourself.

When Charlotte was told the diagnosis of her 7-year-old, she was completely at sea because she didn't know anything about the condition. She felt "stupid" and became angry with herself because she knew so little.

Kathleen "couldn't wrap my brain around what was happening so I couldn't talk to anyone." Her doctor offered to get her help, but she was "so stubborn I wouldn't accept it."

Anger can become a "time bomb" for parents who have no opportunity to air their complex feelings about their child's disability. Sometimes parents are dealing with multiple stressors at the time their child is diagnosed—perhaps a divorce or loss of a job. The care of a child with many extra needs can leave a parent with no time to work through grief or loss. But parents can benefit from channeling their anger constructively. Runner, whose son Lance has a spinal cord injury, says, "My aggressiveness got me answers to questions." Anger motivated him to find the resources to help his son.

Harriette recalls some "gloomy days filled with anger" as she tried to cope with her son's multiple disabilities. But "when I saw that my anger was eating me up alive, I knew I had to direct my feelings in a more positive way." Harriette mobilized her "anger energy" to "nail down the benefits I had to have for my son's medical care and to get help at home."

Separation from Your Child

Most couples expecting a child know that the *mother* may need medical intervention during delivery, such as anesthesia, episiotomy, or C-section. But most parents are unprepared for the possibility that their much-anticipated "bonding" time will be disrupted by the *newborn's* need for medical procedures or surgery.

Separation from their baby due to medical treatments right after birth is hard on new parents. The fact that your baby has been born with a disability may be less distressing than the loss of opportunities to feed, cuddle, and tend to your newborn. You may feel displaced as a parent by the health care providers who hold your child's life in their hands.

Kathleen had an ultrasound just hours before her baby's birth, which indicated fluid around the brain. A neurologist was consulted and diagnosed SB; an hour later, Kathleen gave birth. She got only a "quick glimpse" before they took the baby off to a specialty hospital. She felt as if she were in shock. "My baby was taken away immediately. I couldn't touch him or pick him up." In the specialty hospital, her baby was surrounded by medical machinery, nurses, and doctors, and there were strict rules about how to handle her newborn. "I felt like the nurses and doctors told me what I could and couldn't do. There were oodles of people around. Why couldn't I be alone with my own baby?"

Liz, whose daughter was also whisked away to another hospital for medical care, remained behind in the maternity ward, watching as the other mothers cared for their newborns. In order to get through the ordeal, she turned off her feelings, becoming numb: "I don't think I reacted very much."

When you are separated from your baby (or from your child, who is having surgery or a prolonged hospital stay), it's important to make extra efforts to reconnect emotionally. For Liz the first step was to recognize the feelings of loss she'd experienced when her baby was whisked away. Thankfully, their period of separation was short and they were soon reunited. Grateful to be with her baby, Liz held her close, fed her, and looked lovingly into her baby's eyes; she was emotionally open to her baby's needs and interacted with her as much as she could with a brand new infant. In this way, Liz set the tone of their relationship for years to come.

If you have to be separated from an older child, it is equally important to recognize *the child's* feelings (perhaps separation anxiety, fear of surgery or doctors, or loneliness) and to reassure him or her with a healing dose of TLC.

Grandparents' Emotional Reactions

Grandparents are an important part of their children's and grandchildren's lives and can be a valuable source of support in good times and bad. While they want to be supportive, especially in times of stress, they may not know just what you need. They also have their own individual emotional reactions and may need some time to deal with them, so that they can be supportive of you and your family.

Elsie wanted as much information as possible after learning that her daughter and son-in-law's baby would have a disability; she asked her son to find out what was available on the Internet. At the same time, there was a sense of disbelief: "This can't be happening to us." Elsie asked herself, "What went wrong?" She also wanted assurance that her daughter and son-in-law would be okay. She worried about the impact of her grandchild's physical disability on her daughter's marriage.

Upon her grandson's birth, Elsie was thankful he didn't have brain damage. During the early days while he was in the hospital, she felt fearful about his future. What would he have to face? Would he be able to walk? Would he be accepted? "We were angry at first. But it also made us closer as a family." Elsie and her daughter were able to openly air their feelings, many of which they shared in common, and to support each other.

Ways of Coping

Disability can rock your emotional boat up or down; what is tragedy for one family is triumph for another. We can view events, people, or experiences in our lives, including a disability, as *loads* or *lifts*. One of the tricks to coping with any difficult or novel situation is making the choice to focus on the lifts and to find enough lifts, or positives, to outweigh, or at least balance, your loads. Most parents find their lifts through trial and error, by testing behaviors, parenting styles, and coping mechanisms until they find the ones that work for them and their families.

It's common to focus more on the loads when you first learn about your child's disability. But even at this early stage, there are things you can do to change your point of view and look for the lifts, which will help you begin to move on from your feelings of loss.

Sharing with Your Spouse, Partner, or Closest Friend

After the birth of your baby or when disability occurs in your older child, you seek solace, understanding, and an ear from your mate to "take

Although it is difficult to summon the energy, reach out to the person closest to you—your spouse, partner, or family member. You may find that while you were trying to shield them from your feelings, they were doing the same for you. Acknowledging that you and your loved one are both experiencing emotional upheavals—whether in sync or not—can create a safety zone for each of you to share your feelings and fears.

in" and talk about your feelings and the "flipping over" of your expectations. (If you are a single parent, you can seek the same support from your best friend or closest family member.) But while you both need to reach out for comfort and support, you and your partner may have little time or emotional resources to give to each other. It may require all of your individual resources just to "keep your heads above water" and deal with pressing decisions about your child's physical needs.

You and your spouse or significant other may also be on different wavelengths, experiencing dissimilar initial reactions to the news about your child's condition. You may be out of "sync" emotionally, one feeling anger about the situation, while the other is denying the reality of what is going on. While this is common and expectable, it is important to keep your lines of communication open. Share your feelings with your partner and accept where she is on the emotional roller coaster. During these early stages mothers generally express feelings of grief or sadness and need time to vent and mourn; fathers more often express feelings of anger and want to take steps to change the situation. You both wish you could "do" something to control what's happening and to comfort each other, and it feels terribly frustrating when, at first, there seems no way to do either!

Journaling

Even when you are still reeling from hearing the diagnosis, keeping a journal is helpful. If you don't have much time or feel too fatigued to do it in depth, at least make some quick notes that you can reconstruct later. Journaling about your feelings helps you unburden that weighty load of reactions you are carrying on your shoulders. It's also good to look back

> **T** If possible, keep all the medical information about your child, copies of doctors' reports, and information about medications, reactions, and surgeries in one section of your journal. Use another section of the journal as your "release" valve, allowing you to vent your thoughts and feelings about what is going on.

on later, to see how your feelings have evolved and gain some perspective on your experiences. This is especially helpful if you don't have a partner to share with.

You will be receiving lots of information about your child's diagnosis, how to take care of her physical needs (medicines, equipment, or procedures), and how to use the medical support system. The amount of information can be so large that you can't possibly remember all of it. Making notes in your journal can help you listen better and organize your questions when receiving new medical information and can jog your memory when you need to refer to the information again.

Taking Constructive Action

Many parents cope with painful emotions by taking action—such as surfing the Internet for information on their child's condition, scouting out accessible facilities for family activities (curb cuts, ramps into schools, churches, theaters, restaurants), filling out insurance forms, building a ramp for a child who uses a wheelchair, or doing some other task that will solve a practical problem for their child or family. When Rose learned, while still pregnant, that her baby had SB, she dove into research on the condition and made sure she was fully informed about the latest treatments before her baby was born. She made arrangements to save her baby's umbilical cord stem cells, in case they could be used in the future to promote better function. Over the years, Rose has kept up with all the latest research and treatment innovations, and her daughter will soon be participating in a clinical trial of experimental nerve rerouting surgery.

When D. K.'s son was diagnosed with OI, he did not allow himself a "pity party." He, too, turned his sadness into action, immediately searching for treatments and cures and gathering information about the practical side of dealing with the disorder.

Taking action shifts your attention toward a more positive attitude and results in greater productivity and feelings of accomplishment. Moving from a stance of helplessness to active problem solving helps parents regain a sense of control over their lives and emotions, at a time when everything seems upside down. As one dad said, "The more choices and control you have, the more easily you'll accept and cope with the situation."

Getting Social Support

Take advantage of emotional and social support offered by friends, extended family members, coworkers, or professionals, especially early on when you've just received word on your child's situation. This support helps you feel less alone in the world and strengthens your resolve and ability to take effective action when it is needed.

Gary spent many weeks at the hospital after his newborn daughter had surgery to correct a hole in her heart. His friends were busy working, and most wanted to avoid the distressing experience of visiting the pediatric intensive care unit (ICU). But Gary developed close relationships with other parents of kids in the hospital and soon had a small network of supportive peers. These connections gave him a chance to unburden himself and, later, to get advice about accommodations for his daughter at school and how to find home health aides for her.

Early on, Cindy talked with her friends and also reached out on the Internet to people with similar issues. The voices of experienced parents about how they coped with the initial diagnosis and birth gave her some good ideas and made her feel more supported. These relationships continue to help Cindy maintain her equilibrium and perspective on life.

Rose recalls that right after her baby was born, the hospital staff was "awesome, because they were so professional." The staff suggested that she attend support groups in the hospital even before she took her daughter home. These were helpful to her in coping with her initial emotional reactions to her daughter's diagnosis. They also gave Rose contacts for mental health counselors in case she needed additional help.

Spirituality

When hearing difficult news, most people are sustained by the faith or belief system that has helped them in the past. There is comfort in the known and trusted, and for some parents, this includes spiritual or religious beliefs.

The first question formed by many parents, "Why me, God?" may be both a prayer and a demand for understanding. Some parents find relief, perspective, a sense of hope, and support through their spiritual beliefs or practices. These benefits can come through meditation, prayers, "talking with God," or simply a belief in a benign higher power.

Cindy, whose religion is a source of strength for her, "felt compelled to talk with a priest; he listened and we prayed." Her parents also prayed for their new grandchild, and their priest talked about him at Mass. "I asked for strength to be able to handle this," Cindy says; "I didn't ask for it not to be."

Nasim, upon receiving the call that his son had been paralyzed in an automobile accident, was devastated. He contacted his mosque immediately, and by the time he reached the hospital's ICU, his imam was waiting at the hospital with his wife and her parents. He consoled the family and led them in prayers. Nasim felt that Allah must have some plan for his son. His faith helped him find hope and convey to his 14-year-old son a sense of meaning and purpose.

After hearing during pregnancy that her child would have a disability, Lola contemplated having an abortion. But she heard an inner voice say, "Trust in life." This spiritual experience, which she accepted without question, helped prepare her to accept and love her baby boy born a few months later.

Not all parents believe in a higher power, and parents can certainly find strength and confidence without spiritual beliefs. Alan, for example, did not believe that God had any role in the fact that his son was born with congenital deformities. He simply had "no use for God." Alan felt that it was up to him to carry this load alone—and he firmly believed that his lack of reliance on a higher power made it easier for him to tackle problems and make good decisions.

When her daughter was diagnosed with juvenile rheumatoid arthritis, Rebecca rejected the visits of the clergy to the hospital room. "I have my own beliefs about life and its origins, and they do not include spirituality. I rely on my own inner resources. I know that I have ultimate responsibility for my life; when the doctor gave me the final diagnosis, I knew I would deal with it. I didn't need a higher power to depend on."

After getting the news about their child's disability, parents experience a wide range of emotional reactions, but soon they begin to find ways to cope with their feelings and the practical aspects of this unexpected situation. Around the time that your child comes home from the hospital or rehabilitation center, another phase of family life begins. As you integrate your child's disability into the everyday life of your family, you can anticipate making some changes in your family's activities, attitudes, and timetables. You may need to learn how to provide hands-on care for your child and to manage ongoing physical or medical problems, and you will develop new ways of thinking about your children and your family. In time, all these changes will become routine for your family, as together you find your "new normal."

The Hamiltons: Raising teenagers in a blended family with humor, responsibility, and respect for differences

Evelyn and Scott Hamilton have three children, two from her first marriage and one from his. Evelyn's son Mark is a college student. Her daughter Celeste and Scott's son Richard are both in high school. Scott and Evelyn first met in high school. They dated, broke up, and dated again in college until Scott changed schools. They kept in touch sporadically and were reunited years later.

While still in college, Evelyn met Romi, a foreign exchange student. She became pregnant and married him soon after. Both continued their studies. Romi had a modest student stipend and played in a band at night. Evelyn's family would not help her financially after the marriage, so she had to work. She felt alienated from the rest of the world, pregnant "out of wedlock" and married to a foreigner. Romi slept late during the day and refused to help when their son Mark was born. Evelyn took comfort in her relationship with Mark and found joy in exploring the world with him.

When Mark was 4, Evelyn gave birth—alone—to a daughter, Celeste. Romi was playing a gig that night, as he had been when Mark was born. A physical exam immediately after birth revealed that Celeste's left arm had broken during delivery, and further tests showed multiple fractures in various stages of healing. The sclera of her eyes was blue instead of white. Four hours later, Evelyn was told that Celeste probably had osteogenesis imperfecta (OI). Celeste was flown by helicopter to a specialty hospital.

Evelyn and Romi followed by car the next day. The diagnosis of OI was confirmed. Romi felt responsible, in part because the family doctor incorrectly told him that OI was more common in children of Romi's ethnicity. Romi never held Celeste; their closest encounter was when he moved her from one spot to another. Even when he was alone with Celeste, he avoided touching her.

Evelyn felt abandoned by her husband and her family, who maintained their distance even after Celeste's birth. Friends, too, stood back, hesitant to help care for Celeste because they feared harming her.

Evelyn wrote to her old friend Scott about Celeste's birth. "I panicked," Scott recalls. "I didn't know how to respond. 'I'm sorry' was insufficient. I didn't write back." A year passed before he sent an apology. Evelyn responded, and they began to communicate regularly.

Meanwhile, Evelyn was entering a whole new world of medicine and rehabilitation. Her experiences with Celeste's medical care were "almost all good," but there were some rough times. Many doctors did not accept Medicaid, the only insurance the family had. As a result, Evelyn had to do her daughter's splinting herself. Finally, they were directed to a Shriners Hospital where they found a doctor with expertise in OI, a helpful social worker, and financial assistance to buy equipment for Celeste. Because of these positive experiences, Celeste has little fear of medicine, needles, or hospitals.

Because Romi had become so remote and uninvolved, Evelyn managed life for the children on her own. "I had to grow up really fast. I was doing all the research about OI as well as being the primary caregiver. I was the one in charge, assertive, determined, focused." The upside of this was becoming a better parent, says Evelyn. "It improved the way I parented my son, too." She filled their free time with art, concerts, parades, balloon festivals, and movies. But there was no adult "time-out" because she could not find day care for Celeste.

Evelyn was very conscious of Mark's needs, too. She "didn't want him to become an adjunct of his sister. I had an older sister, second of five, who was given the job of caretaker. She didn't get a real childhood. There was too much stress put on her by our mother." Evelyn made sure that Mark did not become "a slave to Celeste's disability."

One day she discovered an online support group for OI. The other mothers were empathic and offered practical advice on caring for Celeste. Two weeks after joining the group, she started taking Celeste, then a toddler, off the pad where she spent all her time. She found that Celeste began to move around more.

Around this time, Romi's behavior went from remote to threatening, and Evelyn feared for her children's and her own safety. She took the children, moved to her father's home in another city, and soon filed for divorce.

Meanwhile, her friend Scott was on the down slope of his marriage. Although he tried his best, it ended in divorce. A year later, he and Evelyn got together. When Celeste was 5, they married. Their marriage has been close and supportive. Scott loves to make Evelyn laugh, and he "keeps me stable so I can take care of the kids."

Scott now joined the new world of disability and medicine. He and Evelyn followed the advice they'd been given by an easygoing doctor to "let your daughter lead you." They asked Celeste to tell them how to do things so they wouldn't damage her. For instance, Scott asked Celeste, "How can I pick you up?"

Blending the two families was rocky at first. Scott's son Richard stayed with them some weekends during the school year and for an extended time in the summer. At first, Richard and Celeste did not interact. He saw her disability as foreign and a hindrance to having fun. Early on there was a three-way wrestling match, and Mark and Richard clunked heads with their sister. Their parents abruptly put an end to this physical play. Richard said Celeste "spoils all the fun." But as the years have passed, Richard has acclimated to his sister's disability and the siblings have become friends.

Evelyn and Scott are open about their differences in parenting, particularly on the issue of risk taking. Evelyn's son Mark is allowed to take risks within reason; he's able-bodied, thoughtful, and able to judge the risks and benefits of most situations. Scott says that not too much is off-limits with either of the boys. Richard and Mark participate in a variety of sports and physical activities. But Scott is more cautious with Celeste: he is aware of the time a broken bone requires to heal and is afraid of letting Celeste do things that could cause a fracture.

Evelyn wants Celeste to take some reasonable risks, like going sledding and bike riding, where the chance of injury is not too high. When Celeste was small, Evelyn would throw her up in the air and catch her in the pool, just as she did her son. She says Scott can be a "dream crusher. He seems to say 'I love you so much I don't want anything to happen to you.'" Scott has relaxed a bit since Celeste had an operation to put rods in her thigh bones, resulting in fewer breaks. He and Evelyn have taken

Celeste ice-skating in her wheelchair, with Scott pushing hard to make her go fast.

Celeste likes the thought of being close to the edge and feeling the wind in her hair, but at 15 years of age, she hesitates to take risks posing bodily harm. Now Scott's main concern is about her driving a car. "I worry about who gets to her after a crash. Paramedics might harm her, won't know how to take her blood pressure, for instance." Scott is also worried about Celeste's medical care when she goes to college. He fears she will need extra help if she has a break. He wants to have an emergency backup plan, and he hopes she will attend a school close to home so her family can step in if necessary.

Evelyn is more concerned about Celeste having a good social life and wants her to drive for that reason. Celeste is very sociable, a good writer, a violinist, and a Girl Scout. As a child she had more friends, but as a teen, her peers often "blow her off" or cancel plans at the last minute. Evelyn and Scott want Celeste to fit in like everyone else, but also to stand up for her rights. Celeste once told a boy off in the cafeteria for making rude remarks about her. Other students stepped in to stick up for her.

Scott and Evelyn have also encountered some people's negative responses to Celeste. Scott says there are times when he wonders if anyone notices or cares. But then they go into a shop and someone won't stop staring at their daughter. While Evelyn is offended because "Celeste is not on display," Scott sees these situations as "an opportunity to educate." Evelyn disagrees. "I didn't sign up to be a spokesperson for OI. I just want to get my stuff and get out."

As preparation toward independence, all the kids have responsibilities around the house. Chores are matched in time and effort, with Mark and Richard doing the heavy lifting and moving, and Celeste helping with chores such as using the Dustbuster. "We believe in fairness in the world, and no one receives special privileges," says Scott. Evelyn agrees that letting Celeste get off easy, or doing everything for her, would not be helpful. The more she does, the more strength and stamina Celeste will have.

The Hamiltons express affection and cope with stress through laughter and kidding around. "Humor is the primary language in our home," says Evelyn. Sometimes, as a lark, when they are all in the car they will group text chat on their cell phones. Scott's favorite times are family dinners or Sunday brunch, when within minutes everyone is goofing off and joking—a veritable "laugh riot." Scott knows that there is a delicate balance between individual and family needs, and he encourages each child to do solo activities. But in the final analysis, Scott's focus is on family togetherness.

Evelyn believes she still has much to learn about being a parent, but she tries to treat her children as individuals, to recognize their different personalities and help each one become what they want to be. She's also learned the importance of "taking care of myself so that I can be a better, whole, capable person. Parents need to be well rested to do a good job and make good decisions. That makes a big difference in the kids' lives." Evelyn has been pleasantly surprised by how much she enjoys being a mother. "Parenthood defines me," she says; "I love it."

2

Coming Home

"I quit work. I didn't have as much freedom as other young mothers because my baby needed catheterizing."

—KATHLEEN, MOTHER OF SON
WITH SPINA BIFIDA

"There was an adjustment period. His older sister was jealous because he got 'extras.'"

—MARY, MOTHER OF SON WITH
CEREBRAL PALSY

"I put one foot in front of the other. I did what needed to be done. I closed out feelings and concentrated on the next thing to do."

—ABE, FATHER OF A DAUGHTER
WITH CEREBRAL PALSY

"I got more chores but I didn't mind doing them."

—VINNY, OLDER BROTHER OF
A GIRL WITH CEREBRAL
PALSY

When your child finally comes home from the hospital, you feel relieved but nervous at the same time. What's in store now that responsibility for your child rests solely on your shoulders? Some misgivings and fears are common. Life can feel a little different than it was before—or totally "out of whack." You'll confront unanticipated problems that sometimes feel insurmountable. But little by little, you will learn how to manage.

You'll find that challenges come on two levels, the practical and the emotional. Practical problems can be solved with concrete actions, things you can do that have visible results. These might include learning how to care for your child's physical and medical needs, restructuring your work and family schedules, and adapting your home for the needs of your child who has a disability.

Emotional adjustments can be harder than changes in your physical environment or routines. While you physically "put things in their place" by making your home accessible, you'll find it more difficult to do the same with your emotions. Physical fatigue can accentuate feelings of sadness or frustration. You'll need to find some time for rest and a way to make "space" for your emotions, to recognize and cope with them constructively. Eventually, you'll learn how to "put disability in its place," not letting it take over your (or your child's) life.

This chapter explores a number of practical and emotional changes that families experience as a child's disability becomes part of their daily life—new time and energy demands, different family activities, accessibility issues, and getting help from others. It looks at how to manage your child's ongoing medical and self-care needs, work with his medical team, and become an expert on his disability. And it describes the experience, shared by many parents and siblings, of finding a "new normal" as they embrace a child who has a physical disability into their family.

Adjusting to Changes in Family Life
Time and Energy Demands

Parents in families that include a child who has a physical disability wish they had additional hours in their days to do everyday tasks—getting ready to go somewhere, going to the bathroom, dressing, eating. And they note the extra demands on their physical energy. For instance, Pili needs extra time to put on her son's braces and organize the special equipment she needs to have on hand for him whenever the family goes out. Their daily schedule must include time for Pili to catheterize her child every five hours and to locate safe and accessible places to do so. Liz, a single parent, recalls the time and energy demands of caring for her baby daughter with spina bifida (SB). In addition to parenting, Liz continued to work as a writer and college professor; she was tired all the time.

You and your partner and family will need to set priorities to avoid overloading yourselves. Making changes in your work hours, increasing the amount of help you get from others, or simply letting go of less important chores are all ways to cope with the increased demands on your time.

Kathleen gave up her job outside the home to care for her children, and she also missed out on many social events because of her baby's complicated bladder catheterization and bowel care regimens. Kathleen couldn't hire just any babysitter or nanny; caregivers had to be specially trained. Support from her mother and husband helped Kathleen make the transition to being a full-time mother. "I'm not mad," she says; "it's just the way it is."

Runner and April wondered how they could manage 4-year-old Lance's unpredictable and complicated treatment schedule without one parent at home full-time. They weighed various alternatives and decided that Runner would quit his job while April kept hers. Although their income was reduced, their stress was, too. They enjoyed a better quality of life, and Runner loves the extra time he has with his son.

Getting Help outside the Family

Whether you are a single parent or have a partner, extended family and community members can help you lighten your load and make it easier for your family to cope after your child returns home from medical treatment or rehabilitation. They can support you emotionally, physically, and sometimes financially. All parents can benefit from help; some can receive it graciously, while others find it hard to accept.

Angie has "a million friends," says her mother, Mia. "So many people have helped with meals or money. When someone does something for us, it is hard for me to receive their help. I was always the helper; I was the one who cooked for others and gave them money. It's my family pattern."

You might find it upsetting, as Leigh did, if outsiders jump in to help your family without asking whether you want or need assistance. When Leigh's neighbors wanted to throw a fund-raiser for her daughter, Leigh felt angry, thinking the neighbors viewed her family as "needy" and unable to handle her daughter's situation. Even well-meaning neighbors can go overboard when they assume that a family whose child has a disability must be in dire straits. But most neighbors offer to help out of kindness, not because they think your family is incompetent. It is helpful to communicate your wishes to others and let them know when you feel you can handle things without their help. But it's also important to leave the door open to accepting—or asking for—help in the future, should the need arise.

Susie initially found it difficult to accept kindness from others. As a single mother with four little boys, two who had physical disabilities, she had to rely on help from her friends, but she felt uncomfortable with being beholden to them. But she learned to accept help when one of her friends told her, "Someday you'll help someone else, and in that way you'll repay me."

Bobby, whose son lost an arm in an accident, found it easy to accept the help that was offered by his friends and church members. "What goes around comes around," he says. "I've always volunteered with kids at church and helped my neighbors rake their leaves in the fall. So I figured it was my turn—and boy was I grateful."

Family Activities

Many families that include a child who has a physical disability make some changes in the types of things they do together. Sometimes the child who has a disability needs more hands-on help with an activity than the family can provide, or has limitations in how much he can participate in leisure activities that his siblings or parents enjoy. More advanced planning is necessary, reducing spontaneity. Mia says, "It's tough. You can't just run off. We used to go camping but haven't since Angie was born [with osteogenesis imperfect (OI)]. We have to keep her safe." You may need to make adjustments in family outings and vacation plans so that all your children are able to enjoy sports, games, and recreation. Every family has different ways of doing this. You might want to focus on leisure activities that are accessible to *all* members of your family or can be adapted to include your child who has a physical disability. Finding a substitute activity that can give everyone the same excitement or exercise as their old favorite will make this work better—you might take skiing off your list, for example, and focus on water sports and sledding, if they are more accessible or adaptable for your child. Another approach is to give your children who are able to ski the chance to do so and find an equally attractive activity, perhaps horseback riding, for your child who has a disability.

Accessibility

A step is not just a step. There is an old pamphlet with a picture of Itzhak Perlman, the famous violinist, standing with his crutches at the bottom of a flight of steps, saying, "I hate steps!" If you are a parent of a child who cannot climb steps, you understand the depth of meaning behind this statement. Steps, curbs, very steep inclines, and other architectural barriers can convey, particularly to a child, the message that he is unwanted or unworthy to enter. A mother of a son who has a disability says that she has only one friend who has a house without steps. Although she can carry her son up the stairs now, she knows that she will not always be able to do so. How will that limit his ability to hang out with friends at their homes as he becomes a teenager? One solution is to make your home the gathering spot for your child's friends. You might also invest in a portable ramp to use when visiting homes or other places where there are only a couple of steps. Friends might ask about how they can open up their homes; you can refer them to information on "visit-able homes." These homes are based on the barrier-free, universal design concept, meaning they can be used by both able-bodied people and those who have disabilities. Inclusivity is the goal.

Adjusting to Changes in Yourself
Dealing with Your Emotions and Attitudes

Parents need to deal first with the practical aspects of caring for their children after they have a baby who has a disability or an older child has a disabling illness or trauma. There is no time or energy to analyze your emotions when you are swamped by the physical and medical care of your child, especially if you have one or more other children at home. And

---

☞ Grief, loss, and other "negative" emotions are normal. These reactions don't mean that you love your child any less or that you are a "bad" parent. Allow yourself to experience these feelings before trying to "get over" them. Grant your spouse, family, and friends the permission to do the same.

▶ *Working through feelings.* Releasing your feelings, whatever they are, by sharing them with a friend or a counselor can bring some relief. Remembering that feelings can change from moment to moment and that you don't necessarily need to act on them makes them less frightening. Facing your feelings and dealing with them will free up energy for you to better support your child. Crying, sharing your frustration or disbelief, getting mad, and telling your story—perhaps many times—will lighten your load and ease your discomfort and confusion. Allowing yourself to replay, refeel, or rethink your situation will make your feelings less intense, and with time they will gradually fade. As you gain distance, you will develop a new perspective.

you may not be *ready* to deal with emotions that threaten to overwhelm your ability to function in the heat of a crisis. But after your child is at home and life is humming along, your emotions may come back at you full force.

Casey felt sad when one of her twins was born with a spinal cord injury (SCI), but she quickly had to "get with the program" to care for them. A couple of years later, when her family life was finally in order, Casey "fell apart." Like Casey, when you finally have more time and energy, you may experience a delayed emotional reaction to the stress of your child's initial illness and hospitalization. Some people become more depressed, others more nervous or irritable. Some parents have delayed reactions and difficulty accepting their child's disability as a result of negative attitudes about disability or expectations that will not be fulfilled. Understanding and working through these difficult feelings takes work and requires support. It is necessary work, allowing you to gain strength and perspective in order to see and appreciate your *whole* child, who is so much more than his disability.

Although parents often have anxiety after coming home from the hospital, it may occur during other transitions, for instance, when their child who has a disability gets an infection, is assigned a new health aide, starts school, has an operation, reaches puberty, goes to camp, or leaves home for college. Paul, whose son David has complex care needs due to quadriplegia, says there are "so many things to worry about on a daily basis.

T Get some help from your partner or another adult family member who feels more comfortable and accepting of physical differences. Let this person help you by talking with you about their positive feelings and attitudes about disability and by spending time with your child. Watching another adult interact with your child can give you a new perspective on your own feelings and behaviors. He or she can be a role model for you, as well as boosting your child's self-esteem.

Sometimes I feel like I'll lose ten to fifteen years off my life span because of this stress!" Some parents of kids who have physical disabilities worry excessively about their children getting hurt, either physically or emotionally, as the children take steps toward independence. Terry, for example, whose 17-year-old son Jamie has severe juvenile rheumatoid arthritis, was surprised when her husband talked about finding a college with accessible housing for Jamie. Terry assumed that Jamie would live at home and go to a local community college and had even daydreamed about building an apartment on their house so Jamie could live there "forever." Scott, whose stepdaughter Celeste has OI, gets anxious about her doing anything that could cause her physical harm. His wife, Evelyn, describes him, at times, as a "dream crusher," holding back Celeste out of fear of her getting hurt. Anxiety overload can lead to overprotecting your child, preventing him from experiencing life to the fullest. Talking with your partner or co-parent can help you to reduce your anxiety and increase your tolerance for the risks your children *need* to take.

You or your partner may have negative attitudes or stereotypes about physical disabilities which you learned somewhere along the line. Maybe you were horrified when your child was born with or developed a disability but were able to put your attitudes on the back burner immediately after her birth or during his acute illness. You may find them surfacing again after your child comes home, you develop a set of daily routines with him, and the reality of disability sinks in. You may have prejudices against people who have disabilities, or perhaps you had negative experiences with disability in the past. If you see your child's disability as a reflection on yourself, you may feel angry at your child or view his disability

as your personal failure. If these attitudes prevent you from bonding with your child, being a good parent, or enjoying the experience of parenting, you can use some help.

Sam had polio as a child; now a senior citizen, he recalls that his mother saw his disability as an embarrassment and a personal "blow." His father, less concerned with his physical abilities, expressed pride and excitement about Sam's academic achievements. This positive attention from his father helped Sam maintain his self-esteem and achieve success in school and his career, in spite of his mother's negative attitudes.

If you are unable to change negative attitudes that get in the way of nurturing your child who has a disability, even after getting support from a spouse or other adult, you should seek professional help (see below).

Charting Your Emotional Progress and Getting Help When You Need It

One of the ways you can better understand your emotions and attitudes and chart your progress in coping is to keep a log or journal of your reflections and feelings. In your journal, you can pour out emotions and thoughts without someone judging you. Reviewing your journal periodically can show just how far you have come in improving your mood, your attitudes, or how you relate to your family. Or it might help you catch a downward trend and recognize when you are struggling and in need of help.

If you are running an "emotional fever" for more than a week in a row, it's time to look more closely at what's going on. Are you lacking

Feelings thermometer chart. On paper, rate yourself on a 10-point scale from 1 (none) to 10 (most intense) on your feelings of sadness, frustration, isolation, anger, being misunderstood, exhaustion, or other feelings you may have. Take your emotional "temperature" by rating yourself on the 1 to 10 point scale. Retake your "temperature" several days in a row. At the end of this time, look to see if there is an upward or downward trend or if it is stable in one spot.

> ☞ Sharing your feelings with someone you trust is a powerful way to release your feelings, to hear them and assess them. This person can be a friend or family member who is a good listener and can accept your feelings without judging you or dictating how you should deal with them.

momentum to get the laundry done or schedule a date with friends? Are you physically exhausted, depressed, or overwhelmed? Do you need more support from others?

Sometimes you need more than a friend to change your negative thoughts or help you find a way to move forward. Don't be afraid to seek professional help if you find yourself in this situation.

Choosing a therapist who is best suited to your needs is important. Try to get two or three recommendations and call each therapist for a short phone interview to determine your comfort talking to them and if they have experience working with people with your needs. To prepare for your first session, make a list of your feelings, concerns, and questions ahead of time so you don't forget to tell the therapist about them. You will probably feel relieved after the first session because you have taken the hardest step toward changing the way you are feeling.

Grandparents go through their own emotional adjustments as they come to terms with a grandchild's physical disability. Feelings of loss, anger, sadness, and anxiety, among others, are common and to be expected, just as they are with parents. Grandparents may use denial to protect themselves from the emotional impact of a grandchild's disability, or try to reverse events by bargaining with God. Parents' and grandparents' emotional reactions may not be in sync: mother is sad while dad is angry, grandmother thinks everything will get better, and grandfather is full of nervous energy and wants to get going on building ramps. It helps to remember that each individual's feelings are okay and that where a family member is emotionally at any given moment won't last forever. Emotions will change, and you will all move on in time. Rose's family is an example. When her child was born with OI, her husband's family was supportive, stepping in to help care for their two older children and soon to take all three children in order to give the parents some rest. They made their new little granddaughter with OI part of the larger family's life. Rose's mother,

T If you feel stuck, find professional help. You might choose to work with a psychologist, social worker, counselor, psychiatrist, or pastoral counselor. Advocacy organizations and state organizations for various mental health professions can recommend experienced therapists. Friends may also be able to recommend someone to talk with you. Remember: you are not "sick" if you ask for professional help; you are a good problem solver!

on the other hand, had a difficult time adjusting to the fact of her granddaughter's disability and did not help out. After a while, she did sort through her feelings and became a part of the family support team.

When Kelsey was five months pregnant, she told her father, Ned, that her baby had SB. Ned and his wife started reading about this condition and found only negatives. Ned was frightened. "I had a hard time dealing with it. My brother had muscular dystrophy. I didn't know if I could handle this again. I associated hospitals with death, but that changed with Leeann and her surgeries. She adjusts and we adjust. She has had twelve surgeries and is now a candidate to walk. We had to live with it to find the positives."

Despite differences in emotional reactions and timetables, grandparents can be incredibly helpful to your family when you are adjusting to life after the hospital. Many grandparents are willing to educate themselves about your family's emerging needs and help you build an understanding of the complex new situation you face.

Pepere and Memere, grandparents of a child with OI, had previous positive experiences with physical disability before their granddaughter was born. Although they "would have been happier or more relieved had she been born healthy," their past history had given them a good appreciation for the reality of living life with disability. The experience of Memere's brother's life with quadriplegia after a car accident "had already provided us a foundation of compassion and understanding." Their view that disability is just one factor in a person's life, that it doesn't dominate his existence, and that he can enjoy and experience life gave their granddaughter and her family strength and hope to cope with and move beyond their initial fears about OI and disability.

Managing Ongoing Medical Problems

When your child comes home from the hospital, his medical condition is probably stable. But it is likely that he will continue to experience medical complications or surgeries, or need extensive treatments or rehabilitation therapies—for several weeks, months, or years. This is another new fact of life, one you will cope with better as you gain experience.

Parents who go through repeated medical crises with their children—bone breaks, respiratory problems, or surgeries—find that the first episode is often the most trying because everything seems foreign and overwhelming. Often there is no blueprint for what to expect, what to do, or how to respond. But after living through the experience, you learn that your child—and you—can do it!

While your own experience and growing confidence will make things easier, having a good relationship with your child's doctor is also essential to getting good care for your child and supporting you in caring for your child's medical needs. Look for a doctor who is empathic, reassuring, and positive. He or she should be a good listener who can understand your painful emotions and respond to your concerns about your child. Ideally, your child's doctor should include you as a partner in the medical care of your child and boost your confidence in parenting, while providing reassurance when you need it. Your doctor's support for your dream of creating a happy family is invaluable.

Going around the cone. Picture one of those orange cones used to direct the flow of traffic. The bottom is the widest part, and from there it narrows to a point, so that each time you circle it, higher and higher, the circumference grows smaller. Similarly, the first go-around with a child's medical crisis is the most difficult, as you have to learn a great deal of new information and at the same time deal with strong emotions. You'll find that when this medical issue comes up again, it will be less stressful because you're more prepared. You'll know which tools and strategies can bring you full circle, and you'll get to the end point sooner. The trip around the cone grows smaller with each circle, and each time around you can manage the situation better—both physically and emotionally.

Priscilla's baby was diagnosed with SB while she was pregnant. She couldn't imagine how she would cope until she found a doctor who told her, "Wait until you have this beautiful baby. You're going to love him and play with him and cherish every moment you have with him. Leave his medical care to me." This put everything in perspective.

Communication with the Medical Team

Medical care for your child who has a physical disability usually involves more than one doctor. To be successful in navigating complex health care systems and becoming an active participant in your child's health care team, you will need to develop an effective way to communicate with multiple providers and hospitals or rehab centers.

Each parent has a different way of working with medical providers. One study described parents' styles of relating to the medical team along a continuum, from those who try to keep as much control over their child's treatment as possible ("confrontive questioners") to those who accept and go along with every medical recommendation without question ("compliant consumers"). Between these extremes are the "managing partners." These parents form a partnership with the medical team; the parents can make the final decisions about their child's care, but they have the benefit of frequent access to the expertise of the providers.

Any of these styles can be effective at different times and in various situations. When your child has an emergency, you may be more inclined to go along with the doctor's recommendations, but when you have time to consider and choose a treatment from several alternatives, you might want to ask more probing questions about the pros and cons of each choice. A "managing partnership" with your child's health care team is ideal in most situations, although at times you may want to give more weight to the medical team's advice, or at other times you may need to advocate for your child and clearly express your wishes or views, perhaps differing from those of the medical team.

As a parent, you need to know how to handle your child's daily medical care needs, and you probably learned much of this while your child was in the hospital. But now you will have to decide when to seek urgent medical attention and when you can manage on your own. And if your child has an illness, symptom flare-up, or surgical procedure, you need to know how to provide any extra care that's required. As a parent, you are responsible for monitoring changes in your child's condition and communicating with your child's doctor—and for asking questions, expressing your concerns, and voicing your opinions. When you communicate well with your child's doctor, you will develop a mutually trusting relationship and learn to put more trust in your own ability to provide your child's medical care at home and to make good medical choices for her when necessary.

By the time their son was a youngster, Priscilla and Lee were comfortable expressing their concerns and anxieties, asking questions and seeking information from his medical team. If something didn't sit well with them, they could speak up about it. Once effective communication had been established, they were able to rely on the medical team for a sense of security. For example, when they were worried about their son's new pressure sore, the nurse reassured them. "It's okay. It's not major; we'll keep an eye on it." This type of feedback helped them learn that they "didn't have to be alarmist."

Sometimes parents are shy or embarrassed about admitting their confusion, discussing their fears and concerns, or challenging a doctor when they disagree with his opinion. But if parents don't speak up about these things, there can be misunderstandings that lead to serious problems. For Evelyn Hamilton and her first husband, Romi, poor communication with their daughter's doctors led to years of needless guilt and worry.

When his daughter was born with OI, Romi was told that OI occurs more frequently in people of his ethnic group. This information was inaccurate, and it was presented to (or heard by) Romi in a way that made him feel blamed for "causing" his daughter's condition. He felt so guilty and so afraid of hurting his daughter that he rarely touched her. But Romi neither discussed his guilt or fears with his daughter's doctor nor sought other professional opinions or new information about OI. Sadly, this misunderstanding led to increasing physical and emotional distance between Romi and his daughter.

Evelyn, too, suffered for years from a misconception about her daughter's condition. Early on, she received a report of her daughter's genetic testing and misread the numbers coding her daughter's type of OI—she thought it was the most severe type, and for a long time she expected her daughter to die before reaching adolescence. But she never tried to confirm the genetic typing with her daughter's doctor. Years later, when she had to get her daughter's health records to travel overseas, Evelyn discovered her error—and she cried over her "wasted pain."

Things can be especially muddled when a child's disability develops over time and the cause is unclear. Multiple specialists are consulted in these "difficult cases," making it harder for parents to keep track of complex medical information. Communication gaps between the various doctors are also common. Ironically, getting an accurate diagnosis is sometimes *more* difficult when multiple specialists are consulted. This is what happened when Marie's daughter Ashley was injured.

Marie recalls, "I was at work when the call came; I dropped everything and was at the scene in twenty minutes. Ashley was standing there, talking to the police. The car was totaled. She had a headache and was in shock. I took her home." Though Ashley walked away from the accident, three days later she started experiencing bouts of paralysis, involuntary shaking of her body, headaches, and pain. Her parents took her to the ER and told them about Ashley's accident, but a CT scan did not show any injury. Over the next several months, Ashley's condition deteriorated, and she couldn't walk or get on and off the toilet by herself. She saw numerous specialists, but none could make a definitive diagnosis. Ashley thought she heard one doctor say that it was "all in her head," which was disturbing to her. In retrospect, she might have heard him say that she had a mild head injury and misinterpreted his meaning. Another doctor suspected she had transverse myelitis, a disease that damages nerves in the spinal cord. Ashley's inability to walk and do her own personal care led to a stay in an inpatient rehabilitation hospital, where a comprehensive evaluation of her physical, cognitive, and functional abilities led to the final diagnoses of lumbar SCI and postconcussive syndrome.

When the diagnosis is unclear, parents experience the pain of knowing that something is wrong, yet *not* knowing what it is or what the effects on their child or family will be. Sometimes there really are no concrete answers, and you must live with an uncertain diagnosis, do what you can to care for your child, and hope for the best. Unfortunately, when a specific diagnosis has not been made, parents (and kids) may get the message—intended or not—that their child is being "bad" or "acting crazy" or that they are not doing a good enough job as parents. This can damage your (or your child's) self-confidence and contribute to a delay in making an accurate diagnosis of a significant medical problem. In these situations, trust your instincts about your child. As a parent, you know your child best, and if you don't think he's a bad kid, then he probably isn't. Your confidence in him and in yourself as a parent will reassure your child and help you become her advocate. You may need to do some additional research to find a doctor or medical center that can find the reason for your child's symptoms.

Jane's son, Adam, was born with his umbilical cord wrapped around his neck and had to stay in the hospital for six days. He was susceptible to infections as an infant, and they were in and out of ERs for seventeen months. When he was 2 years old, Jane's car was rear-ended, and Adam was hurt. He had been potty trained before the accident but "regressed" afterward. Jane took him to a neurologist, but his diagnosis was unclear. When he was 6 and still unable to control his bladder, she took him to a urologist, who told her that Adam was just "lazy" and "not disciplined." But Jane firmly believed that she was a good mother and that Adam was a good kid, not "lazy." She continued to search for a diagnosis, taking Adam to a number of different specialists. Finally, when he was 8 years old, an MRI showed a cyst in Adam's spinal cord blocking the nerve signals needed for bladder control.

Adam's spinal cord condition is expected to worsen over time, with eventual paralysis of his legs a possible outcome. But now that Jane and her husband have a clear picture of Adam's diagnosis and his expected function, they can make better decisions about how to manage his current symptoms and plan appropriately for his future. Jane advises parents to get a second opinion and not to "take what is said in the hospital as gospel."

After understanding the cause of their child's disability, parents want specific information on the likelihood of the condition improving or worsening and on its long-term effects (prognosis). When information about prognosis is unavailable or confusing, many parents feel more unsettled

---

☞ Remember that no other person possesses the broad perspective and intimate knowledge of your child that you have. Trust yourself to do what's right for your family. Although you can benefit from the advice and input of professionals, ultimately, you must decide what's best for your child.

and anxious. The more detailed this information is, the better you can plan for your child's and family's future needs. Again, it's essential that you keep asking for this information and not give up or accept ignorance. You may have to ask for a separate appointment to speak with the doctor by phone or in her office, because she is probably pressed for time during regular clinic visits. Or you might need to take your child to a specialty hospital or clinic to get clearer information about his prognosis.

Casey had a medical background and knew that her son, who was born with an SCI, would most likely be permanently paralyzed. "I almost knew more than I wanted to know," she recalls. Still, like other parents who are less sophisticated about SCI, Casey needed to hear about her son's prognosis from "the horse's mouth." But she remembers "sitting in clinic waiting rooms for hours, waiting to see a host of doctors to get very little information, other than he is 'doing fine.' Most of the answers to my questions were, 'We'll just have to wait and see.' No one could tell us what his outcome would be."

After moving to a different city with a specialty hospital for kids with SCI, Casey finally felt that she was getting answers; even though she was hearing mostly what she already knew or suspected, it was validating to have confirmation from the experts, and it made her feel more understood and cared about.

How to Get Answers to Your Questions

Most medical professionals who care for kids who have disabilities are well informed and compassionate. They will work diligently to find the best treatments for your child and be responsive to your questions and concerns. If you are frustrated with your child's medical care, consider whether there are ways you can improve the situation. For example, try restating your concerns and questions so your needs become crystal clear. When you have a suspicion that something is wrong with your child, bring it to the doctor's attention and insist on getting her input.

If you don't understand what a doctor is telling you, try asking him to repeat the information using different or simpler words, or to give you written information or instructions. Don't be hard on yourself if you don't "get it" the first time; most parents find that it takes some repetition to absorb complex medical information.

Lynn, who has three daughters who have disabilities, worked in a hospital. She came to parenting with a good medical background, yet she had to pose many types of questions to her children's doctors in order to extract the specific information necessary to manage their medical needs. "This is a good skill I learned in childhood," she says, "to find another way to ask the question." Lynn emphasizes the importance of getting the answers "in language people understand."

One way you can learn to ask better questions is by doing some of your own research at a library, on the Internet, or through the consumer organization for your child's condition (see the Resources section of this book). Once you've read and thought about the information, you will have a much better idea of what you are dealing with—and what you *don't* know. You can then organize your questions, write them down, and bring them to your next doctor's appointment. It helps if both parents make a list; often each parent will think of different but equally important questions. It's a good idea to list *all* your questions and concerns, no matter how trivial they may seem.

Scott, whose stepdaughter has OI, says, "I always do my homework. I go to the doctor with an idea of what's wrong and which options the doctor will present. It is important to me to always ask why he is making a recommendation. It seems you've got to know about the specifics of the disability because of the potential for a bad decision."

Becoming an Expert on Your Child's Disability

One way that medical and rehabilitative care has changed over the past thirty years is that patients (even children) and their families are included in medical decision making more than ever before. In the course of parenting a child who has a physical disability or chronic illness, there are many decisions to be made regarding medical care, surgical procedures, and rehabilitation. Some of these will be no-brainers, like whether or not to set a broken bone. But others, such as whether your child should have a leg-lengthening surgery or a course of experimental therapy, are much more complicated. Such decisions require consideration of your child's and your family's goals and values, emotional and support resources, insurance coverage, and other factors. Understanding the medical information provided by your child's doctors is just one piece of the puzzle. You

☞ Gather up-to-date information about your child's disability. Being aware of the newest medical, technological, financial, and social advances that affect your child's health and well-being enables you to be a true partner in medical and educational decisions concerning your child. Try to keep abreast by reading, researching on the Internet, and going to conferences related to your child's disability.

may need to learn more about your child's insurance and disability benefits, social and community support services, assistive technologies, and educational options, in order to make the best decisions and plans. Casey recalls playing simultaneous roles, as "a mom, a caregiver, and a case manager," while attending to her son's medical needs, negotiating changes in their insurance coverage, and trying to make ends meet on one income.

In addition, parents—and other family members—play a central role as "hands-on" care providers for their children who have disabilities. Fifty years ago, children who had severe physical disabilities living in urban areas were more likely to attend "special" schools or live in institutional settings, frequently with children having intellectual as well as physical disabilities. Now, due largely to advances in disability rights legislation, including the Americans with Disabilities Act (ADA), children who have disabilities are cared for in the "least restrictive environment," and there is widespread recognition that most children who have physical disabilities are healthier and more successful when integrated into regular public or private schools, just like their able bodied peers.

The ADA requires public schools to make accommodations for kids who have physical disabilities, and participation in social and leisure activities is a major goal of medical rehabilitation programs. Other changes in the medical system, including limited insurance coverage for professional caregivers, shorter hospital stays for acute illnesses and rehabilitation, and the increasing specialization of medical care, contribute to the greater role that parents play in the home medical care of their children who have physical disabilities.

Parents of children with complex or unusual medical conditions often learn more details about the condition than are known by any one of the many medical specialists who care for their child. Parents frequently become the "case coordinators" and information specialists on their child's disability. Parents in these roles find it helpful to collect and store information on their child's medical history, surgeries, and current symptoms and make sure it gets distributed to all of his doctors. One father who has a son with complex medical needs keeps a spiral notebook in which he puts all doctor reports, medication and treatment changes, schedules, and problems that arise. You may also need to educate nonmedical service providers (such as teachers, counselors, and aides) and extended family members about his medical needs and care.

Diane and her husband learned as much as possible about managing their daughter's OI—mostly from the OI Foundation—and then they educated their extended families. "The doctor called us after seeing the X-rays and told us of his suspicions of OI, Type 1, and within minutes we had located the OI website, which explained so much. Finally, all of her issues made sense. The dots were connected; everything was clear. We read and read and read—and then we passed the information along to our families."

D. K.'s family, including a son with OI, has moved around and traveled a great deal. If his son needs care in an area where there are no OI specialists, D. K. sometimes instructs the doctor on how to treat him. To further his efforts at educating medical personnel naïve about OI, D. K. printed information about the diagnosis and laminated it to the back of business cards. He is now able to give these out to new doctors and others involved in treating his son.

At times, educating yourself, your family, and your doctors can be exhausting. Becoming an expert on your child's disability—and sharing your expertise with others—takes a huge amount of time and energy. Parents struggling to raise a family, including the extra care needs of a child who has a disability, have a heavy load to carry and shouldn't expect to be "perfect parents" at all times. If you are able to learn the basics necessary to care for your child, and if you are willing to ask questions when you need more information to handle new situations or decisions, you are doing a great job. If, like D. K., you can also bring fact sheets and treatment plans to your child's doctor, give yourself extra credit!

Grandparents may be able to help you gather information or come up with creative ideas about your child's treatment. Weighing the pros and cons of medical decisions is one of the hardest tasks for parents of

> ☞ Stress and anxiety are common when your child is having ongoing medical problems or requires extra care. Remember that there is a connection between your mind and body; stress (or "de-stressing") in one area affects the other. Next time you're worried, try smiling. You will find that your facial muscles relax and, more importantly, the "worry tape" in your head stops running. Pretty soon your body is more relaxed, too. Creating a new and positive mantra or repeated message for yourself is another way to control anxiety—for example, "Things are tough but I can do it." (Repeat as needed!)

kids who have disabilities. Your parents (your child's grandparents) can support you by sharing any information they have found in their own research; when a grandparent has done his homework on a particular treatment, he can make an important contribution to the discussion. Grandparents may also help simply by being the sounding board as you discuss the pros and cons of various treatments.

Sometimes a grandparent feels strongly about a different course of action than you are inclined to take; hashing out your conflicts can help, however, by forcing you to reexamine your decision and be sure it still feels right. Ned, grandfather of Leeann, notes, "I don't always agree with what's going on. I fought against Leeann getting a feeding tube—but it has helped her put on weight. She has reflux that I blame on the tube because she didn't have it before." Still, Ned knows that many factors have to be considered in judging whether the benefits of a treatment outweigh the side effects—and that, after stating his position, a grandparent needs to step back and accept decisions that parents make for their child.

Partnering with Professionals

Marie's introduction to the medical system came when her daughter Ashley had a car accident at age 17. Ashley's medical situation was complex, but as Marie discovered, her insurance coverage was equally complicated and difficult to manage. Marie's biggest frustration during the initial months after Ashley's injury was the fight with her insurance company for coverage of Ashley's extensive medical care and rehabilitation. "I am

> ☛ Other parents of children who have physical disabilities have walked this path before you and are a great source of information. If possible, find other parents of children your child's age with whom you can "co-trailblaze." Parents of children older than your own may also be able to help you by charting what lies ahead.

nesses or disabilities, and some include parents of kids who have a variety of different disabilities.

Pili, the mother of a child with SB, says that counseling from a professional would have been helpful "up front," when her baby was first diagnosed. But although counseling was not available, she found that valuable support "came from other families." She is active in a support group and says, "It's incredible to share your journey with parents of kids who have other disabilities, not just spina bifida. It is good to have someone you can connect with."

Peer support groups can help you become an expert on your child's disability. They can be found through many consumer health organizations, hospitals, rehabilitation programs, and social service agencies. Many are listed in the Resources section of this book.

Finding Your New Normal

Once your family has made some adjustments to the routines of daily life and worked out a way to manage medical problems when they resurface, life begins to settle down a bit. Your focus shifts away from narrow medical and disability-related problems and broadens to include the interests, activities, and relationships that make up normal family life. Despite the media stereotypes of disability as a family tragedy or a badge of heroism, your child who has a disability is an ordinary child—and your family, a "regular" family.

Part of creating this new "normal" for your family involves limiting the role of disability in your child's life and in yours. As an inclusive parent, keeping your child's disability in perspective will allow it to gradually become part of your family's scenery, rather than taking center stage.

> ☞ Maintain a balance of friends who have children with disabilities and those with able-bodied children. This can lessen your feelings of "apartness" or "specialness." It is important to keep the perspective that all children have the same basic psychological and social needs and most parenting and growing-up issues are the same for both able-bodied kids and those who have physical disabilities.

When this starts to happen, it will be easier to focus on your child's needs *beyond* his disability, to give equal attention to all your children, and to take better care of yourself.

As parents, you are not alone in creating a sense of normality for your family. Your other children play a central role in this process. Especially when their brother's or sister's disability was present from birth or started early in life, siblings tend to view the disability as simply a fact of their family life, rather than something weird or a cause of emotional distress. Research shows that people who have one or more close relationships with a person who has a disability have more positive attitudes toward disability and are less likely to view disability as the defining characteristic of a person. This seems to apply to siblings, who often have positive attitudes toward their brother or sister who has a disability and see them as capable, reliable individuals. Most siblings define their inclusive families as "normal."

Erik, whose family includes three younger sisters who have physical disabilities, is right on target when he says that each family has to define its own "normal." Erik's mom and her partner chose to grow their family by adopting daughters who have disabilities, but the family makes room for Erik's needs as well. Disability is a big part of their lives, but not always the main act. Erik's family rejects outsiders' interpretations of their lives; they are comfortable with themselves as a family. "What is normal?" Erik asks. "My family is normal."

Jean thinks of her older brother who has SB as her "best friend" and says, "Disability is normal to us, part of our daily routine." Sukey, the youngest of five sibs, was born years after her eldest sister had polio. She experienced her older sister as "just normal. She was my wonderful big sister who happened to walk on crutches." Paige says that the only times she thinks of her sister as having a disability are when medical questions come up about her care. Otherwise, "she's just my sister."

Able-bodied siblings may look up to their sib who has a physical disability for her exceptional strengths in coping with disability, but more often they value the same personality traits, talents, or intellectual achievements that would make any sibling admirable. As the younger brother of Albert, who has an SCI, Terry thinks it will be difficult to duplicate the achievements of his sibling: "He's a great student, a leader, and is really popular at school. I don't think I will ever be able to do all that he has done." Fred remembers how he "rode on my younger sister's popularity." He dropped his sister off in her wheelchair at middle school each day as he drove to high school. She was well known and liked, and Fred, who was quiet and a bit shy, liked the recognition he received as her brother.

Siblings also understand that a brother or sister who has a physical disability is not mentally limited, and they respect their sibs' intelligence. Zoey recalls that when her baby sister was born with OI, she had to carry her around on a pillow to help avoid breaking her sister's fragile bones.

How can you tell when your child's disability has become a normal part of your family? Creating an inclusive family takes time, but there are some changes you can look for in yourself that let you know you're getting close to a new normal:

- You see how handsome your boy looks in his new suit, not his crutches or wheelchair.
- Your little girl is misbehaving and you feel free to discipline her, just as you do her able-bodied brothers and sisters.
- You call to reschedule your son's orthopedist's appointment because it conflicts with his piano recital or his sister's Little League game.
- You go out for the evening with your spouse or accept a date, leaving your children with a babysitter, and do not worry about them for the entire evening.
- You no longer ask "can" or "should" but instead "how" all your children will participate in an activity or achieve their goals.

"It was upsetting," Zoey says, "but she's smart. It's only physical and she can live a full life."

What's more, many sibs of kids who have disabilities are able to recognize the challenges in their own lives and have a greater appreciation that *all* people have some kind of limitations; they are part of the human condition and therefore normal. Jean observes, "Everyone has an obstacle, but it doesn't change the person's personality." Michelle O'Brien says of herself and her able-bodied sisters, "All of us have 'special needs'; they just may not be apparent on the exterior."

PART II

All in the Family

The Bowers: An athletic couple sort out what works for them in raising their only child, a serious student and accomplished wheelchair athlete

April and Runner married in their late twenties. "I'm in love with my husband," April beams. "I can't say enough about him." Runner agrees that their marriage is "excellent, and it's gotten even better over time. I can't see being without her." April is an occupational therapist, and Runner was a computer programmer before becoming a stay-at-home dad to Lance.

April always wanted to be a parent, but Runner "resisted having children. I didn't want to be pulled from sports and the freedom we had. We were making two good incomes. Parenting was too much responsibility."

"We were married ten years and then . . . surprise!" says April. Runner was "not happy" at the prospect of becoming a father. "But it was the best thing that ever happened to me. The instant I saw my son it was pure love, happiness; everything changed." Lance was "the perfect baby," born happy. He became the focus of their lives, even going for runs with April and Runner in the baby jogger.

When Lance was about 4, they noticed he had some bruising while they were vacationing in Florida. Doctors said it was just "growing pains," but they asked for a blood test, and then a second. The physical exam was repeated. The doctor told April that something was amiss and sent them to a hematologist. A bone marrow biopsy was done, and Lance was diagnosed with leukemia. April recalled the oncologist saying, "'It doesn't look good.' They assumed that being an OT [occupational therapist] I should know the implications."

Lance started chemotherapy. The illness went into remission, but he developed hand tremors that were a side effect of the treatment. Then, while April was at work one day, her sister called to tell her, "Lance is staggering. He can't walk." Runner remembers that when he arrived home, Lance was standing and took a few steps. Then his legs buckled. "We went to the ER."

The doctor wasn't sure if the side effects of chemotherapy were causing Lance's inability to walk—or even stand—but he suspended chemotherapy while he observed Lance's condition. At first, Lance was strong from the waist up and could propel his own wheelchair. Several weeks later he was paralyzed from the neck down and could hardly breathe. Runner wondered, "Is this how his life is going to be? When I saw Lance he smiled and said, 'Can you scratch my nose, Daddy?'"

Life was changing rapidly. For a few months Lance remained paralyzed in all four limbs. Then he slowly began to recover, and a year later he had regained his upper body strength though his legs remained paralyzed. His final diagnosis was paraplegia due to a rare neurotoxic reaction to the chemotherapy.

Each family member was affected emotionally by Lance's illness and paralysis. Going to the hospital for treatments, Lance would get angry, saying he wanted to "blow up" the hospital. April asked him about the people inside, and he would say, well, of course, he would get everyone out first.

"When Lance was going through paralysis, I couldn't stop crying," April remembers. "I went to a counselor who helped me find resources for him. She helped me see I was going through grief." April realized she wasn't crazy to have feelings of loss, anger, sadness, and frustration. April found that her "faith in God" also helped her cope during Lance's health crisis. "I prayed all the time asking God to give me strength. I feel He listened to me." One evening when Lance was in the hospital, April and Runner were in bed, crying. "Then a feeling of calm came over me. A voice said, 'Everything will be okay.' Some people lose faith when a child incurs a disability; others believe more resolutely."

Runner lost faith in Lance's doctors and hospitals. He was angry that Lance had not gone through an inpatient rehabilitation program right after he became paralyzed. After Lance's leukemia stabilized, Runner located a different hospital, which "was like a new family, seventy-five miles away. We drove there three times a week for Lance to begin a new regime of chemotherapy and to get outpatient rehabilitation."

Their families and friends were "in sync" with them, says April. Her mother, whom April thought of as her best friend, had died earlier, and she missed her. Runner says his mother was wonderful; she provided food, watched Lance, and visited in the hospital. She helped when Lance got sick, as did April's father when he flew in. Some siblings visited and supported them; others had difficulty dealing with what was happening and remained distant.

Lance needed full-time care, so April and Runner had to decide who would stay home with him. Ultimately, Runner gave up his career to be a stay-at-home dad. "I was dedicated to Lance. That helped." But it was a difficult choice for Runner and a sacrifice for all of them when their income was cut in half. April became the primary breadwinner, and they had to learn how to balance their new roles. Besides being the at-home parent, Runner does all the bill paying. April is a "clean freak" and has had to let that go. She would like to attend doctor's appointments with Lance but relies on Runner's reports.

When Lance was 8, his chemotherapy came to an end. They had a big party to celebrate. Runner was uneasy during the first year following cessation of therapy because Lance was vulnerable to a relapse. He worried about it day after day until the year passed. Then one day he realized he had gone an entire day without thinking about the possibility of relapse. "That felt good," he says.

Life in the community has not changed for them, other than their realization that "there are lots of great people." April affirms that their experience made her more thankful to people who cared about a child they didn't even know. She says she is sad that there are also folks out there with prejudice against people who have disabilities. "I would take my 4-year-old out in his wheelchair and people would stare and ask, 'What happened?'"

Lance, a teenager now, says, "When you are in a wheelchair, people judge you before they know you. It frustrates me. Once they get to know someone, then they help and are thoughtful."

An outgoing, positive wheelchair athlete, Lance is also in a unique academic high school program focusing on real-world applications of ideas. He describes himself as ambitious and serious about achievement. He is among the top-ranked hand cyclists in a competitive national circuit. He also plays wheelchair basketball competitively and travels to regional tourneys.

Although Lance has several friends at school, he tends not to socialize outside of school. He likes to spend time on his Xbox. His closest friend moved away recently, so they visit a couple of times a year. Most of his good friends are the adult wheelchair athletes with whom he travels and competes. He finds that other kids are not serious or don't care enough in school.

Risk taking is also important to Lance. "I'm a daredevil. I pop wheelies but I'm also safe." Runner says that when Lance goes biking alone, "it's worrisome because he's low to the ground and hard to see." He continually warns his son of the hazards while at the same time trying to let Lance care for himself.

A typical teen, Lance doesn't pick up his room as his parents would like him to—although he feels he helps out a lot, clearing the dinner table, setting out silverware, and keeping his bathroom clean. April and Runner feel they haven't given him enough responsibility and do too much for him. And they also have some concerns about their lack of consistency in enforcing rules or limits for Lance.

As for the future, Lance says he will study aeronautical engineering. He loves airplanes and admires his father's engineering mind. He might also become a professional hand cyclist. He asserts, "Having a disability doesn't mean you can't do anything. You have to find a reason for life and have a positive outlook. Because I was injured so young, disability shaped my outlook and the way I was going to be. I don't take life for granted."

Runner notes, "We search out opportunities to get our son involved in. We want him to participate in basketball and hand cycling. It has shaped all of our lives." He and Lance also do adaptive skiing together. He advises families not to withdraw and close in on themselves, but instead to seek new opportunities for themselves as a family and for their child who has a disability. He and April can see that the many trips Lance has taken with his basketball team have helped him mature and become even more independent.

April has found that "patience with your spouse and yourself helps" with parenting. She has learned not to worry about the little things and become more caring of herself and her family. She agrees with Runner that looking for the best resources is imperative when you have a child who has a physical disability.

3
Inclusive Parenting

Make It Work for You

"Being a parent has given me more to live for, more to appreciate about life. I look at the world with a sense of purpose. Having a child has an impact; having a child who has a physical disability has an even greater impact. I can't separate the two. It's a lot more work, but rewarding. I have to be positive and tough in a way. I have a lot more love than I knew I had."

> —KATHLEEN, MOTHER OF
> A SON WHO HAS SPINA
> BIFIDA

In this chapter we look first at how you can *take care of yourself*, so you can be a more effective parent, and secondly at how you can *build resilience in your kids*. Taking care of yourself means getting enough support (from your partner, family, and friends), finding ways to cope with your emotions, setting priorities and letting go of unnecessary tasks, taking time out for yourself, and learning from experienced parents. Building resilience in your kids involves creating expectations for success, giving them responsibilities, allowing some risk taking, enriching their life experiences, and boosting their self-esteem by being a positive role model.

First Things First: Get Support for Parenting

All parents need to support their children economically (usually by working outside the home), create a safe and secure home, and supply the nurturance, education, and love necessary for their kids to thrive. Each family divides these jobs in different ways. But no matter how you slice it, parenting is one tough job! You need support from other adults to be the best parent you can be.

Support from Your Partner

If you are part of a couple—mom and dad, two moms, two dads, or a parent and stepparent—you support each other, make decisions as a team, and share the task of building an inclusive family.

Working as a Team

When your child is born with or develops a physical disability, having a strong, intimate tie with your partner can help you with parenting. Rose found that learning to confide in her husband and becoming his "best friend" was essential to her parenting success. Paul, the father of twins, one of whom was born with a disability, found that "working as a team" helped him and his wife cope with stress and solve problems. April and Runner, whose son Lance has a spinal cord injury, agree. "We relied on and appreciated one another, and Lance's illness brought us closer," says Runner. Their support for each other sets the tone for the family; "I think it's good for Lance to see how we feel about each other," says April.

D. K. and his wife have a "very good, understanding relationship. We are strong spouses for each other. We are both strong willed, perseverance based, and have a no-quitting attitude. We make our marriage and family work and do not compromise the lives of our children."

In short, support and teamwork strengthen a couple's partnership—and also help them take better care of their kids. Some parents worry that time spent with each other will mean less time for their kids or less effective parenting. But actually, nurturing your relationship with your partner makes you a better parent.

Keeping an Intimate Connection

Parenting seems all-encompassing at times, threatening to crowd out your intimate emotional and sexual life as a couple. Setting aside some time each day to talk with your partner without the kids around, going on "dates," and getting away for a weekend now and then are some ways to avoid losing this vital connection with your partner. Scheduling time for your sexual relationship can also be helpful, as privacy is scarce during the day, and after the kids are asleep one or both of you may be too tired. Getting some extra help with the kids a couple of days a week can leave you more energy for making love on those nights. On other nights, cuddling with your partner before going to sleep can help you feel closer and more relaxed and encourage sharing of intimate emotions. When you feel loved and supported by your partner, you are better able to cope with stress and can bring renewed enthusiasm to parenting.

Support from Other Sources

Grandparents Can Help

Even if you and your partner work smoothly as a parenting team, there are times when both of you run out of energy and need a break to recharge. Getting away from home for a few days is incredibly restorative. Grandparents (or other relatives) can really help, especially when your child has extensive care needs, by caring for your children while you are gone.

Kathleen's son has spina bifida, and there are few babysitters who can handle his needs, but Kathleen's mother has learned to manage his complex care. She stays with her grandson several weekends a year so Kathleen can go away with her husband. Last year she stayed with him for ten days while Kathleen and her husband went on an extended vacation. These special times with her husband help Kathleen enjoy and nurture her marriage, unwind, and gather energy for the next phase of parenting.

Community Resources Can Back You Up

Even if your family members can't take care of your child who has a physical disability, there are other options in the community, including short-term residential services or week-long or weekend camping experiences. These programs, sometimes called respite care, allow parents to get away for a few days, knowing that their child is with experienced caregivers. Many private home care agencies employ trained people who can stay with your child for a few days or a few hours. These services range

---

T Sleepaway summer camps for kids who have disabilities offer sessions of one or more weeks, allowing you and your spouse a much-needed break while providing fun and stimulating activities for your child. Look for camps in the Resources section of this book.

---

from babysitters to certified nursing assistants to registered nurses, depending on your child's needs.

Support for Single Parents

If you are a single parent of a child who has a disability, the support of other adults—family, friends, or hired helpers—is critical to your success, as well as your sanity! When you don't have a partner, you are "it"—the teacher, cheerleader, decision maker, consoler, goal setter, and disciplinarian for your children. Finding support from other adults is one of the secrets to success as a single parent. Some single parents exchange nights of babysitting for each other's kids so each can have some free time. "Bartering" with friends to meet each other's needs is another approach. For instance, Dorothy, an excellent seamstress, often hems a skirt or makes a dress for her friend's daughter, in exchange for her friend's babysitting services.

Susie's experience illustrates how challenging single parenting can be when your family includes children who have physical disabilities—and how, with support, you can do it.

Susie was married and a working mother of four little boys, including twins with a muscle disorder. When her twins were 17 months old, her husband suddenly decided to leave the family. Susie prayed for guidance and believed that God was telling her, "It's not going to work out but you can manage it." In time she "learned that I was stronger than I knew."

After her separation, Susie had no health insurance for herself and her boys. The twins had not yet been formally diagnosed, but they had abnormal muscle tone and weakness. Their condition fluctuated; at one point Susie was told they might die. As babies they had no strength in their necks so their heads needed extra support. One twin had curvature of the spine, and both were delayed in their physical development. Finally, the boys were diagnosed with benign congenital hypotonia and sent to a specialty hospital for treatment. Susie was working part-time and spending two to three hours a day doing physical therapy with the twins. Besides this daily exercise regimen, Susie had to carry the boys when they were sick or when they had used up their limited energy and were too exhausted to walk. Fortunately, she discovered the Mothers of Twins Club, and they helped her out one afternoon a week for several years.

When her husband walked out, Susie was left alone to deal with four of life's biggest stress factors: the birth of a baby (× 2!), disability, the breakup of a marriage, and loss of health insurance for the family. Susie could not do it all alone—and discovered that she didn't have to. She found the emotional and practical support she needed from her family, friends, and volunteers. Susie also coped exceptionally well with this crisis by drawing on her inner strengths and the social values passed down from her parents. With the "hard work" ethic and expectations for success instilled by her own family, Susie had guideposts to follow for raising her children and for continuing to live productively in other ways.

Mia is another single mother of four children, the youngest with osteogenesis imperfecta (OI). After many years of marriage, she divorced her husband, who was an alcoholic and an unreliable father. Mia has to support her family by working full-time plus teaching two nights a week. Although there are downsides—especially the few hours of sleep each night!—she takes pride in the way the family works. They are highly organized, with a schedule of chores for everyone to contribute to running the household. Mia also makes sure that the kids have time to play with friends and do the things they love to do. She brings an upbeat sense of humor to mothering; she likes to "get crazy and play jokes on the kids" to lighten the tone in the family. While Mia's children do not have the benefits of a second parent in the house, Mia feels proud of her resilience as a parent who is able to provide economically for her kids and to nurture and guide them.

Blake is a single father of George, a teenager who has a spinal cord injury. His wife left the family when George was 6. Blake reorganized his life, going from his traveling sales job to a predictable nine-to-five job with good insurance benefits close to home. Blake's sister helped him out by watching George after school until Blake got home from work. After George's injury, at 13, Blake's sister learned how to take care of him, so Blake could get away for a weekend once in a while. As a solo parent of a teen who's campaigning for his independence, Blake has to work a little harder to maintain his role as the family decision maker. But he talks openly with George about problems and takes his opinions seriously. Currently, Blake is weighing George's need to be independent, i.e., drive a car, with concern for his son's safety. They have resolved the problem by scheduling frequent cell phone check-ins (while parked) when George is out with the car.

As Blake and Susie found, extended family can be a vital source of support for single parents, ranging from phone or e-mail check-ins, to dinners or overnight visits, to financial help. Even if they can't provide practical or economic assistance, your family's respect and regard for the job you are doing are very helpful. Let them know when you need some encouragement and approval. When your family's ability to help is limited, friends can be a valuable backup. Members of your religious congregation, parent-teacher association, or community center may offer emotional support or child care while you get some rest. If you are a single mom with sons or a single dad with daughters, you may be able to find a same-sex role model and mentor for your child through the Big Brothers Big Sisters organization in your town.

Step Two: Coping with Your Emotions

Before you can tackle any new job, you need to "clear the decks." Difficult emotions sap your energy and limit your ability to focus on finding solutions. You need to identify and cope with emotional reactions to your child's disability before you can move on to learning about your child's needs and solving problems.

Parents have different approaches to coping with emotions. Some parents need to "let it all out," while others work through their emotional reactions internally. This can be a brief or lengthy process. Priscilla found that just having a good cry after learning that her child would have spina bifida brought relief—enough that she could begin the search for information to educate herself and her husband about this condition. Kathleen allows herself a fifteen-minute "freak-out" when she's "had it" emotionally. She takes a quick run around the block, and the physical exercise gets her off the emotional roller coaster and helps her clarify the problem and find solutions. Mark finds that writing about disturbing feelings and looking for triggers that "set him off" help him understand his emotions and regain composure. Then he's in "a better space" to explore solutions.

Other parents find that working out solutions is, in itself, a way to cope with their feelings about a problem. These parents spring into action from the start, dealing with hurt, anger, or sadness by *doing something*— such as seeking the advice of experts, surfing the Internet for information, building a ramp for a child who uses a wheelchair, or doing some other task that will solve a practical problem for their child or family. Sometimes taking the first step to tackle a problem helps you feel more in control of your life, which can make you feel calmer.

Step Three: Taking Care of Yourself

As a parent, you need to keep a balance between your family's needs and your own; you need to take care of *yourself*, not just your kids! Parents often sacrifice for their kids, neglecting themselves in the bargain. But this can backfire, because if you become ill, exhausted, or emotionally burned out, your parenting will take a nosedive. "Maintain" yourself and your physical and mental health by getting medical checkups, exercising, relaxing, and having some fun.

Take a Time-out

One way to manage the stress of parenting is to take a time-out to focus on what *you* need. Periodic getaways can give you a reprieve from the daily grind. Make sure you don't wait to take a break until you've reached the point of exhaustion! A time-out is not just a chance to collapse, but rather time to kick back and relax, to enjoy your friends, hobbies, or leisure pursuits—and to relish life apart from your role as a parent.

If you have a partner, friend, or other supportive person in your life, they can remind you to take a break and be there to back you up. Evelyn's husband, Scott, is a loving stepdad to her daughter Celeste, who has OI. Evelyn makes sure to take regular "downtimes" for rest and relaxation, free of her usual responsibilities. "I take care of myself so that I can be a better, whole, capable person to care for the kids. Scott's job," she says,

---

Mom's or Dad's time-out. Important for all parents, especially single parents, is a "time-out"—perhaps a movie with friends; a long, relaxing bath; a one-mile run; or ten minutes of sitting in the sun. The important thing is that it's just for you and makes you feel good. This is one of the tricks of a resilient parent—knowing how to create a bit of peace or enjoyment to restoke energy.

"is to care for *me* so that I can do that. It makes a big difference in the kids' lives."

Experienced parents agree that it's important *not* to define yourself solely through your role as a mother or father. Maintaining an identity as an individual contributes to good mental health. There are many ways to do this. Many parents find meaning in getting together with friends, doing volunteer work, joining a book club, or taking a class. Runner loves to read for relaxation and enjoyment. "I go to the library once a week." Lee enjoys shooting and hunting, while other fathers enjoy running or woodworking. When you do things that make you feel good about yourself and the world, you have more energy to engage and be creative with your children.

Take Charge of Your Schedule

"There just aren't enough hours in the day!" is the universal mantra of busy parents. If this is true for most parents, how do those with a child who has a physical disability manage to fit in the needs of the whole family? Susie carved out time in her schedule to fit in her twins' exercise regime while continuing as a volunteer in programs for her two older sons. Since it was impossible to do it all at one time, Susie focused on one of the boys per year, alternating years of being a room mother for the oldest boy with leading her second son's Cub Scout den. Wisely, Susie realized she needed to set some limits on her time in order to protect her health, essential to mothering all her boys.

For many parents, there are times when the needs of their children are greater than they can manage. Both Larry and Pili experienced the time crunch that a child's physical disability adds to the family routine. Larry remembers the frequent feedings his son needed in the first year of life, the nights when he and his wife slept in shifts, and the amount of extra time and energy he spent with his son during his many surgeries. Pili's schedule includes catheterizing her child every few hours plus the extra time it takes to prepare equipment they need for trips outside the home. Liz, a single working parent, agrees that the biggest difference having a child who has a physical disability made in her family life was the need for more time, given the daily routine of dressing and changing her daughter, putting on her braces, chauffeuring her, and trying to meet her son's needs.

For most parents, these times of being overwhelmed by too much to do are temporary, and they can muddle through by putting some non-parenting responsibilities on the back burner. In those families where there's no letup, you need to find additional help or support. Often, the time demands ease as children get older and more independent.

Parents find that, by prioritizing the needs of their family, they can make time stretch. Mary found that with her daughter's disability everything took more time, and life seemed to be moving in "slow motion." But this slower pace had a positive side, too, allowing Mary to really listen and take a good look at what was happening in her family. She didn't want to let the time needed for physical disability–related needs trump activities that each of her other children found fulfilling. But something had to give to make it work. Mary's solution was to figure out which activities were either absolutely necessary or uplifting to the life of the family and to eliminate those activities that weren't. She reset her expectations about what she *had* to do, putting all the unessential tasks in the "optional" column and setting aside certain home chores and projects. Letting go of that perfectionist "getting it all done" mind-set can help you find the time not only for the necessities of life but for the activities that your children—and you—are passionate about and find energizing. Runner and his wife found that parenting their son who has a spinal cord injury was overwhelming with both parents working outside the home. Although Runner always thought he *had* to work, he and his wife agreed that Lance was their priority; ultimately Runner chose to leave his job so he could be there whenever Lance needed him. Though their income "was cut in half," Runner has no regrets. "I like my time with Lance, and this gives all of us a great family life."

Interestingly, some parents find that during their busiest times they are highly efficient and actually get more things accomplished, taking on projects they have not done before. Charlotte, for instance, planted an enormous flower and vegetable garden while she had two toddlers at home and her daughter was going through a series of spinal operations. As the old saying goes, "If you want to get something done, ask a busy person to do it." While some parents benefit from letting go of nonessential activities, others with excessive demands on their time can cope by relying on a high degree of organization and multitasking—and sometimes manage so well that there is time "left over" to take a breather. Sometimes extra activities, like working in the garden, are pleasurable and renewing, making it easier to manage those things that weigh you down. Creating projects that you plan for and control can help you cope better with the unexpected and uncontrollable demands and challenges of life.

Find Friends

Parents who seem to "have it together," able to manage their families under challenging circumstances, are often people who have supportive friends. Friendships improve parents' self-esteem, provide practical help and emotional support, and add meaning to parents' lives.

We all add and subtract friends during different phases in our lives. Parents lose some when their children are born with or develop disabilities; certain friends can't cope with the idea of disability and seem awkward and unsure about what to ask, how to be helpful, or how to interact with your child. Cindy found that friends had trouble both at the time of her son's birth and later, when he had to have treatments. "When people find out about Xavier, they use the typical sayings, phrases like 'hang in there' or 'everything happens for a reason.' Some of the sayings helped when they were sincere. But the best thing anyone did for me was to be there, just sit with me at the hospital, or eat lunch or dinner with me. They really didn't have to say much; just being there was a great support in itself." It's important to find a friend who can listen and try to understand your experience, without judging or trying to change your feelings. This sort of empathy ("I'm in it with you") is a special kind of support that is essential for your emotional balance. Friends can also help with things like babysitting or going to the grocery store for you. You may need to rely on different friends for each of these two types of support—being with or doing things for you. You can also let your friends know which type of support you need (and your needs will be different at different times), for example, by saying, "You know, I don't really need you to *do* anything right now, but if you can just spend time talking with me, listening to me, that would help me so much!" Or alternatively, "I really need to rest today—I'm too tired to even talk. Could you possibly pick up some milk and cereal for me while I get a nap?"

All parents need emotional support from friends and peers, but mothers and fathers of kids who have disabilities need an extra dollop. Men tend to have fewer close friendships than their wives, and many feel alone when coping with the initial diagnosis of a child's disability and during the months or years in which parenting requires the largest share of their time and energy. When you are a new parent, or one whose child has just acquired a physical disability, it's helpful to make new friends with whom you can bond over your common experiences as parents. You will find that many parents are accepting of children who have disabilities and see this as just another individual variation—even if their own children do not have disabilities. Claude felt unsure about how his son—or he himself—would be accepted into a scouting troop. He was pleased when the leader integrated his son into a variety of activities and invited Claude to take a central role in planning. Not only did Claude and the troop leader become close friends, but involvement with the scouts opened up friendships with other fathers who were helping the troop. A key for parents is not to assume that others will have a negative view of your child or the role of disability in your lives. Many families are eager to integrate children with all sorts of unique experiences and backgrounds into their own children's friendships, including kids who have physical disabilities. Parents are wise to assume the positive until proved otherwise, taking the risk to help your child initiate relationships with a variety of people. Although some will not be interested, many will.

Learn from Parents Who Know the Ropes

Being friends with parents whose children don't have disabilities can help you (and your child) keep disability in perspective and lessen your feelings of "other-ness." But it's also helpful to get support and learn from

> **T**Consult a voice of experience. Just as there are "master gardeners," there are "master parents" who have years of experience raising children, one or more of whom have a physical disability. They've been through the ropes of childhood, adolescence, and young adulthood. They've dealt with school systems, worked on social skills with their children, and know how to solve practical problems and technological puzzles. Find one of these "master parents" with whom you feel comfortable to ask for advice and counsel.

other parents of kids who have disabilities. As Pili says, "It's incredible to share your journey with parents of kids who have other disabilities," not only the same disability that your child has. "It's good to have someone you can connect with." Throughout the various stages of your family life, you can benefit from the expertise and advice of parents who have "been there." Having a mentoring relationship, where you can learn one-on-one from a more experienced mother or father, is invaluable.

Building Resilience
Meet Every Child's Needs

"How can I ever meet all their needs?" "How can I make sure each child gets a fair share of my time and attention?" While balancing the needs of each family member is a challenge for every parent, making sure that basics are met is the first priority. Beyond that, parents need to create ways to pay attention to each child, as well as sharing family time. Lola and her husband make a routine of giving their undivided attention to each child whenever he or she has a special event or has accomplished a new goal. For instance, when their older son makes honor roll at school, they celebrate with him; the following week their middle son basks in the limelight at a chess tournament; and their daughter has the focus when she dances in a recital. Extra care and attention are also given to family members when they have extra needs—like when their son needed surgery or when Lola underwent treatment for cancer. Philip and Lola got help from their extended families during these crises, so they could provide extra support to the family member who was hospitalized, while continuing to pay attention to the other children.

Liz has been more concerned at times about the development of her able-bodied son than her daughter who has a disability. She advises other parents to give special time to their able-bodied kids, too.

Liz's busy work schedule meant that often the needs of her daughter who has spina bifida took first priority. But when Liz had sabbaticals from teaching, she took the children abroad with her. During these trips, she had more time than usual to participate in activities with her kids, to listen to and talk with them, and to focus specifically on the needs and desires of her son who does not have a disability. These sabbaticals also gave Liz's children exposure to different cultures and the opportunity to visit historical sites.

Some parents emphasize family unity more than individual relationships between each child and parent. They express inclusiveness by finding ways for their child who has a disability to be a part of shared family vacations and leisure activities and by making sure she plays a meaningful role in how the family works. Lee, for example, takes his family to an accessible beach camp in the summer, where all the children can participate in outdoor activities. Scott likes to bring the whole family together for Sunday brunches, where everyone goofs off and jokes, creating "a veritable laugh riot." He believes that family outings and activities that include all the children create a "more enriched experience" and are vital to family closeness. He's not against doing things individually with one child, but he notes that in his family "if you split up the kids, they wish everyone was doing something together."

After her daughter's accident, Marie worked hard to create family solidarity and avoid sibling rivalry by having big family dinners in the tradition of her Italian parents. "We sit around the table as a family and share the day. Everyone has a chance to talk and communicate." While a sense of family togetherness is emphasized and strengthened by these dinners, Marie and her husband try to make sure that each member of the family is also individually recognized and listened to.

In D. K.'s family, most of the leisure activities are on the water, where everyone can join in. Swimming is relatively safe for Dan (who has OI)

"Look out for the well-being of your children without a disability. Give them time, listen to their emotions. Be mindful of them." —Liz and enjoyed by all the kids. D. K. jokes that he and his wife "created a family of good swimmers" by putting in an Endless Pool. They value boating, because it, too, "keeps the family intact." Once in a while, they split up the family for special outings; D. K. might take Dan to a museum while his wife, Erica, takes their two able-bodied children skiing.

It can be particularly challenging for parents to pay attention to the needs of all children when one has a medical problem or is in the hospital. Advanced preparation for these crises is very helpful. For example, Erica keeps ready a grab bag of games, toys, books, and little gifts for the times when Dan breaks a bone and the recuperation periods that follow. Other parents prepare fun activities ahead of time, such as DVDs and new computer games, which can be shared by the child who is recuperating and his siblings—who are likely to be more limited to home-based activities when their brother or sister is ill.

Expect Success

There are many ways to help your kids learn how to care for themselves and respect the needs of others at the same time. Methods need to be tailored to each child's personality strengths and weaknesses. Some children are self-driven and goal oriented. They may be prone to overreach and feel defeated. Jasmine, a high school student, has rheumatoid arthritis. She is a straight A student taking several honors classes. When she does not meet her self-imposed goals, she becomes overly critical of herself. Her parents try to help her ease up on the high expectations she has for herself. They remind her that they love her for who she is as a person, and that her accomplishments are just icing on the cake. When they think she is overloading herself, they try to "rein her in" by making suggestions for lightening her course load. They help her balance her load so that she can be successful.

Other kids need to be motivated and pushed a bit. Gerald is happy playing computer games and hanging out with his friends, but he has little interest in schoolwork. His parents set up incentives for him (working to get an iPad) to complete his school assignments and disincentives (loss of computer time) for goofing off. They help him through feelings of inferiority that sometimes interfere with his trying to do his best.

Carmen's 7-year-old daughter, Mercedes, home after treatment for a traumatic automobile accident, had grown accustomed to being waited on in the hospital. She began to think that her disability entitled her to special consideration—forever! Back home, however, she had older and younger sisters who had needs of their own. One day she threw a tantrum when she didn't get the Lego kit she wanted at the toy store. Carmen realized that it was time to fit her daughter back into the family system by saying "No" and giving her some responsibilities. She began a "respectful love" regimen with her daughter. Carmen set higher expectations for her daughter's behavior, letting Mercedes know that she respected and believed in her abilities. Soon Mercedes was working in the kitchen in her wheelchair, drying the silverware and putting it in the drawer. This was the beginning of her preparation for independence through developing competency and thinking of others.

Some children find controlling their emotions and behavior difficult and need extra help in changing it. Skip was disruptive at school and alienating friends and family with his outlandish behaviors. His parents had him tested by a psychologist, who diagnosed his problem as attention deficit disorder, manageable with medication and therapy. With this support, his grades are slowly improving and he has started to make some new friends.

Teach Responsibility

Teaching your child that she has obligations to herself and others is a major goal of parenting. How do you teach that we all have duties to our fellow human beings, particularly our parents and siblings? When we hear about "spoiled" children, we are really hearing about children who have not been taught how to think of and do for others. Shaping a child to be responsible begins early in the child's life, and this job rests with the parent.

In most families, parents decide together how chores or responsibilities will be assigned to their children, but often one parent is the "heavy" while the other is the "softie" when it comes to discipline and follow-through. Sean, for instance, would like to demand more from his kids, while his wife, Leigh, he feels, is more likely to be "manipulated" and let the kids slide on their chores. On the other hand, they both enforce high standards of academic achievement and expect commitment from their girls to practice piano and go out for sports. Leigh feels that those standards require time and effort and that home chores rank low on the priority list.

Finding the right combination of love and discipline can be a process of trial and error. Carson believes that consistent but loving discipline is the key to raising responsible children. Part of being an inclusive parent is applying the same standards of behavior (politeness, honesty, timely completion of schoolwork, and so forth) to his son, Brian, who has a severe physical disability, and to his able-bodied daughter, Cory. Carson notes that good discipline leads to good behavior, and he hopes that good behavior will lead to acceptance, respect, and love for Brian from those outside the family circle. This will be essential to Brian's survival, understanding of give and take, and enjoyment of life when he is living away from the family as a young adult.

Let Your Kids Take Some Risks

Parents expose their kids to life experiences that can broaden their child's physical and mental skills, knowledge, creativity, and character. Risk taking is often part and parcel of these experiences. Children learn through trying new activities and relationships and by making (and correcting) mistakes. For example, taking the risk to expand a circle of friends exposes them to rejection, while participating in physical activities strengthens their bodies but also includes the risk of injury.

Parents often hesitate when their kids take risks to expand their worlds with new friends, activities, or sports. This anxiety is doubled when your son or daughter has a physical disability. After the initial attempts at some new activity, your concern is usually overcome when you meet your child's new friends, see him up on stage in the school play, or watch him make his first hit in the Little League game. You will discover that a good experience in one area will increase your (and your child's) openness to other "risks" in different areas.

The support of other adults who interact with your children can help you encourage risk taking and new experiences. Runner's son Lance plays wheelchair basketball, and the first time Lance traveled with his team, Runner was nervous. But Lance's coach told him, "We'll take care of him." Lance has since traveled nationally and internationally; now that Runner knows that Lance can take care of himself on the road, he tries to find other opportunities that will help Lance increase his physical and social independence. The first step in "letting go" is always the hardest.

If you are worried about your child spreading his wings, discussing your fears with your partner, your parents, or another trusted adult can help you assess your child's readiness to take reasonable risks. If your partner also has a disability, she may be more comfortable with risk taking and be able to give you a unique perspective. Jalah and her son Jon both have OI. Jon recalls that it was "harder on Dad" to let him take risks, "harder for him to see me get hurt," while it was "less hard for Mom because she grew up with it." Jalah's confidence in her own abilities provided a role model that encouraged reasonable risks, balancing her husband's tendency to be protective. Jalah advises parents to "let your child set their own limits and not feel sorry for the child because this can cripple them. Let them be who they can be and do what they can do."

Julius emphasizes the importance of helping children with their fears when it comes to risk taking. He knows that his daughter must take some risks to fully enjoy life and gain competence. "You can't ignore your child's fears, but you have to help her focus on what she can do, not what she can't." Julius encouraged his daughter, who lost a leg in an accident, to try out for wheelchair track events in high school. She loved it and became a regular competitor in college. "That's what a little confidence can do for you," Julius says proudly.

> "I don't want my daughter to be held back by her disability and afraid of living. I want her to say, 'That's what I want,' and go for it." —Julius

Broad-mindedness and flexibility help parents find novel activities that expand their children's world of skills and experiences but are not beyond their physical limits. One mother encouraged her son to take a modern dance class when he couldn't "make the cut" for any of his school's team sports. At first her son, a 15-year-old with a muscle disorder, was mortified, but when he realized he'd be getting a great workout—and exercising with a lot of girls wearing tights—he became an enthusiastic dancer.

As your child who has a physical disability matures, he becomes increasingly able to judge his own abilities and limitations; he can collaborate with you in making decisions about risk taking. You can talk directly with him to weigh the pros and cons of various risks—the possibility of

> **T**Children have dreams of what they'll do in life, whether it's going to the moon, being an NBA star forward, or becoming a firefighter. Parents listen to these dreams and set no limits on this imagination. However, when your daughter who walks with braces and crutches dreams of being a prima ballerina, you may want to step in to redirect that dream to protect her from future disappointment. Restrain yourself! Step back as you do with your other children, allowing your daughter to make her own personal discovery of what she is able to do, in her own time.

hurt or disappointment versus the chance to have a special experience or accomplish a new goal. Felicity, a young woman who has a spinal cord injury, advises parents not to "judge the abilities of your child who has a disability." Although parents try to empathize with their child's experience, Felicity says that "they don't really know what the child is going through." She urges parents to let their child try to do the things he or she wants to do, because kids who have physical disabilities are stronger and wiser than others might think. Sometimes, what we think is impossible isn't. Billy had both legs amputated below the knee; he loved baseball and became a star pitcher on his high school team, even running bases without prostheses.

Jon agrees that parents don't always appreciate the strengths of their child who has a disability. He feels that the child should be "a large part of the decision making team" regarding when to let the child take certain risks. Jon's parents let him take a major role in judging risks, and he notes, "I was pretty intuitive about knowing what would hurt." Because he has OI, some bone breaks were inevitable—regardless of Jon's level of risk taking. Jon believes that even the extra breaks were worthwhile experiences— they made him more resilient and determined. "I can stick with something because I had to keep getting back up. It's hard to defeat me."

Boost Self-Esteem with Positive Role Modeling

All kids—whether or not they have disabilities—look to their parents as the keys to creating a positive self-image and self-esteem. For kids who have disabilities, resiliency depends in part on learning to value their own

Parents need to continually weigh the risks and benefits of a child who has a disability joining in activities with siblings or friends. If your child has arm strength but not leg strength, she can bike using a three-wheeled, hand-propelled bike, or sail down a mountainside on a sit-ski, tethered to an able-bodied skier. Even with adaptations, the risks involved in sledding or horseback riding, especially for a child with OI, must be considered along with the benefits to your child: should you err on the side of "staying safe" or risk a little to enhance your child's life experience?

talents, character traits, and abilities, rather than basing their self-worth on how their bodies look or work. Be open to discussing this if your child is grappling with the way he thinks others see him. For example, listen when your child brings up the unfairness of having physical limitations and how hard it is to feel excluded when other kids are playing sports. Tell her she has a right to her feelings and repeat those feelings back to her, so she knows you are really hearing her. When she has finished, remind her of her talents, her abilities, and what is available to her. And reassure your son that he is loved for himself, not his linebacker abilities. Once again, the importance of keeping balanced in life emerges; when your child feels pulled down, you can help him counterbalance by talking about and exposing him to uplifting activities and experiences. Remind her that many other opportunities will come along as she gets older and then the things that are so important now—like running and playing soccer—will not be as important.

Beatrice Wright, one of the first psychologists to examine the psychological experience of living with disability, notes that individuals who have physical disabilities develop a positive sense of self by making changes in their values; rather than measuring their worth through physical prowess, they learn to value their personal attributes—such as intelligence, warmth, humor, and so forth. They focus on what they can rather than can't do, and they evaluate goals more in terms of the ends (can they get the job done?) than the means (did they have to use a brace or walker to do it?).

Parents of children who have disabilities go through a parallel change in values, leading to a different way of defining their own "success" as parents. Many parents measure their own worth by their children's milestones in physical development, achievements in sports, or attaining conventional social goals like driving a car and going to sleepaway camp. But after raising a child who has a physical disability, parents learn to rate their "job performance" by their child's social, emotional, and moral development, the quality of his relationships with other people, and his personal characteristics—like courage, affection, or generosity. This can "rub off" on parents, changing their *self*-evaluation to one based less on their vocational and financial achievements and more on their fulfillment in how they contribute to the world's good, maintain relationships, and follow their passions.

For young children, playtime is an opportunity to develop confidence and self-esteem, especially when a parent shares their special project or hobby. Adam, a 9-year-old who has a spinal cord injury, built an entire Lego city with his father in their dining room. He felt a sense of accomplishment and pride when his father praised his imagination and skill. And from watching his dad's step-by-step approach, Adam learned that patience and care, as well as inspiration, are important to the success of a creative project.

Parents can model attitudes, emotions, a॥
children learn to manage their feelings, behav
of situations, and cope with life's challenges. Ka
multiple disabilities, models humor and an up
with stress. "My positive attitude's rubbed off on
plaining and get on with life.' I was brought up t
and I try to pass that on. Even when Tony's sick,
and laugh at my silly jokes. He'll usually make a
Kaylee is quick to add, however, that she takes To
when he is having a rough time—and does not *exp*
"Mr. Upbeat."

For older kids, parents can also serve as role n
success and be influential in their kid's career choic
Lance, for example, admires his father's quick mind an
electronics and software. Like his "computer whiz" dad,
nology and wants to be an engineer someday.

When a parent has a physical disability, too, his chil
ability may have a unique learning opportunity. Raul, a y
juvenile arthritis, says his father is "my inspiration. Dad
jury that crippled his arms, but I've never looked at him as b
Emma, a young woman who has spina bifida, is now a m
Her father has multiple sclerosis, and as she grew up, he wo
"desensitize me to the ridicule of peers." Jalah, who has OI
"harder letting my son with OI be independent and seeing h
bone than letting myself do the same thing. I was more protect
than her mother had been of Jalah.

Reaping the Rewards of Parenting

Many parents feel unprepared for parenthood and wonder v
they are up to the task. The arrival of a new baby who has a disabil
cause additional feelings of helplessness. Still, most parents "fall in
with their newborns, whether or not they have a disability. Runner re
that, despite his trepidation about becoming a father, Lance's birth
the "best thing that ever happened to me. The instant I saw my son it
pure love, happiness; everything changed." Later, when Lance was trea
for cancer and developed a spinal cord injury, Runner found enormo

tion in watching him recover, grow, and develop into a lively and
d teenager.

rents of kids who have physical disabilities experience many emo-
rewards. Parenting can lead to positive personality changes or a
ened sense of purpose. Sean says that raising his daughter Eliza,
has cerebral palsy (CP), "made me more empathetic; it humanized
'm still a type A, but now I'm more patient." Sean has a rewarding
onship with Eliza. "I like the feedback from Eliza—when she asks
or a hug—when I see how well she is doing in college." Father to three
ger daughters in addition to Eliza, Sean says that parenting is "hum-
g because you realize your own inadequacies. But life is more interest-
with kids than without them. It sucks to get up at 6:40 on Saturday
rning to line the soccer field before the game, but then you drive home
th your child and say, 'Fun game, wasn't it?' "

Debbie found that caring for her son Daniel, who has a disabling
int disorder, improved her relationships with her other two children—
d helped her change for the better. "I'm so much more tuned in to *each*
ild, what they need and their unique personalities. Daniel was the 'baby,'
and before him, the older kids never really saw me express
emotions. I never yelled, but I wasn't a real fun mom either.
My brain was always at work or worrying about the house.
With Daniel, I had to *be there*—and now I've learned how to
do that with all of them. I'm a better parent because of it."

Creating *Your* Unique Family

Like many parents, you may have tried to fit in with the neighborhood's standard of "normal" family life. But when your child has a physical disability, these standards may not be a perfect fit. If you listen to your
own inner radar and challenge social stereotypes, you can arrive at your
own definition of success. When you stop worrying about the guidelines
set by others, you are free to decide what works for *your child or family*.
You can create a "different kind of normal" that allows every member of
your family to thrive. When you believe that *all* of your children can live
meaningful lives and allow yourself to do what is necessary to promote
their success, you create a unique way of being an inclusive family—the
way that works best for *you*.

☞ Here are some tips for making inclusive parenting work for you:

- Become educated about your child's needs. With greater knowledge and experience, your confidence in your own judgments and decisions increases, and you become proactive, not reactive.
- When you feel overwhelmed, reach out to veteran parents. You can learn from their experience and get support from them.
- Parents who find someone with whom they can share their load—whether spouse, significant other, partner, another relative, or friend—have an easier time with parenting. Multigenerational families can help share the load of raising children.
- Making the time to ensure that you feel fulfilled in your intimate life with your partner or spouse gives you more energy to bring to parenting.
- You will make the best decisions and ensure the best care for your child by partnering with professionals—physicians, physical therapists, occupational therapists, nurses, psychologists, social workers, rehabilitation counselors—in your child's treatment.
- Finding activities that give you "breathing room" outside the family is essential to restoking your energies and caring for yourself as a parent.
- Parents can help prepare their children for adulthood by giving them responsibilities to build competence, social skills to engage in relationships, experiences to understand the world, and permission to take risks so they can learn to evaluate their capabilities and what is safe and acceptable for them.
- To build resilient families, parents must use their own internal compass to guide their children and create their own visions and expectations for their children's future. Learning to ignore or counteract negative stereotypes and attitudes is part of this process.

The Fishers: Parents working together to build family unity and protect their children while allowing them to take healthy risks

D. K. and Erica were anticipating the birth of their first child with some anxiety. D. K. felt well prepared to be a parent, but Erica, although eager to begin a family, didn't feel as well equipped to be a mother. When Erica was six months pregnant with their first child, Dan, she and D. K. went for their prenatal doctor visit. After the examination, the nurse told them to wait to meet with the doctor. Because there were some irregularities on the sonogram, he referred them to a specialist, who diagnosed osteogenesis imperfecta (OI) in their unborn baby. They were not prepared for this news.

D. K. remembers seeing the pictures of Dan in utero. "I was shocked because I had been led to believe that all was fine. We had gone through all the checks and balances of pregnancy. My immediate thought was, How do we deal with it? We had no pity party. We didn't allow ourselves." He knew that OI was an uncommon disease that could make life complicated, so he started looking for treatments and cures; he wanted information. For Erica it was a "psychological adjustment."

When Dan was born, he had twelve broken bones. There was a sign on Dan's bassinet at the hospital: DO NOT TOUCH THIS BABY. D. K. and Erica carried Dan on a pillow for a year. Grandmother Ann, D. K.'s mother, was fearful: "How are we going to be able to do this?"

Other parents of kids with OI coached D. K. and Erica on how to explain Dan's fractures to medical personnel unfamiliar with OI. This was important in order to avoid suspicion of child abuse when taking Dan in for frequent broken bones. Because many doctors have no experience with this uncommon condition, D. K. and Erica have had to become very knowledgeable about OI. They have had to instruct doctors, especially in small-town hospitals, exactly how to treat their son. To help in medical emergencies, D. K. made and carries laminated cards with information about his son's diagnosis and treatment.

Erica found that everything in her life changed when she became a mother of a child who has a physical disability. "Nothing was normal." As a baby, Dan was so fragile that they were always on guard, especially around others who might be clumsy or not understand the risks, such as teenagers. They were afraid to use babysitters because of these risks; as a result, they had little couple relaxation time.

D. K. became the sole breadwinner when Erica gave up her profession to be a stay-at-home mother. As they gradually adapted to Dan's frequent bone breaks, their family life took on a routine, and they soon felt ready to have another child. Hank was born about a year later, and several years after that, they had daughter Sophie.

"Dan's brother and sister have been phenomenal. They are fabulous with their older brother." D. K. says that he and Erica have nurtured a sense of responsibility for others among the siblings. Hank and Sophie never let Dan feel he is imposing when he asks for anything. D. K. says that Dan is never a burden as "he has that no-quit attitude."

But Erica says it can sometimes be rough on Hank and Sophie. "Dan gets all the attention and Hank none. Then when there is a bone break I attend to Dan, and Hank has more responsibilities." Erica "coaches" D. K. in giving equal attention to each child. "She says, 'You're showing partiality to Dan'—and the other children have told me to be conscious of this," says D. K. He tries to talk with everyone at the dinner table and to participate in each child's activities. Grandmother Ann says that people pay attention to Dan while his siblings stand by quietly, deferring to their older brother. But that bothers Dan, so he speaks up for his siblings, reminding people who are talking to him that "I have a brother and a sister."

Erica says that she and D. K. help each other deal with Dan's multiple fractures, which come in waves. "We don't allow ourselves to get down. Having a strong spouse who doesn't wilt is a bonus," admits D. K. Erica appreciates that her husband is so even-keeled, keeping things light and happy. She also believes that she is a stronger person because of parenting three children, one who has a disability; sometimes she amazes herself. "Last summer Dan had two broken femurs. I slept on the floor with him. Then he broke his clavicle. People don't believe what I go through." D. K. says that he and Erica are "strong spouses for each other. No matter how painful, never did we show panic or fear. No matter how bad it is, we have it under control."

Erica and D. K. work together to keep the kids' spirits up when Dan has a broken bone. At those times, the family's schedule is often disrupted, and the children feel frustrated and sad when their plans have to be postponed or canceled. To lift the children's spirits, Erica always has special "stuff"—such as puzzles, DVDs, and books—ready for them to enjoy while she is busy attending to Dan.

All three children are good students and have varied interests. Dan, 14, is the family entertainer: "I love to make them smile." Dan also helps the family by using the Swiffer, making his bed, cleaning his room, and tutoring his younger sister. He likes making videos and is a good speaker, debater, and actor.

Hank, 12, says his role is to "help out" by vacuuming, raking the lawn, and helping Dan move around. Sometimes he carries Dan to another part of the room to play with the Xbox. He is close to Dan. He remembers getting upset once when Dan broke a bone; "I cried." Besides making straight As, he plays percussion in the school band and is on several sports teams, one of which is coached by Erica.

Sophie, at 9, says that she is "the one in my family with energy because I'm the littlest. Sleep is totally boring." She swims in the family pool with Dan because she feels that it makes him happy. Like Hank, she also plays on sports teams that Erica coaches or assists with. While Dan tutors her, Sophie likes to open doors for Dan and get him his glasses. Since she doesn't save her money, he uses his money to buy her candy. "His OI doesn't interfere with life. I feel completely good about it because everyone likes him."

The family swims and boats together. They installed an Endless Pool in their basement, forgoing other luxuries. In the summer they travel to their cabin, where they go boating on a lake. They "bubble jump" off the back of the boat. To protect his body against breaks, Dan keeps his limbs together when he jumps into the wake. Grandmother Ann says that Dan is allowed to take a kayak out alone at twilight to fish. "I am proud that his parents allow this."

Erica says that staying fit gives her the stamina to deal with emergencies as they arise. She swims half an hour each day to help maintain strength, and she enjoys running while listening to music. She finds social outlets coaching Hank's and Sophie's basketball and baseball teams and gets support from occasional meetings with friends. "Do for *you* once in a while," she advises. "It's the only way to keep it together."

The Fishers are an open, communicative, and active family. They believe in working for those causes they think are important. Erica and D. K. have been vocal advocates for OI since Dan was born, and their whole family is committed to raising funds for research on OI. D. K. feels strongly that "families have to be proactive about fund-raising in the race to find cures for disabilities." He is reaching out to big companies now, raising awareness of their social responsibility to contribute funds for disability research.

Grandmother Ann contributes to the cause by making baskets of donated goods to raise money for OI. "It keeps me busy. People have been donating to OI through me since Dan was born." She advises other grandparents to help as much as they can and to connect with and learn from others who are going through the same thing. She plays an important role in encouraging her son's family to *be* a family, and helping them to be a supportive one.

4

Brothers and Sisters

Siblings Sharing Family Life with Physical Disability in the Mix

----

"We're all people. We just have different things in common. That's good because otherwise we'd all be the same."

—ISABEL, THIRD OF FOUR SIBS

"We have a good relationship, but we fight like all sisters."

—ELIZA, OLDEST OF FOUR SISTERS

Relationships between brothers and sisters are the most enduring of all family ties, often lasting a lifetime, and yet they've gotten the "short end of the stick" when it comes to research on families. Sibling connections remain somewhat mysterious; no one really knows what's "normal" in *any* sibling alliance. So it's hard to say whether sibling relationships in a family that includes a child who has a physical disability are different from or more "difficult" than those in any other family.

Some research studies have explored experiences of able-bodied siblings who have a brother or sister who has a disability, but very few have included the perspective of the sibling who *has* the disability. Instead of trying to understand the relationship *between* the siblings, most studies focus on how the able-bodied sibling is affected emotionally and socially *by* the brother or sister who has a disability. In the past, most people, including social scientists, assumed that able-bodied children would suffer negative effects as a result of having a sibling who has a physical disability—so that's what they looked for. But this is not the case. In reality, studies that compare children whose sibling has a disability with those who have only able-bodied siblings show that there are no differences in their psychological or social adjustment.

This doesn't mean that relationships between able-bodied siblings and those who have disabilities are all smooth sailing or without challenges. Siblings have mixed feelings about *all* their brothers and sisters. When a family includes a child who has a physical disability, all the siblings have a chance to develop patience, compassion for others, and good social skills, but they may—or may not!—also experience more worry, stress, jealousy, or conflict. It all depends on the circumstances of the family, the way parents handle the situation, and the personalities of each individual child.

This chapter explores how you can set the stage for good sibling relationships among your children by modeling positive attitudes, paying equal attention to each child, including all the sibs in family activities, and assigning age- and ability-appropriate responsibilities to each child. This is followed by a look at sibling relationships from the point of view of both able-bodied sibs and those who have disabilities—how siblings help and share with each other, how they cope with problems, and how they find support.

Parents Set the Stage

Parents' attitudes toward disability have a major influence on the quality of relationships between siblings in families that include able-bodied kids and those who have disabilities. Inclusive parents have a positive attitude toward each of their children and want *all* of them to enjoy the benefits of sibling camaraderie by taking part in family activities. They expect their child who has a disability to share in responsibilities and achieve individual goals, just like his siblings. When parents help their child who has a disability fully participate in his sibling role, his able-bodied siblings are likely to be better adjusted, too.

One way to set the stage for good sibling relationships in your family is by making a conscious effort to give equal attention, affection, and quality time to each of your children, despite extra requirements that your child who has a physical disability may have. Able-bodied siblings may grumble, but deep down they understand that the physical disability of their brother or sister sometimes demands more parental time or energy. They are usually aware and appreciative of their parents' efforts to balance the time they give to each child—even when the results are not perfect. Michelle, whose older sister Eliza (who has CP) is now away at college, was often unhappy about the energy drain on her parents because of Eliza's needs. Yet she valued her parents' emotional involvement with all the sisters, as well as the fact that, for the most part, they "didn't overlook any of our needs, or problems in our lives; they supported our activities." Her younger sister Alice agrees that all the girls "get equal attention. No one person is favored."

Kids who have a disability benefit when their parents include them in the day-to-day life of the family—both routine and fun activities. When you create opportunities for shared sibling experiences, you encourage "bonding" between sibs that leads to closer and more caring relationships. One way to do this is to identify a sport or activity that all children can enjoy together. The Fishers, for example, made swimming a focal point for family fun and exercise, because all their children enjoyed the family pool and it was safe for their son Dan, who has OI. In the Jones family, everyone likes miniature golf, and it's an activity in which all the children are able to participate. They also create a family vegetable garden, a fun family project, where they can spend time together and produce something that everyone shares and enjoys. They prepare the garden plot in the spring and plant their jointly agreed-upon crops; in the summer, they take turns watering and weeding. Angie, who uses a wheelchair, sits on the ground to work in the dirt alongside her older brothers and sisters.

When parents assign similar, if not identical, responsibilities to each child in the family and enforce the same standards of ethics and social behavior for each of them, they set up an inclusive team. Eliza, whose *physical* needs took more parental attention than those of her sibs, appre-

---

To make gardening more accessible, build elevated containers for plants that are at wheelchair height. This creates an "equal opportunity" garden: the whole family can use this raised garden to share in planting, weeding, and playing in the soil!

ciates that when it comes to other areas of her development, "I've had the same guidelines as my sisters; there is no special treatment." Her parents expect her to reach the same goals for academic achievement and uphold the same moral codes as her sisters—and eventually to become a socially and emotionally independent adult, in spite of her physical limitations.

Even with the best of intentions, it's not a good idea to let your child who has a physical disability avoid responsibilities, or to lavish excessive attention on him. In fact, as Fred points out, "doting on the one who has a disability" is not good for *any* of the children. "The one who has the disability doesn't want it, and it causes dependency by the child who has the disability and resentment in the others." This can create a "spoiled" child, whose "special" treatment gets in the way of her ability to develop competence and independence. If your child who has a disability is pampered, protected, and allowed to dominate your attentions, she is more likely to become bossy and demanding—traits not leading to good sibling relationships! On the other hand, she may feel guilty about her siblings' unfair load of responsibilities or their relative neglect by parents and unjustly blame herself for being a "burden." Fred's parents were careful *not* to overindulge or baby his sister who had a physical disability. Because Fred's sister "pitched in to help with the household chores, there was no extra burden on the other kids," and sibling relationships were good.

When you expect your child who has a disability to take on chores and responsibilities equivalent (in proportion to her physical abilities) to those of her able-bodied sibs, your children are less likely to have conflicts or jealousies related to special treatment of the child who has a disability. Priscilla Brandon, whose son has spina bifida, embraces the philosophy of evenhanded parenting. "Don't make the child with the disability the center," she says. "All children need responsibilities and discipline—no one person has entitlements." Priscilla's daughter Jean, who is able-bodied, appreciates her parents' policy of "treating all children evenly and not sheltering either child." She and her brother who has spina bifida were each expected to excel in school, to keep their rooms clean, and to follow family standards for minding their manners and keeping their tempers in check. The Brandons' expectations of each child are coupled with their willingness to give each child the support needed to achieve his or her goals. For Jason this included advocating for accessibility and personal care attendants at his college, while for Jean it meant "pushing me in my chosen path"—to become an actress—and "coming to all my performances." Jean reports a loving relationship with Jason and says that there is little jealousy between them.

The Fishers assign chores to each of their children, based on their abilities. Fourteen-year-old Dan, though physically limited by OI, is expected to sweep floors, make his bed, clean his room, and help his younger sister with her homework. His 12-year-old brother, Hank, who is able-bodied, does more strenuous chores, like raking leaves and vacuuming, while 9-year-old Sophie sets the dinner table and loads the dishwasher. These siblings each describe their relationships as close and loving. Says Dan, "We get along really well; we do well together. Most other siblings aren't as close as we are." Hank enjoys "a lot of laughs" in his relationship with Dan and Sophie, as well as feeling empathy for Dan's struggle. "When Dan broke a bone, I cried. My brother and I are close." Sophie looks up to and feels protected by both of her older brothers. She can count on Dan, the oldest, for special treats. "He buys me candy and we play Xbox together."

Of course, expectations for the child who has a disability have to be realistic. Some families assume that fair treatment means exactly the same treatment for all sibs, and they hold the unrealistic expectation that the child who has a disability must match his siblings' contributions in *every* way. If the child is not able to live up to those expectations, she may blame herself for being a "failure." It is useful for parents to think about giving each child responsibilities that match his or her age and abilities, rather than assigning *identical* responsibilities to every child. Margo has her children change the sheets on their beds on the weekends. Her 12-year-old daughter who uses crutches struggles with this, so Margo had all the siblings work out a swap that they thought was fair—while her sibs changed their sister's bed for her, the 12-year-old sister put pillowcases on all of their pillows and dusted the bedrooms.

When parents raise their children to expect that they will be asked for help at appropriate times, their children, including the child who has the physical disability, can be counted on to help one another when needed. If children regularly help their parents or sibs as part of their age-appropriate role in the family, and if they are rewarded with love and attention, they may become more compassionate and caring adults and learn the value of being responsible for another person.

The trick for parents is identifying chores that their children who have disabilities can do to help siblings and the family. Some parents expect an older sibling who has a physical disability to help with the care or supervision of their able-bodied younger sibs. Chores such as helping younger sibs with homework or babysitting are common. When siblings share in the care of their brothers or sisters, it gives their parents more free time and energy to spend on fun and interesting activities and interactions with *all* the children.

Other things that parents have found helpful in setting the stage for good sibling relationships include encouraging open communication and sharing among family members, making sure that all siblings have ample opportunities for recreation and fun, and using humor to defuse conflicts and bring a healthy perspective to the family.

But parents are only a part of the story. No matter how evenhanded parents are, siblings will still fight with one another, be envious, and feel that another sib was given special attention or treatment that they were not. And in some families where there is not enough attention or support for the children, siblings will band together and become exceptionally close.

Every child's relationship to his parents will be different. Parents gain experience and wisdom as they have more children, mature as individuals, and experience changes in their economic, marital, or other life circumstances. Sometimes family size plays a role; in larger families, the emotional impact of one child who has a disability may be more easily "absorbed" and have less influence on sibling relationships. Finally, each child comes with his own "hard-wired" temperament that interacts in unique ways with parents' and siblings' personalities and relationship styles.

As anyone who has a brother or sister knows, relationships between them have a life of their own, separate from each sib's relationship with their parents. They can love each other to pieces; fight like cats and dogs; share experiences, dreams, and secrets; envy and resent each other; and help, support, and protect one another. In spite—or because—of these early experiences of companionship and conflict, brothers and sisters grow into mature and competent adults.

Jealousy, Guilt, and Sibling Rivalry

The O'Brien family includes Eliza, who has CP, and her three younger sisters. Their parents tried hard to find recreational activities that *everyone* in the family could do together. But this meant that the younger girls had to give up some activities they were interested in, since Eliza was physically unable to do them. They felt that this wasn't fair, even though they knew their parents were trying hard to do the right thing. Sister Alice says that because Eliza's been "confined to her room through so many surgeries," her parents put a TV in her room, while none of the other girls have one. The girls understand the rationale, but they still feel jealous. Eliza is very close to her mother, and Alice worries that mom's intense involvement with Eliza might take away from her relationships with the other sisters. But the girls love Eliza, they want to protect her, and they feel guilty about being able to enjoy so much that Eliza cannot.

Sam, who had polio as a child, recalls that his brothers were jealous of his relationship with their father, while he was envious of the attention they got from their mother (who had rejected Sam because of his disability). But despite vying for parental attention, Sam and his brothers were close; his middle brother in particular was always "nice to me; he was supportive and cheered me up."

Ashley, the youngest of three siblings, was 17 at the time of her injury. Her siblings also "competed" for their mother's attention. Marie recalls that her middle child was jealous because Ashley "consumed my time and energy; she needed me." After the accident, Ashley's parents stopped taking the family on beach vacations because Ashley's disability made it difficult for her to get to the beach. When Ashley's able-bodied sibs had to give up an enjoyable experience, they felt more resentment, and Ashley felt guilty for getting in the way of their enjoyment. Yet when Ashley was a young adult engaged to be married, and her family went to Disney World without her, she still felt "jealous that they could go" and she couldn't. Ashley notes that she and her sibs did not talk openly about these difficult feelings—and that this "made things worse for my family."

Talking Things Through

Communication between siblings is vital for creating close relationships, learning to deal with conflicts, and having fun. Early on, talking allows children to play games, to "make believe," and to develop friendships. In the preteen and teen years, kids love to talk about relationships—siblings enjoy discussing the ways that each one relates to their parents or close friends and dissecting their parents' relationship to each other. Siblings aren't just being nosey. When they "gossip" about relationships, they are actually coping with complex feelings, understanding relationship conflicts, and thinking about solutions. And they are reinforcing a sense of connection to their family.

When a child's ability to participate in sports or other physical activities is limited by a disability or injury, talking can become even more important to forging connections and sharing experiences with their siblings. Alice finds that of her three sisters, she talks the most with Eliza. They share many interests, including history, TV shows, and spectator sports, and Alice says that Eliza "is the calmest in the family, easy to talk with." Eliza and Michelle weren't always able to talk freely, but since Eliza went away to college, she can "talk about more things with Michelle, perhaps because we don't compete for attention at home anymore." With her youngest sister, Sammi, Eliza finds that "I'm able to help her—she talks to me." When Sammi struggles with schoolwork, Eliza says, "I'm more understanding and patient. I'm good at relating to people so maybe I'm the sounding board."

Sharing Experiences

In most families, some activities are shared by all the siblings, while others are one-on-one between a child and a parent. Generally, as children get older, more activities are shared with friends outside the family. A disability can lead to increased social exposure for a child—whether because of more time spent in academic or rehabilitation settings, being involved in disability or advocacy groups, or just responding to the curiosity of people encountering a young person in a wheelchair or on crutches. As Eliza says, "I've met lots of different people through my disability." But having a disability can also limit opportunities to create close friendships, especially if it causes frequent medical problems, hospitalizations, or prolonged periods of recovery. Sibling friendships are especially important in these situations.

Dan, who has OI, has frequent bone breaks and often needs to stay home for several weeks to recover. Although Dan is popular at school, his able-bodied brother Hank says that Dan "doesn't have lots of friends outside of school, so I hang out with him. My brother and I are close. We substitute computer games for playing ball together." When Dan is well, he and Hank go on "boys only" fishing trips with their dad. When the family goes trail riding, Dan joins in with his siblings, riding in a cart pulled by Hank's bicycle.

Sometimes the sib who has a disability enjoys "going along for the ride" even if he can't participate in the chosen activity. Sam enjoyed watching his brothers go sledding, even though he couldn't sled because of having polio. "I admired my brothers; they brought excitement to my life."

Age differences between brothers and sisters can influence the activities they do together. Zoey, a 16-year-old, has a 4-year-old sister who has OI and says, "She loves me to fix her hair and to play dolls with her." At 9, Isabel rewards her little sister by playing video games with her. "I let her play with them when she does something good." Zoey, Isabel, and their brother Joseph enjoy watching movies together and cooperate in cleaning their rooms.

A family's resources also play a role in the types of activities that siblings share. Janet's mother, a university professor, was able to travel extensively during sabbaticals from teaching, bringing the children along. "We went to Scotland when I was 7 and in a wheelchair," Janet recalls. She shared many good times with her brother during trips to Holland and France, where they visited cultural sites and museums, went on tours of the cities, and ate wonderful meals.

> "Siblings should treat the person who has a disability like the others. Go places where people who have disabilities can go; don't go separately."
> —Alice

For Cora, whose dad was a factory foreman, quality time with her sibs was simpler, but just as special—Sunday picnics in the park with the whole family and spring vacations at her grandparents' house near the beach. Cora's big brother Toby would push her in a "sand chair"—a wheelchair fitted with oversize tires—so she could get down near the water. Cora, Toby, and little brother Al spent hours looking for shells and sand dollars, and when it was time to swim, Cora's grandfather would come down and carry her into the water with the other kids.

Helping Each Other

When one child has a physical disability, some amount of help from able-bodied siblings is normal and may be necessary to the smooth functioning of the family. In many families, the degree of help is similar to what happens in any family, where older siblings help younger ones, or sibs work together to complete projects or chores. In others, able-bodied siblings need to go the "extra mile" for their sibling who has a disability. In families where mutual help and support are a family norm, children usually want to help; in these families, the sibling who has a disability, depending on her age and abilities, also helps her able-bodied sibs. Helping a sibling is a source of pride and enjoyment, though in some situations the need to help can cause resentment. Most sibs experience both pros and cons in helping their brothers or sisters.

Erik's parents divorced when he was very young. After living with his dad for a year, he moved in permanently with his mother, Jesse. He was 8 years old when Jesse and her partner, Lynn, adopted a daughter who had multiple disabilities; two more daughters who had disabilities were added to the family over the next few years. Erik was old enough to help out and to appreciate the pressing care needs of his sisters. "I've never felt my needs diminished by my little sisters. Their needs may be life and death. How would I feel if I put my needs first, and something happened to them?" Of course, there were times, when things were particularly hectic, that Erik felt "like a servant" and longed to be "left alone." But since he was so young when his family went through radical changes (his parents divorced, his mother moved in with her partner, and three girls who had disabilities joined the family), Erik "expects chaos in life."

In retrospect, Erik recognizes that he had a tendency to do too much; he had to learn "when my help could be a hindrance and I needed to back off." Erik also knows that his personality makes it easy for people to lean on him, sometimes too much. "I'd sometimes like to feel less appreciated. People think I have the right answer. I listen and don't judge; I don't make waves. I'm the nice guy."

Now a young man, Erik still feels a strong sense of family unity that incorporates his sisters' needs. "Our norms are different. There are challenges we face as a group—we adapt things to fit our life." But he also enjoys an independent social life, has a full time job, and is working on his first novel. Although he was very involved in the care of his sisters, Erik doesn't feel that his family held him back; in fact, he says that they helped him grow "by showing me how life is, and guiding me into the real world."

For Erik, taking care of his sisters was a mixed bag, but on the whole it was a positive experience. At times he felt that too much help was expected of him, and he had difficulty asserting his own needs, which seemed insignificant next to his sisters' life-and-death medical issues. On the other hand, Erik was proud of his ability to adapt to change and to do his part for the good of the family. He developed greater empathy, flexibility, and tolerance that served him well as he became an adult.

Michelle sometimes felt frustrated or resentful as a result of her family's expectation that she help Eliza, especially when she felt she had to put her sister's needs ahead of her own. "Eliza went to physical therapy camps in the summer," she says, "so we had to spend summers in the car taking her there."

For Paige, resentment and anger about taking care of her sister were caused by her parents' inability to create a safe environment for their children and her having to take on more responsibilities than any child should. Her siblings' survival depended on Paige becoming a "step-in mother," and she felt overwhelmed by having to care for them. Children put in this position miss the chance to have fun with their siblings and feel robbed of their childhoods; they can feel, as Paige did, like "the little maid." Family situations like Paige's can cause feelings of deprivation, jealousy, and resentment; create emotional distance between siblings; and make it difficult to form friendships outside the family.

The oldest of three siblings, Paige is now a young woman. She recalls her family as "chaotic, irrational, non-nurturing, and unstable"; she "grew up quickly without much of a childhood." Paige's younger sister had spina bifida, and her baby brother had autism and severe intellectual disability. Her father left the family when she was little, then moved back in, but was abusive to Paige's mother and neglectful of the children. Paige became the "mother figure" for her siblings. She helped take care of them and did many household chores. When she was younger, she felt very close to her siblings, but as they got older, "the relationship soured." Paige resented being the child who always had to "take up the slack," because her parents were inadequate and had low expectations of her sister. "I had animosity, not toward my sister, just about the situation."

Looking back, Paige wishes that her parents had encouraged her sister to take more risks and responsibilities, so she could have become more confident. And she wishes they could have understood her perspective as the able-bodied child. On the positive side, Paige found that as a result of caring for her siblings, she was more prepared to be a mother herself. She makes a conscious effort to raise her own children differently than she was raised, giving them emotional support and attention, respecting their views and feelings, and having regular "family time."

For Zoey, an able-bodied 16-year-old and the oldest of four siblings, helping her youngest sibling, who has OI, has been primarily a positive experience, partly because she shares the job with two other able-bodied sibs. Their parents recently divorced, and their mother has to work long hours. Zoey is in charge when their mother is out. "I'm the oldest. I watch everyone while Mom's at work. I hold down the fort." While this involves some special care for her sister who has OI, Zoey doesn't resent having this responsibility. "If Mom needs me one Friday night, she is lenient on another night"; Zoey is not expected to sacrifice her social life in order to babysit her siblings. Additionally, her mother appreciates Zoey's help and "lets me know I'm a good kid. I don't go un-thanked."

Her 13-year-old brother, Joseph, the only son and self-proclaimed "man of the house," also cares for his two younger sisters, "babysitting and playing board games" with them. When his youngest sister was born with OI, Joseph says he "got more chores, but I didn't mind. Sometimes I was out playing and then I'd have to come inside to watch my baby sister." On the other hand, Joseph thought, "it was cool to have a new member of the family. She looked up to me."

Sister Isabel, age 9, waxes philosophical in discussing their baby sister's disability. "You can't pick everything you want in your life," she says. She knows that "the job of keeping her safe is painful and stressful for everyone in the family." But, like Joseph, she acknowledges that being an older sib who pitches in to help the family run smoothly makes her feel important and valued. "Every day I tell myself to do some extra chore. Sometimes I do extra things to help Mom. I like the feeling of doing something good."

In the Fisher family, younger sister Sophie helps Dan, who has OI, by "opening doors for him and getting his glasses," and younger brother Hank helps move him about, sometimes carrying him. Dan, on the other hand, has the job of helping his younger siblings with their homework. Dan does not see himself as a "burden," nor do his siblings; they consider the different types of helping they do to be part of the normal give and take in their particular family.

In most families, the child who has a physical disability is able to help the able-bodied siblings in various ways, as well as accepting their help when needed. This may be especially true if the sib who has a disability is older than the other children. Janet, who has spina bifida and uses a wheelchair, had a younger brother and stepsister. Although "it was a challenge for me to care for them physically," one of Janet's responsibilities in the family was to help with her little stepsister. Janet appreciated the fact that caring went both ways between her and her siblings. "When kids made fun of me, my brother stood up for me"; as they have grown older, Janet feels that her good relationship with her siblings has become even closer. Janet advises families to encourage able-bodied siblings to help care for their sib who has a disability, but she believes it's equally important for the sib who has a disability to help care for a younger one, if possible. Her experiences of getting help and giving help in her family have made her "a more caring person."

Sometimes the sibling who has a disability becomes responsible for brothers and sisters when parents are emotionally absent, neglectful, or abusive. Even in these situations, the sibling who has a disability, just like an able-bodied sib, can benefit from the chance to be a giver, as well as a receiver, of help.

Emma recalls that her spina bifida was "the straw that broke the camel's back" for her emotionally unstable mother. Her parents fought frequently and were unable to cooperate in her care. They separated, but during a brief period of reconciliation, her mother became pregnant with Emma's brother; he was born when Emma was 8. When her brother was 2 years old, her father left the family for good. Emma's mother was unable to manage the load of work, home, and child care responsibilities; they ate carryout food every night, and Emma's mom would often forget to buy food or to give them lunch money for school. When her mother started dating again, she left the children home alone. So Emma became the protector and substitute mom for her little brother. She took loans from friends to buy him food, and she made sure he was clean and properly dressed for school. She watched over him when her mother was gone and gave him as much emotional support as she could.

Eventually, her mother's boyfriend moved in with them, but he soon became verbally abusive, and the children felt unsafe around him. Emma and her brother went to live with her father at that point. Because he lived in a rough neighborhood, where waiting for the school bus could be unsafe, Emma had to continue protecting both her brother and herself from harm.

Helping her little brother had some benefits –her brother never thought her disability lessened Emma's competence, and caring for her brother helped shape her career choice. Now a mother herself and a school teacher, Emma used her course work in human development to help her design a plan for being a good parent. She is a nurturing mom who tries to be caring and protective without "micromanaging."

Though Emma has a physical disability and Paige is able-bodied, they each played extraordinary roles in caring for a younger sibling, primarily as the result of parental neglect. Like Paige, Emma views her childhood experiences as a model for what *not* to do. "I do nothing like my parents," she says. "My memories guide me day to day, correcting my childhood."

Emma and Paige are among the "invulnerables," children who become resilient and capable adults in spite of neglect or abuse in childhood. In other families where parents are struggling with poverty, divorce, substance abuse, or mental illness, children may experience more difficulty coping with ups and downs in their sibling relationships. Felicity, for example, grew up with alcoholic parents, and her mother was abusive. At age 19, she had a spinal cord injury, and in the absence of any guidance or support from parents, her siblings reacted badly. She recalls that her "youngest sister didn't visit her much" while she was in the rehabilitation hospital, and when she did, "she would complain and whine" about her own problems, unable to offer emotional support to Felicity. Her middle sister "took my injury hard and got into drugs." These sibs had no support to cope with Felicity's injury or to handle life's challenges.

"Cope-ability" for Sibs

When children who have physical disabilities and their able-bodied sibs are raised by caring and capable parents, *all* can learn to cope with problems, thrive, and become productive adults. In addition to good parenting, some other factors that improve the "cope-ability" of siblings are good communication, positive belief systems, the ability to redefine themselves, and support from peers.

Communication

Communication is a cornerstone of resilient families. Siblings who can communicate more openly and directly about their thoughts and feelings are generally better able to cope and solve problems. Sharing feelings with each other, their parents, or friends helps sibs deal with highs and lows of daily life.

Isabel likes "to keep relationships strong in the family, to be a good family," and she is a big fan of communication as a means to this end. But in a busy family with four sibs, Isabel sometimes has to struggle to be heard. "I get upset when people cut me off when I am talking. That happens a lot." Isabel copes by communicating with her mother, even if no one else is listening. This helps her get relief from frustrating situations and figure out how to solve problems in her relationships with her siblings or others in her life. "Sometimes I get so aggravated that things explode in my mind. I don't like holding it in, it's not a way to settle things. I say what's bothering me. I talk with Mom and I let it out. Then it's not all up in my mind." Eliza agrees that sharing feelings is a good way to cope. "Don't bottle up feelings and then explode; communicate," she says. While Isabel finds solace in talking to Mom, her sister Zoey turns to friends and her church community. "I go to Mass with my two best friends. We talk about our problems and it's better than coping alone."

Interestingly, siblings don't always communicate directly about the disability itself. In a study of over forty siblings of children who have a physical disability, almost half said they didn't talk about the disability at all—either because they were uncomfortable bringing up the subject or because the child who had the disability preferred not to discuss it. In some families, it may not be needed or important to discuss the disability, or disability may be overshadowed by other pressing problems. Emma recalls that she and her brother "never had a conversation about my disability. During his formative years too many things were going on: our parents split up, we lived with our mother's boyfriend, and I was my brother's babysitter much of the time." Sometimes the impact of a sibling's disability is communicated in roundabout ways; Janet remembers that although they did not openly discuss her disability, "my brother wrote a story about me and my disability for his college application essay."

Spirituality

Spirituality is one way of coping that is important to many children, as it is to adults. Praying, "talking" to God, and practicing religious rituals can give children a feeling of comfort and security. Zoey, whose youngest sib has OI, describes herself as "the religious one" in her family. "I do a church retreat where the teen group sleeps in the church on the weekend. You have to be sponsored, and then you belong." Zoey's religious affiliation is both an expression of faith and a way to get support from and fit in with her peers, so important to teenagers.

Eliza's faith has helped her deal with disappointments in life, some related to having CP. "When I got mad because life hadn't worked out the way I wanted, I thought of the good things that happened." Eliza's appreciation of the good things in her life is linked with her belief that "someone up there is watching." Eliza goes to church almost every Sunday and belongs to a Catholic club at her college. When she needs help or support, she "says a Hail Mary."

Sam found religion in college. He remembers the night he was "called," sitting in the balcony of a church. He volunteered to be saved and decided to become a minister. After years of exposure to prejudice and social isolation because of his disability, Sam experienced "being accepted and belonging" through religion; it made him feel "at home in the universe" for the first time.

Darlene was raised Catholic but rejected the formal teachings of the church when she was about 12 years old. Darlene found her own brand of spirituality, combining various religious traditions. "I have a touch of Catholicism, a touch of Buddhism, a little Islam. I'm spiritual in my own way. It's made me feel better about helping my sister Wanda, who has quadriplegia. I believe in karma; I do good deeds and hope they will come back to me."

Not all children (or their families) believe in a higher power. But many kids find solace in their connection to the natural world or strength in identifying as a "citizen of the universe," experiences that have a spiritual quality. Nikki, a 10-year-old whose sister Jodi lost both legs in a car accident, says that when she's having a bad day, she goes for a walk in the woods near her house and listens to the birds. "There's a special spot where I sit on a big rock and see rays of light coming in through the trees, and I just feel like I'm part of something bigger than me. I kind of forget to be sad about Jodi and think about how beautiful and amazing the world is." Nikki's brother Bob likes to camp out in the summers, and he took Nikki and Jodi on an overnight trip at an accessible campground he had found. Bob says, "It was awesome. You realize you're all spinning around in space with the stars and planets. It's a great feeling!"

Eli, a teen who walks with crutches as a result of CP, got involved with a nonprofit that provides health care for children in Africa and helps their mothers start small businesses. He started out as a local fund-raiser and eventually traveled to Africa to spend a summer volunteering in a small village. Eli's perspective on his place in the world was totally changed. "I'm not just a 'little guy' dealing with everyday hassles—I'm helping families on another continent, and I'm seeing great results firsthand. It makes me feel stronger; people respect me for what I do and they don't care if I can't walk perfectly. I'm not into religion at all, but I think my life will turn out better because I'm connected to so many people in a good way."

Reframing Who You Are

As we have seen, children who have disabilities and their able-bodied siblings redefine what is "normal" for themselves and their family. They often reframe the disability experience to keep it from "spreading," that is, to make sure the disability—or having a sib who has a disability—won't become the central fact of their personal identity. Frequently, siblings attribute some positive character traits to the positive effects of disability.

Eliza says she knows her "disability is a big deal, but I don't make it a big deal. I always say I may not like being in a wheelchair but if I weren't I would be a different person. I like being me. Disability is just a part of me."

Arthur and his twin brother share a congenital muscle disorder causing weakness and poor coordination. The twins required special medical care and intensive physical therapy in early childhood; his mother gave them little prizes when they did their physical therapy exercises, and Arthur recalls that he never thought about it as being "a drag." As an adult,

Arthur has some weakness that limits his physical abilities, but he defines himself by what he can do and what he enjoys—intellectual pursuits, science, playing the cello, cycling, playing with his dog, and being a father to his children. Having an identical twin who shared his disability made him feel less alone and different; he always "fit in" with his twin. In addition, Arthur had good relationships with his two older brothers and didn't see himself as "a problem" because of his disability. While not the defining force in his life, his disability is a factor in his "forward-looking" approach. "I've developed into a can-do person in every aspect of my life; I don't throw in the towel."

The realization that disability does not define you as a person is important for both able-bodied siblings and those who have disabilities. Seeing yourself as a person who is quiet, interested in sharks, a Yankees fan, a fly fisher, a medium student, and, oh yes, someone who uses a wheelchair helps you incorporate disability into your life without having it take over. You don't deny it, but you don't let it crowd out all the good and interesting things in your life.

As Michelle points out, able-bodied siblings also have weaknesses, challenges, and "special" needs. The experience of having a sib who has a disability can help able-bodied children learn to be more tolerant of their own imperfections or problems and to put them in perspective—focusing more on their strengths and abilities. One expression of their "cope-ability" is siblings' choice of the "lens" that lets them view the person first and then the disability—and not necessarily to identify it as a flaw, but just a part of the bigger picture.

Making Friends with People Who "Get It"

Finding a friend who has a disability or a friend whose sibling has a disability can be difficult, and many children feel somewhat alone with their family's experience of disability. But as Zoey reports, it's easier to find friends who have *someone* who has a disability in their family, even if it's not a sibling. Zoey's kinship with these friends helps validate her ideas about disability, which are at odds with the stereotypes of most of her peers. "I have a different view of people who have a disability. I can share this with people at school who have family members who have disabilities. We have that connection." Friendships with peers who share their disability experience help children feel understood and give them a sense of belonging.

Support Groups for Siblings

Informal support from friends is especially valuable for siblings, since there are few formal support groups available for them. One notable exception, the "Sibshop" program, aims to fill that gap. Its developers note that, "for most parents, the thought of 'going it alone'—raising a child with special needs without the benefit of knowing another parent in a similar situation—would be unthinkable. Yet this routinely happens to brothers and sisters. It is not uncommon for siblings to be in their forties before they meet others who share their unique joys and concerns. Forty years is a long time to wait for validation."

Not all children need or want this type of group experience. Some get adequate support from their friends and family. Others feel uncomfortable in groups and may do better with individual counseling, if they need more support than friends and family can provide. But many children can benefit from peer support, particularly if their opportunity to find understanding friends is limited. If you think that your children would benefit, contact the Sibling Support Project (see Resources section of this book), which conducts Sibshops at locations around the country. Sibling (and parent) advocacy efforts could potentially help to develop more local support programs for siblings of kids who have disabilities. Interested siblings could approach disability organizations or local rehabilitation hospitals to start a support group in their community. Other places to hold informal support groups are schools, churches, and community centers.

Growing Together

Siblings who have a disability frequently experience positive changes in their personality—such as greater sensitivity toward others, increased tolerance for diversity, more appreciation for their abilities, and striving to be better people. Arthur's physical disability spurred his "constant drive to be better . . . to rise above my physical limitations." Eliza's disability has made her more "appreciative . . . a more open person. I'm a lot more understanding." Ashley says that her experiences with disability "showed me that lots of people are better off or worse off than I am. It taught me to deal with things, how to cope." Felicity says, "I am blessed. I may not walk, but I can use my arms and move my legs." Coping with her disability, including the negative reactions of her siblings, has given Felicity a sense of competence and self-awareness. "We're the strong ones," she says. "We're a lot wiser than those walking around looking at us."

Children who have a brother or sister who has a physical disability experience similar kinds of personal growth. When asked about the positive effects of having a sibling who has a disability, they frequently mention increased tolerance for individual differences, greater empathy and compassion for others, and more appreciation of their health and abilities. Other character traits associated with being the sib of a person who has a disability are patience, kindness, insight into coping with challenges, dependability, and loyalty. Siblings who act as advocates can also develop greater assertiveness, self-confidence, and persistence.

> "As a kid I used to play with a little girl who was mentally retarded and it was no big deal. She was one of us." —Michelle, whose older sister has a disability

Jean reports that her brother's disability has had an "impact on our view of the world," making her family more compassionate and concerned, not just about disability but about other social and environmental issues. "It's made our family more emotional about the world. We are disappointed about global warming and wars." Jean feels that her "brother made me a better person."

Charlie, Fred, and Sukey are three of five sibs; their sister had a childhood illness resulting in a physical disability. For them, the impact of having a sister who has a physical disability was woven into their experiences as part of a large, active, and supportive sibling group. Charlie, the third-born, says his interactions with his sister made him more compassionate, "made people respect me," and led to a feeling of solidarity, not just with his sister but with all people who have disabilities. "I am a more humane person; I have more human feelings for those who have less. I side with them."

> "I don't fear disability; I don't look and judge a book by its cover." —Paige, whose two younger sibs have disabilities

Oldest brother Fred, who drove his sister to high school and got her wheelchair out of the car, also feels good about how his relationship with his sister affected him. "I was proud. I made things possible for her, and was happy. It made me a better person." Their youngest sister, Sukey, says, "I grew up during the JFK era—things were to be equal for everyone. I felt that people who had disabilities were part of that." Although she was much younger than her oldest sister, "I felt protective when I walked with her. We would hold pinkies. When kids stared, my sister would look down at me and say, 'It doesn't matter.' Now I go out of my way to acknowledge people who have disabilities."

As adults, Charlie, Fred, and Sukey place a high value on their sibling relationships. Like Jean's family, their worldview expanded, in part because of having a sister who has a physical disability. Fred notes, "The impact on our family was definitely positive. We are all more open-minded and understanding." And Sukey says, "I felt so lucky to have the family I do. My family enriched my life."

The Brandons: A family devoted to faith, education, and unconditional love, inspired by Grandfather's example and bolstered by his support

"Disability is normal to us, part of our daily routine. It's not a bad thing, you know," says Jean, a teen who doesn't view her brother's spina bifida (SB) as a problem. She reflects her family's attitude that Jason's disability is just a part of life.

Grandfather Frank is a vital member of the Brandon family, ready to lend a hand anytime. Frank and his wife were always supportive, stepping in to help whenever the family needed them. But when Frank's wife died several years ago, he admits, "I buried myself in the grandkids."

Frank became a regular part of the family's life. He helped Jason get ready for school each morning while parents Lee and Priscilla got ready for work (Lee owns a construction business, and Priscilla works for the school system), and then he drove Jean and Jason to and from school. Frank continues this routine with Jean, now that Jason is away at college. Although he has a long commute to the Brandon home, the time and effort are worth it to Frank; the love and respect he receives from his grandchildren give him great pleasure and have helped him adjust to life without his wife.

Priscilla's first pregnancy ended in a miscarriage of twins following a car accident. After that, she was cautious and watched her health carefully. She soon became pregnant again, but by the twenty-eighth week, she hadn't felt the baby move. Priscilla pleaded with her obstetrician to prescribe an ultrasound, but the doctor refused because it was not covered by insurance. But the doctor's face revealed concern, and when Lee said he would pay out of pocket, the doctor sent Priscilla for a scan.

At the hospital, medical staff gathered to observe the ultrasound. There was silence except when the technician asked, "What's this?" That night the doctor called to tell the Brandons their baby might have SB. It was the worst day of Lee's life; he felt frightened. He wanted to protect his wife and his unborn child, but there was nothing he could do. Priscilla also felt helpless. After that she had an ultrasound every two weeks to check on the baby's condition.

The Brandons were referred to the local Spina Bifida Association (SBA) chapter and invited to a barbeque to meet other families. They felt overwhelmed by the wide range of abilities of the children with SB and wondered where their child would fit along this spectrum.

They were also referred to a geneticist, who warned them that the baby might have brain damage. After leaving his office, Priscilla cried for forty-five minutes in the parking lot. When she dried her tears, she resolved to educate herself, delving into research on SB.

Priscilla contacted a surgeon, whom she describes as "so wonderful." He explained that hydrocephalus is treatable and that brain damage can often be prevented. "Wait until you have this beautiful baby. You're going to love him and play with him and cherish every moment you have with him. Leave his medical care to me." That put everything in perspective for Priscilla.

Two weeks before the due date, Priscilla delivered Jason by C-section. He seemed so fragile that Priscilla "held him as if he were a doll." She still feels her emotions "like it was yesterday."

Hospital caregivers made the new family feel secure, but leaving the hospital was frightening. "I was so scared when we brought Jason home. This was both our first child and a child with many health issues."

When Jason came home from the hospital, the demands of the "real world" were stressful for Lee. He had to run his business, help care for Jason, and find a new, accessible home for his family. As life settled down, Lee's experience enabled him to offer installation of accessible bathrooms and ramps through his construction company. People told him, "I'll give you the job because your son has spina bifida and you know something about this."

While the Brandons' extended family was supportive, some of their closest friends backed off or drifted away. Relating to people in the community was also challenging. Priscilla didn't want Jason to feel "different"; she wanted him to go to church, get groceries, and go to the toy store like any other little boy. But occasionally when they went out, small children would point at Jason and a mother would say, "Don't look at him!" Priscilla remembers one such occasion when she longed to tell the mother that her children's curiosity was normal and to tell the children that her son's legs just didn't work the way theirs did. But the mother rushed on.

Afterward, Priscilla sat in the mall, crying. How could she explain her feelings to the mothers she encountered? They didn't know what she was going through. They didn't understand that she also found the blessings in mothering Jason. They didn't know that her son had to try on a dozen shoes to find ones that fit his braces. And they didn't understand that sometimes no shoes would fit and she would sit down and cry. But then Jason would do something wonderful and the scale would balance itself. Positive, fearful, thankful, angry, set apart—all those words described how Priscilla came to feel about the world.

Four years after Jason's birth, Jean was born: a bright, alert little girl who adored her older brother from the start. The siblings had a nurturing, bickering, love/hate relationship with a bit of jealousy on each side, a normal brother-sister relationship. Jean was included in Jason's medical care early on. She was too young to stay home alone, and since her grandparents also went to Jason's appointments, she couldn't stay with them. Jean remembers the whole family piling into the car for clinic visits. Although it was hard for everyone when Jason was in the hospital, Jean never felt left out. "He is not a complainer, and he makes me forget he has spina bifida. He makes me feel proud."

Hospitalizations and surgeries, fourteen in all, were part of their family life. Lee says that having his son hospitalized "is the only thing I've ever cried about. It's harder having your kid in the hospital than a spouse." Priscilla agrees: "You prepare yourself and your child, but when they wheel the child away, you cry." Dealing with the physical and emotional impact of surgeries was difficult. Priscilla recalls Jason asking, prior to one surgery, "Am I going to be able to walk?" and not having a clear answer.

Predictions by medical personnel have been both encouraging and discouraging, and not always accurate, beginning with the geneticist who warned of brain damage that did not occur. Later an orthopedist told them Jason could walk—but the braces didn't work, and he continued to need a wheelchair. There were highs and lows. Some doctors focused mostly on the cost of an operation to determine if it was "worth it" for Jason, but this was balanced by others who based their decisions on what was best for Jason's health and well-being.

Grandfather Frank worries about the future. Although Jason has started college, Frank is concerned about whether he will have full access to educational opportunities at his college and beyond. "We've had to fight even for curb cuts for each school he has attended." And "kids," he believes, "don't earn—they deserve."

5

Grandparents

Seeing through a New Lens

"I look at her waking up of a morning. I sit right outside her bedroom door so she'll see me there and feel safe knowing her granddad is there. We'll build tents and take our flashlight inside. It's given me an appreciation for what we have each day."

—NED, A GRANDFATHER

Grandparents can be parents' ace in the hole, ready to stand in or soothe frayed nerves as necessary. Just as you and your children are expanding your views of what is "normal," grandparents will be rethinking and refocusing their lens to frame a different view of both their able-bodied grandchildren and those who have disabilities. Grandparents usually follow the parent's lead in focusing on each child's abilities without losing sight of the fact that disability can add its challenges. And sometimes grandparents are a step ahead, helping you see your family in a new light.

Even though you are an independent adult, you are still your parents' child, and they want to be in on the highs and lows of your life. Grandparents can help in numerous ways: for example, by being a sounding board for decision making without demeaning you or your parental authority. Their sensitivity—knowing when to offer help and when to stand back—is a key to having a healthy relationship with you and the grandchildren.

Many grandparents have natural radar screens that allow them to assess what their children and grandchildren need from them at the moment. Is this a grandparent's "waiting-in-the-wings" role or a "you're-needed-now!" role? If grandparents miss their cue, you can direct them, letting them know when you need their help and when you don't. Flexibility and communication are critical to managing parent/grandparent roles. This is a learning process for parents and grandparents; you will both get better at communicating your needs and defining your roles over time.

Grandparents Near or Far

Grandparents may live in the same house as their grandchildren, in the same neighborhood, in the next county, or a continent away. Each distance creates different hurdles for grandparents in remaining a part of their grandchildren's lives. But with a little effort and good communication, emotional closeness between grandparents and grandchildren is possible regardless of geographic distance.

"In the Vicinity" Grandparents

When grandparents live near you, but not in the same household, they can see you on a regular basis, play with your children, and help out—but still have some distance from the private life of your nuclear family. They can be "on call" for both the up times of your children's lives—dance recitals, holiday concerts, sports events—and down times such as operations and illnesses.

Although you may want your parents to be an active part of your family, you probably don't want to include them *all* the time. But some grandparents who live nearby have trouble respecting the boundaries of their adult children's nuclear family. They drop by without calling ahead, or plan events and dinners without consulting the parents about the fam-

---

Grandparents can establish a running thread through interactions with each grandchild. For example, one child loved jokes, so his grandmother bought a book of jokes and had a new one to share during each phone call. A grandfather and his granddaughter loved to talk about the kinds of birds they saw; at holiday time he sent a bird identification book for his granddaughter to keep a record of her bird sightings. Grandparents whose grandchildren love to read can read the same books and talk about them.

> Grandparents may remember when they taught their child to ride a bike, running alongside him at first, gradually falling back, and finally allowing him to take over. And he did! It is now time for grandparents to fade into the background, believing that their child has the ability to handle new challenges.

ily's schedule. If this happens, you may feel that you are being treated like a child, as if your parents don't consider you adult enough to make decisions for your own family. You will have to remind them that you are in charge of your own home life and children.

If they feel rejected when you claim your position as head of your own family, it may help to remind your parents that this was the goal of their years of parenting: to see you become an independent person, capable of leading your own life and raising your own children. Grandparents will find that when they recognize your right to make decisions and set limits on their level of involvement, you will actually be more willing to welcome them into your life.

Like Frank Brandon, some grandparents have a larger role in their grandchildren's life, by mutual agreement with their adult children. Ned's granddaughter has spina bifida. He drives her to school and picks her up each afternoon, and he cares for her twenty hours a week while her mother and father are at work.

"In-House" Grandparents

When grandparents live with their children and grandchildren, the experience can be fulfilling and helpful to all—*if* relationships and roles are clearly defined. "In-house" grandparents regularly witness the workings of their child's nuclear family and, in some ways, become part of the

> When thinking of the way to treat a grown child, grandparents need to ask themselves, "How would I treat a friend?" Adult children have the same rights to respect, autonomy, and privacy.

☞ If parents are abusive to their children, unable to provide a safe environment for them, or incapable of meeting their basic needs, then grandparents need to step in to protect their grandchildren. Grandparents can report their concerns about parental abuse or neglect to the Child Protection Services Agency in their state. If parents are deemed unfit by the state or voluntarily put their children in grandparents' care, then grandparents who want to do the job may be awarded temporary or permanent custody of the grandchildren.

family system. Yet grandparents are not the parents, and they need to support the parents' rules and roles. Any disagreements with the way parents are dealing with a situation should be discussed adult to adult—and not in front of the grandchildren.

While their adult child may consider grandparents' opinions and advice on parenting, ultimately grandparents must defer to the rules and structure for parenting that their adult child sets for his family.

Finances play a role in the everyday life of every family. Clarifying how household bills and rent or mortgage payments are to be shared by grandparents and adult children is fundamental to the success of multi-generational living. Doing chores or providing services (such as child care) that the family would otherwise need to pay for may be counted as an economic contribution.

Some grandparents may have to live with their children for economic reasons and rely on them for financial assistance; in turn, these grandparents may assume certain responsibilities within the home, such as making dinner or being there for the children after school while parents work. In other families, adult children and their kids get financial help from the grandparents, or live in the grandparents' home in order to make ends

A live-in grandparent is not the decision maker for the grandchildren unless she has been assigned that responsibility. Her mantra should be, "Better ask my son or daughter if it's alright for me to do that with my grandchild."

meet. Often, adult children (and grandchildren) will repay the grandparents by helping with household chores, driving, yard work, or other things they need. Any of these arrangements can work to mutual advantage—as long as roles and expectations are clear and each generation feels they are gaining something through multigenerational living.

Faraway Grandparents

For many grandparents who live far away from their grandchildren, keeping in touch is a challenge. Travel is not always possible, but grandparents can connect through telephone calls, e-mail, and Skype, an Internet video chat service. Tech-savvy grandparents may join the world of cell phone texting—increasingly the communication medium of choice for children. Vern enjoys regular "visits" with his son and his family by Skype. Vern lives abroad and can only travel to see his grandchildren every two years, yet he feels very connected to them. He recently heard and saw his grandson's live performance of "Go Tell Aunt Rhodie" on his new trumpet and watched his granddaughter tell him about her first day of ballet school. He likes the spontaneous exchange and a sense of really "being there" in the children's life.

Genevieve, a Canadian, sees her American family a few times each year and talks with them by phone weekly. In this way she keeps up with the latest interests and developments in their lives. Genevieve makes her-

When a grandchild is going through surgery or a lengthy medical procedure, faraway grandparents can stay in touch by texting, e-mailing, or having "face-to-face" talks via Skype. They can send pictures, videos, or links to websites that their grandchildren will enjoy. These interactions divert the grandchild from what he is going through and give the grandparents an opportunity to entertain him, even if not physically present. Ask your parents to create a direct connection with all the siblings so that each feels involved and cared about. When one of your children requires medical attention because of her disability, your focus is on her, and your able-bodied children may feel left out—that's when they can benefit from extra attention from their grandparents.

T One grandmother who sees her grandchildren only once a year picks up little gifts she thinks the children might like, wraps them, and puts them in a bag until she has the number of gifts corresponding to the number of days she will visit. Every day each child can choose one of the gifts to open. She does this for her "faraway" grandchildren because she does little things regularly for the grandchildren who live nearer to her. If grandparents don't want to buy gifts, they can find things in nature to share, like a stone from the woods, a beautiful bird feather, some seeds from their sunflowers, or some leftover ribbon or lace from a sewing or craft project.

self more of a presence in her grandchildren's lives by sharing jokes and stories about her pets and her local grandchildren—their cousins. She is also a resource for her daughter and a comfort when needed.

Of course, *actually* being with their grandkids is the ultimate goal for most grandparents. But when families live far apart, visits are so special that sometimes they don't seem quite real. There is so much to pack into a concentrated amount of time that visits can become too intense and exhausting. Scheduling in some rest breaks or time alone will give everyone a chance to relax between family activities. If grandparents can also spend some time individually with each grandchild—to talk, take a walk, or go out for a meal—they will strengthen the bonds they have with each child. Grandchildren will value and remember this special time when they are the focus of their grandparents' attention.

Grandparents' Supporting Roles
Support for Adult Children

The American Association of Retired Persons announced in August of 2011 that an increasing number, about 70 percent, of grandparents are stepping in to help with their grandchildren. Grandparents are clearly an important source of support to their children. Their support can be emotional, physical, or financial. Any help from grandparents—when it is wanted by their children—will reduce stress on the family and protect the parents' mental and physical health. Helping also gives grandparents a chance to form closer and more meaningful relationships with their grandchildren.

Emotional Support to Parents

When a group of grandparents get together, the talk is usually about their grandkids. It's easy to get caught up in the exciting world of grandchildren's lives. Meanwhile, the "sandwich" generation—parents of the aforementioned grandchildren—sometimes feel left out. As one son said to his mother, "What am I, chopped liver?" It's OK for adult children to ask their parents to listen or give them advice. Sometimes you just need your parents to "be there" for you when you are either overjoyed by your child's accomplishments or stressed out by life events.

While grandparents' presence at your child's special events will be welcomed by your children, it's also a way for your parents to show solidarity and support for you. Helen finds that even when her grandkids are disinterested, her children "don't want me to miss any of their kids' activities."

Grandparents can also help by giving positive feedback to their adult children. Receiving appreciation from your own parents or in-laws for ways you treat your spouse, care for your children, or care for yourself boosts your morale and self-esteem. Helen's daughter-in-law, Pili, appreciates it when Helen tells her that her child who has spina bifida "picked the right parents." Pili says, "I owe a lot to my supportive in-laws." When adult children know that their own parents trust them to make wise decisions and to do what needs to be done for their families, they are encouraged to assume their responsibilities with added vigor.

Genevieve trusted her daughter's family to use their personal resources to help her granddaughter meet the challenges of living with OI. She believed they could do whatever was necessary. "Everyone in the extended family had great sympathy for the family and, after the initial shock and disbelief, faced it as a fact of life. Our granddaughter is loved and treated the same as all of our other granddaughters, with no special allowances made other than for her safety." Genevieve's belief in her children's abilities made them feel they had been given "the grandparents' seal of good parenting."

> "My Mom knows I can handle this crisis; that gives me the confidence to deal with parenting decisions I make every day."
> —Debbie

Physical Support to Parents

When grandparents are able to give it, physical support (housework, babysitting, chores, and so forth) is invaluable to parents. Earlier, you read about Susie, the mother of four sons, including twins who have physical disabilities. When the twins were 4 years old, Susie had a herniated disc from carrying them up and down stairs in her three-story home. Two years later, the disc ruptured while she was bathing. Her parents, who lived several states away, took the children for six weeks while Susie recovered her strength. Their generous help allowed Susie to rest and recuperate with peace of mind, knowing that her children were in good hands. For the grandparents, this visit was an opportunity to spend "real" 24–7 time with their grandchildren, getting to know each one. This was also a special time for the boys to get closer with their grandparents. Ned also gifts his children with his time when he cares for his granddaughter—and he finds this role a fulfilling part of his life. "She and I are very close."

Grandparents can also help out by structuring playdates or excursions, taking dinner to their grandchild's family, or inviting the children to spend some time at their house while the parents get a rest.

Having a night out is restorative and gives parents a chance to reignite the intimacy necessary to keep their relationship alive. Helen often babysits overnight so her son and his wife can have a complete break from family responsibility. She feels that it's essential for the parents to get a break once in a while, so they can keep their family running smoothly. "The family structure has to work. I don't know what they would have done without us grandparents," says Helen.

Grandparents handy with hammers and nails can help put in ramps or lower light switches to make their child's home more accessible for their grandchild who has a physical disability. A grandchild might ask a grandparent clever with his hands to build a "desk" that fits across his wheelchair for doing work at home or school, or to create custom built-ins in her room, so she can reach her toys and books. Grandparents are prized for the skill they bring to these projects.

Financial Support to Parents

A family's financial resources are a deciding factor in what they can do for or with their children. If a family has a child who has a physical disability, there is usually more financial stress due to the unanticipated and often rising costs of medications, hospitalizations, doctor's fees, equipment, or home modifications. Some families may have times when it's difficult to meet all their needs.

Grandparents can sometimes help in these situations. Though most grandparents cannot afford to make much of a dent in the mountain of medical costs, they may be able to supplement the family's needs in small but significant ways. Elsie, for example, buys clothing for her grandchildren, which eases the stress on the family budget. "My children are grateful if I buy clothes for the grandchildren. They have never told me to back off—but I tell them to set limits on me if I buy too much." While Elsie's help is valued by her family, she's also aware that her children might feel humiliated or obligated if she gives too much. Her sensitivity and keen ear for their priorities are keys to the close relationship she has with her children.

Grandparents might be able to help with the cost of special equipment (such as a ramped van if the kids use wheelchairs or scooters, or balancing balls for physical exercise) or finance the building of accessible accommodations (like a stair climber up to the second level). This type of help is doubly beneficial as it gives their grandchild more freedom and alleviates muscle strain and fatigue for parents.

Paying for tutoring or activities like music lessons, gymnastics, or art classes is a boon to parents who want to give their children these advantages but can't afford them. Elyse, living far from her family, but understanding their constant struggle to make ends meet, sends them a check before each Christmas to cover the cost of gifts they would otherwise be unable to give their children.

Support for Grandchildren

Most grandparents want to meet as many of their grandchildren's needs as possible, and they often stretch themselves, giving more than they thought they could. Helen, with grandchildren both able-bodied and who have disabilities, says, "It's a lot of work, but you do what you have to do." She says that meeting the needs of *all* their grandchildren is important. "We don't limit what we do because of my grandson's disability." The family creates ways to incorporate him into the activities they plan for all their grandchildren.

Most grandparents agree that a cardinal rule is to treat all the grand-children equally. Ned found this important in his own personal develop-ment. "I had a hard time being normal in high school when my brother (who had muscular dystrophy) couldn't be. But my parents treated us the same and that always meant so much to me." Ned carries that into his relationship with granddaughter Leeann; he treats her just as he would an able-bodied grandchild.

Providing Physical Care to a Grandchild Who Has a Physical Disability

Of course, when a grandchild has a physical disability, there are add-on needs—those related strictly to the disability. As a grandparent, it can be challenging—or exhilarating—to learn the new skills involved in caring for that grandchild. "Overnights" with grandparents, special for any grandchild, take on an added dimension when grandparents are learning how to provide hands-on physical assistance and medical care.

Elsie, for example, had to master a few rehab techniques before she could babysit for her grandson Landon. "I took him for ten days so his parents could go on a trip. In preparation I learned how to catheterize and brace him, and get him into his walker. I needed to learn his new enema program, as well as his physical therapy program. I want to be there, to be a good grandma." Elsie enjoys caring for Landon and having some one-on-one time with him, without his parents around. "I like to be fun but also to give him a good example. I find as a grandmother I have time to enjoy him more and I let him try things. He does more than we think he can. He stands on a stool to brush his teeth. I don't stop him from trying."

"My grandfather gave me five cents every time I could walk around the dining room table." —Sam

Elsie and Landon's relationship exemplifies the closeness that can develop when there is the opportunity to care for a grandchild. She has overcome her reservations about meeting his physical needs and feels so comfortable that she can allow him to try things that he has never done before. In the process she has also earned the trust of her children: they know that their son will be well loved and cared for when he is with his grandmother.

Becoming a Stand-in Parent

When grandparents rearrange their lives to care for their grandchil-dren, it is usually their choice. For some, like Ned and Frank, helping their grandchildren has become an avocation, which they find personally fulfilling. But some grandparents become sole guardians and stand-in parents for their grandchildren out of necessity. Naomi, for instance, raises her daughter's two boys, one of whom has cerebral palsy, while their mother is in prison. In addition to acting as a parent to her grandsons, Naomi has a job outside the home. She is sustained physically and emotionally by the strong support of her congregation and friends.

Clara is another grandmother who became "mother" to her two granddaughters after her daughter and son-in-law were killed in a car crash that left one of the girls paralyzed. Elina, the girls' aunt, moved in with Clara to share the load of raising them. When the roles of grandparent and parent are fused, relationships with grandchildren can become somewhat murky and complicated. Grandparents in these families become directors, disciplinarians, and schedulers for the children, where before they had primarily been givers of unconditional love and emotional support. Grandparents will often need time to sort out their feelings about these role changes and redefine their relationships with their dependent grandchildren.

When the focus is entirely on the child's needs, grandparents can lose sight of *their* needs. But taking care of self is vital to maintaining the energy and perspective needed to raise children. Support for grandparents can be found through religious congregations, extended family, friends, and sometimes coworkers. An in-depth discussion of custodial grandparents' needs is beyond the scope of this book, but there are other books that can help. In some communities, social service agencies have special services for families headed by grandparents (see the Resources section of this book for other information). Grandparents who find it difficult to maintain their equilibrium with the children or are depressed or overwhelmed might benefit from additional help from a mental health professional.

Planning for Changes in Grandparents' Ability to Help

Although many grandparents are healthy and active, some will have physical limitations and continue to age as your children grow up. Their ability to help out or to stay emotionally engaged with your children might lessen over time. It's helpful for you and your children's grandparents to anticipate these changes and how they will affect your family, as well as make plans to lessen the impact on everyone.

Helen, for instance, worries about how her son, his family, and she

Traveling

If grandparents are financially able—and parents approve—they can take grandchildren on trips by land, sea, or air. This requires lots of advance planning in regard to accessibility and meeting physical needs, but there is information available to make this possible (see Resources section of this book for travel agencies that specialize in trips for people who have physical disabilities). There is nothing like an adventure to bind the generations together. Traveling is a mind-expanding opportunity for children of all ages, and the memories last forever.

Being Present

"Gram, are you coming to the holiday concert at school?" What your grandchild is really saying is, "Gram, I really want you there to watch me. And I know that you care enough to come." Grandmother's attendance gives the child a sense of belonging to a wider family than just her parents and siblings; it is a lesson in the ways family members support one another. Indeed, a grandparent's presence at the holiday concert is as significant as her presence at the child's bedside when he is in the hospital.

Grandparenting a Child Who Has a Physical Disability

Just as parents experience "extras" in having a child who has a physical disability, so do grandparents. Challenges and rewards, supporting and being supported, keep grandparents focused on helping their families prepare for the future. Faith, a sense of purpose, and flexibility help grandparents in this family mission.

Community Support

Helen's way of grandparenting is an extension of how she's always lived and what she's believed. In her childhood community, people expected life to bring ups and downs, and they were prepared. "If someone caught a big fish, we shared it with everyone; our community shared the good and the bad." When an unanticipated event happened, like the birth of a baby who had a physical disability, the community acknowledged it, consoled the family, and supported the family in coping. Sharing whatever came along, positive or not, was a buffer for the family; what happened to one happened to all, and the community was supportive in fair weather and foul. Because Helen was prepared for life by this balanced, down-to-earth worldview, the impact of her grandson's disability was lessened.

Faith

Elsie's faith is unbroken by the experience of having a grandchild who has a disability. "There is no answer why this happened. There is a reason for everything. Faith has gotten me through so much. If you don't have faith I don't know what you do. This has made us closer. Even if my grandson has a disability, he has a loving family he is part of. No one promised us life would be perfect." Ned's faith is paramount, too. "You have to believe," he says.

While religious faith is central for some grandparents, others put their faith not in a higher being but in their own ability to face life's slings and arrows and in their children's resilience. Marshall believes that events happen randomly, and he can't imagine that there could be a god who would make a child suffer; nevertheless, he has faith that his son and daughter-in-law will raise their children with and without physical disabilities to their full potential.

A Sense of Purpose

Ned and his wife are more aware of other people who happen to have disabilities since their granddaughter's birth. He struggled when Leeann was born as her disability brought up old feelings of loss for his brother who had muscular dystrophy. "I fought it when Leeann was born. Why? I was handed a little girl. I was bitter over a recent lay-off. I was upset at first but then realized there are many worse off. Now I know it had a purpose—so that I could babysit Leann. When I first started I had to learn how to catheterize and give medicine. When you're the only one there, you do it. I'm loving it." Ned realized that a bad event turned into a meaningful relationship, where he both gives *and* receives love, and in which he is growing in his ability to care.

Grandparents Adapt and Grow, Too

Grandparenting presents a unique opportunity to reach one's potential as a human being and to develop personal qualities that may have been lacking earlier in one's life—like patience, giving or receiving, being optimistic and hopeful, or being thankful for the "small things." Having a grandchild who has a physical disability among one's other grandchildren provides a whole new perspective on the possibilities in life.

Generativity

By the time they become grandparents, most people have reached the stepping-stone that Erik Erikson, a developmental theorist, calls the *generative* stage of life. This stage, normally occurring in middle age, is a time when adults continue to develop by being creative and productive in their own lives and by helping the younger generation—in their own family and outside it. Ann expresses this impulse to give and create through her widely known fund-raising efforts for OI, especially "in-door picnics," her signature activity. "I'm making ham, potato salad, everything. It keeps me busy." She has made over seventy baskets of donated goods thus far. "People have been donating to OI through me since Dan was born. As a giver I've had to learn to be aware of other people who give. I have to be thankful to them." But she knows that, even if her grandson had not had OI, she would still be involved. "I like helping people."

Patience

Grandparents who are type A personalities—hard driving, using every minute to its fullest—may feel stressed when they are out of sync with their children's and grandchildren's slower pace. Grandparents may need to slow down a bit to fit in with the rhythm of life for their grandchildren, especially those who have physical disabilities. Children have their own internal clocks (usually moving at a different rate than adults') and their own agendas and priorities. And grandchildren who have disabilities have internal clocks and agendas *plus* the external schedules of medical or rehabilitation care; they learn to slow down, developing the ability to wait, endure, and be steady. Grandparents need to develop patience, so they can enjoy being in the moment with their grandchildren.

"Having a grandchild who has a physical disability made a huge difference. It made us more patient and understanding. Now we understand the struggles parents with kids who have disabilities go through," says Elsie, whose experience with disability has led to greater patience and tolerance for human differences.

Giving and Receiving

Some of us are great givers but feel uncomfortable with receiving, perhaps because we feel unworthy or beholden or have little practice. Others are great receivers but do not know when or how to give, or are uncomfortable deciding what another person would like or needs. Grandparents must train themselves to do both well, since grandchildren love to receive gifts—everything from an autumn leaf to a DVD—as well as to give them. Grandparents' reactions to a scribbled "map of your house," a papier-mâché "ball," or a teen's gift of a psychedelic print scarf will be scrutinized for authenticity; grandchildren will be gratified when they determine that grandparents' appreciation is genuine.

For Elsie, in the giving is the receiving. When she knows that her grandson and his parents are coming to visit, she plans the day around their desires, and that brings her happiness. "I enjoy what they give back to me. When the family comes to visit, and I open the door, I hear that little guy squealing from the back seat of the car, 'Nana, get me out of here!' He wants to be with us."

Helen too enjoys the satisfaction of making her family happy. "You have to say, 'I have the time. Let me have the kids.' I want my son and daughter-in-law to have all the time they can find to spend together."

Optimism and Hope

After resolving some difficult emotional reactions to a grandchild's disability, a grandparent may find that their up-close-and-personal experience of physical disability leads to new levels of optimism and hope—openness to good things, and confidence that one can cope with bad things that come their way. Elsie finds it uplifting that so many people are interested in her life. "People ask about my grandson. People collected money for him. Co-workers bring in things for him. It changed my relationships with others. I am so surprised at how much people care."

Grandparents Have Their Own Lives, Too

Grandparents today are living different lives than those of preceding generations. Increased life expectancy and advances in technology, as well as their health status, abilities, passions, family needs, and economic conditions, all contribute to the variety of lives they lead. Working life is extended for some, by choice or need, while others opt for early retirement to enjoy travel, recreation, or avocations.

Grandparents have more choices than ever about how to spend their time. While they often choose to play an integral part in their families, their pursuit of individual interests and talents is equally important to fulfillment in the "third act" of life. As their children assume the reins of the family, grandparents are free to let go of being "in charge" and give their attention to other interests.

While raising their own family, they may not have had enough time to follow their own passions. But by the time people become grandparents, they often have more "space" in life to pursue their own passions—career, physical fitness, volunteer work, or hobbies shelved while you, their children, were the main focus. Now, even if grandparents are still fully employed, they can finally say, "It is my time."

In fact, it is vital—for the well-being of grandparents and the entire family—that they remain engaged in the world outside the family. Physical and emotional self-maintenance for grandparents is not selfish; it's wise. When grandparents are taking care of themselves, they will be better prepared to help you and the grandchildren when needed, or just to "be there" for you, in both celebrations and hard times.

The time and effort put into keeping physically and mentally fit are well spent, generating the energy and vitality to tackle what *has* to be done as well as the fun things in life. Building a program of exercise and relaxation and pursuing passions for fulfilling activities or ideas (in addition to being an involved grandparent) are prescriptions for a well-rounded and healthy life.

Elsie and her husband own a small resort on a lake. Begun as a hobby, the resort now has five cottages. They lead a happy, outgoing life, and both place a high value on family. Each also holds down another job, Elsie working at a college. Exercise—walking and running together—is part of their life. Elsie also runs 5Ks, finding them a "stress reliever." Last but not least, they relish being with and helping their four kids and grandchildren. Maintaining a good balance of work, family, couple, and individual activities is their goal.

Inclusive grandparents balance giving with receiving. It takes some time and experience for them to fully develop the ability to respond to their own needs as well as those of their children and their families, especially when one of their grandchildren has a physical disability. It takes a good dose of respect and sensitivity not to intrude on their child's family. But inclusive grandparents are ready, physically and mentally, to step forward when their presence is requested. And for most grandparents, that request for participation is a gift.

PART III

Into the Wide World

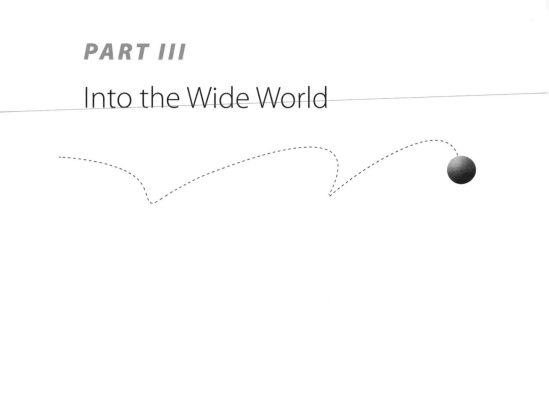

The Sheridan-Wolfe Family: Two women build their family by adopting children who have complex disabilities and helping them reach their potential

Lynn met her life partner, Jessie, at a wedding, and after some time they began a romantic relationship. Lynn had an adopted daughter, Miranda, who had multiple disabilities, and Jessie had two sons; they knew they were creating a "package deal" when they made their commitment to each other.

Lynn had worked for twenty years as an intensive care nurse and then provided home care when children were discharged from the hospital. In time she became a case manager, assisting children with the transition home and helping families understand their children's needs. Meanwhile Jessie had chosen a career as a counselor, and she discovered a special empathy for children who needed help.

Early on in her work in a large neonatal unit, Lynn observed the number of babies who were not able to leave the hospital because their care was too complex for their families. "I started thinking, 'I love kids. I would want to take these kids home.'" A few years later, Lynn became involved with a family that fell apart. The mother left six children in foster care, went into labor prematurely with the seventh child, and then disappeared after giving birth. "The social worker called me and said, 'Would you take the baby home? You're the only person here who is involved with her.'"

Lynn took baby Miranda home when she was 24 weeks old. Lynn did not feel ready for this, but she felt there was no choice. As they were leaving the hospital, a physician told her, "Don't expect much; she is going to be blind and deaf and she won't walk." Lynn was "floored."

Lynn became a single parent, working full-time. But as soon as she started day care, Miranda began to have medical complications, including recurrent pneumonias. She was suffering from broncho-pulmonary dysplasia (BPD), a respiratory condition that affects some premature babies. Lynn was forced to quit her job because she could not get a home care nurse for Miranda eight hours a day. That was the first time Lynn had to quit work to care for Miranda, but it was not the last.

It was during this time that Lynn and Jessie got together. Jessie became a second mother for Miranda while Lynn became close to Jessie's boys. Erik, the younger of the boys, lived with his father for a year before moving in with his mother and Lynn, going from youngest in the family to the older child role. He didn't fully understand Miranda's disability, but he accepted her. "I just saw her as my new little sister."

At age 3, Miranda was placed in a special school for children who have severe disabilities. In retrospect, Lynn regrets that decision because "kids identify with kids they're around." Miranda seemed more comfortable with other kids who had disabilities because she was in the hospital so much. She was a cute little girl, and Lynn says she learned to play the "poor little thing" role.

At age 7, Miranda transferred to a mainstream elementary school. Her speech was difficult to understand and she used a wheelchair, except in the classroom, where she used her walker. She became a social butterfly, was part of the pack, and was included in all activities with her peers.

Lynn and Jessie were eager for Miranda to have a sister. They were considering a foreign adoption, but then they received a call from a local children's hospital: a family had planned to adopt a baby girl but reneged because of "unknown" medical issues, including some type of brain injury at birth. After meeting baby Siobhan, Jessie and Lynn decided to adopt her. When Lynn's mom, Esther, first heard about Siobhan, she wondered about the wisdom of this adoption; but when Esther met Siobhan, she said, "There is something in there." It took Siobhan some time, but then, Esther says, "she broke out."

Siobhan came home at 2 months of age with a gastrostomy (feeding) tube. Life seemed crazy. When she was 5 months old, the neurosurgeon determined that she had had a stroke while still in utero. Only the part of her brain that controls basic functions such as breathing, swallowing, and motor coordination was damaged by the stroke; early in her childhood, it became clear that her intellect was normal. She had various procedures and ER admissions. Doctors said that Siobhan would need a tracheostomy in the future, but they delayed it until after her second birthday because it would make speaking difficult. Since then, she has had numerous other medical interventions, including the use of a bilevel positive airway pressure ventilator, sleep monitoring devices, and a spinal fusion operation to prevent severe scoliosis.

Erik was exposed to the health care system and his sister's medical needs during those years. He says that Lynn and Jessie "had me help out a little, slowly integrating me into the situation." Erik found that patience was the key to not becoming overwhelmed. "The hospital was not a traumatic event for me." He learned that sometimes his attempts to help could be a hindrance and learned when to back off. "I've never felt my needs diminished by my little sisters' needs. Their needs may be life or death," says Erik.

Erik is grateful to his parents for "showing me how life is, to guide me in the real world." He says that the experiences in his family have been the key to his open-mindedness. "Our norms are different. What is 'normal'? My family is normal. I was young when change came. I expect chaos in life. Whenever everyone is in the box, I've stepped outside and can look back at our world."

During the early years, when the girls lived closer to her, Esther babysat. "I consulted and brainstormed with Lynn because we are both nurses and both like to invent. We think outside the box." She helped to create some of the tools Siobhan uses to control her world. Because Siobhan has spasticity, it is hard to cuddle her, so Esther says they have an intellectual closeness, both being passionate about books and learning. Siobhan has become a very curious teen; she often questions what she hears on newscasts and seeks out further information. Esther is her co-researcher. They like to solve mysteries together. When people refer to Siobhan as a "case" or a "disorder," Esther corrects them: Siobhan is a *person*.

Lynn and Jessie learned that Siobhan's brain was actually "in overdrive"—she was intellectually gifted. At age 3, Siobhan would throw fits if not read to exactly as the words appeared on the page. Later, she used a Gemini voice output system (a communication aid that creates audible speech or readable text for people unable to speak), appropriate for her age. Now, as an adolescent, she uses a computer with PowerPoint and other programs.

Despite her intellectual gifts, Siobhan has not been in a mainstream classroom since second grade. Because of her multiple medical problems, she would need a nurse to assist her in class all day, and the cost was prohibitive. So Siobhan has been homeschooled for many years. Lynn now knows what "learning is" and lets her daughter run with her interests. Recently Siobhan has been studying American history to 1865 and learning about Burke, Locke, and Rousseau; she is itching to learn Mandarin Chinese and Spanish. Her homeschool math and language arts curricula come through a top university program for gifted youth.

Teaching Siobhan has taught Lynn that a parent needs the mind-set of "presuming competence" and looking for ways to help her child accomplish all she is capable of. Lynn's attitude is person-centered: "How do I help Siobhan be Siobhan?" This has required adaptation and creativity. For instance, because of a visual impairment, Siobhan has difficulty seeing black ink on white paper; they have found that orange- or peach-colored plastic overlays cut the glare and make reading easier. When working on an adaptation, Lynn tries to use what is commercially available, but sometimes she has to improvise. When Siobhan needed a way to hold down her paper while writing or painting, Lynn, with Esther's help, improvised a tool combining a cabinet door latch, an old computer mouse, some buckshot, and industrial Velcro!

When Siobhan took a class in conflict resolution at a local university, she needed a way to participate in class and gain the professor's attention. Lynn and Jessie rigged a bicycle light to her wheelchair with a touch switch to turn it on. As Jessie says, "If a tool is not out there, how can you help your child be all she can be? You can't stop at 'No, it doesn't exist.' "

With Erik having graduated from high school and working, Miranda in a vocational life skills program, and Siobhan progressing, Jessie and Lynn have recently taken in another little girl, Annette, just 4 years old. Annette had a significant disability; she had been institutionalized and had never used a bathroom, communicated, or even sat upright. But Lynn saw the "intelligence in her eyes" and knew she would fit into their family.

Annette recently had an allergic reaction that resulted in a hospital stay overlapping with her birthday. Lynn took party horns in for every staff member so they could all help celebrate this big event in her life. "People change their behaviors when a child is seen as competent, having opinions, likes and dislikes. Sometimes parents have to lay out those expectations" and show the way.

Lynn says, "I always wanted children. This is the journey of my life. All the pieces come together. I don't think about the physical dynamics of the needs of the girls and my aging. I wasn't planning on this latest little 4-year-old munchkin. And Siobhan is going to be tall; I'm five feet four. Siobhan needs complete physical support."

Mothering the three girls has helped Jessie learn to show compassion, and she has come to experience more compassion for herself, as well—especially since she was struck by lightning a few years ago and can no longer work. She is "different than before. When working for my BA I didn't open a book and got all As. I was struck by lightning while working on my MA; I couldn't do it. I accept myself for where I am."

Lynn's professional background has helped in her parenting, but if people assume she has a huge knowledge base, they are sorely mistaken. Lynn says the secret is to know how to ask questions. "It has to be in language people understand; you need to gauge that understanding. I am often asked by professionals and other individuals if I can find some re sources or documents. I find they are not asking questions in a way that will get the answers they need. This is a good skill I learned in childhood: find another way to ask the question."

Lynn remains sensitive to the issues she recognized in high school, when she first worked with families of children who have disabilities: the lack of communication between families and educational systems, and the need for competent medical care, a family support network, and getting people to listen.

Lynn and Jessie work together to support each other and their children. "We couldn't be without the other person. We are each other's safety sounding board. We are a team, willing to drop everything, to be with the child in the space where they have to be; that comes from having to be there in the ER *now*. We feel compelled to fix, give an answer. We both have the ability to see a puzzle piece, change the interlocking one around, move."

Both find bits of time to replenish themselves, Jessie through Native American spirituality and Lynn through the refreshing practice of Tibetan chanting. "You have to find yourself," even if you can't leave your kids to go on vacation.

Lynn says that for her and Jessie, as it is for other parents of kids who have severe disabilities, it's difficult to imagine what lies ahead. "Families are struggling so hard to just get through the day to day that they can't venture a thought about the future, potential, and possibilities." The future may evoke fear for many families; some are grieving the loss of their child's normal developmental stages and the inability to be parents without providing medical care. Parents need help dealing with grieving and with their feelings about having to cause pain and discomfort in caring for a child's physical needs. Other issues Lynn sees affecting parents are the sense of isolation, advocacy efforts being misunderstood, the psychological impact of "well-intentioned" comments and actions, and the problem of meeting the child's need for touch and physical closeness because of the child's paralysis, spasticity, or rigidity.

What would Lynn and Jessie be doing if they hadn't taken this journey? "Probably working twelve-hour shifts, not having found the everyday human piece of life," says Lynn.

6

Opening Doors to Inclusion

"I worry about what my daughter's life will be like when she grows up."

—MIA, THE MOTHER OF
A DAUGHTER WITH OI

"Most teens 'take' independence; adolescents with disabilities may have to be 'given' independence deliberatively."

—RHODA OLKIN, PhD,
PSYCHOLOGIST

Preparing to Launch

Parenting takes so much energy, love, time, fortitude, and creativity that while you're doing it, it's hard to imagine a time when your full-time involvement will no longer be necessary. Of course, parenting never really ends, but as your children mature and gain independence, your role can become more supportive and less directive. If you are like most families in our society, your ultimate goal as a parent is to see your children become independent and able to leave the nest. Some young adults who have physical disabilities can live independently without any special assistance, but others need help with household chores, transportation, moving about, or activities of daily living (showering, eating, or dressing). If your child needs regular help with these activities, you may be worried about whether she can make it on her own. This chapter explores how you can prepare your child who has a physical disability to be *socially and psychologically independent* even if he needs some help from others to accomplish physical tasks.

Laying the Groundwork

Launching your children—whether able-bodied or having disabilities—from the comfort and safety of home will be more successful when everyone in the family has envisioned their "release" into the wide world and prepared for this early on. As we have seen, parents do this by gradually exposing their children to greater levels of responsibility and to experiences that build their character and support their relationships with peers. Parents lay the groundwork for their children's eventual independence by fighting negative stereotypes, communicating their expectations for competence, instilling values, and reinforcing character traits that will help their children cope with the ups and downs of life. Additionally, parents can help their children gain access to educational, social, and recreational activities throughout childhood and tap into resources that will support them once they leave home.

Combating Stereotypes and Negative Attitudes

"They just don't get it!" As the parent of a child who has a physical disability, you've probably had this thought hundreds of times. You have no doubt met some people who demean your child (or you) with condescending words and attitudes, sometimes unintentionally. They think that your child's disability defines her as a person—and assume you do, too. While you see your child as whole and perfect as she is, others may focus on her orthopedic appliances—and lose sight of the child who's using them.

When Pili encounters these attitudes toward her child, she feels "set apart, fearful, a little angry about the way people look at my son or talk about him. I cry and move on." These are the people who give *sympathy* (they assume that a person who has a disability is inferior, and that *they* *know* what the person needs) when it would be more helpful to express *empathy* (seeing the person who has a disability as an equal, and trying to understand her inner experience). One mother remembers grocery shopping with her daughter who walked with crutches. An older man approached her, saying, "Bless you!" and handed her a card with a religious text promising miracles. The mother was not interested in this man's sympathy; she handed the card back, saying, "Save this for someone who needs it."

There is a little mental trick to distinguish between empathy and sympathy. We call it "the altitude of attitude" because it has to do with the way the recipient of concern feels afterward. Do you feel that the person is looking up to you as if you are a saint in the sky? Do you feel that you are being looked down upon, like a child getting a pat on the head? Or do you feel like you are on the same level, knowing that the other person would "shoot the breeze" with you or tell you the latest joke? This understanding is one to be tucked into your child's toolbox as well; it can help her recognize and gravitate toward people who "get it," and/or to read people more accurately and choose whether or not to educate them or try to change their attitudes.

Liz believes that parents can model positive attitudes for others. "You need to establish the pattern by treating your child who has a physical disability like all other children. People will take their cue from you." Another mom, Kelsey, says that her daughter's disability "is obvious. I used to care what people think and say, but not anymore. Now I just get my daughter out to do whatever girls her age are doing."

Liz and Kelsey have learned to stop asking whether their children *should* do a particular activity, or even whether they *can* do it. Instead, they seek out a variety of life experiences and activities that can enrich their children's relationships with peers and boost their self-confidence and skills. Then they find out *how to make it possible* for their children to take part. By making sure their kids share experiences with their able-bodied peers, Liz and Kelsey give the message—to their kids and others—that their children are "regular kids," neither on higher nor lower planes than their classmates and friends.

Communicating Confidence in Your Child

Communicating confidence in your children's ability to cope, to thrive, and to achieve adult goals is essential to encouraging their dreams. You can open doors for your child by giving her the message that she has the potential to achieve her goals.

One young woman, who developed quadriplegia from a spinal cord injury at age 12, recalls that right after her injury, "I wanted no part of

the life I was enduring and selfishly tried to drag my family into the misery that was overwhelming me. But they refused to go along, challenging me to reach for more than I was willing to believe was possible."

Sam, on the other hand, wishes his parents had praised him more when he was a young boy living with the effects of polio. Sam, now a grandfather himself, advises parents to "pump up your child's self-esteem. Don't give up on the child; they look to their parents to see if they're valuable."

Donny is 13 and has a disorder affecting muscle and joint growth. When he worries about what he can do when he grows up, his parents remind him that his abilities and skills can change as he grows. They encourage him to think about a wide range of possibilities in life.

Recognizing and reinforcing your children's unique assets—intellectual abilities, character strengths, or special talents—is another way to build their confidence. Focusing on your child's positive attributes and abilities can also help him learn to speak up for himself and guide him toward a career or life plan that puts his best qualities to use.

Lynn and Jessie's daughter has multiple physical disabilities but is intellectually gifted, and they have encouraged her intellectual strivings. "She's an awesome student," says Lynn. From her experience teaching her daughter, Lynn has come to appreciate "what learning really is. . . . I let her go with her interests. She reads philosophy, politics, and history books. She's in a gifted youth program and takes math and language courses taught by an Ivy League college. I've learned not to sell her short!"

Some character traits, while "difficult" in the younger years, may help a child strive for independence and self-determination when she is older. Diane recognizes this in her daughter, Rochelle, who has OI. Always "strong willed and determined" as a toddler, Rochelle needed to be watched carefully to prevent accidental injuries. But now that Rochelle is almost a teenager, Diane can see that these character traits "will serve her well in the long run."

Balancing Dreams and Limitations

Encouraging your child to find a balance between "thinking big" on the one hand and realistically sizing up his abilities on the other will help him make career plans and choose hobbies in which he can be successful. Pointing out that everyone is limited in some ways and sharing the history of your own life choices and compromises can sometimes be helpful.

Priscilla Brandon says that she always told her son who has spina bifida "to follow his dreams." However, "when he said he wanted to be a baseball player, we said, 'Let's get a bat and a ball—but remember that I wanted to be a ballerina, but I didn't have the physique or the discipline. I can still have the love of ballet and enjoy it, but it's not for me to do. Just remember if you can't be on a baseball team, you can still love the sport and play it on your own.' "

Priscilla's example works for both able-bodied children and those who have disabilities. As Rhoda Olkin points out, most people don't have the height to play professional basketball or the flexibility to be an acrobat, but neither do they "dwell on these 'limitations.' We all get what we get and then cope with what we've got."

Parents may want to err on the side of letting their kids have their dreams, even if they seem unrealistic at first. If you give your children the opportunity to work toward their dreams or goals, they will find their own "ceiling" through trial and error. More than likely, they will get frequent "reality checks" from other people who point out their inability to meet certain goals—and they will have to make adjustments. But when you listen to your child and encourage her to think creatively and fully explore her interests, she may find a way to realize her dream, in some fashion. Children whose interests and talents are valued by their parents (or other adults) may be able to use their intellect or personality traits to pursue careers or hobbies that would otherwise be closed to them because of their physical disabilities. This is one way to reach the middle ground between dreams and limits.

Sam says he "had great teachers" who saw his talents and potential and who helped open doors for him. "I wanted to be a lacrosse player, but I couldn't play sports, so I became the scorer and manager and did the team's laundry." As a young adult, Sam's intellect, good communication, and social skills allowed him to "identify bridges, key into society, establish presence, give value, and find a way to connect with others." He built a successful, multifaceted career, got married, had a family, and contributed to society at large.

Eliza, a young adult who has cerebral palsy (CP), comes from a family that values academic achievement. Although Eliza has mobility limitations, she is a good writer and has used her talents as the editor of her campus newspaper. She wants to become a newspaper or book editor after acquiring a graduate degree in English. Eliza sees herself "living a good life on my own, not relying on my parents."

Providing Positive Role Models

Donny's dad says that, at 13, "he's getting to an age where it would be eye-opening for him to meet some adults who also have a disability. It would help him see what other people are capable of and expand his horizons."

Finding positive adult role models for your children (besides yourself) can expose them to different interests, hobbies, and occupations. For all children, having adult role models from different backgrounds, including both able-bodied adults and those who have disabilities, leads to appreciation of diversity, debunks stereotypes, and increases tolerance. But when a child is the only person in his family who has a physical disability, exposure to adults who have disabilities may be especially helpful for him. Ideally, when introducing your children to an adult who has a disability, you want to choose someone whom you admire and respect as a total person—not only because of his or her success in living with a disability—and who can be a role model for your able-bodied children as well. If you don't have a friend who has a disability, you may need to introduce your child to disability organizations or recreational events where adults who have disabilities are active.

Lance, a high school wheelchair athlete, was unique in his school. His same-age peers were able-bodied teenagers whose opportunities for success in athletics were much more varied than his. When Lance started traveling with a wheelchair cycling team, he met adult athletes who had disabilities, who introduced him to the excitement of competitive cycling and provided role models for success as a differently abled cyclist.

Giving Your Child Responsibility

Having consistent expectations for responsibility instills confidence and is crucial in preparing your child for independent adult roles—work, parenthood, and managing a home. Along with insisting that their children do for themselves, some parents find it helpful to remind their kids that they won't be around to "be there" for them forever. This can spark a series of discussions about the habits and responsibilities the children must cultivate to be independent and a realistic exploration of the kinds of resources and assistance they will need after leaving home.

Candy, a college sophomore who has CP, says, "I am who I am today mostly because my parents refused to baby me. They didn't spoil me or treat me like I couldn't do anything. They made me do what I could. My dad's motto was, 'Seize the day!' They expected me to try new things and work hard." Candy sometimes got angry when her parents wouldn't help her, but now she thinks she's a stronger person because they made her do everything she could for herself. "My parents made me accountable—just because I'm in a wheelchair didn't mean I could get off easy on responsibilities." Candy's mom also encouraged her to go to social events, telling her, "I won't always be here to hold your hand—you need to make friends your own age."

Like Candy's mom, Liz expected her daughter Janet, who has spina bifida, to have responsibilities as she was growing up—to help care for her younger sib, practice her musical instrument, do some light housekeeping chores, and cook dinner once a week. But Liz says that, even though Janet was "determined to be independent and go to college, she wouldn't always take care of herself." Her mom sent Janet for counseling as a teen, to help her become more responsible for her own physical care.

Sometimes it's hard for parents to keep up consistent expectations for their child who has a physical disability. It's tempting to cave in, when you see your child struggling. Liz notes that it took "patience and stamina" for her to "stick with the program" with Janet, "but the result was worthwhile," as Janet is now an independent, married woman.

Sam's family also assigned chores for him as well as his able-bodied brothers. "I had work to do—a lot was expected of me." These responsibilities contributed to his strong work ethic and self-confidence, which served Sam well as an adult with a challenging career and a family.

Giving your child responsibility in any area of life will help build his belief in himself. Although she may have only a small range of responsibilities at home, your child's definition of herself as a *responsible person* will tend to spread into other areas of her life. As they grow, kids who were given responsibilities at home will be more comfortable accepting the variety of responsibilities they need to take on adult roles in the future.

For example, older siblings who help care for younger ones—babysitting, driving them to school, or helping them with homework—learn important adult skills, such as safety awareness, being on time, and communicating their expertise to others. These can help them succeed in college, on the job, and when they become parents. Summer jobs for teenagers, whether they are paid or volunteer, give them another chance to increase their range of responsible behavior. Although jobs are harder to find for teens who have disabilities, you may be able to help your teen find volunteer or paid work in a friend's business, at a local hospital or non-profit organization, or in his or her high school's office or library. Many parents pay their teens for babysitting younger sibs or doing other chores around the house. This is another way to reinforce their sense of responsibility and prepare them for adulthood.

Allowing Your Child to Take Risks

Helping your children assess and take some risks and gradually take on responsibility for the consequences of their risk taking is another way to work toward independence. These risks can be social, emotional, or physical. All children benefit from "stretching" themselves by risking rejection in an attempt to make a new friend, ask for a date, apply to a difficult academic program, or participate in a sport where there is a small risk of getting hurt. Parents find it particularly daunting to let their children who have physical disabilities take risks, especially when bodily harm may result. But, like all children, these kids need to explore the limits of their bodies, minds, and emotions—and find their own comfort zone for acceptable risk.

Jon recalls that he never rode a bike as a child, because of the risk of falling and breaking a bone. But he was allowed to make this decision himself. "I was pretty intuitive about what would hurt. I wasn't stopped from doing things by my family." Jon believes that "kids need to do normal things" and that parents shouldn't be so protective that they prevent them from doing any activity that poses a small degree of risk. Jalah, Jon's mom, who also has OI, agrees with him that "you need to let your child set their own limits."

The same applies to social and emotional risks. When your daughter who uses a wheelchair wants to ask a boy she likes to the junior prom, she is risking the pain of rejection, just like her able-bodied sister or friends.

But only by asking does she have any chance of success! You can help boost her confidence and, if she does not succeed at first, encourage her to try again. It's important to remember the old saying "nothing ventured, nothing gained."

Teaching Your Children to Ask for Help

Teaching your child to ask for help might seem like an exercise in dependence, but knowing when and how to ask for help is actually critical to the psychological and social *in*dependence of all children. Children who are not encouraged to ask for help when they need it—or who are pressured to "be strong"—may reject assistance and suffer needlessly.

Sam had polio as a child but was never told what was wrong with him or what to expect. He learned to "fight" his disability, hoping "others didn't see me limping so they wouldn't pity me. I wouldn't dream of being a burden. I didn't use assistive devices until I was 45 years old."

Had Sam been given a more positive message about the use of assistive devices (such as his crutches) as tools for independence and freedom, he might have walked more efficiently or with less pain.

Knowing when and how to get help in a variety of situations (not just with physical activities) is a basic part of becoming an adult. For example, when your able-bodied son is away at college and starts failing a math class, you won't be there to help him. To solve this problem, he needs to find out where he can get help on campus—perhaps from a tutor, teaching assistant, or a fellow student—and he needs the social skills to explain his need, ask for help, and use it most effectively. When your child has a physical disability, he is likely to need the same types of help as his able-bodied peers. But if he also needs physical assistance on a regular basis, learning how to ask for help will be essential to his ability to function without parents.

As a parent, you can help your growing child develop an awareness of what she can do on her own and what she needs help with and make sure she has an accurate understanding of her physical and medical care needs. You can "reframe" your child's ability to ask for help as a sign of his increasing knowledge, competence, and maturity. You and others who help your child while she's growing up can teach her how to direct her care, so that by the time she is an adolescent, your child will be able to tell another person exactly *what* she needs done and exactly *how* to do it—

for example, the methods used for bladder care or for safe transfers in and out of her wheelchair.

Of course, you also need to teach your child when it is *not* appropriate or necessary to ask for help and encourage him to do as much as he can reasonably do for himself.

Special Considerations for Launching a Teen Who Has a New Disability

When your child acquires a physical disability in the teen years, you have less time to prepare him for living successfully as an adult and coping with his disability. Although a teenager already has more life experiences and social connections than a child who acquires a disability in elementary school, it may be hard for him to leave the nest so soon after experiencing this life-changing event.

This is partly because, in most families, control gradually shifts from parents to child during the teen years—but this process is delicate and easily disrupted by stressful events. When a physical disability unexpectedly enters the picture, both teens and parents experience feelings of loss and anxiety that can interfere with the progress of this normal transition. Families tend to revert to an earlier mode of interacting—with parents grabbing the opportunity to take back control and teens taking advantage of the chance to be relieved of difficult responsibilities.

Felicity is a young woman who has paraplegia from a spinal cord injury at 19. After her injury, Felicity recalls that she "regressed in my parents' eyes." Her parents started treating her more like a child than a teenager about to leave home, constantly nagging her to "take my medicine, push myself harder, do more exercises!" rather than allowing her to be responsible for herself.

Ashley had a similar experience. She had a car accident at 17 and developed weakness and difficulty walking, ultimately diagnosed as a spinal cord injury. Because her family felt sad about her accident and disability and wanted to protect her, "they treated me like a child."

If you can resist the temptation to treat your injured teen as if he had suddenly become a toddler again, he will be more likely to continue on his course toward psychological and social independence, despite his physical impairments. When you help your teen with her physical care, you may be reminded of how you cared for her in early childhood and the tender, protective emotions you felt back then. But it's important to remember that your child is still the same teenager he was before his injury—intellectually, socially, and emotionally. While you may need to help her or to "cut her some slack" with physical chores or jobs she can't do as efficiently (or at all), you can help your teen to maintain her steps toward social and psychological maturity—and to keep herself moving forward.

Making a Plan

By the time they are teenagers, each of your children should be putting together a practical plan (with your assistance) for venturing out into the world beyond the family—to college, vocational training, work, or another productive adult role—and becoming independent in managing daily life activities, health needs, and social life. This plan should include vocational goals (such as getting an education, a job, or a volunteer position), social goals (such as dating, living with friends or roommates, traveling, or getting married), and recreational goals (such as involvement in sports, arts, or hobbies), as well as an assessment of the economic, social, and other resources your child needs to achieve those goals.

"Slow down and get to know your children individually. How can you support and help them build their individuality? Strategize, triage, and help them reach what they want." —Mary, a mom

When your child is a teenager, you should answer these questions together: What is my child's plan for the immediate future? Where does she see herself five or ten years from now? What skills and resources does he need to make his goals possible? If one of your children has a physical disability, you may have an additional layer of questions: Will my child need physical assistance from others (such as a PCA or part-time aid) in order to live away from home? Will he need special accommodations or technological aids at college or in the workplace? Does she need disability-specific education on sexuality or birth control? Once you have answered these questions, your child's plans for the future will start to take shape. Then you can set about finding the resources and providing the specific tools she needs to reach her goals.

Getting Off the Ground

Most teenagers begin to plan for their immediate post–high school future by talking to their parents and scouting the Internet to find the most compatible colleges or job placements. Arthur, a young father who has benign congenital hypotonia, points out the benefits of "seeking the counsel of other people in making choices about education, and what to focus on." Teachers, guidance counselors, peers, clergy, and extended family members can act as "consultants" to help you and your teenager figure out the best educational or vocational path.

Most teenagers have no major health problems, and just making sure they have health insurance through their parents, school, or employer is sufficient to send them on their way. But for a teenager who has a physical disability, relocating for college or work may necessitate finding a new doctor or health care team who has expertise in their particular disability. As importantly, these teenagers, especially if they have acquired a disability recently, need to become familiar with laws that protect their rights to equal education and employment and with the resources (such as offices for students who have disabilities, which exist on most college campuses, and departments of vocational rehabilitation, which exist in every state) that can ensure they get the best education or training.

Landing Gear: Tools for Independent Living

Getting your child ready for success "on the ground" requires motivation, determination, and *information*! Familiarity with resources is essential to open the doors of opportunity for your child. In the rest of this chapter, we discuss how you can help your child participate in the essential activities of adult life that parents of able-bodied children take for granted—social and recreational pursuits, education, vocational training, dating and intimate relationships—and teach them to manage their own medical and health needs. Along the way, we give some examples of parents using their skills as public advocates to improve access and inclusion for their own kids—helping others in the process.

Social Life and Recreation

"Lance has had one best friend since fourth grade," says his mom, April. But he has not been included in many social activities with his peers.

"He doesn't get invited to parties; he has never been to a birthday party," says April. Lance and his parents have put more energy into his involvement with athletics as a wheelchair cyclist, but even in this arena, Lance's social connections have been mostly with adults, not other teens.

Kids like Lance, who use wheelchairs or crutches, face architectural barriers to attending birthday parties and other social events, but attitudinal barriers are more likely a factor when a child who has a disability is never even *invited* to a birthday party. How can you help your kids get included in the social life of their peers? Some parents take the lead, by regularly inviting their child's classmates to their home (or another accessible location) for playdates, parties, and sleepovers. Others talk to the parents of their child's classmates or teammates and answer questions about their child's disability, to put them at ease. If your child is invited to a friend's party at a location that is not accessible, you can suggest an alternative venue that is. But when that is not possible, you might be able to "bump" your child up the steps in her wheelchair.

"The accessibility issue is big. It's like you don't belong and in general things aren't made for you." —Pili, a mom

Teaching and modeling social skills for your child, such as how to start up and how to take turns in a conversation, will make him a more attractive playmate or friend. If you have helped her develop varied interests—so she has something to share with other kids—your child will have an easier time joining in with social groups. Because kids who have disabilities often have extra "appendages," like wheelchairs or crutches that draw negative attention, it's helpful (especially in the teen years) for them to dress according to the latest fashion trends and express themselves through clothing and accessories that they and their friends think are cool.

It's also important to talk to your child about how things are going with his peer group and friends. Bullying has become an unfortunately common problem for school-age kids, and your child who has a physical disability may be picked on or bullied at school and need encouragement to talk about it and to let you help him find solutions. Or he may be trying to connect to other kids through inappropriate means, such as becoming the aggressor in school or on the playground. He might try to get attention by being the class clown but never make friends with an individual classmate. You can work directly with your child's teacher to create a more accepting atmosphere in her classroom, to encourage social interaction between your child and her classmates during recess or team projects, and/or to help your child learn better ways to initiate social contacts and make friends.

It may also help to explore places for your child to meet and socialize with peers, outside of school. Taking music, art, or swimming lessons; joining 4-H, the Y, or a scouting troop; and going to summer camp are some examples.

The earlier you begin supporting your child's social relationships with peers, the better. Friendships and recreational activities help kids develop essential social and communication skills. When your child has a variety of social opportunities early in life, he is more likely to develop mature social skills and have more enjoyable relationships as an adult. Encouraging your teenagers—whether able-bodied or who have disabilities—to participate in social activities and develop friendships will help them build the social support they need to make their transition to independence.

Encourage your kids to be a part of whatever their peers are doing—at school, at their community center, or in their neighborhood. Creating a skit for a talent night at school, going to the school dances with a group of kids, or asking a girl for a date may be challenging for your child, but with your help, he can find a way to participate.

When transportation to special events (like a scouting trip) is a problem, your child may be able to find a sponsor to provide an accessible bus or van. If he can travel in a car but cannot drive, he may be able to get a ride with another teen or a parent.

Finding recreational activities and sports that work for your child who has a disability can sometimes be challenging. As we have shown throughout this book, many kids who have disabilities participate in swimming, baseball, cycling, horseback riding, skiing, and other sports, either with or without special equipment or accommodations. Many recreational organizations, for example, the Boy Scouts, Girl Scouts, 4-H, and YMCA programs, are open to children who have physical disabilities. These kids deserve equal rights to be part of mainstream groups and teams. Parents sometimes have to step in to advocate for their inclusion. When joining an inte-

Advocating for Inclusion

When Judy saw the obstacles her son faced after becoming a wheelchair user, she was determined to open up the world to him. After tackling the accessibility problems in her own home to allow him more freedom to get around in the house, Judy began to identify barriers in and out of their neighborhood. Armed with the knowledge of what was needed, she searched funding sources in the county and advocated at public meetings for curb cuts to be placed at various intersections, so that her son could travel from block to block in his wheelchair without assistance. Ultimately, Judy campaigned for a playground in her neighborhood; its universal design allowed both able-bodied kids and those who have physical disabilities to play together. Judy became a powerful role model for her son; as a teenager, he started his own advocacy website for people who have physical disabilities.

Advocating for Access

Tony's son relied on the para-transit system to get around, since they couldn't afford a wheelchair van. Tony was fed up with frequent bus delays and cancellations that caused his son to arrive late to class parties and Saturday swim sessions at his local pool, which were his main opportunities to socialize with friends and meet girls. Tony joined his county's commission for people who have disabilities and led a campaign to reform transportation services for citizens who have disabilities in his city. With an increase in the number of para-transit buses and more frequent stops, Tony's son and others relying on the system gained better access to their favorite social and recreational activities.

grated ability group is not feasible, your child can gain access to a variety of activities through organizations devoted specifically to adaptive sports, recreation, and camping experiences. (Many of these are listed in the Resource section of this book.) For some kids, this feels like segregation and stigmatizing; but for those who are comfortable joining in, it feels liberating. You should discuss this with your kids and honor their preferences and reasoning. If your child needs such extensive assistance that only a special disability program will enable his participation in sports or recreation, it is probably beneficial for him to give it a try. Being with other kids who have physical disabilities is a supportive experience for some kids and can potentially bolster your child's self-image and give him perspective on his particular disability.

Education

ACCESSIBILITY Several important federal laws protect the rights of people who have disabilities and ensure access to education and vocational opportunities. The Individuals with Disabilities Education Act of 1990, which was revised in 1997, requires schools to provide a free and appropriate education to all children who have disabilities. School systems must make reasonable accommodations (that is, modifications in the way children are taught, the amount of assistance they are given, the technologies they use to do their work, and so forth). Children who have physical disabilities cannot simply be sent to a "special school," but must be included in mainstream education (regular classrooms and schools) whenever possible. This is consistent with the concept of raising children in the "least restrictive environment" and allows them to share as fully as possible in the same educational opportunities that are available to able-bodied children. Schools must be made physically accessible to children who have disabilities, or if they cannot be fully accessible, then accommodations must be made. For example, if your child who uses a wheelchair goes to a public high school with multiple floors, there must be an elevator, or the school must offer any class your child wants to take on the first floor of the building.

Some parents of children who have physical disabilities choose to do homeschooling, sometimes for the same religious, practical, or philosophical reasons that parents homeschool their able-bodied children. While homeschooling allows parents to individually tailor their child's educational program and avoids certain hassles, like transportation to school, it may make it even harder for your child to form friendships or learn the social skills he will need to live independently as a young adult. (If your child has been attending public school and develops a new disability, he may qualify for home tutoring through the school system during his period of recovery from acute illness or trauma.)

ACCOMMODATIONS Your child's physical disability may not be obvious to the school, especially if she is able to walk without assistance. Perhaps she

☞ Even if your child is in his senior year of high school when he has a disabling injury or illness, it is helpful to go through this process with the school, because an IEP can be your child's "ticket" to use her college's disability services and may be used by the college to begin planning for your child's needs even before she arrives on campus.

has weakness in her hands and needs to use a computer for writing or a tape recorder to "take notes" in class. Or perhaps he has difficulty with bladder control and needs permission to use the bathroom on demand. These issues—and any other special needs related to your child's disability—should be brought to the attention of the school, so your child can be evaluated for accommodations. The school is obligated to evaluate your child's abilities, disabilities, and medical needs (sometimes using outside experts, such as your child's doctor or physical therapist). Within thirty days of the school's deciding that your child is eligible for services, they will prepare an Individualized Educational Plan (IEP). This written document describes your child's needs, based on professional evaluations and your input as a parent, and details the school services or accommodations that will be provided to meet them. Parents are included in the initial and subsequent IEP meetings; discussion of the plan and your agreement with the recommendations are necessary for implementation. If you and the school cannot come to an agreement about what your child needs, you may seek independent medical evaluations, use mediation services, or ask for a hearing. The IEP is reviewed periodically and can change over time as your child's needs change; keeping the school informed about changes you believe are necessary is vital to the process.

HELPERS, ATTENDANTS, AND AIDES Kids who have physical disabilities and need physical assistance or accommodations at college can usually find resources on campus. Almost all colleges in the United States now have an office on disability to serve students who have special needs. While there is no obligation to report a physical disability during the application process, students who are admitted to a college should contact the disability office as soon as they enroll—especially if they will need regular assistance (such as a personal care assistant, a reader, a person to help transport them on campus, special access to elevators). Early planning will help avoid situations where your child is stuck in his dorm room without an aide to get him ready for class, or has to spend the first two weeks of the semester "bumming" rides from classmates who can push his wheelchair to classes across campus. As Arthur points out, it's important to "accommodate the disability without making it a distraction."

In some cases, your state's department of vocational rehabilitation (see the next section) will work with your child's college to arrange for a personal care attendant (PCA), ensure that your child has access to dormitories and classes, or provide other types of special assistance. For teens like Jason, who has spina bifida, a PCA is a necessity at college—or anywhere he goes without parents around to provide his care.

Kevin, who has quadriplegia from a car accident, emphasizes the importance of hiring one's own attendant, rather than relying on a family member to provide personal care. If your child needs a PCA, learning how to negotiate his relationship with the attendant and to hire, fire, and arrange backup care is essential to his success in college and/or the work world. Your child's relationship with his PCA requires a certain amount of emotional distance (your child is the employer/boss, the PCA is the employee) but can feel quite close in terms of the intimate personal care the PCA provides. While having a respectful relationship with one's PCA is a good thing, your child needs to be aware that problems will result if their roles become blurred by romantic or sexual entanglements, or if he and the PCA become too emotionally involved in each other's lives.

Vocational Training and Employment

Not all kids who have disabilities go to college; some will transition to the work world right after high school. And many who do go to college

☞ A listing of every state's vocational department can be found on the U.S. Government Department of Education website: www.workworld.org/wwwebhelp/state_vocational_rehabilitation_vr_agencies.htm.

will need assistance finding a job afterward. There are several sources for vocational training and job placement that may be helpful for kids with either a high school or a college diploma.

Each state in the United States has a department of vocational rehabilitation (sometimes called "vocational services") whose mission is to help people who have disabilities become employed.

Any adult who has a disability is eligible for services. Benefits vary but may include evaluation of work skills and preferences, financial assistance with job training programs, partial payment of college tuition, assistance with job placement, and help negotiating accommodations with an employer.

Private, fee-for-service vocational rehabilitation and/or employment agencies and those located in freestanding rehabilitation centers, faith-based family service agencies, and nonprofit community agencies (such as Goodwill Industries) may also be helpful. If your child is enrolled at a college, the office on disability may provide career or job counseling and a job bank or list.

In addition to helping your child gain access to these vocational services, you can help prepare your child for working life by discussing a variety of career options. Your child who has a physical disability should be encouraged to follow his dreams, but you can also help her find a match between her interests and goals on the one hand and her abilities and disabilities on the other. Donny's parents, for instance, want him to

☞ Your child may also be eligible for vocational services through your state's Department of Developmental Disabilities. A listing for each state is available through the federal Administration on Developmental Disabilities: www.acf.hhs.gov/programs/add/state.html. Although the term "developmental disability" is often used to mean a disability that impairs cognitive function, it can also refer to any disability that begins before the age of 21.

know that there are "many choices he will have in life." But they tend to praise Donny for his intellectual abilities and social skills and have encouraged him to think about a career that relies on "brain power," like teaching. Donny is fascinated with engines and, like many boys, would like to be a mechanic or work on race cars. His parents support this interest but have suggested that he think about becoming an engineer or automotive designer, since his ability to use his hands is limited.

Susan, a young woman who has paraplegia, says she was interested in becoming a large animal veterinarian before her injury. After her injury, she rethought her options. She wanted to do something interesting and make a good income, "knowing I'd always have to work sitting down," so she "picked a practical major" (information technology) in college.

Teaching your children about disability laws, especially the Americans with Disabilities Act (ADA), can help them understand and take advantage of their legal rights in the areas of employment (the ADA also addresses access to public services and transportation). The ADA was signed into law in 1990, but its application continues to evolve based on new legal challenges. It provides protection against discrimination in hiring based on disability status and mandates that employers make reasonable accommodations for an employee who has a disability, as long as he can do the basic functions of his job. As a young adult applying for her first job, it's particularly important to know how to avoid discrimination in employment, beginning with the first interview. While employers may ask whether she can do the basic functions of the job (for example, can she use a computer for word processing), asking questions about your daughter's health or disability status is not allowed during the interview stage. Once offered the job, your son or daughter can decide whether to request accommodations (for example, a voice activation program or modified keyboard for the computer). There is no requirement to divulge any more information about one's health than is necessary to justify the request for these accommodations. Keeping abreast of the current interpretations of the ADA and other disability laws can add to your child's success in the work world (see the Resources section for the ADA website).

Managing Medical and Physical Care

Scott, whose stepdaughter Celeste has OI, wants her to enjoy the independence of driving a car but worries about "who gets to her after a crash. Will the paramedics know how to treat a woman with OI?" Similarly, when he thinks of her going to college and living independently, he anticipates "no problems when she is healthy" but worries that if she has a bone break, she may not be able to fend for herself. While he thinks that a PCA might solve the problem, he still hopes she'll go to college close to home, so he and his wife can be her "emergency backup plan." His wife, Evelyn, on the other hand, is less concerned and thinks Celeste can go to college wherever she wants.

As they get older, giving your children some basic education about common health problems and gradually allowing them to have more input on medical and treatment decisions will help them learn how their bodies work, develop their own values and preferences regarding medical care, and ultimately take over responsibility for their own health management.

Jon, an adult with OI, says, "I appreciate that my family included me in treatment decisions, that they were straightforward and honest. That built trust. Parents should let kids be a large part of the decision-making team."

By the time *any* child goes to college or leaves home for a job, he should know how to take care of minor health problems himself and when to seek professional care. Every young adult should be able to recognize symptoms of strep throat, allergic reaction, and common viral infection; clean and dress a cut or scrape; be aware of situations that need emergency medical attention; know which over-the-counter medicines to take for minor illnesses; and so forth. Young people should also know about how to prevent illness—through regular exercise, weight control, moderate alcohol use, and safe sex. In addition to these basics, children who have physical disabilities need information specific to their physical or medical conditions; they have a right to be told the truth about their disability and will benefit from understanding the full range of medical and rehabilitation options available to them.

Ken's family began asking his opinions about his medical treatment when he was in elementary school. Although they made the ultimate decisions then, it was clear to Ken that his input and preferences were valued and taken into consideration. When Ken was in high school, the doctor proposed an operation that would have taken him out of school for half of his senior year. The family convened to look at all the pros and cons of the operation and considered its impact on Ken's life. They left the final decision up to Ken, figuring that he was old enough to make decisions about his own body. Ken didn't think the time away from friends and school was a good trade-off, since the potential improvement offered by the operation was small and there were some substantial risks. So he opted against it.

As part of the transition to adulthood, teens who have disabilities should become knowledgeable and responsible about their own health issues, developing a collaborative relationship with their health care providers. As parents, you played a role as a partner in your child's health care team; now it is up to your child to become part of the team herself. Teens can be encouraged to do things such as ordering their own catheter supplies, refilling medications, and scheduling their own medical appointments. Even before the teen years, all children can be given some responsibility for health behaviors (like doing exercises) and taught to do some of their own medical care (for example, using a glucometer to monitor blood sugar or taking regular medications independently). In fact, when kids establish a good routine of self-care before the teen years, they may be less likely to use neglect of their self-care as a means of rebellion against parents.

Connie, an able-bodied 21-year-old, was on a cycling trip miles from home when she suddenly came down with a severe sore throat. "I remembered my mom telling me how strep throat can go 'dormant' and later you can get kidney problems. I sort of heard her voice in my head saying, 'Get checked!' So I went to a local clinic right away. And it was a good thing, because I needed antibiotics."

Connie had both the information about the dangers of sore throat and the skills to find a health care clinic in an unfamiliar city. She did not need to call home for help, because she had been adequately coached by her mother in the past and knew what to do.

When your child has a physical disability, she will need to know all of these things—and more. Understanding his unique medical or physical vulnerabilities and knowing how to care for routine physical problems are essential. Celeste, for example, will need to learn how to manage her OI while she is away from home, especially what to do if she breaks a bone. On her own, or with her parents' input, she can create a plan that might include which doctor or hospital to call, when to call an ambulance, where she will recuperate, and how she will complete school assignments during her recovery. Celeste could carry an emergency information card with her at all times, giving basic information about OI, a website address for more information, the phone number for her primary doctor, and some basic steps for how to treat her in an emergency like a car crash. Most importantly, Celeste's knowledge of her physical and medical care needs should be so complete that she can explain to any health care provider what she needs.

Taking care of medical equipment is also important—for example, regularly cleaning a continuous positive airway pressure (CPAP) device or other respiratory machine, checking wheelchairs for loose screws or deflated tires, keeping the battery charged on an electric scooter, or checking for worn-down crutch tips. Once away from home, a young adult will need to be familiar with companies that service his special equipment and can supply backups while his equipment is being repaired.

Sexuality, Dating, and Marriage

Donny, a 13-year-old who has a muscle disorder, just went to his first boy-girl party. He wants to get married and become a dad someday. Priscilla wondered whether her son Jason, who has spina bifida, would get a date for his senior prom. Sean hopes his daughter, a college senior who has CP, will find a marriage partner to share her life with. And Elsie is "concerned about my grandson finding someone to love him and to have a family."

Sexuality, dating, and marriage are essential aspects of adulthood. Most parents look forward to the day when their son or daughter gets married and starts a family. Parents want their child to have the fulfillment and security of a loving partnership—and they want to become grandparents!

But kids who have physical disabilities often face barriers to dating, sexual intimacy, and finding a marriage partner. They are bombarded with media images of physical "perfection" and may feel—even more than able-bodied kids, who also struggle to fit in—that they are unattractive or unlovable. As a parent, your acceptance of your child as a sexual being and your expectation that he will find a mate are essential in counteracting social stereotypes. You can help your child feel that she is lovable and has the qualities and abilities to be a good and competent partner or spouse.

> "I want to walk down the aisle at my wedding, want to dance with my husband."
> —Ashley, a young woman with paraplegia

Teens who have physical disabilities may have fewer opportunities for sexual "play" or experimentation than able-bodied kids and teens, and the standard sex education curriculum does not address all of their particular needs and concerns. Though teenagers who have disabilities have the same risks as other teens for getting a sexually transmitted disease or having an unplanned pregnancy, their ability to use the usual methods of prevention may be limited, requiring special education and coaching. Teens who have disabilities, especially girls, are also vulnerable to sexual exploitation and need to be taught to recognize and avoid sexual manipulation or abuse.

You can help promote your child's sexual health by filling in the gaps in her sex education, preferably before she becomes sexually active. Many parents talk with their kids about the "birds and the bees" before they reach puberty, as part of preparing them for the physical and emotional changes they will soon experience. Immunization against the sexually transmitted diseases hepatitis B and human papillomavirus are given routinely to boys and girls in middle school; these vaccinations can be springboards to conversations with your child about sexuality and dating.

Beyond the basics of safe sex and birth control, it's important to convey the information and values about love and relationships that you feel are essential, to share your hope that your child will one day have a loving relationship or marriage, and to educate your child (or help him find resources for education) about any sexual health or sexual function issues related to his particular disability.

Listen to your child's point of view, try to understand the attitudinal and physical barriers that make dating difficult for your child, and work with him to find solutions. This is another place where adult role models—individuals who have physical disabilities who are in intimate relationships, are married, and have children—can be helpful to your child.

> "I would like to get married—although I would like to return home for the holidays like a normal person!"
> —Eliza, a young woman with CP

Alma was dating Lenny, and they were thinking about marriage and children. Alma worried about how she would care for babies because she used crutches and braces. She remembered meeting Lauren, another young woman who walked with crutches, at a conference the previous year. She had heard from mutual friends that Lauren had recently had a baby. So Alma asked Lauren if she could visit her; she hoped to see how Lauren managed to care for her baby. Alma saw that Lauren had a lower, side-opening crib, allowing her to sit down to care for the baby. She could easily transfer him to a stroller, which she pushed around the house with her abdomen. Lauren was a happy and confident new mom. This visit gave Alma the confidence that she could manage being a mother, too. A few weeks after the visit, Alma and Lenny got engaged.

"When I'm 29, I want to be working as an engineer, be a professional hand cyclist, and be married— possibly with children."
—Lance, a young man with paraplegia

The Next Step (for Mom and Dad)

Now that your kids are embarking on their own lives, you can take a moment to savor their incredible accomplishments—and your own! As your child who has a disability becomes an adult—not fully formed, but with definite personality characteristics and more mature ideas—you may be amazed by all that he *can* do. But as you did when you first found out that your child had a disability, you will once again have to reconcile the ideal with the real, let go of some old dreams, and celebrate the reality of your young adult child, with all his strengths and challenges.

In the next chapter, we explore this letting go—how parents move on from full-time parenting and gradually shift the focus from their children to themselves. Parents reflect on the personal growth they've experienced in the process of raising children, as well as the new process of building a life for themselves that goes beyond parenting.

The O'Briens: Parents working together to help their daughters develop individual talents, support one another, and practice their faith

Leigh and Sean met in college; they married right after Leigh's graduation and Sean started his military career. Leigh got pregnant sooner than expected. It was a difficult time for her; she missed going skiing or having a drink with Sean at the officers' club. It was a "downer" to have so little time as a young couple without kids, yet they were excited about starting a family. Because Sean's career involved frequent travel, they agreed that Leigh would be a stay-at-home mom.

Their daughter Eliza was born prematurely at twenty-eight weeks. Sean "didn't expect the severity of what was to follow": at two days of age, Eliza had a brain hemorrhage. Sean remembers their two-and-a-half-pound baby wearing an oxygen mask; the "good news" was that she didn't need a breathing tube. Leigh remembers that "all the other mothers were moved off the maternity ward with their babies; I was not."

Eliza stayed in the hospital for a month after the hemorrhage. Doctors said that the hemorrhage would cause motor skill problems, but no specific diagnosis was given. At first Sean demanded to have all the information, but a nurse in the neonatal unit cautioned him, "You don't want to know too much." She encouraged him to let things be revealed when it was timely. That helped Sean stop dwelling on the unknowns.

Leigh's mother traveled to see them, and they assumed she would be helpful because of her experience with Leigh's brother, who had Down syndrome. But when she heard about the brain hemorrhage, she became faint. She told them, "I can't believe this is happening to *me* again." Seeing that Leigh's mother could not be helpful to them, Sean put her on a return flight. "The baggage you have either helps or hurts you," he says. Sean's older brother also had a cognitive disability, and although his family was not able to give them "hands-on" help, they were emotionally supportive to him and Leigh.

Leigh began to notice physical differences between Eliza and other babies her age, including an inability to sit up unsupported. When she was 9 months old, with Sean recently deployed overseas, Leigh took Eliza for her first physical therapy evaluation and came home with a diagnosis: cerebral palsy (CP). She remains grateful to the therapist for her honesty and remembers that it was "nice to know what it was . . . but shocking to hear it without Sean there." Sean heard the news from Leigh on a long-distance phone call; he, too, had to cope with his feelings alone.

When Sean returned home, he became actively involved with Eliza's care. He experienced his own confrontations with the medical system, finding both "saints and morons in clinical garb." After watching Eliza go through a number of operations and uncomfortable procedures, Sean learned to make his own judgments of what would be helpful to his daughter. "I always ask myself, 'Does she really need this?' " He wonders if clinicians have to numb themselves to the impact of the treatments they administer, and he respects those who remain truly caring and humane toward the children they treat.

Leigh recalls a couple of bad experiences at the hospital. There was a resident who failed to check medicines when Eliza was in pain, and an inept technician who tried to insert an IV four times—until Leigh banned her from the hospital room. But in general, Leigh experienced the medical system as supportive and helpful. When she took Eliza for therapies, she was often told, "You are so lucky to have this little girl, bright and alert." She felt that, too.

Leigh and Sean were nervous about having another child, but Eliza was very social and they wanted her to be surrounded by siblings. They were five months pregnant with their second child when Sean was deployed to combat duty. Leigh sent him photos of 2½-year-old Eliza, driving her electric wheelchair around the house, occasionally bumping into walls and furniture.

Michelle was born while Sean was overseas. She was a quiet child. "I was more scared than willing to talk to strangers." As a little girl, she had few close friends but was part of the neighborhood group. She often mediated their disputes because she was sensitive and didn't like to see people get upset.

In the first grade Michelle first recognized that her sister had a disability. Eliza attended an accessible school outside the neighborhood. For convenience, Michelle went there, too, riding the bus with children who had disabilities. She found that the kids had good senses of humor, and she liked going with them. When Eliza started middle school, Michelle enrolled in the neighborhood elementary school.

Alice joined the sisterhood five years after Michelle. Self-motivated, she was always busy, into her own projects. Two years later, Sammi was born. Sean and Leigh had consistent expectations for all four girls: study hard, attend church services, participate in sports and music, and have dinner with the family every night.

Relationships with their parents are different for each sister. Eliza says her disability made it more difficult to connect with peers, and she feels lucky to have a close relationship with her mother, whom she considers her best friend. "I tell her most of what's going on. This is not a normal thing with my other friends." Still, there have been some "on and off" moments in their relationship. Leigh would like to see Eliza, now a college graduate, take more steps toward independence and stop procrastinating about getting a job. Eliza admits she's avoiding the job hunt, which she fears will be highly stressful.

Michelle and Alice are closer to their father. Michelle's role in the family parallels Sean's role in his, the second sibling in a family where the oldest had a disability. He and Michelle each felt they had to fill the role of the "oldest," taking on extra responsibility without, as Michelle says, "getting the glory of being first." She felt that her father wanted her to do the activities with him that required physical skill, such as woodworking, that he would have done with Eliza, if it were possible. Michelle says she's the one who takes the "heat" when there is any discord among the sisters.

Alice says, "Me and my dad are closer because we share sports and our games." Sean coached many of her teams over the years. "I took the blame for things the other players did. He talked with me about that; he said I would take the blame because he couldn't say those things to the other players." Although she understood Sean's rationale, sometimes it felt unfair.

The girls know that Leigh can easily get angry or sad, but that she quickly forgets about it. Having a stay-at-home mother is appreciated because she's there to listen or to take them shopping for shoes or "things for projects." They all admit that there are certain subjects they don't discuss with their mother—and that are shared just with friends.

The sisters have had their share of fights, but these lessened as they grew and the older ones moved on to college and beyond. The younger sisters credit their older siblings for listening to them and helping them with homework.

They are sensitive to each other's feelings. Eliza says, "If I weren't around, people would be able to go off and do things. They've never made me feel that way, I just know it." Michelle says that her sister's physical disability hasn't made a difference in their day-to-day lives, but it has kept them from sharing some experiences. "I always wanted to go skiing. Obviously Eliza's disability is the reason we didn't do it. But I don't want to hurt my sister." She also feels that because of Eliza, she is more sensitive to issues such as people illegally parking in disabled parking spots; "That bothers me," she admits.

Alice adds, "I do think about the way I talk, and what I say in front of Eliza and how it must make her feel, like 'Oh I hate to go to soccer practice.' Eliza says, 'At least you can play soccer.' " Alice advises siblings not to go places where their sibling who has a disability can't go. She also recommends helping younger children to deal with unusual situations affecting their sibling who has a disability. She recalls, for example, that her little sister, Sammi, "freaked out when Eliza had surgery and they put screws in her head."

Sean and Leigh tried assigning household jobs to each of the girls (for example, putting away their laundry); however, the girls often avoided doing their chores, and Sean admits they were terrible about enforcing it. He disagrees with Leigh about this area of parenting. Sean wants the girls to help more and is willing to reward them with an allowance. But Leigh thinks it's enough if the girls are good students and athletes and keep up their musical practice, so she asks Sean not to harangue them about chores. Alice agrees that chores are too stressful, added to the pressure to keep up her grades and do well in sports. But once Eliza and Michelle departed for college, Alice helped with the lawn mowing, and Sammi with dinner.

Leigh and Sean believed in promoting physical risks that made their daughters stronger. They allowed fewer risks in social activities. The daughters could go out only in groups until age 16; then they could date, but their parents controlled where they could go.

Sean says he has tried to do the same things with all four girls, and the sisters agree that their parents give them equal attention, and "no one person is favored." Eliza's disability influenced the choice of shared family activities but didn't prevent each girl from enjoying sports and recreation. Sean says, "We live our lives. We had a routine. We got Eliza out to watch her sisters in their sports, but then she did what she wanted to do, like horseback riding." He walked her on the horse, just as he coached the younger girls' teams.

As a teenager, Eliza had treatment for scoliosis, including halo traction (using a brace screwed into the skull); this felt so unfair to Leigh, after all Eliza had been through. Sometimes Leigh finds herself thinking about the imperfect world. "Why? Why you? Why her? Sometimes I feel angry." But then Leigh says, "We are more caring, and I attribute that to Eliza. Religion gives me hope and a reason for why things are the way they are. If I didn't have my faith I would see pain, hopelessness. Every life has meaning. You give something and you get something back." Although Sean has had some conflicts about his faith, he participates with Leigh in their religious community. "The tenets of my religion have helped. When you think of Christ's life, it was perfect. He truly lived by example. That brings you back to where you need to be. He was my philosophy teacher."

The daughters also find religion meaningful. Eliza still attends church weekly. "When I got mad because life hadn't worked out the way I wanted, I thought of good things that happened. So someone up there is watching. When I need help, I say a prayer." Michelle, now a college student, goes to church with her friends, sometimes more out of habit than belief, "but I feel guilty if I don't go." She relies on her faith during times of desperation. Alice, 13, and Sammi, 11, attend church with their parents and participate in religious education classes.

Sean appreciates the rewards of raising a family that includes a child who has a disability. He tells other fathers to accept their sons and daughters as individuals, not to let others' expectations about physical disability change the way you see your children, able-bodied or not. "Don't change them," says Sean. "Realize the gift of intellect. Our daughter who has a disability has bettered our family."

Leigh says that the experience of raising Eliza "has made me the person I am. I'm not shallow or self-absorbed. I have an appreciation of what she can't do and how well she handles it. Eliza's taught me." Sean agrees, saying, "Eliza made Leigh grow up. She began to stand up for herself and the children. It made her stronger, solid on her own two feet. I can't hold a candle to her."

By the same token, Leigh thinks that "parents have a right to enjoy themselves, to take needed breaks, to be who you are, not Eliza's or Melissa's, or Alice's or Sammi's mother." She does this by running and taking long walks. Now she's looking for a part-time job, after years of being a full-time mother.

When asked her perspective on mothering a "mixed bag" family, Leigh relates the story of raising a child who has a disability to planning a trip to Rome and ending up in Holland. "It's okay to wish you were in Rome, but you would miss the tulips and windmills of Holland. We have to accept where we are."

7

Letting One Dream Go to Let Another Grow

"Looking back, I wouldn't have changed a thing. Jason's disability made me a better person."

—LEE, A FATHER

"I'm more insightful, recognizing that life is not a bed of roses but it is still good. I'm thankful I'm alive."

—SUSIE, A MOTHER

"If you are selfish, when you have a child who has a disability, your self-centeredness will go out the window."

—MIA, A MOTHER

L ife moves on and so do you! Once your children have left the nest, you begin a new phase of your journey, one in which the spotlight shifts from your children's lives to your own. Along the way, the dream of the *ideal* family has been discarded in favor of your *real* family. Your dreams for your children have been redefined, replaced by the ones *they've* dreamed for themselves—and are now making reality as they venture out into the world on their own. This is a transition point, a time to take stock, to envision what you want and to plan the next step forward in your own life. You let one dream go to let another grow, for both your children and yourself.

Swinging that spotlight from your children's lives to your own is both exciting and daunting. You may have a jumble of feelings, from sadness over the loss of your children from the nest (perhaps mixed with frustration about those who can't seem to fly away!), to pride in your children and happiness for them, to a sense of personal parental accomplishment.

For Priscilla, parenting was "the most important part of my life—

devoting time and effort to raise confident, well-educated, and happy individuals." She expected that both her children would go to college, and the whole family was overjoyed when son Jason, who has spina bifida, was admitted to a university far from home with a full scholarship. Priscilla was exhilarated by Jason's ability to move on with his life, relishing his success. "It's a huge accomplishment for him. It's normalcy, what every kids wants. He is able to do it!"

You may also feel some anxiety about how to pursue—or create—goals for your own life when responsibility for your children is no longer its chief focus. Deciding how to let your new dreams grow, using your talents and skills, is a journey to the unknown. It's filled with possibilities, but a little scary.

NOTE: Not all young adult children move out on their own entirely; some boomerang back home, especially in economically depressed times, when jobs are hard to find or may not pay enough to support an independent apartment, or when working full-time is impossible while pursuing an advanced degree. Some adult children have medical problems that bring them home, either because their parents can provide the best care or because they can't afford to hire private nurses or attendants. Dora and Ted's daughter is in her early thirties and has osteogenesis imperfecta (OI). Several times, after a medical situation requiring care, she moved into her parents' home until the problems resolved and then returned to her apartment. A key for parents in these situations is to treat returning adult children like adults—with both respect and expectations for grown-up behavior and responsibilities—and for their kids, in turn, to be respectful of their parents as people with their own lives.

If you live in a multigenerational family, you also need to have some boundaries for yourself, your grown children, and/or your parents, making sure everyone is clear about their responsibilities and that there is mutual respect for privacy. George and Elena share a home with their daughter and her family. Recently their young adult son Matt, who uses a wheelchair, returned home as he searched for a job. His parents told Matt that he would need to take his turn cooking and helping with upkeep of the house like everyone else in addition to taking care of his own personal needs. Expectations would be the same for all the adults in the family.

Looking Back at What You've Learned

Raising a child who has a physical disability offers parents opportunities for personal growth. You are forced to rethink values, change priorities, and decide just how you want to spend your finite stores of time and energy. Having a child who has a disability leads parents to shuck old ideas of "normal" or "perfect" and redefine what is worthwhile and valuable.

While parents usually dwell on how their *children* react and adjust to life's challenges, you can also benefit from looking back on *your own* track record on life's roller coaster. You'll be surprised to see the many ways you've matured; for instance, Erica points out that she became less self-absorbed and shallow. The challenges of family life spur parents to grow and develop their capacity as human beings—to become more involved, patient, tolerant, or thankful for the "small things" in life.

Reviewing the character strengths and coping skills that helped you raise your family can embolden you, providing the confidence to move forward into the next phase of life.

Confidence in Yourself

Being a parent to that mixed-bag family of able-bodied children and those who have physical disabilities, you've grown many capacities, including belief in yourself. This self-confidence developed—sometimes through trial and error—as you mastered the skills necessary to raise *all* your children and accumulated the unique knowledge and technical know-how to meet the needs of your child who has a physical disability. You've managed difficult medical and physical routines, learned the professional lingo, and made tough decisions.

In that process, you've collected a toolbox full of capabilities and "cope-abilities" to help you over the physical and emotional bumps in the road. Remember "going around the cone"—the first time an emergency or unexpected medical problem arose, and the exhaustion and self-doubt you went through? But each time you went around that "cone," you felt more confident in your ability to handle the situation because you survived the previous trip and had your own personal book of remedies. In coping with an array of problems and emergencies and—oh yes!—

triumphs, you developed your own patterns to guide you. These patterns became models for your children, too, showing them how to be proactive, to rely on experience as a guide, to be flexible in considering their options, and to act decisively in emergencies.

You've made decisions, created your own expectations of family life, adapted to unfamiliar medical and rehabilitation care routines, taken frequent detours (ramps in hidden places!), and met a slew of professionals (brace makers, surgeons, rehabilitation counselors) you never thought you'd need—all in a day's work! You are well prepared for your next steps into the world beyond parenting.

Trusting Your Instincts

Like Kelsey, whose daughter has spina bifida, you developed more trust in your own inner voice or gut instinct as time progressed. "At one point we felt something just wasn't right with our daughter, and it turned out we were correct—she needed surgery." Often "gut instinct" reflects the deep personal knowledge you have of your child—which you may not be aware of on a conscious level and can't fully explain. You just *know*. By listening to your gut or inner voice, you learned to trust your judgment about your child's condition, to know when to get help.

"Gut checks" are important not only in decisions about your children but also in many other decision-making situations. Now you can apply this tool, along with others that have worked in the past, to decisions you make about yourself in this new, more "adult-centric" stage of life.

We can judge our satisfaction with decisions we make with our brains by listening to our guts. Think back to a decision you made recently and how you felt in the pit of your stomach at the time. If you felt queasy or jittery inside, it may be because you weren't ready to make the decision owing to lack of information, or because you were making a decision for the wrong reasons—perhaps to please someone else or as a result of pressure from peers or a professional. But if your "insides" feel settled and calm after making a decision, it is probably the right one for you.

Balancing Self-Sufficiency with Help from Others

Living life well requires balance. As a parent of multiple children, one of whom has a physical disability, you've had to build self-sufficiency, resilience, and confidence in your independent judgments. This had to be balanced by a certain amount of support from others. In the beginning, you might have been uncomfortable accepting help because you felt unworthy, didn't want to feel beholden to someone else, or were afraid of being a burden. But as you recognized your limits, you learned to ask for help, allowing yourself to rely on others when necessary. Mia, a single mother whose youngest child has OI, says, "At first I had to prove I could do everything. Now I can accept help. I rely on others. You have to build your support system so you are not all by yourself." Susie, whose twins have physical disabilities, became a gracious recipient of help when she realized that she could repay that help in the future by giving the gift of her time or presence to someone else in need. Pili found her help through a support group of parents with both able-bodied children and those who have physical disabilities. "It's incredible to share your journey with parents of kids who have other disabilities."

Balancing may also involve getting professional help, which is beneficial, even to expert parents, when they are feeling bogged down by life. Opening up to a mental health professional or parenting expert helps some parents get the breathing room to assess their options in a tough situation, often leading to better understanding of the issues and a change in how they handle the problem or cope with their emotions. Emma, a teacher and now a parent herself who has spina bifida, had parents who divorced when she was young. She wishes her parents had reached out to experts. "You can't meet the needs of your family if your head is not clear, if you don't have strategies. Dealing with professionals can be a huge support for overwhelmed parents."

Professional counseling can also be useful when you first find yourself in an empty nest and feel unsure of how to get on with your life. Valerie, the mother of five children, including a son who uses a wheelchair, was a stay-at-home parent who gave up her real estate business to care for her family. When her youngest daughter left for college, Valerie felt depressed, unanchored, and useless. After some weeks of tearfulness and withdrawal from her usual social schedule, her husband encouraged her to "go talk with someone." Once she examined her feelings of loss and abandonment with her therapist, Valerie was able to see that her children felt free to "fly solo" largely because of the good job she had done as a parent. She also came to understand that the skills she had given to her children were the same ones she herself could use in this next stage of life—in order to fly on her own or in tandem with her husband.

Turning Anger into Action

You've found that the energy behind negative feelings can be used for positive results if harnessed creatively. As the parent of a child who has a physical disability, you know the frustration and anger you've felt when your child was excluded from activities, exposed to prejudice or teasing, or unable to get around barriers to play, socialize, or go to school with his peers. Although anger is usually seen as a "negative" emotion, its bound-up energy can actually be channeled into constructive action. Runner found that when he turned his anger into fuel for the fight to meet his child's medical and social needs, he was able to conquer his feelings of helplessness. An everyday "anger arouser" is the abuse of handicapped parking spaces by people who do *not* have a disability. Marian turned her ire into action by putting official-looking notices on the windshields of cars illegally parked in these spaces. It was a small constructive gesture, but she was taking action. She hoped it would make people think twice about what they were doing and perhaps change their illegal parking habits.

Some parents get angry and frustrated with the obstacles faced not only by their own children but by *all* kids who have disabilities. Their anger motivates them to advocate for better services, increase awareness, and support legislation that can improve the lives of all children. Regina, energized by her indignation at the fact that her child had no accessible entrance to the municipal pool, led a letter writing campaign to the town council, resulting in the installation of curb cuts and an accessible bathroom. Other parents have taken a similar route, writing to legislators requesting power-operated doors, accessible bus routes, special walkways into parks and recreational areas, and many other accommodations.

If you've raised a child who has a physical disability amid your brood, you may have a built-in radar screen for social justice and child welfare in general. Luke, whose teenage son was born prematurely, gets angry when other parents act without regard for the well-being of their kids, "for example, when I read an article about a pregnant woman using cocaine." Billy feels his "blood boil" when he sees parents yelling at or slapping their children. Once your own children are out on their own, you may contribute to the well-being of other children and their families, perhaps through organized political action or through one-on-one help.

Increasing Patience and Tolerance

Hard-driving parents who felt stressed when they had to adjust their busy schedules to the slower timetables of children, especially those who have physical disabilities, found that their patience grew through parenting. In addition, the external demands of the medical or rehabilitation system required them to slow down and helped them develop the ability to wait, endure, and be steady. Veteran parents say they had to "pump up" their patience and learn greater tolerance.

As the father of four daughters, Sean often felt his patience tried—and worked at increasing it. He developed the awareness that every person has "trials and tribulations"; it's the way we deal with our circumstances that determines how they affect us. Sean was active in his daughters' lives, coaching soccer and joining in therapeutic horseback riding; he turned what others might perceive as a "trial" into a positive experience, learning to adjust his timetable to each daughter's different tempo and be tolerant of their varying needs.

Cindy also found greater tolerance and empathy for others through her experience as the mother of a child who has a physical disability. She accepts certain behaviors she formerly would not put up with, understanding that a person might just be having "a bad day." She knows that when people are dealing with events in their lives that are beyond their control they may not act in a civil manner. "I'm easier on others," she says.

Lee says that joining his son Jason in activities such as going to the rifle range in his wheelchair has made him "more understanding, patient, and flexible." Mary agrees; although parenting a child who has a physical disability involved more work and fatigue, she says that her patience and tolerance have grown and she has learned to reach out to others. "You grow with it or you grow bitter." Mary has learned to be more gentle and understanding not only with others but with herself as well.

Grandparents often go through positive changes that parallel your experience as parents. Elsie says that "having a grandchild who has a disability made a huge difference. It made us more patient and understanding of other people who also have something to carry." This understanding brought her greater tolerance for human diversity beyond her family. As she reached out to her community, Elsie's faith in people and hope for the future were bolstered by discovering how much other people cared for her grandson and their family.

Looking Ahead to What You Want

When you find yourself in your new post-active-parenting status, you feel a bit rudderless, as if your focus is fuzzy. You may still be working outside the home, and there are likely to be some needs you continue to fill for your kids or other family members. Perhaps you remember a similar time as you transitioned from single to married or from being a couple to having children. But this phase of life has a different tone; you are a different person, intellectually and emotionally, as a result of your life experiences. Your interests, occupation, ideas, and belief systems have evolved, changed, or solidified over time.

One of the biggest challenges for parents at this stage is to define where they want to go, what they want to do. Do they want a sea change or to stay steady? Do you feel stumped by the question "What do I want out of life?" Are you sure of your dreams and how to reach them? Do you stay with familiar horizons or explore new ones?

Shifting away from 24/7 parenting allows you to put into effect the plans you've been waiting to execute, or to invest your energy in figuring out a new dream or goal. Whether your goals are clear or you are still searching, the next phase of life will likely bring something new in work or study, hobbies or interests, reconnecting with your spouse or partner, rebuilding your social life, taking care of yourself, or pursuing your passions. There is a world of possibilities ahead of you.

Working and Studying

Do you want to devote more time to your career, or start a new one? If you were a stay-at-home mom or dad, decisions about returning to work can be perplexing. Do you return to what you did before having children or go in another direction? Runner, a stay-at-home dad and computer expert, found that by the time he was ready to go back to work, his skills were out of date in the fast-changing field of computer science. If you experience something similar, more education or skills training may be what you need. On the other hand, you may decide that your former job doesn't sound fulfilling or exciting anymore. Perhaps your interests have changed; maybe you were a nurse and no longer want to be a caregiver. Or, like Susie, whose twin boys had physical disabilities, you might choose to turn your knowledge of parenting and disability into professional advocacy work for other families in need of education and support. If you are financially and physically able, you might want to push the envelope even further—join the Peace Corps or do missionary work abroad or begin a non-profit group—or just retire! Leigh, with two kids in and two out of the home, prepared herself early for the empty nest to come by looking for part-time work, so she could gradually reorient herself to the workaday world, figure out what type of work she wanted to do, and be ready to take on a full-time job after all her daughters were living away from home.

Hobbies and Interests

Parents who stay involved with their hobbies, athletics, arts, reading, and other interests during the children's growing-up years will be in a better position to make the transition from full-time parents to parents of young adults. They have their sources of enjoyment ready to fill the time that is freed when children are grown. Rather than feeling that time is weighing heavily on their hands after the kids leave, these parents report that they become so engaged in pursuing their interests that there just aren't enough hours in the day to do all they want. Priscilla, for instance, always nurtured herself with supportive friends, involvement in volunteer work, church activities, and scrapbooking, even while raising Jason and

Jean. Although still employed, she has time to become more deeply involved with these activities that she finds so satisfying.

Reconnecting with Your Spouse or Partner

Perhaps in the turmoil of raising a family, you had little opportunity to talk to your cocaptain about your own relationship. You may have grown apart in your ideas and attitudes, or you may not have had the energy to be there for each other in difficult times. When your child was going through a medical crisis, you and your spouse became focused on his ordeal, at times leaving you without each other's emotional support. Later you talked about it and apologized to one another, working out ways to do better next time. Now you have time to put in the effort to reconnect and strengthen your bonds of trust and intimacy.

Rebuilding Your Social Life

Now that you are less connected on a day-to-day basis with your children, you can focus on nurturing other relationships, not only with your partner, but also with family members and friends. You may be a single parent and want to find someone with whom to share your life. Some single parents have found others in the same boat at national disability group meetings. Other parents have joined faith-based adult groups, interest clubs, and athletic teams, as well as online dating services.

Friendships—old and new—can be more fully developed and savored. Now you have more time for dropping by a friend's home for coffee or going to a movie in the middle of the day or having a gossip session with friends on the front porch. You probably have friends who are "mine" and friends who are "ours"—those you like to have lunch with on your own and others whom you and your significant other enjoy together. Whether single or married, getting into the swing of things with other people breathes new energy into your life—mentally, emotionally, and physically. You can deepen your existing friendships or widen your social circle by talking about books with friends, analyzing movies you've seen together, learning to salsa dance, participating in political campaigns, organizing a gourmet dinner club, going on a weekend retreat, rooting for your favorite teams, teaming up to help build homes for those in need, or playing in a community band—the list of possibilities goes on.

Taking Care of Yourself

Whether a single or co-parent, you may not have had much—or any—time to take care of yourself while on full-time parent duty. Now there may be extra time during the week or on weekends, formerly taken up by kid-oriented activities, in which you can think about your body's needs—exercise, diet, skin care, relaxation. Some parents are able to make this a priority even while raising kids; Evelyn's husband Scott always supported her so she could get plenty of rest and care for herself by exercising and eating right. But most parents have not been able to accomplish this when their time and energies were concentrated on their children's needs. It may feel strange at first to give yourself permission to work out at the gym, go for a run, or take a long walk. Some couples build an exercise program for two, going for long walks, jogging, swimming, playing tennis, or working out in the gym together. They find increased levels of energy and a general feeling of well-being. As one parent observed, "It helps sustain my sense of self." April and Runner, both avid physical fitness advocates, found that running, both together and solo, helped reduce the stress of the tough medical events they went through with son Lance. It is still an integral part of their lives.

Pursuing Your Passions

You are fortunate if you have interests that are engrossing and engaging. But if you can go beyond that and find your *passion*, life is even better! Passion is a compelling desire to be involved in something you can "lose yourself" in. Have you ever felt like the world, with all its demands and questions, melted away? Maybe in the thick of a math problem, or working out the next line of a poem, or finding the right blue for the sky in your painting, you suddenly found that time had flown by. Your passion might be adding to your knowledge about the Mayan culture, learning to play *Rhapsody in Blue* on the piano, visiting all the state capitols, or compiling your family history. Exploring (or perhaps discovering) your passion keeps you developing and thriving when your children have left home. Jana, whose daughter has rheumatoid arthritis, found that, partly as a result of parenting experience, she was able to build her confidence as a sculptor and to pursue this passion after her daughter went to college. Jana applied the four elements she used to raise her resilient daughter to her own life—she took responsibility for her work ethic, experienced many aspects of her work, took risks on "beyond the realm" pieces, and expanded her social life by reaching out to others through her art.

Giving Back

When Susie was a newly divorced young mother of four, her wise friend advised her to accept help because she could repay it by helping others later. Susie listened: she has helped link numerous people who have disabilities to the services they need and to each other. She channeled her professional expertise and her volunteer energy into her passion, giving back what she was given tenfold.

Giving back is a fulfilling aspect of many parents' lives. A kind word or gesture that shows understanding for those in the same boat, especially young families, is a simple way to help others.

Many parents, like the Fishers, make fund-raising a key component of their giving back. The whole family is involved in fund-raisers, including Grandmother Ann, who solicits "goodies" to make baskets that are auctioned to raise money for the OI Foundation. D. K. actively solicits contributions from big corporations to fund research on OI.

Moving Forward

You've been gifted with both able-bodied children and those who have physical disabilities. You've discovered that children are children, but the child who has a physical disability has extra unknowns to deal with. You've raised your kids, coped with ups and downs and medical "surprises," made sure each child was included, instilled in them your knowledge, helped them develop their own value system, prepared them with competencies, created fun times for them, laughed with and listened to them, and finally helped them out of the nest—in short, you have cared well for your gifts. You've discovered what inclusive parenting is all about. Now it's time to direct that caring energy toward yourself, to grow the dreams that will fulfill your potential and increase your resiliency as you move forward with your life.

Remember that, as you go about the business of life after parenting, you are still a role model for your adult children—just as you were a model for parenting when you raised them. You will continue to create new patterns of living that your children can learn from and emulate—if they choose. And wouldn't it be wonderful if, when your kids reach the empty nest stage themselves, they remember the joy and gusto with which you embraced it?

Resources

Accessibility

Accessible Home Design: Architectural Solutions for the Wheelchair User, 2nd ed.
Published by Paralyzed Veterans of America
801 Eighteenth Street NW
Washington, DC 20006-3517

Amherst Homes, Inc.
7378 Charter Cup Lane
Westchester, OH 45069
Phone: 513-891-3303

The Center for Universal Design
North Carolina State University,
   Box 8613
Raleigh, NC 27695-8613
Phone: 800-647-6777
www.design.ncsu.edu

Concrete Change
600 Dancing Fox Road
Decatur, GA 30032
Phone: 404-378-7455
www.concretechange.org
Mission is to make every home
   "visitable."

Lifease, Inc.
2451 Fifteenth Street NW
New Brighton, MN 55112
Phone: 612-636-6869
www.lifease.com

United States Access Board
www.access-board.gov
An independent federal agency whose
   primary mission is technical assistance
   on accessibility for people who have
   disabilities.

Accessible Transportation and Travel

Access-Able Travel Source
PO Box 1796
Wheat Ridge, CO 80034
www.access-able.com

Accessible Europe
Phone: 011-39-011-30-1888
www.accessibleurope.com
Travel agencies specializing in accessible
   tours and travel in Europe and
   beyond

Accessible Journeys
Phone: 800-846-4537
www.disabilitytravel.com
Organizes wheelchair travel for groups
   and individuals, including cruises.

*The Air Carrier Access Act:
   Make It Work for You*
Published by Paralyzed Veterans of
   America
801 Eighteenth Street NW
Washington, DC 20006-3517

Emerging Horizons
www.emerginghorizons.com
Accessible travel news and information
for travelers who have disabilities.

International Association for Medical
Assistance to Travelers
Phone: 716-754-4883
www.iamat.org
Provides access to English-speaking
medical care providers for English
speakers traveling in foreign countries.

*New Horizons: Information for the Air
Traveler with a Disability*
United States Department of
Transportation
Aviation Consumer Protection Division,
C-75
400 Seventh Street, SW
Washington, DC 20590
http://airconsumer.ost.dot.gov/
publications/horizons.htm
The website has the full text of the
document.

Society for Accessible Travel and
Hospitality
www.sath.org
A nonprofit organization for travelers
who have disabilities.

Travelin' Talk Network
www.travelintalk.net
A network of over one thousand people
who offer help and services to
travelers who have disabilities.
Membership benefits include discounts
at various motels.

Assistance Dogs
Assistance Dogs International, Inc.
www.assistancedogsinternational.org/
assistancedogproviders.php
Accredits guide dog programs involved
in training either service or hearing
dogs.

Becoming a Parent When You Have a Physical Disability
http://raisingchildren.net.au/articles/
parents_with_physical_disability.html
Australian parenting site with stories of
parents who have physical disabilities
and have raised families.

www.lookingglass.org
Organization focusing on parents or
children who have disabilities which
provides training, does research, and
disseminates information.

Books and Magazines for Teens Who Have a Physical Disability
Cheney, Glenn Ann. *Teens with Physical
Disabilities: Real-Life Stories of
Meeting the Challenges.* Springfield,
NJ: Enslow, 1995.

Kriegsman, Kay H., Zaslow, Elinor L.,
and D'Zmura-Rechsteiner, Jennifer.
*Taking Charge: Teenagers Talk about
Life and Physical Disabilities.*
Bethesda, MD: Woodbine House,
1992.

New Horizons Un-Limited Inc.
www.new-horizons.org/libmag.html
Lists magazines and periodicals for
people who have disabilities.

Stewart, Gail B. *Teens with Disabilities.*
San Diego, CA: Lucent Books, 2001.

Thornton, Denise. *Physical Disabilities:
It Happened to Me: The Ultimate
Teen Guide.* Lanham, MD: Scarecrow,
2007.

Books for Children Who Have a Physical Disability
Carter, Alden R., and Carter, Carol S.
*Stretching Ourselves: Kids with
Cerebral Palsy.* Park Ridge, IL: Albert
Whitman, 2000.

Dobbs, Jean. *Kids on Wheels—A Young Person's Guide to Wheelchair Lifestyle*. Horsham, PA: No Limits Communications, 2004.

Heelan, Jamee R., and Simmonds, Nicola. *Rolling Along: The Story of Taylor and His Wheelchair*. Chicago: Rehabilitation Institute of Chicago Learning Books, 2000.

Lutkenhoff, Marlene, and Oppenheim, Sonya, eds. *SPINAbilities: a Young Person's Guide to Spina Bifida*. Bethesda, MD: Woodbine House, 1997.

College Resources
Disability Friendly Colleges
www.disabilityfriendlycolleges.com

"Finding the Right College Fit for Students with Physical Disabilities"
www.klemmerec.com/resources _reading_article_disabilities.htm

HEATH Resource Center
www.heath.gwu.edu
A national clearinghouse on post-secondary education for individuals who have disabilities.

Dating, Sexuality, and Marriage
American Association of Sexuality Educators, Counselors, and Therapists
PO Box 1960
Ashland, VA 23005-1960
Phone: 804-752-0026
www.aasect.org

American Society for Reproductive Medicine
1209 Montgomery Highway

Birmingham, AL 35216-2809
Phone: 205-978-5000
www.asrm.org

Ducharme, Stanley H., and Gill, Kathleen M. *Sexuality after Spinal Cord Injury: Answers to Your Questions*. Baltimore: Paul Brookes, 1997.

A Guide and Resource Directory to Male Fertility following SCI/C: A Miami Project Resource. www.themiami project.org

Kaufman, Miriam, Silverberg, Cory, and Odette, Fran. *The Ultimate Guide to Sex and Disability: For All of Us Who Live with Disabilities, Chronic Pain and Illness*. San Francisco: Cleis, 2003.

Rogers, Judith. *The Disabled Woman's Guide to Pregnancy and Birth*. New York: Demos Medical, 2006.

Diagnosis-Specific Books and Resources
Determined 2 Heal
8112 River Falls Drive
Potomac, MD 20854
Phone: 703 795-5711
www.determined2heal.org
Information on psychosocial recovery, support, research, and prevention of SCI.

Dollar, Ellen Painter. *Growing Up with OI: A Guide for Families and Caregivers*. Tampa, FL: Osteogenesis Imperfecta Foundation, 2001.

Hill Foundation
737 N. Michigan Avenue
Suite 1560
Chicago, IL 60611
Phone: 312-284-2525
www.facingdisability.com
A website that provides information
about families living with spinal cord
injury, as well as peer role modeling,
support, and peer counseling.

Lutkenhoff, Marlene, ed. *Children with
Spina Bifida: A Parents' Guide.*
Bethesda, MD: Woodbine House,
1999.

Palmer, Sara, Kriegsman, Kay H., and
Palmer, Jeffrey B. *Spinal Cord Injury:
A Guide for Living*, 2nd ed. Baltimore: Johns Hopkins University Press,
2008.

Thompson, Charlotte. *Raising a Child
with a Neuromuscular Disorder.*
New York: Oxford University Press,
1999.

Disability Rights
Americans with Disabilities Act (ADA)
Information
Phone: 800-466-4ADA
www.ada.gov

Disability Rights Education and Defense
Fund (DREDF)
2212 Sixth Street
Berkeley, CA 94710
Phone: 415-644-2555
Provides information on disability
rights laws and policy. Publishes a
free newsletter, *Disability Rights
News.*

Driving and Vehicle Adaptation
*Adapting Motor Vehicles for People
with Disabilities*
www.nhtsa.gov/cars/rules/adaptive/
brochure/brochure.html
A brochure published by the National
Highway Traffic Safety
Administration.

*Adaptive Automotive Equipment:
A Consumer's Guide*
www.unitedspinal.org/pdf/ahc.pdf
A brochure published by the United
Spinal Association.

Association for Driver Rehabilitation
Specialists (ADED)
PO Box 49
Edgerton, WI 53534
Phone: 608-884-8833
www.driver-ed.org; www.aded.net

Family Village
www.familyvillage.wisc.edu/at/driving
.htm
Adaptive driving and vehicle adaptation
sources.

Equipment and Technology
Abledata
8455 Colesville Road, Suite 935
Silver Spring, MD 20910
Phone: 800-227-0216
www.abledata.com
Maintains a database with over 15,000
listings of adaptive devices for all
disabilities.

Assistive Technology News
www.atechnews.com
Featuring articles on new assistive
technologies for people who have
disabilities.

Karp, Gary. *Choosing a Wheelchair: A Guide for Optimal Independence.* Sebastopol, CA: O'Reilly and Associates, 1998.

Sammons Preston and Enrichments
PO Box 5071
Bolingbrook, IL 60440-5071
Phone: 800-323-5547;
    fax: 800-547-4333
A mail-order catalog for accessibility aids.

Grandparents Raising Grandchildren
AARP Grandparent Information Center
www.aarp.org/relationships/friends
    -family/grandfacts-sheets
Information and links to a variety of resources for grandparents. Includes fact sheets that list resources in each state in the country.

Grandparenting Today
www.uwex.edu/ces/flp/grandparent/
Run by the University of Wisconsin Extension Service, this website offers links to national resources and publication. Includes a listing of books about grandparents raising grand-children at http://learningstore.uwex .edu/assets/pdfs/B3786-9.pdf.

www.grandparents.com
Offers information and links to a variety of resources for grandparents.

Housing Assistance for People Who Have Disabilities
Fair Housing: How to Make the Law Work for You
Washington, DC
Available electronically from Paralyzed Veterans of America at www.pva.org.

United States Department of Housing and Urban Development
Office of Fair Housing and Equal Opportunity
451 Seventh Street, SW
Washington, DC 20410
Phone: 202-708-1112
www.hud.gov
Provides information on housing rights and resources for people who have disabilities and for those who encounter discrimination in housing.

Medicaid Information
Centers for Medicare and Medicaid Services (CMS)
United States Department of Health and Human Services
www.cms.hhs.gov
Information on Medicare and Medicaid benefits and programs, the Medicaid Waiver, and other programs and services provided by these government health insurance programs.

National Mental Health Organizations
American Association of Marriage and Family Therapists
112 South Alfred Street
Alexandria, VA 22314-3061
Phone: 703-838-9808

American Psychiatric Association
1000 Wilson Boulevard, Suite 1825
Arlington, VA 22209
Phone: 800-35-PSYCH
www.psych.org

American Psychological Association
750 First Street, NE
Washington, DC 20002
Phone: 800-374-2721
www.apa.org

National Association of Social Workers
750 First Street, NE, Suite 700
Washington, DC 20002
Phone: 202-408-8600
www.socialworkers.org

Organizations and Foundations
Amputee Coalition of America
900 East Hill Avenue, Suite 290
Knoxville, TN 37915
Phone: 888-267-5669
www.amputee-coalition.org

Arthritis Foundation
PO Box 7669
Atlanta, GA 30357
Phone: 800-283-7800
www.arthritis.org

Muscular Dystrophy Association (USA)
3300 East Sunrise Drive
Tucson, AZ 85718
Phone: 800-572-1717
www.mdausa.org

National Organization for Rare
   Disorders
55 Kenosia Avenue
Danbury, CT 06810
Phone: 800-999-6673
www.rarediseases.org

National Spinal Cord Injury
   Association
75-20 Astoria Boulevard
Jackson Heights, NY 11370
Phone: 718-803-3782
www.spinalcord.org

National Stroke Association
9707 East Easter Lane, Suite B
Centennial, CO 80112
Phone: 800-787-6537
www.stroke.org

Osteogenesis Imperfecta Foundation
804 West Diamond Avenue, Suite 210
Gaithersburg, MD 20878
Phone: 301-947-0083
www.oif.org

Spina Bifida Association
4590 McArthur Boulevard NW,
   Suite 250
Washington, DC 20007
Phone: 800-621-3141
www.spinabifidaassociation.org

United Cerebral Palsy
1825 K Street NW, Suite 600
Washington, DC 20006
Phone: 800-872-5827
www.ucp.org

www.disaboom.com
Website with links to a variety of
   disability organizations.

Parenting a Child Who Has a Physical Disability
Albrecht, Donna. *Raising a Child Who Has a Physical Disability*. New York: John Wiley and Sons, 1995.

Balshaw, Mark L. *When Your Child Has a Disability*. Baltimore: Paul H. Brookes, 2001.

Brooks, Robert, and Goldstein, Sam. *Raising Resilient Children*. New York: McGraw-Hill, 2011.

Children and Physical Disabilities
www.findingdulcinea.com/guides/Health/
   Physical-Disabilities.pg_02.html
Provides information dealing with all aspects of physical disability, as well as resources for sports, activities, socialization, camps, etc.

National Dissemination Center for
Children with Disabilities
www.nichcy.org
A central source of information on
disabilities in children of all ages.
Includes easy-to-read information
on IDEA, the law authorizing early
intervention services and special
education. State Resource Sheets help
you connect with disability agencies
and organizations in your state.

www.fathersnetwork.org
Resources for fathers of children with
special needs.

Sports, Recreation, and Camping

Active Living Magazine: Adapted
Activities, Products and Places
Disability Today Publishing Group, Inc.
PO Box 2660, Niagara Falls, NY 14302
www.activelivingmagazine.com

Adaptive Outdoorsman
www.adaptiveoutdoorsman.com/
handicaphunting
A website for hunters who have
disabilities.

American Canoe Association
7432 Alban Station Boulevard,
Suite B 226
Springfield, VA 22159-2311

Buckmasters American Deer Foundation
www.badf.org

Handicapped Scuba Association
International
1104 El Prado
San Clemente, CA 92672-4637
Independent scuba diver training and
certifying agency. Offers Dive Buddy
Program.

International Paralympic Committee
www.paralympic.org

Mersey River Chalets
Nova Scotia, Canada
www.merseyriverchalets.ns.ca
Accessible accommodations and nature
activities.

Murderball (film, available on DVD and
video). Codirected by Henry Alex
Rubin and Dana Adam Shapiro.
Produced by Jeffrey Mandell and
Dana Alex Shapiro. Documentary
about wheelchair rugby and the
journey of the American "quad"
rugby team to the Paralympics.
(See also United States Quad Rugby
Association, below.)

National Ability Center
Park City, UT
Phone: 435-694-3991
www.discovernac.org
Specializes in accessible recreation,
sports, and leisure activities.

National Association of Handicapped
Outdoor Sportsmen, Inc.
RR 6, Box 25, Centralia, IL 62801

National Center on Physical Activity
and Disability
Phone: 800-900-8086
www.ncpad.org

National Foundation of Wheelchair
Tennis
940 Calle Amanecer, Suite B
San Clemente, CA 92672

National Wheelchair Basketball
  Association
110 Seaton Building
University of Kentucky
Lexington, KY 40506
www.nwba.org

North American Riding for the
  Handicapped Association, Inc.
  (NARHA)
PO Box 33150
Denver, CO 80238
www.narha.org

Rocky Mountain Village
PO Box 115
Empire, CO 80438
www.eastersealsco.org

United States Golf Association
PO Box 708
Far Hills, NJ 07931
Modified rules for golfers who have
  disabilities.

United States Handcycling Federation
PO Box 2245
Evergreen, CO 80437

United States Paralympians Association
  (part of the United States Olympic
  organization) www.teamUSA.org/
  US-Paralympics.aspx
The Paralympics provides appropriate
  levels of competition within sports
  categories for athletes who have
  various types of disability.

United States Quad Rugby Association
5821 White Cypress Drive
Lake Worth, FL 22467-6230
www.quadrugby.com

Wheelchair Sports USA
10 Lake Circle, Suite G19
Colorado Springs, CO 80906
Information on archery, shooting,
  swimming, table tennis, weight lifting,
  track and field, and specifics on local
  competition.

Wilderness Inquiry, Inc.
1313 Fifth Street, PO Box 84
Minneapolis, MN 55414
Phone: 800-728-0719
www.wildernessinquiry.org
Land and water wilderness excursions
  for both able-bodied people and those
  who have disabilities.

Wilderness on Wheels Foundation
7125 West Jefferson Avenue, #155
Lakewood, CO 80235
Accessible camping, hiking, and fishing.

www.kidscamps.com/special_needs/
  physical_disability.html
Lists of camps for kids who have
  physical disabilities (can filter by
  region, age, length of stay, or camp
  type).

Support for Siblings
Sibling Support Project
A Kindering Center Program
6512 23rd Avenue NW, #213
Seattle, WA 98117
www.siblingsupport.org
Sibshops and other resources for siblings
  of a child who has a disability.

Visual and Performing Arts
Encore Studio for the Performing Arts
www.encorestudio.org
A professional theater company for
  people who have disabilities.

Mouth and Foot Painting Artists
2070 Peachtree Court, Suite 101
Atlanta, GA 30341
Phone: 770-986-7764
www.mfpausa.com

National Arts and Disability Center
www.semel.ucla.edu/nadc
Working for full inclusion of artists and
audiences with disabilities in the arts
community.

That Uppity Theater Company
4466 West Pine Boulevard, Suite 13C
St. Louis, MO 63108
Phone: 314-995-4600
www.uppityco.com
A theater company for both able-bodied
actors and those who have disabilities.

VSA Arts
818 Connecticut Avenue NW, Suite 600
Washington, DC 20006
Phone: 800-933-8721
www.vsarts.org
This nonprofit organization provides
opportunities for people who have
disabilities to learn through, participate in, and enjoy visual and
performing arts.

Vocational Rehabilitation and Employment
State Vocational Rehabilitation
www.workworld.org/wwwebhelp/state
_vocational_rehabilitation_vr
_agencies.htm
Under the provisions of the Rehabilitation Act, every state government offers
vocational rehabilitation services to
help people who have disabilities
obtain education and job training and
return to gainful employment. A list of
state vocational rehabilitation agencies
can be found online.

United States Department of Labor's
Office of Disability Employment
Policies
www.dol.gov/odep
Provides technical assistance and
information for individuals who have
disabilities.

www.jobaccess.org
A website where people who have
disabilities can post their résumés
and connect with employers to find
jobs.

Youth Organizations
These organizations welcome all young
people, whether or not they have
physical disabilities. Find listings in
your local phone directory or in your
school or community.

4-H Clubs
Boy Scouts of America
Girl Scouts of America
YMCA
YWCA

Notes

Introduction: Raising Children—Resilient and Ready for Adulthood
p. 6: Christopher Nolan's experience of feeling the cold stream on his feet was described in his book *Under the Eye of the Clock: The Life Story of Christopher Nolan* (New York: St. Martin's Press, 1987).

Two: Coming Home
p. 57: The different styles that parents use in working with their children's health care teams are described in Susan A. Snell and Karen H. Rosen, "Parents of Special Needs Children Mastering the Job of Parenting," *Contemporary Family Therapy* 19, no. 3 (1997): 425–42.

Three: Inclusive Parenting: Make It Work for You
p. 97: Beatrice Wright was a pioneer in the study of the psychological experience of living with a physical disability. In *Physical Disability: A Psychosocial Approach* (2nd ed.; New York: Harper and Row, 1983), now a classic in the field, she said that the development of positive self-concept in a person who has a physical disability comes through changes in their values.

Four: Brothers and Sisters: Siblings Sharing Family Life with Physical Disability in the Mix
p. 106: Twenty-one research studies on the psychological impact of physical disability on siblings were reviewed in Angela Dew, Susan Balandin, and Gwynnyth Llewellyn, "The Psychosocial Impact on Siblings of People with Lifelong Physical Disability: A Review of the Literature," *Journal of Developmental and Physical Disability* 20 (2008): 485–507. The authors concluded that siblings of people who have physical disabilities are mainly positive about their experience, and that there is little difference between siblings who have and who do not have a brother or sister who has a physical disability. They were able to identify only two studies that included the perspectives of the siblings who had the disability and recommend that their input be included in future studies.

p. 107: Parents' attitudes toward their child who has a physical disability is an important factor in sibling adaptation, as discussed in Ineke M. Pit-Ten Cate and

G. M. P. (Ineke) Loots, "Experiences of Siblings of Children with Physical Disabilities: An Empirical Investigation," *Disability and Rehabilitation* 22, no. 9 (2000): 399–408.

p. 120: The finding that physical disability of a sibling was discussed less frequently with his able-bodied siblings than other everyday topics was reported in Ineke M. Pit-Ten Cate and G. M. P. (Ineke) Loots, "Experiences of Siblings of Children with Physical Disabilities: An Empirical Investigation," *Disability and Rehabilitation* 22, no. 9 (2000): 399–408.

p. 124: The Sibshop model of sibling support was developed by Donald Meyer in Seattle, Washington. Sally Conway, in the UK, adapted the program for siblings of children who have developmental disabilities and attend a residential treatment program. The model is described in Sally Conway and Donald Meyer, "Developing Support for Siblings of Young People with Disabilities," *Support for Learning* 23, no. 3 (2008): 113–17.

p. 125: Positive characteristics associated with having a sibling who has a disability are discussed in Paula Dyke, Seonaid Mulroy, and Helen Leonard, "Siblings of Children with Disabilities: Challenges and Opportunities," *Acta Paediatrica* 98 (2009): 23–24.

Five: Grandparents: Seeing through a New Lens

p. 148: By the time they become grandparents, most people are in the stage of life which Erik Erikson, who proposed a stage theory of adult psychological development, called generativity. At this stage, adults who are beyond child-rearing age continue to be productive in other areas of their lives while also helping the younger generation. Erikson's theory is described in Erik Erikson, *Identity and the Life Cycle* (New York: W. W. Norton, 1994).

Six: Opening Doors to Inclusion

p. 164: The young woman whose family challenged her to "reach for more" after her spinal cord injury was Kris Ann Piazza, whose story appears in Gary Karp and Stanley D. Klein, eds., *From There to Here: Stories of Adjustment to Spinal Cord Injury* (Horsham, PA: No Limits Communications, 2004), 71.

p. 164: The point that every individual, whether or not he has a physical disability, has some "limitations" that affect his career and avocational options was made by Rhoda Olkin, a psychologist, in her book *What Psychotherapists Should Know about Disability* (New York: Guilford, 1999), 103.

Index

----

with emotions, 31, 37, 39, 47, 66, 79, 84–85, 187, 196; of friends, 88; of grandparents, 149; by journaling, 36–37, 53; parental modeling of, 99, 162; of parent partners, 80–81, 159; by sharing feelings, 35–36, 51, 58, 95; of siblings, 15, 70, 107, 113, 119–20, 123, 125; social support for, 38, 126; with time demands, 47–48; ways of, 35–39, 53

counselors, 55, 66–67, 76, 155, 196. *See also* mental health care

creativity, v, xiii, 21, 64, 86, 94, 98, 148, 158, 161, 165, 197

crutches, x, xi, 50, 70, 96, 110, 113, 122, 162, 169, 173, 183, 184

Cub Scouts, 23, 86

curb cuts, 37, 132, 175, 197

cycling, 6, 13, 77–78, 94–95, 114, 123, 158, 166, 168, 173, 174, 182, 185; resources for, 212

dance, xi, 5, 90, 95, 134, 144, 174, 184, 201

dating, 15, 168, 171, 183–85; resources for, 207

day care, 42, 155

denial, 20, 29, 36, 54, 123

Department of Developmental Disabilities, 179

depression, 31; after children leave home, 196; of grandparents, 143; medications for, 22; of parents, 20, 22, 51, 54; at time of diagnosis, 27

diagnosis of child's physical disability, 26–40; uncertain, 59–60. *See also* news of child's physical disability

diagnosis-specific resources, 207–8

disability rights, 63, 172, 176, 180, 208

discipline, 60, 70, 82, 93–94, 109, 130, 143, 165

discrimination, 180

divorce, 1, 33, 43, 67, 83, 115, 117, 119, 196, 203

doctors/medical team: for college students, 172; communication with, 57–61; getting answers to your questions from, 61–62, 159; mental health professionals, 54, 55, 66–67, 196–97;

parents as educators for, 63–64, 102; partnering with, 65–67, 101; relationship with, 56. *See also* medical care

dreams: balancing with child's limitations with, 164–66, 179–80; of parents after children leave home, 192–93

driving, xi, 44, 83, 98, 137, 174, 180–81; parking in handicapped spaces, 189, 197; resources for, 208

dysreflexia, 22

education of child with physical disability, 176–78; accessibility in schools, 52, 109, 132, 176; accommodations at school, 38, 63, 171, 176–77; attendants and aides for students, 109, 131, 171, 177, 178, 181; at college (*see* college attendance); free and appropriate public education, 176; homeschooling, 158, 176; Individualized Educational Plan for, 177; in least restrictive environment, 63, 176; mainstream, 156, 157, 176; about sexuality, 184; in special schools, 63, 156, 176

emotional reactions: charting emotional progress, 53–55; coping with, 31–32, 37, 39, 47, 66, 79, 84–85, 187, 196; dealing with, 50–53; delayed, 51; of grandparents, 20, 34–35, 54–55, 187; to news of child's physical disability, 14, 19–20, 31–33; seeking professional help with, 54, 55. *See also specific emotions*

emotional support, 84, 88–89, 201; from grandparents, 133, 139, 143, 186; from siblings, 117–19

empathy: of doctors, 56; of friends, 88; of parents, 24, 96, 100, 155, 198; of siblings, 110, 116, 125; of support group members, 42; vs. sympathy, 162, 163

employment: of parents, 20, 21, 33, 48, 77, 79, 83, 87, 117, 155–56, 196, 200; of person with physical disability, 15, 66, 158, 178–80, 193; protection against discrimination in, 180; resources for, 213

empty nesters, 15–16, 196, 200, 204

equipment and technology, 183, 208–9

Erikson, Erik, 148, 216n

ethnicity, 11, 41, 58

expectations: for academic achievement, 7, 92, 93, 109, 130, 165–66; behavioral, 24, 93, 94, 108, 168, 193; for child with spina bifida, 109, 167; positive, x–xi, 2, 3, 92–93, 108–9

experiences: family activities, 49, 91–92, 108, 113–14, 130; participation in, 4–7, 101; shared by siblings, 113–14

faith. *See* spirituality and religious beliefs

family interviews, x, xii, 2–3, 7

family life: activities, 49, 91–92, 108, 113–14, 130; adjustments in, 14, 47–50; finding new normal in, 68–71, 157; vacations, 6, 22, 49, 75, 81, 91, 112, 114, 130, 159

family unity, 91, 102, 115

fatigue, 36, 47, 80, 89, 141, 198

fear(s), 19, 32, 46, 103, 127, 128, 129, 162; discussing, 36, 51, 58, 95; about future, 35, 44, 159–60, 161, 188; of grandparents, 30, 55, 102; of medical procedures/doctors, 34, 42; of risk taking, 11, 95; about safety, 42, 52, 95; of siblings, 125

feeding tube, 65, 156

feelings thermometer chart, 53

financial assistance, 41, 42, 48, 63, 66, 84; from grandparents, 15, 136–37, 140–41; for job training, 179

foster care, 29, 155

4-H Clubs, xi, 174, 213

fractures in osteogenesis imperfecta: at birth, 41, 102; child abuse suspected by, 102; medical care for, 43, 62; parent management of, 56, 103; parents' anxiety about, 43, 181; protecting child from, 70, 99; recuperation from, 92, 113; risk taking and, 12, 13, 168; sibling responses to, 104, 110, 113; susceptibility to, 7, 96; unawareness of, 29; in young adult away from home, 181, 182

friendships: of child with physical disability, 9–11, 44, 50, 77–78, 92, 93, 94, 112–13, 172–74; of parents, 23, 30–31, 32, 35, 38, 42, 48–49, 50, 54, 79, 82–86, 88–89, 201; of siblings, 123–24

frustration: with child's medical care, 61; of child with physical disability, 77;

fatigue and, 47; helplessness and, 32; with insurance company, 65; about obstacles faced by child, 197; of parents, 20, 24, 36, 76, 192; rating feelings of, 53; sharing feelings of, 51, 120; of siblings, 104, 116; at time of diagnosis, 29

fund-raising, 48, 105, 122, 148, 203

gardening, 7, 88, 108

Gemini voice output system, 157

generativity stage of life, 148, 216n

Girl Scouts of America, 44, 174, 213

giving back, 203. *See also* advocacy; fund-raising; volunteer work

God. *See* spirituality and religious beliefs

Goodwill Industries, 179

grandparents, 14, 15, 133–51; anticipating changes in ability to help, 143–44; assistance provided by, 19–21, 76–77, 105, 127, 132; babysitting by, 81, 140, 142, 147; being present for grandchildren, 146; community support for, 146–47; emotional reactions of, 20, 34–35, 54–55, 187; faraway, 137–38; financial help from, 136–37, 140–41; fitness of, 150; in generativity stage of life, 148, 216n; giving and receiving by, 149, 150–51; handing down of family story by, 145; having a grandchild with a physical disability, 146–47; "in-house," 135–37; optimism and hope of, 149; patience of, 148; personal lives of, 149–51; protection of child by, 136; religious faith of, 131, 147; resources for, 209; role in enriching grandchildren's lives, 144–45; role in grandchild's medical care, 64–65; sense of purpose of, 147; sources of support for, 143; as stand-in parents, 142–43; support for adult children by, 133, 138–41, 143, 186; support for grandchildren by, 141–44; traveling with, 146; in the vicinity, 134–35

grief, 32, 33, 36, 50, 76, 160

guilty feelings, 190; of parents, 12, 29, 58; of siblings, 109, 111–12

Handicapped Is Only a Word (HOW) Conference, xii

intimate relationships: of parents, 80–81, 101, 140, 201; of young adults with physical disabilities, 15, 172, 183–84
isolation, 53, 121, 160

jealousy of siblings, 46, 107, 109, 110, 111–12, 116, 129
jobs. *See* employment
journaling, 36–37, 53

laughter. *See* humor/laughter
learning: about your child's physical disability, 28, 37, 42, 62–68, 102; about health insurance, 63; from other parents, 89–90
least restrictive environment, 63, 176
legal protections, 63, 172, 176, 180, 208, 209
leg braces, x, xi, 5, 7, 12, 13, 47, 87, 96, 97, 129, 184
leukemia-related paralysis, story of family who has child with, 75–78
living independently, 171, 181, 193. *See also* independence, preparing child for
loneliness, 14, 32, 34
looking ahead to what you want, 199–203
loss, feelings of: after children leave home, 192, 197; of grandparents, 54, 147; of parents, 28, 33, 50, 76, 160; related to teen with a new physical disability, 170; due to separation from child, 33, 34; at time of diagnosis, 29, 35

marriage: of parents, 80–81; preparing teens with physical disabilities for, 15, 171, 183–85; resources for, 207
Medicaid, 42, 209
medical care, 2, 13, 56–62; adoption of children with significant physical disabilities, 155–58; communication with medical team about, 57–61; getting answers to your questions about, 61–62, 159; grandparents' role in, 64–65; including child in decisions about, 62, 181–82; partnering with professionals for, 65–67, 101; peer support and education about, 67–68; teaching teens to manage, 180–83. *See*

also doctors/medical team; hospitalizations; surgeries
mental health care, 3, 54, 55, 66–67, 93, 97, 101, 196; resources for, 209–10
multigenerational families, 101, 135–37, 193
muscular dystrophy, 55, 142, 147
music activities, x, 5, 12, 86, 94, 104, 141, 144, 167, 174, 188, 189

neonatal intensive care unit, 19–21
new normal for your family, 68–71, 157
news of child's physical disability, 26–40; grandparents' emotional reactions to, 20, 34–35; parents' initial emotional reactions to, 14, 19–20, 31–33; receiving after birth or later in childhood, 28–30, 41, 187; receiving before birth, 26–28, 33, 102, 127–28; ripple effects of, 30–31; separation from child and, 33–34; ways of coping with, 35–39
Nolan, Christopher, 6, 215n
nurses, 21, 28, 34, 58, 101, 186; cost of hiring, 157, 193; for respite care, 82

Olkin, Rhoda, 161, 165, 216n
optimism: of grandparents, 148, 149; of parents, 28, 29. *See also* hope
osteogenesis imperfecta (OI): advocacy and fund raising for, 105, 148, 203; fracture risk in, 12, 13, 41, 43, 56, 62, 70, 92, 96, 99, 102–4, 110, 113, 168, 181, 182; grandparents of child with, 54–55, 105, 139, 148; medical care for, 42, 62, 64, 181, 183, 193; misinformation given to parents about, 41, 58–59; negative attitudes about, 44; online support group for, 42; parents educating doctors about, 64, 102; parent self-care and, 85; parents learning about, 28, 37, 42, 62, 64, 102; preparing young adult for independence, 161, 164, 174, 180–83; psychotherapy for person with, 66–67; receiving diagnosis of, 28–29, 41, 102; resources for, 207, 210; risk taking and, 13, 95, 96–97; safety concerns for child with, 49, 52, 70, 91, 95, 97, 108, 181; siblings of child with, 70, 104, 113–14, 117, 121;

single parent of child with, 83, 196; socialization of child with, 174; sports participation and, 13, 91, 108; stories of families who have a child with, 41–45, 102–5; young adults with, 193

Osteogenesis Imperfecta Foundation (OIF), xiii, 64, 203, 210

paraplegia, 1, 76, 165, 170, 180, 184, 185. *See also* spinal cord injury

para-transit system, 175

parents: balancing self-sufficiency with help from others, 196–97; becoming experts on your child's physical disability, 28, 37, 42, 62–68, 102; building resilient families, 1–16, 79, 90–99 (*see also* resilient families); as case managers, 22–23, 63, 64, 155; divorce of, 1, 33, 43, 67, 83, 115, 117, 119, 196, 203; emotional reactions to news of child's physical disability, 14, 19–20, 31–33; employment of, 20, 21, 33, 48, 77, 79, 83, 87, 117, 155–56, 196, 200; empty nesters, 15–16, 196, 200, 204; friendships of, 23, 30–31, 32, 35, 38, 42, 48–49, 50, 54, 79, 82–86, 88–89, 201; grandparents functioning as, 142–43; hobbies and interests of, 16, 85, 199, 200–201; inclusive, 14, 79–101 (*see also* inclusive parenting); intimacy between, 80–81; learning from other parents, 89–90; looking ahead to what you want, 199–203; meeting each child's needs, 2, 24–25, 90–92, 103, 107–8, 189–90; moving forward, 203–4; patience and tolerance of, 15, 78, 98, 100, 167, 194, 198–99; peer support and education for, 67–68; personal growth of, 190–91, 194–99; positive role modeling by, 96–99, 162, 163; preparing child for independence, 161–85; protectiveness of, 12, 52, 95, 96, 99, 102–5, 109, 119, 168, 170; pursuing your passions, 202–3; rebuilding your social life, 201–2; reconnecting with spouse or partner, 201; resources for, 205–13; retirement of, 12, 16, 30, 144, 150, 200; self-confidence of, 3, 15, 39, 56,

59, 95, 101, 139, 185, 194–95, 196, 203; siblings functioning as, 116–17, 118–19; single, 21, 35, 47, 48, 49, 82–84, 85, 87, 155, 196, 199, 201, 202; support for, 14, 79–84; taking care of yourself, 85–90, 104–5, 202; teamwork of, 80, 102–4, 159; thankfulness of, 77, 129, 192, 194; time management for, 14, 47–48, 86–88; trusting your instincts, 13, 15, 58, 60, 195; turning anger into action, 197–98; volunteer work of, 49, 86, 200, 203; who have a physical disability, 99, 206

parking in handicapped spaces, 189, 197

parties, birthday, 158, 173

pastoral counselors, 55

patience: of grandparents, 148, 199; of parents, 15, 78, 98, 100, 167, 194, 198–99; of siblings, 107, 113, 125, 157

pediatric intensive care unit, 38

peer support and education, 67–68

personal care attendant (PCA), 109, 131, 171, 177, 178, 181

personal growth of parents, 190–91, 194–99

physical therapists, 101, 177

physical therapy, x, xi, 6, 82, 116, 122, 142, 187

physicians. *See* doctors / medical team

polio, x–xi, 26, 53, 69, 112, 114, 164, 169

positive expectations, x–xi, 2, 3, 92–93, 108–9

positive role models, 96–99, 162, 163, 166

postconcussive syndrome, 59

pragmatism, 3

prejudices, 52, 77, 121, 197. *See also* attitudes about physical disability; stereotypes

premature birth, 155, 186, 198

pride: of child with physical disability, 13, 83; of grandparents, 104; of parents, xi, 30, 53, 83, 95, 192; of siblings, 115, 116, 125, 129

priority setting: grandparents' role and, 141, 148; to meet family needs, 90, 94; to meet immediate needs of child with physical disability, 2, 87, 91; to meet parents' time and energy needs, 47, 79, 87, 194, 202